Anders de la
MOTTE
DEAD of
WINTER

Translated by Marlaine Delargy

ZAFFRE

Originally published in Sweden by Bokförlaget Forum in 2018
First published in Great Britain in 2022 by
ZAFFRE
An imprint of Bonnier Books UK
4th Floor, Victoria House, Bloomsbury Square,
London WC1B 4DA
Owned by Bonnier Books
Sveavägen 56, Stockholm, Sweden

Translation by Marlaine Delargy

A CIP catalogue record for this book is
available from the British Library.

ISBN: 978-1-78576-946-7

Also available as an ebook and an audiobook

1 3 5 7 9 10 8 6 4 2

Typeset by IDSUK (Data Connection) Ltd
Printed and bound in Great Britain by Clays Ltd, Elcograf S.p.A.

Zaffre is an imprint of Bonnier Books UK
www.bonnierbooks.co.uk

To Annette, for everything we have done together.
And everything that still awaits us.

Prologue

She had always loved the lake. For almost half a century this place had been her sanctuary, a world that was not free from sorrow, but a haven where evil had never gained a foothold. At least that was what she had told herself. Now she knew better.

She shivered as she perched on the edge of the pontoon, and lifted her legs out of the ice-cold water. Wrinkled skin, crooked toes, varicose veins forming thin purple spider's webs over her calves. When had this happened? When had she acquired an old woman's feet and legs?

When it came to the ageing process, it wasn't possible to pinpoint a specific moment when it began. It was a change that came creeping in, just like the way the autumn leaves slowly drifted to the ground, then you woke up one morning and it was winter around the lake.

The ice had already drawn a thick chalk circle along the shore, and the bare branches of the tall trees that extended almost as far as the sauna next to the pontoon were highlighted starkly against the night sky. The colony of crows, the only residents of the holiday village these days, were observing her from above with their watchful little peppercorn eyes.

It's fine, she thought. *I'm not going swimming. You don't need to worry.*

She tucked her feet beneath her and wrapped the towel more tightly around her body. The movement made the pontoon bob up and down, and the rusty chains attaching it to the stakes protested hoarsely. The warmth from the sauna leaked out from under the towel, turning into steam as it met the cold winter air.

She ran a hand over the grey, split planks. They should have been cleaned and creosoted at least a month ago, meticulously prepared for the winter as in years gone by, but like so many other things in the holiday village, she had long since given up the struggle. Resigned herself to the inevitable. Or maybe she'd simply lost her spark.

After the heart attack in the early autumn – her second and probably penultimate, as Dr Olsson had acidly informed her – he had forbidden her from swimming in the winter.

'Your heart won't tolerate any more strain, Hedda. Not of any kind . . .'

She really ought to have surgery. There were several letters to that effect among the piles of post in the house, but she loathed hospitals as much as she loathed doctors.

Which was why, until a few weeks ago, she had ignored both the letters and Dr Olsson's exhortations. Her life consisted of sitting in front of the television with the cat on her lap, allowing her morning, afternoon or evening drink to transport her to a different, happier time. Evoking faces, voices, laughter. Memories of summers and winters gone by. Memories of the children. Her children, that was what she'd called them. Laura, Jack, Peter, Tomas. And Iben, of course. Poor, poor little Iben.

On some winter evenings she almost thought she could hear them outside. Car doors opening and closing, cheerful conversation, feet stamping off the snow on the porch. Occasionally she even got up to welcome them home, tell them how much she'd missed them, longed for them to return. But when she opened the front door the yard was always deserted. Thirty years of emptiness. Of yearning, of guilt. Why draw it out? Sacrifice the few pleasures she still had, in order to live for another couple of years? The doctor could go to hell. That was what she thought.

Until the morning when a car had arrived. It was one of the few occasions when she had agreed to receive a visitor. Reluctantly stayed sober, even had a shower and put on clean clothes. Told herself everything would be sorted out in no time.

But when the car door opened it was as if something clicked inside her head. Brought a flash of light so bright that she had to cover her eyes with her hands.

For a brief moment she thought she'd had another heart attack. Thought she was going to drop down dead on her own doorstep before she'd exchanged a single word with her visitors, but then everything went back to normal, and she was looking out onto a grey November day. Polite exchanges, introductions, business proposals and figures, exactly as planned.

And yet a faint perception lingered throughout the entire conversation, a voice in the back of her mind that she hadn't heard for many years. When she was young she had allowed that voice to guide her, but after the Lucia fire, when she realised that her intuition had failed her, she had stopped listening. Suppressed it with alcohol and self-pity. Until now.

Because in the days following the visit, the voice had grown louder, insisting with increasing vigour that the impossible had become possible. That after all these years, she'd been given a chance. A chance to return to the past. A chance to put right some of her mistakes, to protect those she loved.

As long as she proceeded cautiously – avoided the flames.

She looked down at her damaged left hand. The pattern of scars across the back, the two stumps – all that remained of her

3

little and ring fingers. With the other hand she picked up her evening joint and the lighter she'd placed on the edge of the pontoon. She'd been growing her own marijuana in the greenhouse behind the toolshed since the summer of '75, or maybe it was '76. She really ought to give that up too, but grass helped her to gather her thoughts. Consider what to do next.

Her first instinct had been to call Laura, but she hadn't done it. Maybe she was afraid? Probably. Afraid of being dismissed like a crazy old woman before she had the chance to explain the incredible thing she'd discovered. Or maybe she was afraid of something even worse – that Laura would simply slam down the phone. Which would be entirely understandable, of course.

She'd let Laura down back then, let them all down. All her children.

She held the sweet smoke in her lungs before exhaling, allowing it to drift into the night sky. The moon, slowly rising above the lake, gradually transformed the surface of the water into liquid glass. On the northern shore directly opposite her, the ridge loomed like a steep shadow. Only a solitary lamp shone at the water's edge, breaking the compact darkness. Drew her eyes inexorably, as always.

She should have sold the holiday village, of course. They'd offered her a lot of money, more than she would ever need.

A sensible person would have signed right away. Left the crows, the house and the dilapidated pontoon to spend her final years in a more comfortable place. Paid no attention to the intuition that had remained silent for so many years, refrained from digging up the past.

A sensible person.

Once again she gazed across at the north shore. At the solitary light.

Thirty years – had so much time really passed? She would have to call Laura, regardless of her fears. Explain what was going on, warn her to be careful, but first she had to be certain. Replace intuition with concrete proof. Because the truth was so painful, and it could be dangerous. After all, one young person was already dead, and several others scarred for life. Maybe others were at risk? That possibility couldn't be excluded.

Once again she looked at her burned hand. Stretched the pink finger stumps.

A gust of wind passed through the treetops, and at the same time the crows began to move agitatedly, flapping their wings and emitting harsh warning cries. A fox, maybe, or an owl that had come too close? In which case the birds would soon settle down, once the threat had gone.

But the warnings continued, growing louder to form a cacophony of sound and movement.

She knew what it meant. Someone was approaching. Someone the crows didn't recognise.

A stranger.

She turned her head towards the edge of the forest, but the faint light from the lamp outside her house was swallowed up by the darkness.

For a few seconds she hoped she was mistaken, but the raucous cries went on, with no sign of diminishing.

She hadn't heard a car engine or the crunch of footsteps on gravel, so the stranger was coming through the forest. She rarely had visitors out here, and certainly not those who came sneaking in the night.

It could mean only one thing: she had been too eager. Dug too deep. Given herself away, somehow.

5

Her chest contracted, a sharp burning pain with which she was unfortunately all too familiar.

What was she going to do now?

The phone was up in the house, and even if she got there before her visitor, who would she call? What would she say?

That the past had returned. Who would believe her?

And starting to run towards the house would reveal how frightened she was.

Because she was frightened, there was no denying it. Frightened for herself, but mostly for Laura. The pain in her chest increased, making it difficult to breathe.

Flight was out of the question, so all she could do was sit here and finish smoking her joint. Hope that good would triumph in spite of everything. Especially in a place like this.

She focused her attention on the lake once more, took a deep drag. Tried to stop her hands from shaking.

A slight vibration in the pontoon made the chains resume their litany of complaints, joining the cawing of the crows and her own erratic heartbeat. She suppressed the urge to look around. Stayed exactly where she was, looking out over the dark water.

The footsteps stopped right behind her. The pontoon continued to bob gently up and down, then grew still. The crows fell silent at almost exactly the same moment – as if they were curious, wanted to hear what was said.

She gazed at the yearning light on the far shore. Took one last drag and tossed the stub into the lake. The glow formed an arc before it was swallowed up. *An offering to the nymph, the mistress of the lake,* she thought. Suddenly she was filled with a strange sense of calm, a kind of sorrow that slowed her racing heart.

'I know why you're here,' she said without turning her head. 'You want to find out how much I actually know.'

No response.

Slowly she looked around.

The visitor was no more than a metre away, looming over her like a shadow. The hood was pulled up, the face in darkness.

'I've worked it all out,' Hedda said slowly. 'The offers, the building project, who's behind it all.'

The visitor remained silent and motionless.

Hedda wondered whether to go on, but it was too late to stop now. Too late to change her mind. The truth must come out. For Laura's sake. For the sake of the other children. For her own sake.

She filled her lungs with air. Swallowed.

'The Lucia fire,' she said, and saw the visitor's head come up a fraction. 'That's what it's all about.'

She turned back to the lake, fixed her eyes on that solitary light far away on the opposite shore.

'I know what really happened that night,' she said. 'And why . . .'

1

She hates the winter, has done ever since she was little – or almost. Once upon a time there was ice skating and sledging, camp fires, a flask of hot chocolate and friends to share it with. But that was a long time ago, before the Lucia Day fire.

Now there is only the cold.

'So . . . Laura.'

Her table companion glances at the place card next to her wine glass for at least the third time. His name is Niklas, and so far he's turned out to be both dull and nervous. He's managed to spill something on his tie – or even worse, he chose to put on a tie with a stain already on it when he was dressing for dinner.

'How do you know Stephanie?'

The question is almost laughably predictable.

'We met through work a few years ago, but now we're good friends.'

Laura is trying to be polite. She doesn't say that Steph is her best friend, sadly perhaps her only friend. Except possibly Andreas.

Niklas asks her something else, but the loud alpha male opposite them, who has been holding court ever since he made his ostentatious entrance three-quarters of an hour ago, says something funny and the laughter from the other guests drowns out Niklas's voice.

She should have turned down this invitation, explained that she has a headache and too much work to do, but she had promised Steph. Promised to behave herself and give nervous Niklas a chance.

'It's important for you to get back in the saddle, Laura. Find somebody new. Yeehaa!'

To be fair, Steph didn't actually say 'yeehaa', that was Laura's own addition. She takes a big gulp of her wine and decides she's being unfair. Steph grew up in the USA, and tends to speak both Swedish and English at the same time. Sometimes Laura thinks she does it deliberately, exaggerating her use of Swenglish to make her stand out from the crowd, which really isn't necessary.

She glances over at the head of the table. As always, Steph looks good in a dress that shows just the right amount of décolletage. Her blonde hair is perfectly styled, and she is sitting with her head tilted to one side in the way that makes every man in her vicinity want to be of service. Steph is two years older than Laura, but the cosmetic procedures she's undergone are so discreet and professional that no one would think she's a day over forty.

Laura, on the other hand, definitely looks forty-five. She has crow's feet at the corners of her eyes and a furrow in her brow that shows up particularly well on the kind of alabaster skin that only redheads have. She inherited her hair colour and skin tone from her father, but she alone is responsible for the grim set of her mouth.

She is wearing a long-sleeved shirt beneath a cashmere cardigan, and even though the warmth in the room has already prompted a few of the gentlemen to loosen their ties, her fingertips and the end of her nose are freezing cold. They always are, all year round, thanks to the winter fire. Or rather because of it. She feels no gratitude towards it whatsoever.

She and Steph are the polar opposites of each other in many ways. Steph is open and extrovert; she's built up her own business from scratch. Laura took over her father's company. *Handed everything on a plate,* as her mother points out on a regular basis.

Steph must have felt Laura's eyes on her; she looks in her direction and nods meaningfully. Laura gets the message. *Pull yourself together and give the guy a chance.*

She sighs and turns back to Niklas. Tries to avoid fixating on the stain on his tie.

'Sorry, I didn't hear what you said.'

Niklas blushes.

'I was just wondering if you worked in investment too?'

'No, my speciality is risk management. Mainly the soft sector.'

Niklas looks puzzled, and she realises she needs to expand on her answer.

'We assess people – to see if they're suitable to be taken on, or promoted. You might have heard of screening?'

'You mean you find out if they have a criminal record, that kind of thing?'

She can hear from his tone of voice that he doesn't understand, which is hardly surprising. Her area is narrow, to say the least.

'That's just a small part of what we do. We aim to form a more comprehensive picture of the person. Look into their finances, family relationships, talk to their former teachers, employers, colleagues. We carry out over a hundred different checks, and sometimes we even conduct in-depth interviews.'

She doesn't mention that this is in fact her own area of expertise; no point in scaring him unnecessarily. She's already worked out most things about Niklas - mainly that she has absolutely no intention of seeing him again, whatever Steph says.

'Who are your clients?'

A good question, she has to give him that. If this were an interview she would have made a little squiggle in the margin of her assessment form to indicate that he was brighter than he looked.

'Usually recruitment firms, but also companies, agencies or government bodies that are considering internal promotion to the leadership team or other key posts. Sometimes it's investors who want to know who they're dealing with.'

'Like Stephanie?'

'Exactly.'

Just as Laura is about to return the favour and ask Niklas about his job, the alpha male opposite breaks into their conversation. He must be fifty, and she doesn't need to look at his place card to know his name.

'Did you say you worked as a headhunter?'

He already has the attention of everyone around the table, which means they are now focused on her.

'No,' Laura says curtly, because she already knows where he's going with this.

However, he's not so easily dismissed.

'I'm actually looking for a new challenge.'

Laura shakes her head. 'As I said, that's not what I do.'

He's not listening. 'I usually increase turnover by at least ten per cent in the first twelve months,' he informs her. 'There was an article about me in *Industry Today* the other week - did you see it?'

Laura demonstratively turns to Niklas, but the alpha male still doesn't get it.

'The headhunters call me once a week, if not more often,' he boasts. 'You wouldn't believe the salary they offer – but I need the right kind of challenge. What company did you say you worked for, Lena?'

Steph intervenes before Laura bites his head off.

'*Laura* runs her own business, Tobias. She assesses people like you, searches out their weaknesses. The skeletons in your closet. You need to watch yourself.'

There are odd bursts of laughter, and if Tobias had any sense he would drop the whole thing. Instead, he leans across the table.

'Do I, indeed? So how would you assess me, Laura? What are my weaknesses?'

He beams at her, showing his recently whitened teeth, and she can see that a number of the guests are on his side. Steph is giving her a look, and Laura knows she ought to keep her mouth shut, but alpha-Tobias is wearing the smug expression favoured by only a certain kind of man. He really is asking for this.

Steph shakes her head almost imperceptibly, but to no effect.

'I've met so many people like you,' Tobias goes on. 'Cod psychologists who think they can judge someone by getting them to fill in a fucking form. *Can you list your three greatest weaknesses? What colour do you associate with your personality? If you were a car, what make would you be?* Bullshit, pure and simple.'

He laughs loudly, and once again several of the other guests – mainly male – join in. Buoyed up by their support, he leans even further forward and extends an index finger with a faint sticky film covering the nail.

'Go on, Laura – give me your best shot!'

'OK, but remember this was your idea.'

She takes a sip of her wine, puts down the glass while observing Tobias closely. Follows the tell-tale redness at his hairline, down over his upper body, his hands. You could hear a pin drop around the table.

'You're married,' she begins. 'But that's not your wife.'

She nods in the direction of his companion, who is at least twenty years his junior.

'You drove here because you wanted to show her your expensive car. It could be an Italian make, but it takes time to learn to drive them properly, and you don't have the patience, so I'll go for a slightly more easy-to-handle Porsche.'

Tobias's eyes are darting from side to side.

'You've already drunk too much, but you're still intending to drive home, because you don't want to leave your precious toy parked on the street. Which means you don't really care about risks or consequences for yourself or others. Since you came by car, you don't live in town, but in Lidingö or Djursholm. Judging by the exaggerated way you pronounce the letter *i*, I'd go for the former, but the cadence of your sentences suggests that you were born and grew up somewhere on the west coast.'

She pauses, leaving him to squirm for a few seconds. She avoids catching Steph's eye. This is too easy. And so much fun.

'Your suit is Brioni, your watch Rolex, your tie Fendi. Red, of course, because you read in someone's autobiography that it's a power colour. Autobiographies are all you read, by the way. And you recently had a hair transplant.'

She leans back, trying not to look smug.

'To summarise, Tobias: you're a walking, talking, risk-taking, middle-age crisis. What do you think of my assessment?'

No one speaks. Tobias is gasping for air, as if he's about to explode.

Suddenly Steph begins to laugh, a loud, infectious belly laugh that draws everyone in, and the atmosphere lightens.

'Don't say I didn't warn you,' she says as the laughter gives way to an amused hum of conversation. 'Laura's fucking lethal.'

Tobias knocks back the contents of his wine glass.

'How the fuck did you know all that?' He sounds annoyed, but reluctantly impressed.

'Do you really want to know?' Laura says.

The conversation dies away. She gazes steadily at him.

'I read the article about you in *Industry Today*. It told me where you come from, where you live, and that you've been married for many years. But your companion this evening isn't wearing a wedding ring.' Once again she nods in the direction of the young woman, whose hands are clearly visible. 'Plus, you had a much higher forehead in the photograph in the magazine.'

And there's something sticky on your fingers which I'm guessing is Regaine, just in case the transplant doesn't succeed, because you can't think of anything worse than going bald. She decides to keep that little snippet to herself. There are limits, after all.

Tobias's face is bright red. He has got over the shock and surprise, and now he's furious, humiliated. He's probably wondering whether to call her a bitch and storm out, or pretend to turn the other cheek and be a good loser. She thinks he'll go for the latter option; anything else would be stupid.

'And the car?' the man next to her asks. 'How did you know he drives a Porsche?'

Laura shrugs.

'He arrived just after me and parked by the door. I saw them getting out of the car as I was walking in.'

Another burst of laughter. Tobias grins, looking embarrassed but doing his best to join in the merriment. A wise decision.

One of the women is laughing so much she can hardly breathe. She reaches for her glass of water and knocks it over. When she leans forward to retrieve it, one of her curls gets too close to a candle.

Laura can see what is about to happen and opens her mouth to warn the woman, but it's too late. A flash of fire, then a scream.

It's over in a second. The hiss of burning, the flame is extinguished. All that remains are agitated voices and the acrid smell of burned hair.

Everyone's attention is on the woman, so no one notices when Laura gets up and hurries out of the room. Her stomach contracts, she can feel the sweat on the back of her neck.

She just manages to lock the toilet cubicle door, turn on the cold tap and sweep her hair out of the way before she throws up in the hand basin. She swills out her mouth, blows her nose several times to try to get the smell of burned hair out of her nose, but somehow it is still there.

She looks in the mirror. Notes that she is even paler than usual, if that's possible.

'Calm down,' she murmurs. 'Just calm down.'

After a while she feels better. The voices in the dining room have died down. A slight draught indicates that someone has opened a window.

With hindsight, she realises it wasn't a good idea to take Tobias down like that. If she hadn't been showing off, the woman wouldn't have set fire to her hair, and she wouldn't be standing here throwing up in Steph's marble hand basin.

Her headache has got worse, and all she wants to do is to go home, close the door, not see anyone. But she can't let Steph down.

She takes out her phone. One text message, two missed calls. The first is from a contact called Andreas ex-husband/stalker.

One of Steph's little jokes that she hasn't had the energy to correct. It's her own fault for leaving her phone unattended for a few seconds. Plus, it's not entirely untrue.

A year after the divorce, Andreas still calls her almost every day. Over the last few weeks, he's been calling even more frequently. She ought to ask him to stop, of course. Explain that they both need to move on. And yet she hasn't done it.

The other missed call is from a number she doesn't recognise. A landline with an area code that looks vaguely familiar.

She opens a search app. The number belongs to a firm of lawyers called Håkansson in Ängelholm, and as soon as she sees the name of the place, a faint warning bell begins to ring in the back of her mind. She makes the call before she has time to think, not really expecting anyone to answer at eight o'clock on a Friday evening.

'Håkansson.'

The man on the other end of the line speaks with a rough Skåne accent.

'Hi – my name is Laura Aulin. I think you tried to contact me about an hour ago?'

'I did, thank you so much for getting back to me.'

She hears the rustle of papers.

'It's about your aunt. Hedda, Hedda Aulin. Have you spoken to her recently?'

The warning bell is louder now, and the nausea comes flooding back.

'We . . . We're not in touch.'

'No?'

16

'No, we haven't been for many years. Has something happened to her?'

The brief silence answers her question. She swallows hard.

'I'm very sorry, but your aunt has passed away.'

'When?'

'At some point during the early hours of Monday morning, we think.'

Without warning the skin on her back begins to crawl, a painful mixture of heat and cold that she hasn't felt for many years. At least not while she was awake.

'So anyway . . .' Håkansson goes on. 'Your aunt spoke to me not long ago. She wanted to make a will. You're her only heir.'

He falls silent, waiting for Laura to say something, but she is lost for words.

'As I'm sure you understand, there are a number of practical decisions that will have to be made concerning her estate,' he continues.

'I . . . I understand,' she manages to say. 'Can I call you back tomorrow?'

'Monday will be fine – there's no hurry. Once again, my condolences. Your aunt was . . .' He pauses, searching for the right words. 'A very special woman.'

He ends the call, and Laura stands there with the phone pressed to her ear. The skin on her back is burning like fire, drops of sweat are trickling down towards the waistband of her trousers. The rest of her body is ice-cold.

2

Water is nothing to be afraid of, Laura. Not as long as you respect it.

Hedda's words echo in Laura's mind as she swims.

The pool in the apartment block's spa and gym complex is twenty metres long, and Laura covers a length in fifteen seconds, breathing only after each tumble turn. Her movements are even and economical, using up no more oxygen than necessary. Length after length, usually with nothing else in her head except the sound of the water and her own heartbeat. Today it's different. Her thoughts are all over the place, bringing up voices, memories.

She was never any good at sport, particularly anything involving teamwork. The expensive private school gave her plenty of opportunity to find that out.

Swimming was different. There were no team mates, no balls. No visible opponents. Just herself and the water.

It was Hedda who taught her to swim properly. She'd already had swimming lessons in Singapore, managing exactly one panic-stricken length of doggy paddle with the teacher beside her in the pool, while her mother sat on a sun lounger flicking through *Vogue*.

Hedda had seen how afraid Laura was, and one summer's evening she took her out in the little rowing boat. Laura was seven, but she can still remember every detail. The full moon and the starlit sky above them. The silence when Hedda stopped the oars in the middle of the lake.

'The water will hold you up,' she said. 'If you just have the courage to trust it. And I'll be right behind you. All the way home.'

She pointed to the shore and the lights of the holiday village.

'Are you ready?'

Laura inhaled, nodded. Then Hedda capsized the boat.

As always, Laura showers in the cubicle on the far left, where the grouting between the tiles is clean, the stream of water is steady, and the drain operates efficiently. She meticulously sprays the walls and floor before stepping in. The black bottle she has brought with her contains a fifty per cent dilution of chlorine, guaranteed to kill most micro-organisms that could be lurking on the tiles. She keeps her flip-flops on, just in case.

Her swimsuit has long sleeves and bears more than a passing resemblance to a wetsuit. She doesn't take it off until she has locked the door behind her. No one can see her in here, and she doesn't need to turn her back to the wall while she showers.

She and Hedda repeated that first swim every single summer. Capsized the boat together, even though there was no need. If the water was really warm, they would take their time making their way back to the shore, floating on their backs while she pointed out the different constellations and told Hedda their names.

The little rowing boat would be bobbing by the shore right outside the house next morning.

The boat knows the lake as well as I do. It can find its own way home.

*

When she has finished showering she wraps herself in her bathrobe, pulls up the hood and takes the lift straight to her apartment. The cleaner has been in while she was swimming, leaving behind nothing but the faint smell of detergent.

Laura kicks off her flip-flops and walks barefoot across the smooth limestone floor. Straightens the little Guan Yu statuette that protects the entrance against evil spirits; it is a millimetre out of position thanks to the cleaner's efforts with the duster.

The under-floor heating is on, the thermostat shows twenty-five degrees. There is a stove in one corner, but the fire itself is actually gas, controlled by technology and contained behind reinforced glass. She switches it on with a remote, avoids looking at the flames. Then she slips her feet into her sheepskin slippers.

It is just after three o'clock on Saturday afternoon. The darkness is already beginning to gather over Stockholm's snow-clad roofs. The apartment is silent; the only sound is a faint hum of traffic from far below. She decides not to turn on the lights just yet. She picks up her phone from its charging dock. No messages or missed calls. Not that she was expecting any, but there is a call she has to make. She should have done it this morning, but she's put it off for as long as possible.

'Madeleine Aulin.'

The buzz of conversation in the background.

'Hi, Mum, it's me. Are you busy?'

'Pierre and I have guests.'

'From Sweden?'

'Yes. Some old acquaintances.'

Laura immediately sees through the slight change in tone.

'Is Marcus there?'

The brief pause gives her the answer.

'They arrived yesterday – a last-minute decision. He's been so stressed, and the au pair will take care of the girls until the Christmas holidays begin.'

Laura clamps her lips together in a thin line. Technically she is Marcus's boss, but needless to say her little brother hasn't said a word about his plans to take some time off. Or that he was going to join their mother and Pierre in Majorca.

Madeleine draws her own conclusions from Laura's silence.

'We thought you couldn't come. Marcus said you were very busy. But of course you're welcome any time – you know that.'

Laura moves her jaw from side to side in an attempt to release the tension. She can't say yes, partly because the invitation was forced out, but mainly because she can't think of anything worse than celebrating Christmas in Mum and Pierre's flashy Spanish villa with Marcus's noisy kids. But if she refuses – blames work as she usually does when it's time for a family gathering – she'll prove that they were right to exclude her.

'By the way, have you spoken to Andreas?' her mother says before Laura has worked out what to say.

'Why?'

The question surprises her, and yet it doesn't.

'Marcus bumped into him near Stureplan the other day, with a woman. He seemed a little embarrassed?'

Mum manages to make the last sentence sound like a question, as if she's expecting some kind of explanation.

'It's over a year since we divorced. Andreas can see whoever he wants.'

A brief noise on the other end of the line, possibly a snort.

'Hmm. Not even his patience lasts forever.'

Laura has been expecting the comment ever since Andreas's name came up. The acidic little remark, reminding her that she's being ridiculous, that she ought to stop messing around and beg Andreas to take her back, before it's too late.

'Did you know that Aunt Hedda has passed away?'

The click of a cigarette lighter. Her mother still smokes, even though Laura's father died of lung cancer. A long exhalation, a sigh filled with nicotine as Laura's brain automatically computes the risk of disease after fifty-five years of smoking.

'Yes, I heard something about that. Such a shame.'

'Why didn't you call and tell me?'

Silence, another exhalation.

'It didn't occur to me. Pierre and I have had a lot to do in the house, and you always have your hands full with work. How did you find out?'

'A solicitor contacted me last night. Hedda's left Gärdsnäset to me in her will.'

'I see.'

Laura can sense unease in the neutral words.

'Why do you think she did that?' she asks.

'I've no idea. Hedda's always been a little ... different. As I'm sure you recall, she didn't even have the decency to get in touch when your father died. Her own brother. After everything we've done for her. What on earth are you going to do with a rundown holiday village?'

The sharpness was back, the implication that Laura has done something wrong. She chooses to ignore it.

'I thought I'd go to the funeral. It's next Saturday.'

'Do you think that's a good idea?'

'I'm Hedda's closest relative.'

'So that's the only reason you're going? Because you're so kind-hearted?'

Laura clamps her lips together again.

'It's because of him, isn't it?' her mother continues. 'The orphan.'

The feeling of being caught out makes Laura's cheeks flush red.

'His name is Jack.'

Another snort. 'He disappeared, don't you remember? Left you when you were at rock bottom.'

Her mother's words slice through her, mainly because they're true.

'I remember.'

'You were only just sixteen, it was a stupid teenage crush. And yet you still can't stop thinking about him. No doubt you're hoping he'll turn up at the funeral.'

Laura forces herself not to respond.

'If I were you, I'd stay away. Gärdsnäset is a terrible place, and after everything that's happened I can't imagine why you're even—'

Her mother breaks off, takes two quick drags.

'What I'm trying to say, Laura . . .' Her tone has softened, there is even a hint of sorrow. 'Is that you shouldn't dig up the past. It rarely leads to anything good, believe me.'

Laura stands in the bedroom in front of the full-length mirror. Hesitates for a moment before opening her robe and letting it fall to the floor. The last of the warmth from the shower fades away, and she shivers.

The room is in darkness, with only a small amount of light filtering in and making her skin look whiter than usual. She unties her hair, lets it fall over her shoulders, then folds her arms over her breasts. Without taking her eyes off the mirror, she slowly turns her upper body. The mark begins halfway down her left shoulder blade. She keeps moving, watching it grow into a large patch of rough scar tissue, spreading diagonally downwards across her spine. She shivers again.

For a few brief moments, she remembers it all. The roar of the flames, the smell of soot, burned hair and flesh so intense that she can taste it.

The pain in her back that is both heat and cold at the same time.

Then the floating sensation as someone carries her over the ice, closer and closer to the black, cold water out there. And finally the screams. Her own and someone else's.

3

The juice bar is on Birger Jarlsgatan, right next to Steph's gym, and is full of women who could have been cloned. Padded jackets over workout clothes, perfect haircuts, a glass of juice in one hand, phone in the other. Conversations that are more like monologues, because no one looks anyone else in the eye.

Steph differs from the other customers in one important way. She has actually been working out; this is clear from both her clothes and the sheen of perspiration lingering on her forehead. She doesn't do anything by half measures, which is one of the things Laura likes about her. *Go big or go home,* that's Steph's mantra. Laura never goes to the gym. Sweaty machines, communal changing rooms, open showers and curious eyes.

'So to summarise: you're thinking of travelling to some backwater in Skåne to bury an aunt you haven't seen for years and years, just to annoy your mother, whom you hardly ever see either?'

Steph takes a swig of her juice, which has so many ingredients that it took the man behind the counter four minutes to blend it.

Laura doesn't answer, partly because Steph has a point, partly because she can't tell her friend the whole story. She rubs her hands together, trying to warm her fingertips. It's below freezing outside, and even though it's not yet December, the piles of snow at the side of the road have already turned a dirty brownish-grey.

'How long have we known each other?' Steph goes on. 'Didn't we meet the year I came here?'

'The following year. You moved to Sweden in September 2015, we met in January 2016.'

'So almost two years. It feels like longer. Anyway, you've listened to me droning on about my ex-husbands and the difference between Americans and Swedes until your ears bleed. I know all about your peculiar relationship with your mother and your useless kid brother. I also know about your divorce and Andreas the stalker. But you haven't said a single word about a rich aunt in Skåne.'

Steph raises her eyebrows, but her forehead remains smooth.

'Hedda wasn't rich.'

'No? I thought you said you were her sole heir?'

'I had an email from her solicitor this morning. Hedda was more or less broke. There's a piece of heavily mortgaged land, but that's all.'

'I stand corrected. You have a *poor* aunt that you've never mentioned before. Why not?'

Because I've put all that behind me, Laura wants to say. But of course it's not true. Instead, she simply shrugs.

'You know we moved around a lot when I was growing up. Dad worked all over south-east Asia, so I started in a new school virtually every year.'

Steph nods.

'During the longer breaks I stayed with my aunt at her holiday village in Skåne. Hedda didn't have any children of her own, so she was like a second mother to me. I had friends there; I loved the place.'

'Oh yes?'

The perfect eyebrows are raised. Laura takes a deep breath.

'There was an accident one winter, when I was fifteen. A fire . . .'

Steph leans forward, interested to hear more.

'My friends and I had a Lucia party in the dance hall, which was closed for the winter. A typical teenage idea. Suddenly a fire started.'

She stops, wondering how much to tell. Settles on the official version.

'The dance hall was burned to the ground. There was so much smoke, so much confusion with everyone trying to get out. One of my friends didn't make it.'

The colour drains from Steph's face. Her eyes shine with unshed tears.

'How terrible!' She places a hand on Laura's arm, which is quite touching. Steph can be as hard as nails in business, and she swears like a trooper, but that's all superficial.

'Her name was Iben,' Laura adds. 'She was my best friend.'

Steph squeezes her arm, and they both sit in silence for a little while.

'What . . .' Steph clears her throat. 'What happened next?'

Laura braces herself. The rest is easier to talk about, but it's still challenging.

'My parents took me back to Hong Kong a few days later. I got sick almost right away. I was struck down by a virus – meningitis – and I was in hospital for months. When I got back on my feet, Mum and Dad refused to talk about the fire, or Aunt Hedda. There was no question of my being allowed to go back there.'

I call the virus the winter fire, it fucked up my inner thermostat, among other things, which is why I'm almost always cold.

27

She keeps this to herself, along with the fact that she has been on medication ever since in order to keep the nightmares at bay. Instead, she underlines her story with a melancholy smile, which isn't difficult to produce. Steph looks badly shaken.

'Jesus, what a story. You must have felt like shit.'

Laura shrugs again, for want of a better reaction.

'It's a long time ago. I haven't thought about it for years.'

A lie, but in her present mood, Steph doesn't notice.

'And your aunt never tried to contact you?'

Laura shakes her head.

'We used to exchange letters, but I didn't hear a thing from Hedda during all those months in hospital. I was upset, of course, but I kept writing to her even though I never got a reply. I must have stuck at it for a year before I gave up. Not a letter, not so much as a postcard – and like I said, I'd thought of her as my second mother.'

'And when you grew up?'

Laura's jawline is tense.

'I haven't heard a word from Hedda since the winter of 1987. I have no idea why she chose to leave the holiday village to me, but then Hedda was always different . . .'

'In what way?'

'She was into pottery, painting, she made her own clothes, that whole '68 vibe. My dad used to call her a superannuated hippie.'

'Sounds charming, if you ask me.'

'It was, at least when I was a child. I loved staying with her. There were no rules, no . . .'

Laura realises she's smiling, quickly adjusts her expression.

'But Hedda was also incredibly stubborn. And she knew how to bear a grudge.'

She thinks about all the times she checked the neat pile of post on the hall stand. About her mother's irritated little shake of the head when she asked if there really wasn't a letter for her. *How can you do that to a fifteen-year-old? To someone you treated like your own child?* She rubs her fingertips together. The cold won't go away.

'And now it's too late for a reconciliation. All that's left is a final farewell. So sad.'

Steph picks up her juice and pensively chews her straw.

'Will your brother be at the funeral?'

'No. Hedda and Marcus never met. He's seven years younger than me, and Mum didn't want to send both of us away for the holidays.'

'You mean she didn't want to send Marcus away.' Steph pouts, puts on a babyish voice. 'Couldn't bear to be parted from her little prince for all those weeks.'

Laura can't help smiling this time.

'Mum and Hedda never really got along.'

'I'm liking your aunt even more.'

'There's another reason why I want to go.'

She hadn't intended to say anything, but Steph always has the ability to put her in a good mood.

'Aha. The plot thickens.'

'There was a boy ... We also lost touch after ...' Laura searches for the right words. 'Everything that went on.'

Steph lifts her chin a fraction, studies her face, which makes Laura nervous for some reason. Steph's eyes seem to burn right through her skull, into her mind. There's so much she hasn't shared, so much that she's kept to herself, suppressed.

Steph suddenly laughs.

'And now you're hoping that Prince Charming will turn up at the funeral? So you can revive a romance from thirty years ago?'

'Maybe.' Laura sighs quietly to herself.

'So when are you going?'

'After work on Thursday. Back Sunday evening.'

Steph takes another sip of her juice.

'Do you want me to come with you?'

'Thanks, but I know you hate funerals.'

She really appreciates the offer, but Laura can't let her come along under any circumstances. What if Steph finds out the truth about what really happened on that Lucia night? About what Laura did?

4

Aulin Consulting is in a beautiful old building in Öster-malm. Stucco on the ceilings, dark wood, crystal chandeliers and Persian rugs. Laura would have preferred something more modern, more functional and less expensive. She makes the suggestion at the beginning of every financial year, but her mother flatly refuses to change a single thing from the way it was when Laura's father was still around, and Marcus always backs her up.

The company has nineteen employees, eleven of them part-time: law and journalism students who check registers, request various documents in the public domain, and go through CVs. In addition there are four risk consultants and an actuary on the payroll, plus Gunvor, who was taken on by Laura's father as his secretary when they returned from Asia in the mid-Nineties. Laura knows that her mother and Gunvor speak virtually every day, and that if she so much as changes the brand of coffee in the staff room, the information will be passed on.

Changing direction and concentrating on risk assessing people rather than buildings and vehicles was Laura's idea. Her father reluctantly agreed the year before he died. She knows that her mother blames her, believes that it was the restructuring that broke him rather than the cancer. In fact, they had no choice. Her father had lost his grip, and the company that is now flourishing and supporting both her mother and Pierre,

Laura and Marcus, was about to go under. However, that particular aspect is never discussed. Dad was perfect, a saint. Saint Jacob. End of story.

Laura's office, which was once his, is at the far end of the corridor. On her way she passes Marcus's closed door. As usual he's managed to slink away while she was busy with something else. He has an uncanny ability to do that.

She's first in as always. She woke with her mouth guard beside her on the pillow, which means she has to start the day with a couple of painkillers.

Grinding your teeth and tension headaches – good for you! You're entitled to free Botox!

Steph means well, but Laura would never subject herself to having a toxin injected into her face. Nor operations, vaccinations, sunbathing or any other kind of physical or mental stress that she can avoid. Stress that could trigger the virus hidden deep inside her. Pregnancy, for example.

She forces her mind to change direction, tugs at the sleeves of her cashmere cardigan until they reach her knuckles, then switches on the heater under her desk before logging onto her computer.

She googles 'Gärdsnäset holiday village', and to her surprise finds a link to a homepage. However, when she clicks on the link a message informs her that the page no longer exists, and that the domain name is available.

Instead, she tries 'Vintersjön'.

The lake, according to Wikipedia, is in the district of Vedarp in north-western Skåne.

Vintersjön is twenty-three metres deep, has a surface area of five square kilometres, and is situated sixty-six metres above sea level. Its waters come from the streams that

run down the slopes of the Halland Ridge, as well as from
an underwater spring that rises in the middle of the lake.

The community of Vedarp, comprising 4,058 inhabit-
ants, lies in the inlet that forms the lake's western shore.

The northern aspect, the Halland Ridge, is largely unin-
habited and is mostly given over to a nature reserve. There
are a number of holiday homes along the southern shore, as
well as some permanent residences. Vintersjöholm Castle,
on the eastern shore, dates back to the sixteenth century.

Laura gazes for a while at pictures of the lake and the castle.
Eventually she gathers her courage, leaves Wikipedia and
searches for 'Vintersjön fire'. Just as she had suspected, there is
no direct hit, but she's not giving up that easily. She looks up a
newspaper that covers the area, finds her way into its archive of
pre-internet articles that have been digitised. Chooses 'October
1987' from the menu, then local news. Scrolls down the list.

The first article isn't particularly ominous.

Electrical fault probably to blame for fire in summer cottage by Vintersjön.

The next is dated a couple of weeks later, and is given more space.

Second fire in holiday cottage by Vintersjön. Cause
unclear.

The third headline is in a much bolder typeface, and she feels
the cold beginning to spread through her body.

Yet another fire at Vintersjön. Police cannot discount arson.

And finally, she reaches the headline against which she has no defence. The one that makes the cold penetrate deep into her heart.

Tragedy at Vintersjön. Young woman dead in fierce blaze.

She is about to enlarge the article so that she can read it when there is a knock on the door.

'Good morning!'

As usual Gunvor has walked in without waiting for Laura to say anything.

'Your morning tea.' She moves behind the desk and places a steaming cup next to the keyboard, while unashamedly staring at the screen. Laura quickly minimises the window.

'You look tired, Laura dear.' Gunvor tilts her head on one side and gently strokes Laura's hair. 'I hope you're taking good care of yourself.'

Laura doesn't reply. Both the gesture and the comment infuriate her. She's the company director, but Gunvor still talks to her as if she is little Laura, coming to work with Daddy.

'It's not easy being left alone,' Gunvor goes on. 'I remember how your mother felt when Jacob passed away. She cut herself off for months, hardly ate a thing.'

Gunvor drones on, but Laura is no longer listening. She's heard all this before. She would like to snap at Gunvor, tell her that Andreas isn't dead, they're just divorced, and that she definitely doesn't want to be compared to her mother. It would be pointless, of course. Such an outburst would immediately become another topic of conversation around the dinner table in Majorca.

'. . . so lucky to meet Pierre. Such a stylish, refined gentleman – exactly what she needed.'

And broke, Laura adds silently to herself. But that doesn't stop him from spending her mother's money, not to mention dispensing advice on how the company should be run.

When Gunvor has left the office Laura works her way through her emails, makes a number of calls. It is difficult to concentrate, and she keeps glancing at the screen. In the end she brings up the newspaper article.

It's not very long. The sensational headline, a grainy picture of tree trunks, snow, and a building in flames.

During the night of the feast of St Lucia, a fire broke out in a dance hall at Gärdsnäset holiday village. A group of six local young people were allegedly having a party inside the hall, which was closed for the winter, when tragedy struck. Four were injured and a fifth, a sixteen-year-old girl, lost her life. According to Chief Fire Officer Arne Jepson, the rapid acceleration of the blaze and the fact that the victims were trapped inside the building suggests that the fire was started deliberately. The police have opened an investigation into suspected arson, and it is possible that this incident is connect to the fires that have plagued the area around Vintersjön during the autumn and winter.

Laura stares at the screen. The articles about the fire are pretty hard to track down, which means that Steph won't be able to find them through a quick search. And so far there are no inconsistencies, nothing she hasn't already told Steph. It's the final piece that worries her.

Suspect arrested in Lucia blaze case

The police have confirmed that they have arrested a person suspected of starting the fires in the Vintersjö area. According to reliable sources, the suspect is a local youth, and it seems likely that he was also involved in the tragic Lucia fire that cost a young woman her life.

Andreas calls her when she is on the way home from work. She rejects the first two calls, but he refuses to give up. Laura adjusts her woolly hat and tucks in the hands-free earpiece. Those brief seconds in the cold are enough to make her fingers go stiff.

'I heard about your aunt. Just wanted to check that you're OK.'

Laura sighs to herself. She knows exactly who's behind this, and she doesn't have to wait long for confirmation.

'Your mum said you're going to the funeral.'

'Yes . . .' The headache is still clouding her thoughts, but she knows exactly what's coming. 'And she wants you to persuade me not to go.'

A silence that can only be interpreted as a yes. Andreas is a nice guy – much too nice.

'I just thought it might not be a good idea, this close to . . .'

He breaks off, waits for her to say something.

'She would have been two last Friday,' he goes on in a thick voice when she doesn't speak. 'I tried to contact you, I thought we could go to the grave together.'

Yes, Andreas, I can count too. I know how many years, months and days have passed. I might even be able to give you the number of minutes and seconds. But that's no help at all, is it?

She doesn't say any of that out loud, of course. Never, not to anyone. She simply says quietly: 'I was out.'

'I'm worried about you, Laura. You seem so . . .'

'So what?'

'I don't know. Closed off.'

'Closed off?'

'Yes. For God's sake, you didn't even take any time off last year when . . .'

As usual he can't say the words.

'We got divorced, Andreas. Remember? And yet you keep on calling me.'

'I still care about you. I worry about you.'

'In that case I think you should stop. Get on with your own life and let me get on with mine.'

Another silence. There's something he wants to say, and she thinks she knows what it is. She decides to help him out.

'I believe you've met someone.'

A faint gasp. 'Who told you that?'

'My mother, of course. Apparently, you bumped into Marcus the other day.'

'Well, yes, but . . .' She can hear how uncomfortable he is. 'I wanted to tell you myself. She's a former colleague and . . .'

'You don't owe me anything, Andreas,' she interrupts him. 'Not a single thing.'

She stops walking, makes a huge effort to sound calm and composed.

'I'm very happy for you, but please stop running errands for my mother.'

She ends the call outside the door of her apartment block. Swipes her fob over the card reader, passes through the locked doors and pauses briefly beneath the camera in the spacious lobby. In the lift she hesitates, then presses the bottom button instead of the top one.

The storage area in the basement is a little unusual. No wire netting cages with cross-country skis sticking out, no piles of banana boxes crammed with Christmas decorations, offering an unwanted insight into other people's lives. Instead, there is a series of neatly numbered steel doors each with a keypad, in an air-conditioned corridor monitored by CCTV.

Her own storage unit is empty except for two identical plastic boxes. She hasn't been down here since she moved in last year.

All the furniture in her apartment is new, ordered from the NK department store on the day she signed the contract. Andreas tried to get her to take a load of stuff with her – things they'd bought together, presents he'd given her – but she said no. All she wanted was the little Guan Yu statuette from her father, and these two boxes.

She runs a hand over the box on the left, caresses it tenderly. Inside it is a tiny sleep suit, a flannel rabbit, and a piece of paper with two small prints on it. A hand and a foot. She doesn't open the lid, just makes sure that the two plastic clips at the sides are holding it in place.

The contents of the box on the right are much older.

Two frames protected by bubble wrap, two diplomas: a second and a third place in the university swimming championship, which once hung in her student room. A pile of textbooks on behavioural psychology, risk management and interviewing techniques. Beneath them she finds what she is looking for: *The Great Gatsby*. The cover is battered, the pages yellowing. Inside the front cover is a stamp: ST PAUL'S HOSPITAL HONG KONG. The name makes the skin on her back begin to burn.

She was a patient at St Paul's for almost three months. She could hardly move her arms and legs; she was in so much pain that she couldn't bear anyone touching her. In the end they put her in an induced coma for two whole weeks.

An enterovirus, the doctors said. Not uncommon in young women. Presumably the virus had got into her body while she was vulnerable to infection because of the burns she'd suffered in the fire, and it had then led to severe meningitis. Her mother had threatened to sue the hospitals, both the one in Ängelholm and the one in Hong Kong. She said their hygiene routines must have been unsatisfactory.

Laura knows better. Knows exactly where the winter fire came from, and why.

Gently she lifts the back flap of the dust jacket. There is a dog-eared photograph tucked inside. Pressure and age have made the photo stick to the cover, but with a little persuasion she manages to free it.

Six people on a jetty. It is the summer of 1987, and she is fifteen years old. The sun is shining; everyone is happy. No one has any inkling of the catastrophe that is just a few months away. Jack is on the far right. She runs her index finger over his smiling face. His eyes make her heart flutter in a way that she hasn't experienced since that night in the hospital when she saw him for the last time.

They're after me. I have to get away from here!

5
Winter 1987

'What a lovely picture – where was it taken?'

The woman in the adjoining seat was pointing to the photograph in Laura's hand.

Her name was Ewa, with a *w*, according to the boarding card she was using as a bookmark. The book didn't have a dust jacket, and Ewa seemed to be at pains to hide the title. It was probably *The Valley of Horses*, or the latest Jackie Collins.

'Vintersjön – it's a lake in northern Skåne.'

Laura and Ewa had ended up side by side when Laura changed planes in Frankfurt. She had observed the older woman discreetly, just as she assessed her classmates every time she started at a new school. Tried to work out who Ewa was by listening and watching. Committing every detail to memory: clothes, accessories, interests.

If they'd been the same age and in the same class, Laura's next move would have been to sit near Ewa and her friends in the dining hall. Listen to their conversation, smile in the right places, try to be let into the group. Shed the label of 'the new girl'. Be accepted.

'That must be your mother.'

Ewa pointed to the woman on the far left.

'No, that's my Aunt Hedda.'

'Oh – there's definitely a resemblance. You've got the same hair colour. I think it's lovely,' Ewa added hastily.

Laura didn't tell her how many times she'd wished she didn't have red hair. Her mother had even suggested having it dyed so that she wouldn't be teased in her next school, but Hedda had persuaded her to leave it.

People don't like anything that's different, but that just means they're idiots, not that there's something wrong with you. You're perfect as you are. My little princess.

The flight had seemed extra long this time. Admittedly the first film had been *Dirty Dancing*, which Mum had refused to let her see in the cinema, but the rest of the films had been soooo boring, and even the paperbacks she'd brought with her hadn't held her attention.

'Are any of the others your cousins?'

One of the holidaymakers had taken the picture last year, a few days before Laura flew back to Hong Kong. Aunt Hedda, herself and the whole gang out on the pontoon. Summer colours, big smiles, laughter that you could almost hear.

'Aunt Hedda calls us her children, but she doesn't actually have any of her own. She was a childminder – she looked after Iben, Peter and Tomas when they were little, and Jack is her foster son.' Laura pointed to Jack. 'He's lived with her since he was eleven.'

Her finger lingered on his face for a second before she moved it to the dark-haired girl in dungarees in the middle of the group, between her and Jack.

'Iben's family live at Källegården, next to Aunt Hedda's holiday village.'

Iben had put her arms around their shoulders, pulled their heads close to hers so that their cheeks were touching.

41

'She looks sporty.'

Laura took a closer look at Iben. How she seemed to be pressing herself a little harder to Jack's cheek than Laura's. Unintentionally, of course. She'd been telling herself that ever since Aunt Hedda enclosed the photo with a letter.

'She is. She's broken almost every school record in athletics. And she got full marks in her standard achievement tests. In every subject.'

'Wow – that's impressive.'

Laura quickly moved her finger to the stocky boy with cropped hair who was standing behind Iben and slightly to the side, almost on the edge of the pontoon. He was staring at the ground, as if he wanted to avoid the camera. Some people in the village called Tomas names because of his tics. Sometimes they made sure he could hear them.

'Tomas lives further away, out in the forest at a place called Ensligheten. He and Peter are best friends. They usually help out in the holiday village over the summer.' She pointed to Peter, who was next to Tomas. He was grinning, holding his fingers behind her head like bunny ears. 'They run the kiosk and the minigolf, cut the grass and hire out the boats.'

Laura almost said that Peter called them the Goonies, but she was pretty sure that Ewa had never seen the film. Peter's uncle owned a video rental store in Helsingborg, and secretly gave his nephew a copy of the latest films when his parents weren't around.

'The Lord Jehovah doesn't like movies,' Peter would joke. 'But he has no problem with putting kids in a suit and tie and getting them to doorstep people they don't even know.'

Peter loved *The Goonies*.

'We're just like them – a gang of outcasts. I'm Mouth, Tomas is Chunk and Jack is Brand. The girls are Andy and Stef...'

'Can I see?' Ewa put on her reading glasses and Laura handed over the photo. 'It looks so beautiful, with the lake and the ridge behind it. Absolutely idyllic. Do you go there often?'

'Almost every school holiday. My dad works very hard,' Laura added in the apologetic tone that always came creeping in whenever she talked about her father.

'And your mother?'

'She's very busy too.'

Laura didn't explain, but Ewa seemed to understand.

'Have the schools in Hong Kong already broken up for Christmas?'

Laura shook her head. 'No, but I go to an international school. A lot of families go home over Christmas, so we finish earlier and have a week's less holiday in the summer.'

Ewa handed back the photograph.

'I can see that you love spending time by the lake. You all look so happy, you and your aunt and your friends. I'm sure you'll have a wonderful Christmas together.'

6

Your mother wanted to call you Jacqueline, can you imagine that? After Jackie Kennedy. How pretentious is that? Fortunately, I managed to change her mind, and that's why you're called Laura after my grandmother, your great-grandmother.

Laura's white SUV is far too big for one person. It consumes too much fuel, and definitely causes too much pollution. But of all the cars that have been crash-tested in recent years, this model is the safest. A great big four-wheel drive tank with a double air-filtration system and a computer that notes and assesses all risk factors through a multitude of sensors and cameras.

When she's sitting in her car, nothing and no one can get to her. She likes that thought.

Three nights, that's how long she's staying in Skåne. That will give her time to bury Hedda and sell Gärdsnäset. She's spent the last few days trying to get ahead. She's conducted two in-depth interviews, dealt with all her emails, prepared the office for two days without her.

In spite of her efforts, she only gets as far as Linköping before her work phone rings. It's Ola, her deputy. He sounds stressed, and Laura immediately knows why.

'What's Marcus done now?'

It takes her half an hour and three phone calls to sort it out. Marcus isn't answering his phone, of course; no doubt he's fully occupied with being fussed over by their mother.

The third time she tries his number she's so cross that she almost has a collision. She's halfway through changing lanes to overtake a lorry when the car's warning system starts flashing and beeping, and at the very last second she sees the black BMW in her blind spot. The driver sounds his horn and flashes his lights as he sweeps past, and it takes quite a while for her heartbeat to return to normal.

Blind spot. She doesn't like that expression. Marcus is almost always in her blind spot, at the very edge of her peripheral vision, beyond her control, yet way too close.

Laura stops for fuel just after leaving the motorway, then sits in the car for a while with a cup of disgusting petrol-station tea that's no use for anything except warming her fingers. There is considerably less snow in Skåne than in Stockholm, only about five centimetres, and the thermometer on the display is showing a couple of degrees below freezing. However, the wind and damp air make it feel significantly colder. The odd snowflake drifts down, and the clouds suggest there is more to come. Apparently six hundred kilometres isn't far enough to escape the winter.

The resolve that has brought her here has gradually begun to waver. After all, there was a good reason why she left Vintersjön and Gärdsnäset. She's not here to dig into the past. Only to see Jack.

Hedda was like a mother to him, and if he knows she's dead, he ought to turn up to the funeral on Saturday. And what then? Would she recognise him? A person can change a great deal in half a lifetime. What if he's bald, with a beer belly? Or even worse – what if Jack has a wife and children? What if he's happy and living a good life? What if he hasn't thought about her in the way she's thought about him?

She has no answer to these questions. The last trace she found of Jack Gerhard Olsson was a note stating that in 1989 the tax office had transferred him to the database of those with no known address, which means he is no longer registered in Sweden, and that they don't know where he's gone. From then on there is no one by that name in any Swedish records, nor the overseas records she has been able to access, although those are not comprehensive. The late Eighties and early Nineties were a little chaotic in Europe. Entire nations ceased to exist. It was a good time if you wanted to acquire a new name, a new identity. A new life.

Laura closes her eyes, pictures his eighteen-year-old face as he perches on her hospital bed. The terror in his eyes, the fear that almost makes his voice break as he says goodbye. The sensation of his lips on hers. Then he's gone. Vanished without a trace.

Will Jack really dare to return to Vintersjön? Will she?

It would be so easy to rejoin the motorway and head back north. No one would criticise her, and she doesn't owe Hedda a thing.

Not a single letter or postcard in thirty years. No indication whatsoever that Hedda has thought of her, missed her, longed to see her again, as she longed to see Hedda.

Is that why Hedda has left Gärdsnäset to her? As a way of asking for forgiveness? It's an appealing thought. And besides, she and Jack aren't scared teenagers anymore; they're two adults, each with half a lifetime of baggage.

She puts the car in gear and slowly drives out of the petrol station.

As Laura approaches Vedarp, she realises that the place doesn't look familiar at all. The road is wider, and the industrial estate, the Lidl store and the residential area opposite weren't here back in the day.

Dusk is falling, and the gathering darkness combined with the falling snow make it difficult for her to orientate herself. The grey façades that once dominated the village are gone, covered by less dangerous material that has been painted in brighter colours.

But the ironmonger's is still there, with a brand-new sign. She wonders if Sven-Erik is still behind the counter, then it occurs to her that Sven-Erik, if he's still alive, must be over eighty, which seems unreal.

The haberdasher's is gone, replaced by a modern building housing a pizzeria and a solarium. Where the post office once was there is now a gym and a funeral director's. She looks for the neon WOHLIN's sign, and discovers an Espresso House instead. A group of kids on mopeds hanging around outside stare at her car as she passes by.

Even the church looks different from the way she remembers it. The old green copper roof has been replaced by black metal that makes the building look furious. The Christmas tree outside is smaller than it used to be, the glow of the lamps colder.

On some subconscious level she had stupidly assumed that Vedarp would look exactly the same as in her childhood memories, preserved in amber at the moment she left the village. Life has gone on without her, of course, which makes her feel childishly disappointed.

A sign at the roundabout points left down to the lake, right towards the castle. She chooses right, passing dirty brown Seventies houses that look more familiar. Peter's family lived in one of them. The village's only Jehovah's Witnesses, who would hardly let him build his models because they were afraid he'd become intoxicated from the glue.

She wonders if Peter's still around, if he'll come to the funeral the day after tomorrow. The prospect cheers her up a little.

She thinks about the last time they met. The conference room at the hospital. The lawyer her father had flown down from Stockholm, the big, unpleasant policeman with the boxer's nose sitting opposite them.

OK, kids. So who do you think did it? Who started the fire at the dance hall?

She shakes off the unpleasant memory. Tries to focus on Jack instead. Will she recognise him? Will he recognise her?

Beyond the houses she can just see the sports hall. There's a sign, and she's driven past before she registers what it says. She slams on the brakes, checks her mirrors and reverses.

The sign is white with black lettering, and it looks quite new. It is pointing in the direction of the sports hall, the swimming pool and what used to be Vintersjö School. But not anymore.

THE IBEN JENSEN SCHOOL. That's what it says.

'Fuck,' Laura mutters to herself, without really knowing why.

The winding route to Gärdsnäset isn't totally familiar either. Maybe it's because the surrounding forest has grown taller, encroached more. The main road, as it was once known, feels like a ridiculous description of the strip of grey, bumpy asphalt that doesn't even have a white line down the middle.

The bus stops are gone, and it looks as if the 132, on which she travelled so many times between Gärdsnäset and Vedarp, doesn't seem to run anymore.

Another memory pops up. Deer on the road, a car in the ditch. Herself, running along the road, caught in the headlights like a frightened animal.

Was that the evening when it all started? The first step towards disaster. Or was it before that? Maybe it was.

Maybe it all started at Kastrup.

7

Winter 1987

Jack was waiting just outside the doors in the arrivals hall. He looked exactly the same as last summer. Blond hair, those blue eyes that made something soft stir inside her breast.

'Hi, Princess!'

She longed to tell him to stop using that childish nickname, tell him that she's a young woman now, not a little princess, but before she could say a word he'd picked her up in a great big hug. She closed her eyes, let her nose brush against his throat, inhaled the smell of him. Aftershave, cigarette smoke. And something else, something that made the soft stirring grow stronger. She'd spent the last twelve hours imagining this moment. She wanted to make it last for as long as possible.

But then she realised they weren't alone. Iben was there, tugging at Jack's sleeve, throwing her arms around Laura's neck as soon as he let go.

'You're here at last! I've missed you so much!'

So Iben had accompanied Jack on the long journey from Vintersjön. Laura should have been pleased. And she was, she told herself. Really pleased.

'It's great to see you too,' she managed to say, forcing a smile to make the words seem more sincere. At the same time, she couldn't shake off a nagging feeling of disappointment. When she'd imagined this reunion, it had been her and Jack – alone.

Jack picked up her bag and headed for the exit, while Iben slipped her arm through Laura's.

'How was your flight?' she said. 'Have you missed us?'

Something had happened to Iben since last summer. She'd got rid of the braces she'd worn since she was twelve, and she was wearing makeup, which was unusual for her. There was something else too, something Laura couldn't quite put her finger on – as if Iben had grown up a lot in just a few months.

A thin sleet was falling outside the terminal. Laura immediately spotted Jack's white Saab. She'd been with him when he bought it in the summer, helped him to wash it and clean the inside, bought new seat covers from Biltema.

'Shall I buy you a Wunderbaum?' she'd laughed, pointing to the display of tree-shaped air fresheners at the checkout. Jack had grinned and shaken his head.

But now there was a red air freshener dangling from the rearview mirror, filling the interior of the car with a nauseating, artificial strawberry smell. She tried to catch Jack's eye, but he was busy putting her case in the boot. For some reason the ugly air freshener had annoyed her. She rummaged in her rucksack and dug out his present, an American car magazine.

'Here – I bought you this at the airport.'

'Thanks!'

He took the magazine and was about to say something else when Iben grabbed Laura's hand.

'Come and sit in the back with me so we can talk.'

Laura's irritation continued to grow. This wasn't how she'd pictured the drive home. She and Jack were supposed to be sitting side by side in the front, maybe they'd even talk about what had happened the night before she left. He'd kissed her. Or maybe she'd kissed him, depending on your point of view.

Instead, she was sitting next to Iben, and all she could see of Jack was the back of his head and the occasional glance in the mirror.

Iben got him to put on some of their favourite songs from the summer, and after listening to her chatter on for a while, Laura began to feel a little less cross. There would be more days, lots of days to be alone with Jack before the Christmas break was over.

She and Iben started singing along to the chorus of 'Last Christmas', louder and louder until they were almost screaming at each other.

Jack caught Laura's eye in the mirror and smiled. The softness in her breast stirred once more.

On board the ferry to Helsingborg they bought sweets, as usual. Yankie bars for Laura, a box of Fazer's sweet liquorice for Iben, while Jack opted for a carton of Prince Red cigarettes.

As they left Helsingborg, the warmth and the movement of the car made Laura's eyelids grow heavy.

'I'm just going to close my eyes for a few minutes,' she murmured.

When she woke up, they were leaving the motorway. Iben was asleep, her head resting on Laura's shoulder. Jack was smoking, with the window open a couple of centimetres. Laura sat quietly, studying him in secret. The blond hair curling into the nape of his neck, his slim fingers holding the cigarette. In the background the radio was playing 'I Want to Know What Love Is' by Foreigner.

Her eyes began to close again. The last thing she saw was Jack's face in the mirror; to her surprise, he looked worried.

The second time she woke up they were almost there. The sleet from Kastrup had turned into heavy snow, and she would have liked to see the Christmas displays in the shop windows as they drove through Vedarp, and the pretty lights on the big Christmas tree outside the church. Unfortunately, they'd already passed the centre, and were on the winding, unlit track beyond the village.

Jack had noticed that she was awake. 'Not long now,' he said.

Iben was still asleep, and Laura kept very still so as not to disturb her. At last they were alone. Nearly.

Jack smiled at her, but that air of worry still lingered in his eyes and in the line of his jaw. In fact, the closer they got to Gärdsnäset, the worse he looked.

'What's wrong?'

'Sorry?'

'Come on, Jack. I can tell there's something.'

He shuffled in his seat, moved his head as if he wanted to check that Iben really was sleeping.

'Everything's kind of . . . different,' he said quietly.

'What do you mean?'

He focused on the road ahead. The forest was closing in around them now, interrupted less and less often by open ground.

'Things have happened around the lake. Things that . . .'

They were passing the big sign showing symbols for the holiday village, swimming and camping. Jack slowed down and turned off for Gärdsnäset.

'What things?'

Laura spoke a little louder than she'd intended, and Iben stirred. Jack clamped his lips together.

'It doesn't matter – forget it.'

Iben sat up, stretched. 'Are we there already?'

'Yes,' Jack said, with a little too much enthusiasm. He shook his head faintly at Laura, making it clear that the conversation was over.

They passed the fir plantation, and after a few hundred metres they reached a tall deciduous forest where the snow had formed a white carpet beneath the straight tree trunks.

The headlights picked out the archway that had been their summer project. It had started out as cut-out pictures and sketches on Hedda's planning board, and ended with them helping Jack to build it.

'It's good to have you back,' Jack said in his normal voice.

And there was Gärdsnäset, twenty or so pretty little red cabins distributed among the trees. Every external light was lit, spreading a welcoming glow that was brightened by the thin covering of snow.

It was so beautiful that Laura almost forgot what Jack had said.

Rows of burning torches lined the track. They passed the big cabin in the centre and pulled up in the turning circle outside Aunt Hedda's house. Laura could see the lake beyond the house and the jetty. There were several metres of ice extending out from the shore, then dark water reflecting the lights from the village.

'Welcome home, Princess!' Jack said, back to his usual self.

Hedda's front door flew open and Laura's aunt came running out, followed by Tomas and Peter – and someone else. A young woman about the same age as Jack, who stopped on the top step.

'Who's that?' Laura asked.

'That's Milla – she moved in back in the autumn. Didn't Hedda tell you? Tomas and Peter are already crazy about her.'

Laura shook her head. Noticed out of the corner of her eye that the worried expression was back on Jack's face.

8

Laura is so lost in thought that she almost misses the turning for Gärdsnäset. The big sign with the symbols on it is gone, there's just a faint, barely perceptible gap between the tall firs.

The forest has closed in around the track. The potholes are so deep that even her big car jolts and judders. The snow is dying away, but the odd flake still drifts down.

When the evergreens give way to deciduous trees, she finally knows where she is. She catches sight of the archway, or rather the remains of it. It was once their summer project, but now it just looks sad.

The framework is still there, but most of the carefully crafted wooden letters are broken or missing, and it is no longer possible to make out the words GÄRDSNÄSET HOLIDAY VILLAGE. The pretty little rose bushes that she and Hedda planted on either side have grown into huge hedges, their sharp fingers clawing at the car's wing mirrors.

It's almost completely dark among the trees, but her headlights pick out the silhouettes of dilapidated cabins. Gaping holes where there were once windows and doors make them look like skulls. She passes the biggest cabin, the central point of the village. The roof has collapsed, the windows are boarded up. The front door is ajar, probably stuck that way. She keeps going, avoids checking to see if the phone box is still there.

Almost the entire village is in darkness. The only light is a solitary lamp down by the water's edge.

The forest opens out into the turning circle, and she sees the familiar building down by the water. Hedda's house, with the lake beyond. Ten to fifteen metres of ice extending from the edge, then black water. The light from Miller's boathouse over on the north shore is reflected in its surface, making it resemble a giant eye, silently watching her.

'Welcome home, Princess,' she murmurs to herself.

Kurt Håkansson's car – a Mercedes – appears after only five minutes – at exactly the time they'd agreed on the phone, which Laura appreciates.

The family solicitor looks more or less as she'd imagined – in his sixties, short, slightly overweight, with glasses. He's wearing a flat cap and driving gloves. He makes small talk for thirty seconds about how the track is in need of repair, then chats for exactly thirty seconds more about the weather, while retrieving a bundle of papers from the back seat. He opens the boot and spreads the papers on the floor.

'Wouldn't it be better to go indoors?'

Håkansson grimaces.

'No, your aunt . . . collected things. It's a bit of a mess in there, which is why I suggested . . .' He leaves the rest of the sentence hanging in the air. It was Laura's idea to meet this evening, rather than at his office tomorrow. She was the one who couldn't wait.

'Besides, this won't take long. I just need your signature in three places. As I said, there was a small insurance payout that will cover the cost of the funeral – a headstone, a simple coffin and a wreath. The only other asset in Hedda's estate is the land, as you can see.'

He points to the property designation on one of the papers.

'We've already had a couple of expressions of interest. Is that something you'd like me to take care of, or would you prefer to deal with it yourself?'

'I'm happy for you to do it. I'm not intending to keep anything.'

'Sounds sensible.'

Håkansson finds the right page and puts a cross by each line where Laura needs to sign. Judging by his body language, he doesn't want to hang around any longer than necessary.

'Thank you for coming,' Laura says when the paperwork is done. She feels a little guilty for dragging him out here in the dark, but she could never have imagined that Gärdsnäset would be so rundown.

'No problem. We have a summer cottage closer to the village, and I usually come over to check on it a couple of times in the winter anyway. Run the water for a little while, empty the mousetraps and so on.'

Laura pulls on her gloves. Her fingers are already stiff.

'How long have you had the cottage?'

'Since the early Eighties. My wife and I used to come dancing here in the summer. That's how I got to know Hedda.'

He breaks off, realises he's gone too far. Strayed into a topic he wanted to avoid.

'Tragic, that fire in '87,' he says quietly. 'Gärdsnäset was never the same after that. Nor was your aunt.' He waves a hand in the general direction of the dilapidated holiday village. 'You could say it was the beginning of the end.'

'Who found her?' Laura asks, mainly to change the subject.

'The postman. The mailbox up by the road got knocked down a long time ago, so he used to drive down on the few occasions when Hedda received post. He realised something was wrong when the door was unlocked but no one was home, then he spotted her down there.'

He points to the pontoon, which is no more than a dark silhouette extending across the ice.

'In the water?'

Laura recoils involuntarily.

He nods. 'She was lying right next to the pontoon. Her heart had given up. Apparently, the doctor had forbidden her from swimming in the winter, but Hedda wasn't the type to listen to anyone's advice, was she?'

'No ...' Laura's gaze lingers on the black water, shimmering at the very edge of the pontoon. 'Hedda loved the lake,' she murmurs.

Håkansson gathers up his papers.

'So,' he says in a businesslike tone, holding out a bunch of keys, 'Gärdsnäset belongs to you now. I'll see you at the funeral on Saturday, and I'll be in touch with regard to the sale. Good luck. With everything,' he adds after a brief hesitation.

9

Winter 1987

They had dinner in the main cabin, a square building with a flat roof that was more like a barracks than anything. It contained a large dining room, a kitchen and several toilets.

Laura liked it very much. Liked the feeling of community that radiated from its walls, the aroma of hundreds of meals that had impregnated the linoleum flooring and the pine panelling on the walls.

Hedda's paintings were everywhere. Laura's particular favourite was right in front of her. It showed the lake early in the morning, with the ridge in the background looking like the outline of a sleeping giant.

Laura had longed for this moment. Iben and Jack on either side of her, Aunt Hedda opposite, Peter playing the fool, Tomas listening quietly.

And yet she wasn't quite as happy as she'd expected to be.

Milla seemed OK, although her style was way too cool for both Vedarp and Gärdsnäset. She had backcombed hair with pink streaks, and she was wearing dark-framed glasses, a denim jacket over a mint-green hoodie, and ripped, stonewashed jeans. The very ones Laura's mother had refused to buy her.

'Hi, Laura. Good to meet you at last,' she'd said when they were introduced.

Her eyes were dark and alert, and her accent was very similar to Laura's own, a pretty neutral standard Swedish. She'd tried to read Milla as she did her classmates, but it was difficult to pick up anything beyond the colourful façade.

Milla also kept a low profile. She didn't say much, she simply listened, which made her even harder to work out.

Just as Iben had said, Peter and Tomas seemed to be competing for Milla's attention, Peter by being funny, Tomas by doing errands.

Laura hadn't managed to ask Hedda why she hadn't mentioned Milla in her letters. She had, however, learned that Milla wouldn't be staying at Gärdsnäset for very long, so maybe that was why?

It wasn't Milla that was preventing her from feeling happy, but what Jack had said in the car. Things had happened around the lake – what did that mean? Things he obviously didn't want to talk about while Iben was listening. And why was he so anxious, almost scared?

Laura's train of thought was interrupted as Hedda got to her feet and tapped her spoon against her glass.

'Darling Laura – you're here at last! We've missed you so much. Gärdsnäset isn't the same without you, but now all my children are back home, and I'm so happy ...' Hedda's eyes shone with unshed tears, and she cleared her throat. 'So we raise our glasses to your homecoming, Laura – *skål!*'

After dinner they settled down on the sofas in front of the open fire. The flames danced, and the heat made their cheeks red. Jack fetched his guitar, and he, Laura and Iben sang 'Hold Me Now' and 'You're the Voice' just as they had in the summer. Hedda, Tomas and Peter applauded enthusiastically after every song, and for a while everything was just as it used to be. However, Laura couldn't help glancing at Milla from time to time. Making fresh attempts to read her.

Milla still wasn't saying much, but after a while Laura got the feeling that she was watching Jack and Iben. Following their movements, observing their expressions, leaning forward a fraction, listening in to their conversation.

Were they sitting a bit too close together? Looking at each other more than at anyone else? Laura thought about the photograph she'd taken out on the plane. Iben's cheek pressed against Jack's.

The nausea came from nowhere. She stood up, mumbled that she had to go to the toilet, but slipped outside instead.

The snow had stopped falling, the air was clear and cold in the way that was unique to Vintersjön. The only sound came from inside the cabin, and a bird calling in the distance. In Hong Kong, Singapore and all the other places she'd lived it was never quiet, and Laura realised how much she'd missed it. She leaned back against a tree trunk, turned her face up to the sky and let out a long breath as she tried to sort out her thoughts.

What exactly did she suspect? That Jack and Iben were in a relationship? Was that what Jack had meant in the car?

Just putting it into words was so painful that she clutched at her stomach.

Jack was playing his guitar again. Laura didn't recognise the song, but Iben clearly did. She joined in the chorus, singing the harmony so beautifully that Laura could hardly breathe.

She pushed herself away from the tree and began to run, away from the cabin. The tears burned behind her eyelids, and she bit her lip to stop them from falling.

*

Hedda's house had red walls and white window frames, just like the cabins in the holiday village. There wasn't a scrap of moss or algae on the roof; Jack must have pressure-washed it when he was doing the end-of-season cleaning.

Inside there was a kitchen, a living room and three small bedrooms. One of the bedrooms had been Jack's before he moved into the apartment above the boathouse. These days Hedda used his old room as a combined office and studio.

Everything was clean and tidy as usual. The smell was a mixture of creosote, oil paints, cat and lake. Laura always associated that smell with Hedda, and it made her feel calm and safe. Tonight, however, it wasn't working quite so well.

'Hello, George, have you missed me?'

The grey tabby cat wound herself lovingly around Laura's legs. She picked George up and hugged her as tightly as she dared. The pain in her stomach eased a little.

Her own room was full of things that she and Hedda had created together over the years. Drawings, ceramics, even paintings. Hedda had framed Laura's best painting and hung it right in the middle of one wall. It depicted a woman sitting on a rock, gazing at her reflection in a lake. Long blue-black hair reminiscent of seaweed covered the front of her body, so that it was only possible to glimpse her nakedness.

Hedda swore that she'd seen the nymph with her own eyes early one morning, sitting on the flat stone by the eastern shore just below the castle. Ever since, she'd tossed a sandwich into the water before she went fishing, to make sure the nymph was in a good mood.

A sandwich for father, a sandwich for mother. And one for the nymph who lives down below.

Laura liked all of Hedda's stories, but the one about the nymph was her absolute favourite. Sometimes, especially in the winter, the nymph even came ashore, searching for someone to lure into the deep water. She was very beautiful, but her burned, pitted back gave her away, which was why she rarely revealed it. Not even in Laura's painting. All that could be seen was the hint of an ominous dark patch near one shoulder, and Laura was particularly pleased that she'd managed to convey her secret.

She went over to the desk and took down the framed photograph from the shelf above. Jack was eleven, she was eight. He had his arm around her, and was looking straight at the camera. There was anxiety in his eyes; his expression reminded her of how he'd appeared in the rear-view mirror just a few hours ago.

The tears threatened once more. She hugged George, buried her face in the soft fur.

The sound of a powerful engine made her look out of the window. She saw headlights over by the cabin, the outline of a familiar truck. It belonged to Iben's father. The rear lights glowed like two angry eyes.

10

Laura waves to Håkansson as he drives away. She lingers for a moment in the gathering darkness. The best thing would be to jump in her car, turn up the heat and head for the hotel in Helsingborg. Come back first thing in the morning, rested and in daylight, as planned.

But something is niggling away at her, something she can't shake off. She gazes at the pontoon.

'The water will hold you up,' she murmurs to herself. 'As long as you have the courage to trust it.'

Nonsense, of course. Words to reassure a child.

Back then, all those years ago, they had worked. As soon as Hedda capsized the boat and they found themselves in the water, Laura had felt something down there lift her up towards the surface. She'd believed that Hedda had a special relationship with the lake. She'd even heard her talking to it sometimes, singing little songs to it.

The conclusion that the cold, dark water had made Hedda's damaged old heart stop beating is entirely logical.

And yet it seems unthinkable, in a way she can't explain. Maybe it's the child in her, refusing to accept that everyone grows old and dies.

Even those we once thought were immortal.

She weighs the bunch of keys in her hand. They are smooth from years of use.

The door is only a few metres away. There's a cat flap near the bottom, and a couple of empty cat food tins beside it. Laura knows what that means. She climbs the steps, finds the right key at the second attempt.

The door opens, letting out a stale, unpleasant smell that makes her step back. She remains in the doorway, peering into the darkness. Glimpses the wooden screen separating the front door from the generous living room beyond.

'Puss puss,' she whispers.

A grey shape materialises.

'Hello, George,' she says as the tabby cat rubs herself against Laura's legs, miaowing loudly.

This George is almost identical to the cat Laura remembers, but of course she knows it's not the same animal. From a purely mathematical point of view, there must have been two or three Georges since 1987, and yet she's behaving as if Laura were an old friend, not a stranger. Probably because she's hungry. The poor little thing must be starving.

'Let's see if we can find you something to eat.'

She feels for the light switch. Takes a deep breath and steels herself. The sight that meets her eyes is worse than she could possibly have imagined. The living room is crammed from floor to ceiling. Chairs, bathroom equipment, boxes, a couple of beds piled on top of each other, and behind them yet more objects so tightly packed together that she can't even make out what they are in the faint light from the bare bulb on the ceiling. And then there's the smell. A mixture of rotting food, damp, dust, drains, rubbish – and someone who hasn't washed for a long time. The smell of human decay.

A narrow passageway leads through the piles and into the rest of the house. The cat follows as Laura reluctantly makes her way to the kitchen, where she finds heaps of papers: yellowing catalogues, junk mail, official-looking brown envelopes. The draining board is crowded with plastic containers and empty spirit and soft drink bottles. Her flesh creeps; she breathes through her mouth, tries to touch as few surfaces as possible in spite of the gloves. Sweat is pouring down her back.

'Calm down,' she tells herself.

George's bowls are on the floor, licked perfectly clean. Fortunately, she's been able to use the cat flap to get in and out and to find snow or rainwater to stop her dying of thirst. The empty cans on the porch looked pretty new; someone must have taken pity on her. But who? The kindly postman, perhaps.

Laura checks out the fridge. A selection of ready meals, bottles of grape tonic, a carton of milk, long since out of date. She finds the cat food in one of the cupboards and has to remove her gloves in order to open the tin. She tries to fork the pinky-brown fishy contents into a bowl without throwing up.

George hurls herself at the food, gobbling down half by the time Laura has filled her water bowl from the tap. She stands in the middle of the room, watching the cat eat, comparing her once again with the George she remembers. Hedda always chose her new cat with great care. George is a female, named after Georgina the tomboy in the Famous Five books, which Hedda used to read to Laura when she was little.

The feeling of revulsion begins to diminish. It is replaced by something else, something more complicated. She looks out of the kitchen window. The glass is thick with dirt. On the sill are four china figurines, a broken candlestick, a plastic thermometer and a pair of military binoculars covered in green rubber. The moon has emerged from behind the clouds, making the water sparkle. The lamp at Miller's boathouse glows far away on the northern shore. She wonders whether Johnny Miller still lives in the big, gloomy house, and if so whether he still cultivates the myth of the reclusive former rock star, hiding behind high walls with his long hair and his beard.

When she and Iben were small, they used to pretend that Johnny Miller was a troll, guarding his treasure. Sometimes they fantasised about rowing across the lake to steal the treasure. They would buy Vintersjöholm Castle and live happily ever after. Everything was so simple when you were a child. Treasure, a castle and a best friend were all you needed to be happy forever more.

She returns to the living room, switches on another inadequate light and picks her way among the chaos. The sofa by the back wall looks familiar, but much dirtier and worn down. There is a pillow and a blanket at one end. The coffee table is full of magazines, empty bottles and glasses, cigarette packets and overflowing ashtrays. A stack of dusty canvases are propped up against the wall behind the television.

The uncomfortable feeling grows stronger. For many years she tried to imagine what Hedda was doing that was so important that she never had the time to contact Laura. She came up with a multitude of excuses for her aunt, each more fanciful than the last, so that the situation was less painful. Now she knows better. Hedda spent her days wallowing in booze, cigarettes, crap food and self-pity until her body couldn't cope anymore. The will is not a gesture of reconciliation, it's just a way of dumping the whole lot on Laura.

Look what I've done, Princess. You'll have to clear it all up – because clearing up after other people is what you're best at, isn't it? Your mother, your father, your little brother. So why not me?

Her mother had been right. She should have settled for her childhood memories, all those lovely times with Hedda that were now tarnished by this misery. And for what reason?

A fucking teenage crush.

George rubs up against her legs again. Maybe she wants more food. Laura heads back to the kitchen, but the cat scurries off towards the bedrooms. Stops and looks at her, as if she's expecting Laura to follow.

However, Laura has had enough. All she wants to do is get in the car, sanitise her hands until they sting, then drive to the hotel. Shower off the wretchedness and the stench and have her clothes, including her jacket and gloves, collected by the dry-cleaning service. Tomorrow morning she will call Håkansson and ask him to sell Gärdsnäset to the highest bidder as quickly as possible, and once the funeral is over she will never set foot in this place again.

She empties the rest of the cat food into the bowl and waits for George to come racing in, but there is no sign of her. Laura washes her hands and wipes them on her trousers before she goes looking for the cat. George is sitting in the hallway. She looks at Laura and miaows loudly.

'Bye, puss,' Laura says, heading for the front door.

But the calculator in her brain has kicked in. How long does a tin of cat food last? How many days can a cat survive in the middle of winter?

Gärdsnäset belongs to her now. The land, the house, all the rubbish, and the cat. Besides which, it's not fair to take out her anger on poor George. Maybe she could ask Håkansson to find a new owner?

She sighs and turns back.

'OK, George, you're going for a ride in my car,' she says, trying not to think about all the cat hair that will end up on the white leather upholstery.

However, just as she's about to grab the cat, George shoots off through a door that is standing ajar.

Laura swears. Maybe it would be easier to leave George here, get Håkansson to collect her. But then she hears the miaowing again, louder this time, as if George is calling to her. Hesitantly she follows the sound, ducking to avoid the cobwebs hanging from the ceiling. She nudges the door with her toe to avoid touching the handle. The hall is so full of crap that she doesn't realise which room it is until the door swings open.

She inhales sharply.

The fitted carpet, the ladybird wallpaper that has begun to come away just below the ceiling. Her old drawings, the shelf of childish pottery, the little oil painting that she was once so proud of. Everything is exactly as she remembers it. The moonlight shining in through the window reinforces the sense of unreality.

She takes a couple of steps into the room.

The floor is clean, the bed neatly made. There is a toothbrush on the bedside table. Waiting for someone. For a guest who never came.

Laura perches on the edge of the bed. The duvet cover is faded from frequent washing, she can't make out the motif, but she knows that it was once a unicorn. She runs her hand over the soft fabric.

George jumps up onto the bed, rubs her face against Laura's arm, then settles down.

Laura unbuttons her jacket, lies down and curls her body around the cat. The bedclothes smell of soap powder, as if they were washed not long ago. George begins to purr.

The nymph is reflected in the picture above them. In the moonlight it is just possible to make out the dark patch on her shoulder.

She did the painting two years before the fire, and yet it is impossible not to see the young woman with the burned back as a kind of horrible omen.

She closes her eyes, draws George closer. The cat continues to purr. The smell of the room and the warm body beside her is so very familiar. For a few brief moments it is as if time has stood still. She is fifteen, almost sixteen, and 13 December 1987 is still to come.

There is still a chance to put everything right.

To avert the disaster.

11

Winter 1987

Iben's father's truck was parked right outside the cabin. Laura didn't really want to leave her room, but she knew that Hedda and the others would find it strange if she didn't come to say goodbye, so she dried her tears, splashed her face with cold water, pulled on her jacket and went out.

Ulf Jensen was tall and muscular, with an angular face. As usual he was wearing a tracksuit and a woolly hat with the athletics club logo.

'Hi, Laura – welcome home,' he said. 'Are you still trying to teach people how to talk properly?'

Laura smiled dutifully. One summer when they were little, she'd tried to teach Iben to speak Swedish without a Skåne accent. Ulf clearly enjoyed the memory. Unlike Laura, who was finding it difficult to look at Iben right now.

Ulf had an air of confidence, something that made everyone listen to him without any need to raise his voice. People liked him, but at the same time they were a little afraid of him. He owned a construction company, was a member of the local council, and also worked as a trainer in the athletics club. No one ever talked about Iben's mother; Laura didn't know why. She'd heard Hedda say that Sofia Jensen had left the family when Iben was little, and never contacted them again.

Ulf had built a small training facility for Iben and her half-brothers at home at Källegården: a running track, a long-jump pit, a concrete circle for discus and shot put. Laura had occasionally wondered what it would be like to have Ulf Jensen as a dad instead of her own.

'OK, Iben – time to go home.'

Laura stiffened as Iben put her arm around her.

'We haven't had the chance to talk properly, just you and me.'

'No . . .' Laura tried to sound normal.

'I've got training tomorrow evening, but maybe we could meet at Wohlin's after school? Four o'clock?'

'Great.'

'Thanks for this evening, Hedda,' Ulf said as he got in the truck. 'And don't hesitate to call me if you see or hear anything. We have to catch that bastard.'

'What did he mean by that?' Laura asked when they'd left.

Her aunt took a deep breath.

'There have been a couple of fires around the lake during the winter,' she said. 'Ulf and a few others have got the idea they weren't accidental.'

'What, you mean somebody started them deliberately?'

'That's what they're saying.' Hedda shrugged. 'But there's no evidence. Just a lot of talk.'

She put her arm around Laura and led her towards the house.

'Time for bed, I think. Jack's going to lock up the cabin for me. You must be worn out, my little princess.'

Laura looked around for the others. She could hear Jack moving around inside the cabin, keeping out of Ulf Jensen's way as usual. She didn't know why, but right now it felt kind of nice.

Peter and Tomas were already on their mopeds. Milla was standing between them; she seemed to be saying something quietly, because both boys were leaning towards her.

'Goodnight!' Hedda called out. All three waved in response.

Laura wanted to ask her aunt about Milla – what she was doing here, why Hedda hadn't mentioned her in her letters, but she felt completely exhausted. All she wanted to do was collapse into her bed and put this evening behind her.

Laura woke in the middle of the night, as she often did after a long-haul flight. She lay there for a few minutes, then realised she wasn't going to be able to get back to sleep.

Her mind was racing. She replayed the afternoon and evening, analysed every comment, every glance, every little gesture.

Iben knew how she felt about Jack. Jack knew how she felt about him. And yet they'd gone behind her back. The thought was so painful that she had to get up.

Quietly, she slipped out of bed, taking care not to disturb George, who was curled up in a ball by her feet. She opened the walk-in closet door. There was a piece of foam rubber stuck to the bottom – a relic from the summer when Laura had caught her leg on the sharp corner. Her mother still didn't know about the incident, or the two stitches she'd needed in her shin.

Under the plastic matting inside was a wooden hatch. When she pulled it open, a gust of cold air struck her.

She'd discovered the crawl space under the house a few summers ago, when Hedda had needed her help to fix a blocked drain. She'd seen the inspection hatch and worked out that it must lead straight into her bedroom.

Ever since then, the crawl space had been her secret hiding place. She lowered her upper body through the hole and directed the beam of her torch at the nearest pillar. She groped behind it and brought out an old cigar box with the word MONTECRISTO on the lid.

The box contained all kinds of treasures: letters that she and Iben had written to each other, a friendship ring that Hedda had helped them to craft out of silver wire. And a long black feather they'd found in the middle of the lake.

'A swan's feather,' Hedda had said. 'From a black swan. A *cygne noir*.'

'What does it mean?' Laura had asked.

'That nothing is impossible,' Hedda had replied with the smile that meant you couldn't tell if she was joking or serious. 'I think it's a present for you from the nymph.'

To be honest, Laura was pretty sure the present was an ordinary crow's feather. She'd never seen a black swan, not in a zoo or on TV, and certainly not here at Vintersjön. But she kept the feather anyway.

Outside it had begun to snow again, bigger flakes this time. Laura stood by the window contemplating the snowfall for a while, rolling the feather between her fingers as her breath misted up the glass. The lake shimmered faintly, and against the sky by the western shore it was just possible to make out the lights of the village. Opposite the house, far away on the northern shore, the solitary lamp on Miller's boathouse shone out as usual. Laura breathed on the glass and wrote her initials, then Jack's, in the condensation with the feather. She just had time to draw a heart around them before the whole thing disappeared. The silent snow was falling more thickly now.

She was about to go back to bed when she saw a movement outside. Some of the exterior lights in the holiday village were still on, and for a second she glimpsed something among the trees – a silhouette with flowing hair, moving almost unnaturally quickly through the shadows before being swallowed up by the darkness. A young woman.

Laura gasped.

Sometimes, especially in the winter, the nymph comes ashore, searching for someone to lure into the deep water. In order to ease her loneliness.

She pressed her face to the glass, but the forest was once again dark and still.

12

Laura is woken by George the eighth, or whatever number the cat might be, rubbing her face against Laura's own. It is light outside, and it takes a few seconds before she realises that she's slept the whole night on top of the covers.

She needs a pee, her mouth is as dry as dust, and her jaws and teeth ache because she didn't use her mouth guard.

She pushes the cat away and drags herself to her feet. The bathroom is more or less what she'd expected. A single dirty towel, yellow stains in the washbasin from the dripping tap. The toilet seat is broken. She puts paper around the rim of the bowl before cautiously sitting down. The bath tap is within reach, and she can't resist trying to turn it, but it refuses to move. She can't see any soap, shampoo or bath towels, so presumably Hedda used to shower in the sauna block by the pontoon.

Somehow the house looks even more depressing in daylight. The knowledge that she's slept here makes her skin crawl. She ought to go to the hotel and scrub all this misery away, as she'd planned to do last night, but her curiosity has been aroused again, and mixed with a dose of nostalgia, it keeps her here.

She nudges open the doors to the remaining rooms. Hedda's bedroom door barely moves because of all the crap. Judging by the blanket and pillow on the sofa, she's been sleeping in the living room for the past few years. It's possible to get into the studio/office, but it's full of cardboard boxes, one piled high with blue bookkeeping files in no particular order.

Laura goes into the living room, gazes at the chaos. Most of the stuff has probably come from the holiday cabins. She thinks she recognises some pine chairs and various items of kitchen equipment, and when she spots several of Hedda's home-made ashtrays on top of an old fridge, she's certain.

Presumably Hedda had tried to salvage anything worth saving. She might even have had a plan for all this stuff, at least in the beginning – but that must have been many years ago.

Laura goes back to her bedroom, an island of tidiness in a sea of chaos. She runs her fingers along the bookshelf and finds only a thin coating of dust. Hedda must have cleaned in here quite recently, maybe only a few days before her death.

But why?

Why clean a room for someone who never comes? Someone whom Hedda has made no attempt to invite for thirty years, yet she still seems to have been expecting Laura.

Yesterday's anger has given way to other feelings.

Mainly melancholy.

The faded photograph of her and Jack as children is still on the shelf. They are very much alike. Both blue-eyed, Laura with red hair, Jack blond. Her eight-year-old self is smiling, stealing an admiring glance at Jack out of the corner of her eye. He is three years older, and has just moved in.

This is Jack. He's going to be living with us.

Why?

Because this is his home now. We're his family.

She's never actually heard the full story from Jack. Hedda simply said that Jack's mother couldn't take care of him, and that he'd been with a couple of foster families. At Gärdsnäset Jack had finally found a place where he was welcome. Loved.

She puts down the photograph and goes over to the wardrobe in the corner. Inside she finds a pair of dungarees and a T-shirt that must have been hers. It's covered in a multitude of stains in different colours, and the sight of it makes her heart contract.

Oil paints, pastels, charcoal.

Even strokes, my little princess. Be patient.

She kneels down. The piece of foam rubber is still there. She lifts the plastic matting, opens the inspection hatch and uses the torch on her phone to illuminate the crawl space.

The first thing she sees is a large, unfamiliar object. Some kind of fan, humming quietly. Beyond it a metal ventilation shaft stretches all the way to a grille on the side of the house facing the lake.

Laura tries to find her treasure, but the cigar box is gone. It doesn't really matter. She can hardly remember what was in it, apart from the black feather that her aunt claimed came from a black swan. A *cygne noir.*

These days Laura knows exactly what the term means. She's heard it used in business circles. A black swan is an anomaly, something that is totally unexpected and has far-reaching consequences. Like getting pregnant when you're over forty, even though the doctors had said it was impossible.

Nothing is impossible, my little princess. Not even the impossible.

As soon as Laura steps outside, the crows begin to caw loudly, sounding the alarm. The darkness of the previous evening had hidden all the nests in the trees near the house and the pontoon. The black birds with their almost ridiculously large beaks sidle to the ends of the branches, flapping their wings and staring at her. Some of the more nervous ones are already circling in the air above. To her annoyance she discovers that she has parked her car right under one of the trees. Needless to say, the roof is spattered with bird shit, which contains not only harmful bacteria, but also corrosive ammonia.

She must find a car wash, as soon as possible. But there is one more place she needs to check out before she leaves.

The steep wooden steps on the side of the boathouse are covered in snow, and the wooden handrail is broken in places. She begins to climb, then stops and flexes her knees to assess the stability. The steps don't move, they merely creak a little.

The door to the upper floor is locked, and the window beside it is covered with a sheet of plywood. She tries the keys in the bundle Håkansson gave her, and finds the right one at the fifth attempt. The handle squeaks as she cautiously opens the door.

The apartment where Jack used to live consists of a single room, which takes up the whole of the top floor. She helped with the conversion – well, Hedda and Jack did the construction work, while Laura's contribution was painting the sloping ceiling and the beams. Jack even let her choose the colour – a white glaze that brought out the grain in the old wood, and made the room lighter.

Now the walls are grey with dirt and dust. All the windows are boarded up, and even though two of the bulbs on the ceiling actually work when she flicks on the light switch, the place still feels dark and gloomy.

She takes a few steps. The floor creaks, her feet leave marks in the dust. The air smells of dampness and desolation.

Hedda obviously decided to store some of her crap up here – minigolf clubs, a big ice-cream sign featuring a man in a striped outfit, and various other things from the kiosk. However, more than half the space is empty. Presumably Hedda didn't have the energy to haul any more items up the steep steps, and started taking them into her house instead.

Laura pushes open the bathroom door. The water in the toilet bowl has dried up, and there is an unpleasant smell of drains. The cabinet is empty, except for an ancient rolled-up tube of toothpaste. The mirror is dotted with fly shit. The water has been turned off, both here and in the little kitchenette. The kitchen cupboards contain nothing but dead mealworm larvae.

Jack's bed is at the far end of the apartment in an alcove, but it holds no attraction for her. The sheets are stained, and a huge cobweb extends from the bedhead up to one of the beams.

There is an American car magazine on the bedside table. The pages are curled, the cover faded with age, but she can still make out the date: December 1987.

Here – I bought you this at the airport.

She touches the magazine, smiles to herself. Remembers the journey from Kastrup with Jack and Iben. How young she was back then. How stupid.

The guilt comes flooding in, which is hardly surprising. She's already missed her evening pill, and needs to dig her morning dose out of her bag pretty soon, or she'll start having nightmares.

She closes the door behind her. There is no trace of Jack here – did she really think she was going to find something?

From the top of the steps the wretched state of the holiday village is even more evident. The roofs of Hedda's house and the sauna block are covered in a thick layer of moss and algae. The sun has turned the red walls pink, and the door of the ladies' changing room is hanging off its hinges. And yet there is something beautiful about it all. Beautiful, and sad.

This was once a much-loved place.

*

The crows resume their cacophony as Laura descends the steps. On an impulse she continues past the changing rooms and the sauna, and walks out onto the pontoon.

The thin covering of snow makes the green wood treacherous. The chains between the drunkenly leaning poles are rusty and make a screeching noise that upsets the crows even more.

She remembers sailboats and rowing boats being moored along the length of the pontoon in the summer. She and Iben were allowed to name them, and Tomas and Peter painted the names on the gunwales with the help of templates that Jack made.

She passes the mid-point, reaches the new section. Extending the pontoon was one of Jack's many ideas.

People will want to sail out here, have an ice cream and play minigolf. We might even get a passenger boat from the village when there's a dance on.

It had all become a reality.

Hedda had convinced the village committee to hire a flat-bottomed summer boat that shuttled passengers who wanted to go dancing back and forth on Wednesday and Saturday nights, but the berthing quay is gone. Maybe it tore itself free of its moorings during an autumn storm and ended up in the bay over by Alkärret, halfway between the holiday village and the castle? Lay there like a beached whale as nature slowly broke it down. Or maybe it just sank. Became an offering to the nymph.

She can still hum the song.

A sandwich for father, a sandwich for mother. And one for the nymph who lives down below.

Hedda claimed she'd heard it from an old fisherman who'd learned it from his great-grandfather. Pure fiction, of course, just like the swan's feather. To think that she once believed such nonsense!

She gazes down into the dark water at the bottom of the ladder. The slight current driving towards Alkärret meant that the water at the very end of the pontoon rarely froze, and even if it did, it was easy to break a hole in the ice. Sitting in the sauna until the heat seared your skin and the sweat poured down, then a quick dash.

Don't hesitate, just jump in!

And then the shock, the feeling of a thousand needles pricking your skin, your heart pounding against your ribs. And finally the endorphins racing through your bloodstream as you clambered back up the ladder, overwhelmed by the experience.

They always waited for each other before going back to the sauna and the shower, and afterwards they would drink hot chocolate in front of the fire in the living room. The bathing book would be filled in while the euphoria of the dip still lingered, added to the happiness of sitting there together.

Laura shivers. In spite of her thick jacket, she's freezing again. The network of scar tissue on her back has woken up, reminding her that her last encounter with the icy waters of the lake was neither euphoric nor happy.

Laura sanitises her hands before asking the satnav to direct her to the nearest petrol station with a car wash. She starts the engine and tries not to think about all the bacteria only centimetres above her head, already eating their way through the car roof.

The holiday village looks even worse by daylight as she heads back to the main road. Vegetation is growing through virtually every one of the small cabins that were once so lovely. Some of the roofs have collapsed, either from the weight of the thick layer of moss and leaves that has accumulated on top of them, or because of fallen branches. Nature is well on the way to reclaiming the whole area. Maybe it's for the best.

As she drives she thinks about Hedda. About the fact that she died in the lake she loved. That ought to be a consolation, and yet there's something that doesn't feel right. A vague, nagging sensation that she can't shake off. It's annoying.

At work she pulls up her colleagues when they talk about abstract concepts like instinct and intuition. Tells them to produce the facts, or let it go.

Good advice, which she ought to follow.

The petrol station is by the motorway. When the rotating brushes have removed the corrosive bacteria bombs from the car roof, Laura buys breakfast for herself and food for George. The shop assistant is a young woman in her twenties with an exaggeratedly friendly smile.

'A yogurt drink and four tins of cat food. Will there be anything else?'

Laura mumbles a response, suppresses the urge to explain that the cat isn't hers, she's not a 'cat lady'. Even though that's exactly what she is. She digs out her bottle of pills and washes one down before starting the car. No one except Andreas knows that she's on antidepressants – a weak dose that she's been taking ever since her university days to keep the nightmares at bay. A dose she's doubled over the past few years in order to avoid other thoughts. Thoughts that are linked to the box containing baby clothes and tiny hand- and footprints, which she's locked away safely in her storage unit in the basement.

Back at Gärdsnäset she parks under a tree without nests. The birds greet her with the same deafening racket as this morning.

She checks her phone before she gets out of the car. Discovers that while there's hardly any coverage out here, one text message has made it through.

Hope everything's OK down there in the provinces. Keep in touch! Love Steph

Everything's fine, she replies. As usual she finds it hard to decide on an ending. Goes for a dutiful *Love Laura*, then puts her phone away and opens the car door.

She's had a rethink. Instead of taking George with her, she's going to feed her, then fill up the bowls so there's plenty of food to last into next week. Then she'll go to the hotel to have a shower and change her clothes before sorting out a wreath for Hedda. If she can get through the funeral tomorrow, she'll be able to leave this sad place for good and return to her normal life.

Unless Jack turns up, of course. The thought is still strangely appealing. Or irritating, depending on your point of view.

Without warning her feet go from under her. She sees her toes in the air in front of her before she lands on the ground with a heavy thud. The sudden movement frightens the crows; they take off from the treetops in a flurry, filling the air with their discordant noise.

She lies there on her back gasping for air as she tries to assess the damage. Her lower back hurts; has she broken anything? Is she capable of crawling to the car and driving to the hospital, given how little coverage her phone has?

After a couple of minutes the pain begins to ease, and she manages to get to her feet. She brushes snow and frozen leaves off her jacket; her back really hurts. The patch of ice she slipped on is hidden beneath a thin layer of snow, but that's not what catches her attention. Next to the patch, at the foot of a large beech tree, are several cigarette butts.

She crouches down, examines them closely. Five Prince Red on top of the snow. It stopped snowing around the time she arrived yesterday evening, which means that the butts are fresh.

She straightens up. From here she can see Hedda's front door and some of the windows. So someone stood out here last night, or even this morning. Stood for long enough to smoke five cigarettes. She looks for footprints, spots them right away. Thick soles, heading this way from the forest in a meandering line, then back again.

A smoker who came here for only one reason.

To watch her.

13
Winter 1987

Laura slept late, stayed in bed for a while listening for Hedda, but the house was silent. She couldn't stop thinking about the figure she thought she'd seen during the night. Had it been a dream? She didn't think so.

So what was it? Or rather – who?

She looked out of the window. A grey mist hung low over the lake, carrying with it a disturbing smell of smoke that had somehow penetrated her bedroom.

She went into the kitchen and found George, who immediately started winding herself around Laura's legs.

There was a note on the worktop.

Good morning, darling Laura!

A water pipe in the boiler room has sprung a leak, so I have to go to Ängelholm to pick up a few things. You were fast asleep, so I didn't want to wake you.

Back soon,

Hedda

She peered outside; both Hedda's and Jack's cars were gone.

George seemed to sense her disappointment, and kept rubbing against her legs as if to console her.

Beneath the note lay the bathing book, a ledger with squared pages in which Hedda meticulously documented every swim. Dates, times, temperatures, who'd swum.

More fun than a diary, she always said. *And it's become a bit of an obsession.*

This year's book was green. The past few weeks and months contained only Hedda's and Jack's names, but when Laura turned back the pages it was summer once more, and there were other names.

Laura, Iben and Hedda.

Hedda, Laura and Jack.

Hedda, Jack, Laura, Iben and Peter.

The only name that never appeared was Tomas.

He certainly wasn't afraid of the water, because he rowed, sailed and fished. He could even wade out a short distance from the shore if necessary, but he had never, ever had a sauna or taken a dip from the pontoon. Even Peter didn't know why.

Laura made herself some toast and flicked through the local paper as she ate. Almost half the paper was taken up by adverts from various businesses, wishing their clients Merry Christmas. There were a couple of small articles, one about a car accident and one about a fire in a deserted house. Surely such fires didn't break out by themselves, so could Ulf Jensen have been right? Was someone deliberately starting fires around the lake? The thought was unpleasant yet exciting at the same time.

On the next page there was a picture of Ulf himself standing in a gym, hands spread wide.

**Record year for Vedarp Athletics Club. Successful
trainer heading for bigger things.**

Laura skimmed the article, in which Ulf proudly listed the
medals the club had won in various competitions. Iben was
responsible for over half of them. The previous day came into
her mind once more. The gestures, the looks. The songs Iben
and Jack had practised together.

The pain in her stomach was back.

There was still no sign of Hedda by three o'clock, so Laura
walked up to the main road and caught the bus. The driver recognised her, asked her to pass on his best wishes to her aunt,
and let her travel for free.

Part of her wanted to stay as far away from Iben as possible,
but another more insistent part wanted to know the truth.

Peter was sitting on his moped outside Wohlin's. He didn't
notice her approaching, and jumped when she tapped on his
helmet.

'Hi – what are you doing?'

He took off his helmet, gave an embarrassed smile.

'Waiting for Tomas. How about you?'

'I'm having coffee with Iben, but then she has a training
session. Shall we meet up later?'

'Me and Tomas have things to do.'

'What kind of things?'

He shuffled uncomfortably, couldn't look her in the eye.

'Just a couple of errands.'

'For Milla?'

She didn't know where the question had come from.

He still refused to meet her gaze. She was about to say something else when they both heard the sound of another moped. Peter quickly crammed on his helmet.

'See you!'

He kick-started his engine and took off as Tomas appeared.

Laura remained standing on the pavement, watching them go.

Wohlin's café and bakery dated from the 1940s, its décor favouring dark wood and brass. The whole place smelled old-fashioned in a homely, comforting way.

'Hi, Laura – so you're back!'

Ella Bengtsson, who must have run Wohlin's for twenty years, was a strong woman with sparkling eyes and a loud laugh.

'You've grown since the summer – how old are you now?'

'I'll be sixteen in March.'

'Sixteen, who'd have thought it! I remember the first time Hedda brought you in. You can't have been more than four or five. You were so sweet, with your hair in plaits – and now you're a young woman.' She stroked Laura's cheek. 'I bet all the boys in school are after you!'

Laura blushed.

'I go to a girls' school. There aren't any boys.'

'What a shame! But I'm sure you have plenty of admirers here in the village. Peter Larsson has always followed you around like a faithful puppy, and then there's that other boy . . .'

'Tomas.'

'That's it, Tomas Rask.'

A small furrow appeared in Ella's brow. Laura knew it was because of Tomas's father. A lot of people were afraid of Kent Rask.

She ordered a cinnamon bun and a soft drink, then sat down at a table by the window with a view of the square. The Christmas tree lights were already on, brightening the December darkness.

She glanced at her watch. Iben was ten minutes late, which wasn't like her. The pain in her stomach was coming back. Part of her wanted to get up and walk out, but she had to know.

Iben came rushing in at quarter past four.

'Sorry I'm so late!'

There was a distinctive whiff of cigarette smoke as Iben pulled off her jacket and hat and draped them over an empty chair. She noticed it herself.

'I was talking to my friends in the smoking area at break time,' she said. 'I'd better air my jacket before I go home to Dad!'

Iben didn't smoke; her father would never allow it. Laura had heard what happened when Ulf caught Iben's brothers smoking. He'd forced Christian and Fredrik to do fifty laps of the athletics track. Fifty laps, that was twenty kilometres. It had poured with rain for the last half-hour, but Ulf had insisted they carry on.

She could see Iben's lips moving, but she wasn't really hearing what Iben was saying. She was too busy studying her face. Iben was wearing makeup again today. Her cheeks were pink, her eyes were shining. Another, fainter smell drifted across from Iben's jacket. A smell Laura recognised all too well.

The cloying scent of a strawberry air freshener.

'You've been with Jack,' she interrupted Iben mid-sentence. 'You're together . . .' Her voice gave way.

'Oh, Laura . . .' Iben had gone pale. 'A lot of things have happened over the past few months.'

She placed a hand on Laura's arm.

'Dad's saying I can't go to the sports college in Malmö, even though he promised. He thinks it's better if I stay at home and train with him, but I can't stand that dump any longer. I have to get away. Jack . . .'

She faltered.

'Jack's the only one who understands. The only one who backs me up.'

Laura pushed her hand away.

'You knew how I felt. You knew what happened between me and Jack in the summer.'

Iben shook her head.

'You don't understand, Laura. You're only here in the holidays, when everything's fine. You don't see . . . the rest of it.'

'What do you mean, the rest of it? You winning every competition, getting top grades in every subject? Is it all so fucking stressful that you have to go behind my back?'

Iben was still shaking her head. Tears had begun to trickle down her cheeks, but Laura didn't care. Actually, it felt good to have swapped places. To be the one who was dishing it out instead of being hurt.

'You don't understand,' Iben said again.

Laura got to her feet. Her chest was burning, her throat, her cheeks. Iben had betrayed her, and yet she was trying to make Laura feel sorry for her. This was one competition she wasn't going to win.

'You can go to hell, Iben. I never want to speak to you again, is that clear? I hope you die!'

She noticed Ella Bengtsson watching them from behind the counter as she grabbed her jacket and ran out without making eye contact with anyone.

14

I'll always love you, Princess!
Always? Even when you're dead?
Yes. Even then . . .

Vedarp church looks exactly as she remembers it. White-washed walls, dark wooden pews that feel rock-hard to her sore tailbone. An altar covered in a white cloth, a cross and two candlesticks, with an altarpiece sufficiently nondescript not to divert attention from the sermon.

The coffin is simple – smooth, white-glazed pine, allowing the age of the wood to show through. It reminds Laura of another, smaller coffin. She tucks the memory back in the box where it belongs.

The funeral director and his assistant have wheeled the coffin to the front of the church on a trolley.

'Would you like to see her?' he asks. 'We've got time.'

Her first thought when he opens the lid is, *That's not Hedda.* In Laura's mind Hedda is just over forty, with long red hair and freckles. She's strong and wiry and can tell anyone to go to hell, then tell them in the next breath how much she loves them.

The woman in the coffin is old, with long grey hair. Her skin is pale and wrinkled; it looks as if it still bears traces of the cold from the water. The hands folded over her chest are bent, the backs marked with dark liver spots.

The little finger and ring finger are missing from the left hand, the stumps covered in a network of scar tissue that Laura recognises all too well. Her back begins to burn. The memory is vivid. The roar of the flames, the stench of burned flesh. The screams that slice into her ears. Her own screams, but someone else's too. Someone carrying her across the ice. The sense of floating on a cloud of white-hot pain.

And finally, the moment before the icy waters of the lake extinguish the whole world: Hedda's face above her. The tears, the anger. The pain.

You burned your hand for my sake, she thinks. *To save me. Is that why you were angry with me? Why you never contacted me again? Or was it because you knew it was all my fault?*

Hedda doesn't answer, either in Laura's head or in the real world. Dead people don't usually respond.

'You can close the lid now,' Laura says.

The hotel has cleaned and pressed her shirt and black trouser suit. There was really no need. She's careful with her clothes, always uses a garment bag to minimise the risk of creasing. However, everything smells fresh when it comes straight from the laundry service, still covered in plastic and with a faint aroma of chemicals.

There's a pool, which is why she drove an extra sixty kilometres to stay here. She did three thousand metres yesterday after dealing with four work calls. She was hoping to wash away the final traces of Gärdsnäset and Hedda's house, but didn't really succeed. The problem is that it's her house now, her rundown holiday village, her scruffy possessions. A horrible mess that is corroding the inside of her head just as the bird shit ate away at the roof of her car, a mess she is desperate to get rid of as soon as possible. She's gone over the events of the previous day several times, trying to work out what was nagging away at her, but it's still there. She keeps remembering those cigarette butts she found. Prince Red, the brand Jack used to smoke.

Is he the one who's been at Gärdsnäset? Is he the one who stood among the trees spying on her, but didn't have the courage to come and knock on the door? Is he going to show up in a little while?

Fifteen minutes before the funeral is due to begin, Laura is a bundle of nerves, yet at the same time inappropriately excited.

The door of the church creaks open and she eagerly turns around, but it's only Håkansson. He gives her a brief nod and sits down at the back. He is followed by three tall men in dark suits. Two are in their fifties, the third in his seventies. They make a beeline for Laura as if they know her, and she gets to her feet.

The older man's hair and eyebrows are chalk-white, and the expression behind his glasses is intense and familiar. She knows who he is before he opens his mouth.

'So, little Laura. It's been a long time. Are you still trying to teach people to talk properly?'

'No, not anymore,' she replies. She immediately realises two things about Ulf Jensen. The sunken eyes, the sallow skin, the false teeth that have become slightly too big for his mouth, the exaggeratedly erect posture – they all tell their tale. Iben's father is seriously ill, but he's trying to pretend that everything is fine.

'My condolences,' he says. 'Hedda was a wonderful person.'

'Thank you. And thank you for coming.'

The words are hollow, and that's the way she feels. Cold, hollowed out.

She hasn't seen Ulf since before the fire, but she remembers what Peter told her at the hospital: Iben's brothers had to wrestle Ulf to the ground to prevent him from running straight into the blazing dance hall. He'd bellowed like an injured animal.

The unpleasant memory causes her to miss a couple of sentences.

'. . . hear you're doing well, Laura. We always knew you'd be something special. You and Iben.'

Laura swallows, doesn't know what she's expected to say. She glances at Iben's half-brothers, but they're no help. In fact, they seem to be avoiding her gaze. Maybe that's not surprising, given what happened at their last encounter.

'Well, we'd better go and sit down,' Ulf says. 'Have you got time for a chat after the service?'

'Of course.'

She tries to sound nonchalant, but doesn't really succeed. Should she say something else, apologise – and if so, for what? How can she explain that what happened thirty years ago was her fault?

The door creaks again and she turns, but she is disappointed once more. This time it's two elderly ladies, clutching their handbags at chest height. She nods to them, but receives only long stares in response.

The cantor begins to play the prelude, and the sound of the organ means she won't be able to hear the door anymore.

She sits down, contemplates the coffin only a metre or so in front of her. There are three wreaths. One is part of the funeral package, the second is the one she ordered at the florist's yesterday, but she doesn't know where the third and largest wreath has come from. It is made up of beautiful red and white roses,

95

but there is no silk ribbon carrying a final greeting, a 'Rest in Peace' or 'In Loving Memory'. No name.

Maybe it's from Ulf Jensen, but in that case why is there no card? Who orders a great big expensive wreath without saying who it's from? Maybe someone who doesn't want to make his presence known, someone who hides in the shadows while he . . .

'Laura?'

The voice belongs to a man in police uniform who has suddenly appeared beside her. For a second she thinks something's happened – to the business, her mother, Andreas. But then she realises the man has said only her first name. He's about the same age as her, his cropped hair is greying and receding. The look in his eyes is a mixture of pleasure and sorrow.

'Don't you recognise me?'

It's the smile that gives him away. She's seen it a thousand times.

'Peter,' she says.

Without thinking, she throws her arms around him. It's not like her, and she quickly lets go.

'I just wanted to say hello.' He sounds embarrassed and turns away.

She grabs his sleeve. 'Won't you sit beside me? You're part of the family too.'

Peter hesitates. His face is a little flushed.

'Of course,' he says, sitting down.

Laura tries not to sound too eager. 'Are any of the others coming?'

It seems as if Peter doesn't hear the question over the organ music, because he simply smiles at her once more. Before she can ask again, the prelude dies away. She looks back at the door, but apart from Håkansson, the Jensens and the elderly ladies, the pews are empty. No Jack. She feels a stab of disappointment. Thinks about the cigarette stubs. The anonymous sender of the wreath.

Maybe Jack just doesn't like funerals?

The priest keeps the ceremony blessedly short. His eulogy is so general it could apply to just about anybody.

Her father's funeral was the polar opposite. St Oscar's Church was packed, and a whole series of people had spoken about what a fantastic individual and entrepreneur Jacob Aulin had been. Her mother had thoroughly enjoyed herself, nodding in agreement at every other word, playing the role of the grieving widow to perfection. No indication that the company had been on the brink of bankruptcy under his leadership. No hint that she and Jacob had slept in separate bedrooms for the past twenty years. Or that he'd regularly spent time with a woman twenty years his junior. A woman she had discreetly but firmly excluded from every aspect of the funeral.

Laura remembers only fragments of that other funeral, the one with the tiny coffin. She was in a grey fog of grief and pills, and she has no intention of going back there.

All ceremonies end the same way.

Three small shovelfuls of black earth, one last hymn, then it's over.

One day we shall all turn to dust, Princess. Me too. That's just the way it is. But before that we're going to have a long and happy life.

Had Hedda enjoyed a long and happy life?

Was Laura happy?

Once again she looks back at the door, but there's no one there. Peter notices, smiles sympathetically.

She can't quite believe he's become a police officer. Peter was always the clown, the one who tried to entertain the rest of the gang. In addition, their shared experience of the police wasn't exactly positive. Sandberg, wasn't that his name? A tall guy with a shaven head and a boxer's nose who scared the shit out of her.

Are you sure it was him? Did you actually see him start the fire?

Peter's smile hasn't really changed, but apart from that he seems much more serious than the boy she knew back then. Maybe it's because of his uniform – and they are at a funeral, after all. However, Laura is pretty sure the seriousness goes deeper.

She steals a glance at Peter as they mouth along to 'Härlig är jorden'. He's not wearing a wedding ring. His nails are cut short, his hands are spotless. His face is clean-shaven. His shoes are well polished, his shirt neatly pressed, his tie is not the cheap kind on an elastic that the police often wear. His watch is a Patek Philippe, which surprises her. That kind of ridiculously expensive time-piece is usually worn by men like alpha-Tobias at Steph's party, and is definitely not something you could afford on a police officer's salary.

As they chat outside the church, she learns that he has a teenage daughter. Otherwise he's the one who asks most of the questions, wanting to know about her work, where she's staying while she's here.

She tells him about Gärdsnäset and George, which evokes another smile.

'So the George dynasty continues. Do you remember when we went on a reincarnation trip?'

'Which one?'

'I only remember the time when George the fourth got run over. We must have been about ten.'

She nods. 'That was my second George trip. We went all the way up to Halland before Hedda found the right cat.'

Peter laughs. His expression is warm, shy and a little bit sad.

'Tomas got carsick and we had to pull over. Hedda said it was a sign. She made you, me and Iben ring the doorbell of the next farm we came to and ask if they had any kittens. That was how she found George the fifth.'

He pretends to hold a kitten high in the air, and for a brief moment he is the Peter she once knew.

'Welcome back to our family, little George.'

He falls silent, as if he's done something wrong.

'Hedda was definitely special . . .' he murmurs.

That's the third time Laura has heard someone use that word about her aunt in just a few days.

'How often did you see her?' she asks.

'I haven't seen her for years. Hedda kept herself to herself. She wouldn't open the door if anyone came knocking – especially the police.'

'Why not?'

He doesn't reply. He pulls a face that could mean anything.

'What about shopping?'

'You remember the mobile grocer?'

Laura nods.

'His son took over, and Hedda bought what she needed from him. As far as I know, she never set foot in the village after the fire. There were those who held her responsible . . .'

He falls silent, then almost seems to recoil, as if he's seen someone in the shadows beneath the pine trees a short distance away in the churchyard.

'Excuse me,' he says. 'There's someone over there I haven't seen for ages.'

Before Laura can respond, he heads quickly down the path. She can just make out a man, and her heart begins to beat faster. She's about to follow Peter when Iben's father and half-brothers intercept her.

'So you've met that poor bastard.'

Ulf waves a hand in Peter's direction. Laura wants to ask what he means, but Christian Jensen gets in first.

'Nice ceremony.' He smiles warmly, while Fredrik keeps his eyes fixed on the ground.

'Thank you.'

'What's happening with Gärdsnäset?' Ulf's abrupt question takes her by surprise.

'Hedda's solicitor is sorting out the sale as soon as possible.' She points to Håkansson, who is standing by the gate.

'Who are you selling it to?'

'I think there have been a couple of offers. If you're interested, speak to Håkansson.'

Ulf shakes his head. He is clearly annoyed.

'I thought Hedda had made a decision. Didn't she leave any papers?'

'Not as far as I know.'

Laura sees no reason to mention the chaos in the house.

Behind the Jensens she sees Peter approaching with the stranger. He's wearing a suede fringed jacket and a baseball cap pulled well down over his forehead. The rest of his face is almost completely covered by a large pair of sunglasses and a bushy beard.

'Are you staying long?' Christian asks.

Laura hears herself replying that she's leaving tomorrow, but all her attention is focused on the man with the beard.

'That's a shame. We were hoping you'd have time to call and see us, just like you used to do.'

Ulf's tone has softened. Laura manages to summon up a vague smile as she continues to stare at the man.

'Excuse me,' she says. 'Nice to see you again.'

She slips past the three men and sets off towards Peter and his companion, but as soon as she gets closer she can see that he's much too old to be Jack. He and Peter shake hands, and just before he turns to leave he meets her gaze and gives her a brief, respectful nod. She watches him go. He wears his grey hair in a ponytail that reaches halfway down his back. There can only be one person in Vedarp who goes for the ageing rock star – or old troll – look.

'Was that Johnny Miller?'

Peter nods.

'Do you two know each other?'

'He's my father-in-law,' Peter explains. 'Or rather he was.'

'Are you divorced?' Laura asks. Too late she remembers the lack of a wedding ring on his finger.

'I was widowed two years ago.'

'Cancer?'

She doesn't know why she said that. The word just came out. He shakes his head. 'Car accident.'

'I'm so sorry.'

A widower with a daughter – so that's why Ulf Jensen referred to him as 'poor bastard'. They've both been grieving for the same amount of time, she and Peter, and she almost shares her story. Tells him about the box with its precious contents. But she stops herself.

'Have you heard anything about the others?' she says when enough time has passed to be able to change the subject.

'Tomas's father still lives out at Ensligheten, that's all I know.'

He clearly doesn't want to say any more. She's about to mention Jack, but he gets in first.

'Shall we go over to Iben's grave?'

She'd like to say no. She hates churchyards and graves, but Peter has already started walking. He turns down one of the paths and stops in front of a huge memorial in marble and metal.

The Jensen family grave. A list of Danish names in ornate writing, dating from the early seventeenth century. Down at the right-hand side, a little white stone is sticking up in the snow.

Iben Margarethe Jensen
2 January 1972 – 13 December 1987

Even though Laura is prepared, her body reacts violently. Her scars feel alive, as if they are crawling all over her back, eating into her until she is as hollow as the nymph in the painting above her bed.

Iben is lying here beneath the snow, while she herself has lived half a life. In more ways than one. Neither she nor Peter says anything, they simply stand in silence, side by side.

The covering of snow on the grave is untouched. She looks around for Iben's father and half-brothers, but they've already left the churchyard.

Peter reads her mind.

'Rumour has it that she's not actually buried here. That Ulf scattered her ashes in the lake instead. It's illegal, but I don't think anyone would have objected. Ulf's always done exactly what he wanted.'

Laura nods.

It somehow feels right that Iben isn't lying here in a windy churchyard, by a ghastly monument to a load of dead ancestors.

Iben is resting in the lake. *Well done, Ulf.*

Maybe she should do the same with Hedda's ashes? Let Hedda and Iben rest in the lake together.

She closes her eyes, pictures her aunt and Iben out on the pontoon, just a few paces ahead of her, on their way to the ladder and the water.

Come on, Princess, don't hesitate – just do it!

From out of nowhere, the niggling feeling is back, even stronger now. The feeling she refused to pay attention to, because unlike Hedda she doesn't believe in inklings or intuition, but in facts. In things that can be seen, measured and proved. And yet it just won't go away. It keeps whispering that there's something about all this that doesn't add up, that something is going on below the surface, something she's missing.

She opens her eyes and turns to Peter.

'Is there a police report on Hedda's death?'

15

Winter 1987

Laura had just missed the bus to Gärdsnäset and had no desire to wait an hour for the next one. Besides which, the bus stop is the first place Iben would come looking for her.

Iben who had betrayed her, gone behind her back. It must have been Iben she'd seen in the middle of the night. Iben who had slunk out of Källegården when her father and brothers had fallen asleep so that she could spend a few more hours with Jack.

The pain in her stomach had become an agonising cramp that was making her feel sick, forcing her to stop from time to time and bend forward, hands resting on her knees.

Tears were searing her throat, but she refused to cry. Not yet, not until she was back home with Hedda. She straightened up, kept walking. It was less than four kilometres from Vedarp to the holiday village; she could usually cover the distance in half an hour.

She'd just passed the spot where the street lamps ended and the forest took over when she started to shiver. Her body hadn't got used to the difference in temperature between Sweden and Hong Kong, and after a few minutes her legs began to tremble.

She increased her speed, kept looking over her shoulder in the hope that a car would appear.

Before long she saw lights approaching among the trees. She raised her arm and waved. The car was moving fast; now she could see that only one headlight was working, which made the vehicle look as if it had one eye. She took a cautious step into the road so that she could be seen better. The sound of the engine changed as the car slowed down and stopped. It was a battered old Volvo that she didn't recognise. The side window was wound down.

'Want a lift?'

The driver was a man in his mid-forties with slicked-back hair and a moustache that went all the way down past his chin. Beside him in the passenger seat was a big black dog. Now she knew whose car this was. Kent Rask. Tomas's father.

She swallowed.

'Where are you going?'

Laura glanced around anxiously. The narrow road was dark and deserted. Her knees were twitching with the cold.

'Gärdsnäset,' she said as firmly as she could.

Kent Rask looked her up and down. Curled his lip in something that might have been a smile.

'Hop in.'

He shooed the dog into the back seat and opened the passenger door. Laura perched on the edge of the stained seat; the car stank of animals, cigarette smoke, sweat and oil.

Kent lit a cigarette, watching her with amusement as she fumbled for the seat belt.

'I took the belts out,' he informed her with a grin. 'They got in the way.'

There was a horrible grating noise from the gearbox, and the car began to move.

'You're Hedda Aulin's niece.'

A statement, not a question. He took a deep drag on his cigarette and blew the smoke in the general direction of the partly open window, as Jack always did.

'Mmm,' Laura said. In spite of the unpleasant smells, it was good to be in the warm.

The car picked up speed. The broken headlight meant that only half the road was visible. The dog had plonked himself in the middle of the back seat, with his nose just centimetres from Laura's left ear, tongue hanging out of his open mouth. He had big, sharp teeth.

'The girl from the city, whose daddy is rolling in money.'

He was teasing her. She didn't reply, but it didn't seem to bother him.

'Your aunt's doing well too. Fully booked for the whole summer. She and the orphan kid have done a good job with Gärdsnäset.'

Laura couldn't let that go.

'His name is Jack.'

Kent grinned. 'Is it now?' He took a fresh drag, his other hand draped nonchalantly over the wheel. He had a tattoo – three dots – in the fold between his thumb and forefinger. On the back of his hand there was a triangle, or maybe it was a pyramid.

He put his foot down. The road had been cleared, but there were still patches of packed snow.

'You've got your own little gang out there. You, my Tomas, Peter Larsson, Ulf Jensen's girl. Hedda's little flock of daycare darlings. And Orphan Jack, of course.'

Laura looked away. They'd already covered a kilometre; one more to the turning, and she could get out.

'You and Iben Jensen are best friends, aren't you? Her father's a stroppy bastard. All the times I've had to listen to the fucker going on about how Källegården has been in the family since sixteen hundred and something. You must have seen the coat of arms he claims they found on the wall when they were redecorating the farmhouse.'

He snorted, wound the window down a little further and flicked the cigarette butt through the gap.

'He's trying to claim that the family's descended from nobility, but I'm sure he painted that fucking coat of arms himself. Made the whole thing up to attract attention.'

He took a bend so fast that the car skidded. Laura clutched the seat. They were nearly at the turning; he ought to start slowing down at any second.

'And he watches that girl like a hawk. God help the boy who tries to get anywhere near her. Unless he's got a fancy surname, he won't be good enough in Ulf's eyes, I can promise you that. No village mongrels sniffing around his purebred show bitch. What do you think, King?'

The dog pricked up his ears at the sound of his name.

'Mind you, there's no denying that Iben's turned into a pretty girl,' he went on. 'So have you. What was your name again?'

He placed his right hand on the gear stick, his little finger almost touching her knee. She moved both legs as close to the door as possible.

'Laura,' she managed to say.

The sign for the holiday village must be coming up, but Kent showed no sign of slowing down.

'Laura, that's it. Laura Aulin. How old are you, Laura?'

'Nearly sixteen.'

'Aha – then you'll be legal.'

He grinned again, more unpleasantly this time.

Laura quickly looked away. In spite of the broken headlight, she could see the sign less than a hundred metres away.

'You can drop me off here,' she said.

Kent still didn't slow down.

'I've got a little errand to do first, Laura. A couple of things I need to pick up for your aunt. I thought we could go and fetch them, then I can take you all the way home.'

'There's no need, I can walk the last bit. Aunt Hedda's waiting for me, she'll be worried if I don't . . .'

'I'm sure quarter of an hour here or there won't make any difference. It will give us a chance to get to know each other better.'

They sped past the sign. The next turning was for the Jensens' farm.

'Please stop!'

'Calm down – this won't take long.'

Her fear seemed to amuse him.

Laura groped for the door handle, glanced out of the window at the trees swishing by. She would never dare to jump out at this speed, and if she did, she'd hurt herself badly. But after Källegården there were only forest tracks. No neighbours, no one anywhere near, apart from the castle.

Suddenly, the dog began to bark. Laura almost screamed.

'Quiet, King!'

Kent turned around and shook his fist at the animal.

Up ahead Laura saw several grey, four-legged shapes. Three large deer came into focus, standing in the middle of the road with their heads up, making no attempt to move out of the way.

'Look out!' she yelled.

Kent slammed his foot on the brake. Laura was hurled forwards and banged her head on the dashboard. Noises reverberated inside the car – Kent swearing, the dog barking, the squeal of the brakes, the tyres screeching on the tarmac, then on snow and gravel.

A thud, then everything went quiet.

Laura felt for the door handle. The cold night air cleared her head. The car was at an angle, the left front wing down in the ditch. A cloud of steam was rising from the bonnet. She scrambled out, slipped a couple of times before she managed to get onto the road. There was a smell, a taste of burning in the air. Her head was pounding after the encounter with the dashboard. Kent was still swearing as he tried to open the driver's door, which was blocked by the ditch.

Instinctively she began to run in the direction of Gärdsnäset. The turning was five hundred metres away, but before that there was a path through the forest; she and Iben used it when they were cycling to each other's houses. She could follow it in the pitch dark if necessary.

Behind her she heard a car door slam, then the grating sound of the starter motor.

'Don't start, don't start, don't start,' she prayed, on the verge of tears.

The roar of an engine made her glance over her shoulder, and she saw the reverse and brake lights through a thick fog of exhaust fumes. They were moving slowly, then faster and faster as the car regained purchase on the road surface. Laura tried to speed up. The path was still over a hundred metres away, and the road was surrounded on both sides by thick, almost impenetrable fir trees.

She looked back again. Kent had managed to turn the car in her direction. The single headlight shone through the darkness as he set off – but there were lights approaching from the opposite direction too. A car with its lights on full beam.

She raised both arms, waving frantically to get the driver to stop. The one-eyed Volvo was right behind her now, but she kept on running, made sure she was clearly visible to the oncoming driver. She heard the sound of brakes, first from the Volvo, then others that were definitely newer. With a huge wave of relief she recognised Iben's father's pickup truck. The door opened and Ulf Jensen climbed out.

She ran straight to him, threw her arms around his neck and promptly burst into tears.

'What on earth has happened, Laura? Are you OK?'

She sobbed into his chest, incapable of saying anything.

The door of the Volvo opened.

'What the hell are you up to, Kent?' Ulf asked.

'There were deer on the road. We went into the ditch. I think she's just a bit shocked.'

Laura still couldn't catch her breath or speak, just stood there shaking in Ulf's arms.

'Is that really what happened, Laura?' Ulf said.

Laura kept shaking. Kent came closer, with the big black dog beside him.

'Like I said, she's had a shock. She's not used to life in the country. I'll drive her back to Gärdsnäset.'

Ulf held up his hand.

'You've done enough for tonight. I'll take Laura home, and you can explain yourself to Hedda tomorrow morning.'

Kent glared at Iben's father. The dog began to growl.

'She's my responsibility. I'm taking her home.'

The two men stared at each other, neither prepared to give way.

'You sanctimonious bastard,' Kent muttered. 'Swanning around on your farm, boasting about your fine ancestors. But don't forget – I know about the skeletons in your closet.'

'What the fuck do you mean by that?'

Ulf's face was red with anger.

'Nothing.'

Kent took a step back and grunted a command that made the dog shut up.

'You drive her home if you're so keen, Ulf. I've got better things to do than take care of silly little girls.'

He spat out a gob of phlegm that landed centimetres from one of Ulf's shoes, then he turned and headed back to his car.

16

The police station in Vedarp is next door to the town hall, and consists of only two rooms with a kitchenette in between. The outer room is a small reception area, the inner is Peter's office.

A notice on the door informs her:

Open Tuesdays and Thursdays 12.00 – 14.00.

At other times please contact the police station in Ängelholm, or call 114 14.

In an emergency call 112.

'So this is where I work,' Peter says, spreading his arms wide. 'Coffee?'

'I'd prefer tea.'

'No problem. Go on in and take a seat.'

There are two armchairs, a desk and a bookcase. On the top shelf is a model aeroplane from the Second World War, so detailed and cleverly made that you can even see the tiny pilot giving the thumbs-up inside the cockpit. Peter has obviously carried on with the model making he did as a boy, and taken it to a new level. It's kind of sweet, Laura thinks.

On the shelf below is a large school photograph of a teen-age girl, who must be Peter's daughter. She has short, coal-black hair, heavily made-up eyes, and two rings in her right eyebrow. Her expression manages to combine defiance and utter boredom.

There is also a wedding photo. Peter is probably about thirty. He is wearing his dress uniform and a white peaked cap, gazing at the camera and looking very happy. The woman beside him can't be more than twenty-five. She is platinum blonde and very beautiful, in a cool and slightly impersonal way. Her dress looks expensive, as does the ring on her finger. Presumably Daddy paid. Johnny Miller might not be a troll, but he's as rich as one, as the saying goes. Laura thinks about Peter's expensive watch. Guesses it might have been a wedding present.

There are several framed diplomas on the walls: Interpol, Europol, the UN.

She finds it difficult to reconcile all this with the Peter she used to know. Judging by the diplomas, he's a talented police officer who's travelled the world, and yet now he's working here, all by himself in a tiny local station in the middle of nowhere.

He reappears with two mismatched mugs, puts them down on the desk and holds out a small box of assorted teabags.

'Where did you work before you came here?' Laura asks.

'The National Crime Unit, until two years ago.' He sits down. 'After Victoria passed away, I took some time off. I didn't go back to work until last spring.' He takes a sip of his coffee. 'This is a good job. It might not be exciting, but I have a lot of autonomy, and I can cycle to the station. I'm home when Elsa finishes school. Are you married, by the way?'

She shakes her head, surprised by the sudden change of subject.

'Divorced just over a year ago.'

Her turn to change the subject – and quickly, before he asks if she has children.

'Your daughter's very pretty,' she says, nodding in the direction of the photograph.

'Thank you.' Peter's face lights up. 'She's had a tough time since we lost Victoria, but we're getting there. She starts university in September.'

He puts down his mug and taps away at the computer keyboard. A printer in the corner of the room comes to life.

'I was first on the scene at Gärdsnäset. The postman found Hedda early in the afternoon. He rang the emergency services, and I got there just before the ambulance and the fire service.'

He collects the printout and hands it to her.

'This is the initial report and my notes. That's all there is. A post-mortem isn't required when someone dies of natural causes. Hedda had had two heart attacks, the latest in the early autumn. Dr Olsson had warned her against taking saunas and swimming in the lake in the winter, but you can imagine Hedda's reaction to that.'

'I expect she told him to go to hell.'

Peter gives a wry smile. 'Something along those lines.'

Laura likes his smile.

Back in the hotel room she spreads out the documents on the desk. Her phone rings, as it's done a couple of times during the drive from Vedarp. It's Andreas, but she has neither the time nor the inclination to talk to him right now.

She doesn't actually know what she's looking for; maybe it's just a way of silencing that irritating little voice.

Peter's report is brief and impersonal, written in dry official language.

```
Detective   Inspector   Peter   Larsson   was
called out today to Gårdsnäset holiday vil-
lage because the body of an elderly woman
had been found in the water by the pontoon.
The discovery was made by John Elwin, the
local postman.
```

He then lists the subsequent course of events. Hedda's body was recovered by the fire service, the ambulance was sent away because it wasn't required, the duty doctor officially confirmed what everyone already knew.

```
Duty Dr G. Olsson pronounced the victim dead
at 14.43. In his opinion, the body had been
in the water since at least the previous
evening. He identified the deceased as Hedda
Aulin, aged 72, one of his patients who was
resident at the address in question.
```

And then the last line, in summary:

```
At this point there are no suspicious cir-
cumstances surrounding the death.
```

Laura reads the interview with the postman, who tells the same story she's already heard from Håkansson. He drove up to the house, knocked on the door but didn't get an answer. He real-ised the place was empty, then spotted something in the water. Realised what it was and called the police.

The last sheet of paper is a detailed analysis of the scene, and several digital photographs that Peter must have taken.

She steels herself.

The first shows the body in the black water. Hedda is face down, with only her upper back and the back of her head and arms above the surface. Her skin is chalk-white, the grey hair is studded with fragile ice crystals, and the image is horrific, beautiful and unreal, all at the same time. It reminds Laura of a picture in an old book of fairy tales.

The current has pushed the body against the ladder rather than carrying it across to Alkärret. There is something pale by one leg. She leans closer. It's probably a towel – but why is it in the water, partly wrapped around Hedda's leg? It could have blown in, of course. Hedda was lying there all night and for most of the next day, plenty of time for the wind to pick up the towel.

She reads through Peter's comments on the photographs, including the changing room in the sauna. He checked the heating element, and established that it's linked to a timer that begins to warm up the sauna at five thirty each evening, and switches it off at ten. Hedda's clothes were hanging on one of the hooks.

She moves on to the last photo – the pontoon, from a slight distance away. A light mist hovers over the lake, and far away on the other side she can see the outline of Johnny Miller's house.

The picture is lovely yet disturbing, although she's not sure why.

She leans back and clasps her hands behind her neck. There's nothing out of the ordinary here. An old woman takes a sauna then goes swimming in the middle of winter, in spite of two heart attacks and her doctor's specific orders. Why can't she accept that?

She is beginning to suspect that it's really about something else, that it's her disappointment at Jack's failure to show up that is eating away at her. She's come down here, put herself through all this, and there's no Jack. Maybe he didn't want to come, but it's more likely that he lives abroad and has no idea that Hedda is dead. He probably hasn't given Vintersjön, Gärdsnäset, Hedda or Laura herself a thought in years. And why would he? Jack was virtually chased away from here, in fear of his life.

What about the cigarette butts? whispers a little voice in her ear. Five Prince Red, the brand Jack used to smoke.

Then again, Prince Red isn't exactly an uncommon brand. Maybe it was some curious local who wanted to take a look at her. It's a feeble explanation, she can see that, but right now it's all she has.

She gets to her feet. Her swimsuit has dried off in the bathroom, and she decides to swim a few thousand metres to clear her head. Put Jack, Peter, Hedda and Vintersjön behind her once and for all, before she goes home tomorrow morning.

Unfortunately, there is a noisy family with small children in the pool. Laura waits on one of the benches for a while, but when the family is joined by a couple of businessmen with hairy beer bellies, she decides to give up.

On her way to the changing room, she passes the sauna. It's empty, so she slips inside. Keeps her swimsuit on in spite of the notice saying it's forbidden. Sits down and enjoys the heat and the smell of warm pine.

Eighty-five degrees, according to the thermometer on the wall. The perfect sauna temperature, as Hedda would have said.

And suddenly Laura realises what she's missed.

What it is that doesn't feel right.

17
Winter 1987

The next morning, the ice extended further out into the lake. 'If it carries on like this we'll be able to get our skates out at the weekend,' Hedda said, putting her arm around Laura. 'I hope you haven't forgotten how to skate!'

They were walking through the holiday village on the eastern path, following the shoreline, passing cabins ten and twelve, then the snow-covered minigolf course and football pitch. Laura had glanced up at Jack's window when they reached the boathouse, but the lights were out and the curtains closed.

It was only seven fifteen, and the sun was beginning to rise. Hedda was pulling the sled, with the axe resting on top.

Vintersjöholm Castle had a large Christmas tree plantation beyond Alkärret, at the eastern corner of the lake. Every year, early one morning in the days leading up to Lucia, Hedda and Laura sneaked in. When they'd located the perfect tree, Laura kept watch while her aunt wielded the axe. Then they hurried home with their booty before anyone spotted them.

The outing was usually one of Laura's favourite traditions, but on this particular day she was finding it hard to get in the right mood.

'How's the bruise?'

Hedda stopped and gently ran her hand over Laura's forehead.

'OK.'

Laura hadn't revealed all the details of the previous evening; she'd simply agreed when Ulf Jensen gave his version of events. She'd accepted a lift from Kent Rask, they'd ended up in the ditch, and the bang on her head had left her a little confused. She didn't want to tell Hedda that Kent had frightened her, or why she'd set off for home on foot instead of waiting for the bus.

Fortunately, Hedda hadn't said much. She'd thanked Ulf for his help, examined the bump on Laura's forehead and shone a torch in her eyes to make sure she hadn't suffered a concussion. Then she'd made macaroni cheese for supper and sat with her arm around Laura on the sofa until the girl fell asleep, as if she realised it was closeness that was needed rather than a cross-examination.

'Do you feel sick?'

Laura shook her head.

'Ulf said you came off the road just before Källegården's drive. Why didn't Kent drop you at the turning for Gärdsnäset?'

A good question, one that Laura had asked herself several times. Why had Kent Rask kept going? What would have happened if the deer hadn't appeared in the middle of the road?

'He said he had to pick up a couple of things for you.'

'I see.'

'Do you know what he meant?'

Hedda nodded. 'It's something and nothing – I thought he'd forgotten about it. Forest business, you know?'

Forest business – the kind of business you kept to yourself. Like when Hedda taught her to make 'elk poo' out of mud and fir needles and put it in jars to sell in the shop to German tourists.

Laura wanted to ask what forest business Hedda and Kent were involved in, but her aunt had sped up and was now several metres ahead. Laura felt relieved, and a little stupid at the same time. Kent really had had a legitimate errand. She'd been scared for no reason.

'Jack wants to start draining here in the spring.' Hedda had stopped and was pointing in among the trees. 'He thinks we've got room for eight or ten caravans and at least as many tents if we can just get rid of the ground water from the marsh.'

Jack's name made Laura's heart skip a beat.

They reached the stone wall that formed the border between the holiday village and the marsh. A set of steps with sturdy railings on either side made it possible to get over the wall.

'Grab the back end.'

Together they managed to lift the sled over. The snow made the wood slippery, and it was a couple of minutes before they were safely on the other side.

Alkärret was Källegården's only contact with the lake. A few hectares of low-lying marshland, squeezed in between Gärdsnäset and the castle, no good for agricultural use or construction. Ulf Jensen grazed his sheep on the marsh, a rare breed that could stay outdoors all year round. Their name was difficult to pronounce. Laura and Iben had always found the sheep a little creepy, with their blue-black heads and bulging eyes, but the animals tended to stick to the area nearest the main road, where the ground was less muddy.

The path gave way to an overgrown duckboard footbridge that wound its way between the trees. Here and there the snow had been blown away, exposing dark patches of frozen water. Hedda pointed to them and said: 'The eyes of the nymph. So be careful what you do.'

She nudged Laura in the side with her elbow.

Laura pulled a face to show that she didn't care about old superstitions, yet she couldn't help glancing at those black patches from time to time. They really did look like eyes.

The marsh was quiet; the only sound came from their own footsteps and the sled scraping along the footbridge. Occasionally a few crows who were up early struck up their own dissonant version of the dawn chorus.

Laura wanted to tell Hedda about the previous day. About her meeting with Iben. About Iben and Jack. Yet at the same time she didn't want to, oddly enough. Maybe she was afraid of what her aunt would say? Instead, she decided to bring up something else that had been bothering her.

'Why didn't you tell me about Milla in your letters?'

Hedda stopped.

'Oh – I thought I had done, but it's been such a busy autumn.' She made an apologetic gesture. 'An old friend of mine who's a social worker got in touch. Milla was only meant to be staying for a few weeks, but things became difficult, so I've agreed that she can stay until she turns eighteen in January. We've got plenty of room in the winter – there's only me and Jack.'

'And me!' Laura snapped.

Hedda smiled and stroked her forehead again.

'And you, of course. I should have said something. Can you forgive me?'

Laura would have liked to sulk for a while longer, but Hedda was smiling in the way that made it hard to stay mad at her.

'Of course,' she muttered.

Hedda flung her arms around her niece and dug her fingers into her ribs.

'I didn't hear you. Do you forgive me?'

Laura stepped off the bridge, lost her balance and fell into a snowdrift with Hedda on top of her. Her aunt carried on tickling her.

'Say you forgive me! Say it!'

Laura wriggled and kicked and tried to keep the mask in place, but it was impossible. She was very ticklish, and Hedda knew exactly what she was doing.

'OK, OK, I forgive you!' Laura laughed.

The tickling stopped, Hedda rolled to the side and they lay there next to each other in the snow.

'I love you, my perfect little princess.'

Laura didn't answer. The happiness she'd been searching for ever since she arrived finally seemed to be within reach, but then she thought back to yesterday again.

'Why did Milla have to move?' she asked, trying to keep the unpleasantness at bay.

'She had a few problems. She needed to get away for a while.'

'What kind of problems?'

'She was mixing with the wrong people. Made a few mistakes. It's easily done when you're young and stupid and think you're immortal. I was the same.'

'So what did you do?'

Hedda didn't reply. Instead, she scrambled to her feet, brushed off the snow and held out her hand to Laura.

'Come on – let's go and chop down that tree before the forest ranger wakes up!'

They clambered back onto the footbridge and set off towards the castle. Laura took the lead, and Hedda followed on behind with the sled. The hoarse, agitated cawing of the crows grew louder as they approached an ancient oak tree growing on solid ground. They could see black, flapping wings among the branches; the birds were so busy they barely registered the presence of strangers.

Then, as if from nowhere, came a stench that took Laura's breath away. Paraffin, singed hair, burned meat.

'Laura,' Hedda said warningly, but it was too late. She'd already looked up.

A body was hanging by a noose on a branch. Laura gasped, saw a triangular, blue-black head with the tongue hanging out. A torso, white ribs, the remains of charred black wool.

One of the crows was perched on top of the sheep's head, repeatedly driving its sharp beak into the empty eye socket. It pulled out something grey and wobbly, which it swallowed with a jerky movement.

In spite of the cold, the smell seemed to be getting stronger with every second. Laura's stomach contracted. She forced herself to look away and staggered over to the nearest tree trunk. She stumbled, landed on her knees and just managed to avoid throwing up over her jacket.

'Not again,' she heard Hedda murmur. 'Not another one . . .'

18

Dusk has begun to fall and the exterior light comes on just as she parks outside Hedda's house. The crows welcome her with their usual warning cries.

George bursts out of the cat flap as if she recognises Laura's footsteps. She winds herself around Laura's legs with such enthusiasm that Laura trips and kicks the empty cat food tins by the door. One, two, three, four – two more than yesterday.

She looks over at the forest, but it's already dark among the trees.

'Hello? Anyone there?'

Nothing. She stands, listening for a minute or so, but all she can hear is the wind, soughing in the treetops.

She opens the door, goes inside and locks it behind her. In spite of the fact that she's ready for the chaos, the sense of revulsion is almost as strong as before. She picks her way between the furniture and the piles of crap, flicking on every light switch she can find.

The thermometer is on the kitchen windowsill, next to the binoculars and the china figurines, exactly where she saw it on her previous visit. It is showing nineteen degrees, which means it's working. At one end there is a float with a plastic loop, so that you can secure the thermometer with a piece of string to stop it drifting away.

So why is the thermometer in here, instead of tied to the ladder off the pontoon as it's always been, summer and winter? There is a rational explanation. Maybe Hedda had lost interest in the temperature of the water? It's not difficult to check. Laura picks her way to the woodburning stove in one corner of the living room. The bookcase beside it is crammed with books covered in dust, cobwebs and dead flies. The bottom shelf contains green- or blue-backed notebooks. There must be well over forty.

More fun than a diary. And it's become a bit of an obsession.

Laura takes out the book on the far left. It is less dusty than the rest, which means it ought to be this year's.

The pages are ruled into columns, just as she remembers. Date, time, who swam, air temperature, water temperature.

1 January 2017 19.32, Hedda, air 0 degrees, water +2 degrees, says the first entry. It is followed by a second, almost identical.

2 January 2017 19.26, Hedda, air -1 degree, water +2 degrees.

Laura turns the pages. Hedda swims virtually every evening. The date changes, the temperature of the air and water slowly rises. The only column that remains the same, as the days become weeks and months, is the one containing the name. Hedda swims alone, evening after evening, but she still feels compelled to note that fact in the same meticulous way as the other data.

There is something manic and sad about the whole thing, a record of a lonely person's life.

She continues to turn the pages. The only real break comes in late September. It lasts for almost three weeks, which surprises Laura until she realises that must have been when Hedda was in hospital following her second heart attack. Towards the middle of October, she's back, defying her doctor's orders and continuing to subject her heart to high and low temperatures, which she records in the book with the same meticulousness as before.

And then on 12 November, exactly one week before her death, the notes stop. There are two possible explanations for this. The first and most straightforward is that Hedda simply grew tired of making notes about her daily swim. Without warning, she broke off a routine she'd maintained for at least forty years.

The second explanation, and the one that Laura is convinced is correct, is that Hedda took the thermometer out of the water for some reason and decided to stop swimming in the winter. But why?

If the heart attack in September didn't persuade her to listen to her doctor, then what did?

She thinks back to the photographs, the towel partly wrapped around one leg. It looked as if it had been around Hedda's body when she went into the water, rather than as if it had blown off the pontoon. She gets out her phone and calls the number Peter gave her. He answers almost right away.

'Hi, it's Laura. I think you're wrong about Hedda's cause of death.'

There's a rustling sound on the other end of the line.

'Why do you say that?'

She tells him about the bathing book and the thermometer. The towel that shouldn't have been in the water. He listens without interrupting her.

'There's something I haven't mentioned,' he says quietly when she's finished.

She hears him moving around the room, the sound of a door being quietly closed. He clears his throat.

'There was a lighter on the pontoon. When I checked the house I found a packet of cigarette papers and a pretty substantial bag of marijuana on the kitchen table.'

Laura is taken aback.

'Why isn't that in the police report?'

'Because I got rid of the lot – flushed it down the toilet. People were already only too keen to bad-mouth Hedda. But I should have told you at the station. By the way, do you remember the greenhouse behind the toolshed?'

'Of course. Hedda grew magic herbs in there. Mandrake and belladonna. That was why we were definitely not allowed to go in. Because—'

'—magic wasn't for children,' Peter finishes the sentence.

They are both silent for a few seconds, until Laura's brain finally catches on.

'So the magic herbs . . .'

'Turned out to be good old *cannabis sativa*. A very professional little home business.'

The revelation surprises Laura – and yet it doesn't.

'That does clarify a few things,' she says after a moment. 'The padlock on the greenhouse, the hand-rolled cigarettes Hedda smoked out on the pontoon when she wanted to be left in peace. The fact that her clothes sometimes smelled a bit odd.'

'I thought the same thing. How come we didn't realise?'

'We grew up in Hedda's world, Peter. Magic herbs, the nymph, black swans, reincarnated cats. That's just the way it was.'

She pictures Hedda sitting on the pontoon on a summer's evening, alone with a joint in her hand. Feet dangling in the water as she gazed across the lake.

Sometimes, Princess, you need to be alone with your thoughts.

'Do you think she had more secrets?' she asks.

ANDERS DE LA MOTTE

'Maybe. We'll probably never know.'

Laura hears a door open, then a girl's voice.

'Just a minute, Elsa. I'm on the phone.'

The door slams shut.

Peter sighs. 'I have to go, Laura. I'd be grateful if you could keep quiet about this. Technically I'm guilty of professional misconduct, but I did it out of consideration for Hedda.'

'Absolutely. You can trust me.'

'Thanks. And listen – it was good to see you again. Give me a call if you're ever in the area.'

They say their goodbyes. Before Laura can put down her phone, it begins to vibrate. She assumes it's Andreas and is about to reject the call, but then she sees it's Steph.

'So did he turn up?'

'Who?'

'Who do you think? Prince Charming. The boy you've been pining for over the past thirty years.'

'No. No, he didn't come.'

She hears the disappointment in her voice before she feels it.

'Maybe it's just as well,' Steph says. 'He's probably married, overweight and has a hairy back. Or even worse . . .'

'What could possibly be worse than that?'

'He might be a supporter of the Sweden Democrats. Or one of those people who makes a heart shape in the air with their fingers and thumbs.'

Laura can't help laughing.

'Shall we meet up for lunch on Monday, so you can tell me about your inheritance in detail?' Steph suggests.

'Good idea. It won't take long.'

They end the call, and Laura stands there with the phone in her hand. She's still trying to digest what Peter told her.

When she started working for her father in the early 2000s, she'd soon realised that his frequent business trips weren't just about work. He had a life of his own outside the family, he smoked and drank way too much, and he had relationships with other women. Things she'd taken for granted as a child were nowhere near as clear-cut when seen through the eyes of an adult.

However, until now she had never turned those eyes on Gärdsnäset and Hedda. What other secrets had her aunt had?

She looks around at the mess. Dust, cobwebs, dead flies, rubbish and scruffy possessions in such quantities that it's difficult to see what's there. She suppresses a shudder.

The crows strike up, their cacophony mixed with the sound of a car engine. Laura peers out into the darkness through a dirty window. A white Skoda emblazoned with the council's logo pulls up next to her car. A portly man climbs out, looks up anxiously at the cawing birds. He must be about sixty. He's wearing a long coat and a fur hat, which makes him look vaguely amusing. She meets him at the door.

'Kjell Green from the council,' he says. His handshake is damp. 'I just wanted a few words. I won't take up much of your time.'

Laura hesitates. Can she really invite him in, given the state of the place? Then again, standing out on the steps doesn't feel right either.

Judging by his expression, Green doesn't like the inside of Hedda's house any more than Laura does – but he doesn't seem surprised, which means he's been here before. She shows him into the kitchen and manages to free up two chairs.

He takes off his fur hat, revealing a comb-over and a shiny forehead. He looks nervous.

'First of all I'm sorry for your loss. Your aunt was . . .'

He gazes around the kitchen, searching for the right word.

'Special?' she suggests.

'Exactly!'

He nods gratefully, and Laura silently notes that this is the fourth time that word has been applied to Hedda.

'We'd been in touch a few times during the late autumn,' Green continues. 'Hedda was interested in selling Gärdsnäset. We'd more or less reached an agreement when she . . .' He clears his throat. 'Anyway. I just wanted to call by and offer my condolences.'

'Thank you.' Laura waits for the inevitable follow-up.

'You wouldn't believe how quickly the community is growing. This is a positive thing, of course, but we need land for houses, schools and nurseries. Gärdsnäset is in such a beautiful location – it would be perfect. It would attract new residents, breathe life into the whole area.'

He sighs with relief, as if he's delivered a speech.

'When did you last speak to Hedda?' Laura asks.

Green shuffles uncomfortably.

'At the beginning of November. A week or so before she . . .'

He still can't say the word 'died'.

'Was Håkansson involved?'

Green shakes his head. 'Not as far as I know. I delivered the council's offer directly to Hedda, but I have spoken to Håkansson in the past few days.'

'Yes, he mentioned that. Apparently there's another interested party.'

She can tell from his expression that he's well aware of this fact.

'Vintersjöholm.' He shuffles again. 'Yes, Hedda mentioned that the castle had made enquiries.'

The answer surprises her. After their conversation at the funeral, she'd assumed it was Ulf Jensen. So where does he come into the picture?

Green leans forward, lowers his voice.

'As I understand it, the castle offered more money. A lot more. But Hedda wanted what was best for the community. She didn't like the idea of Vintersjön becoming a playground for the rich. She thought it should remain an oasis for ordinary people.'

She notices the change in his language. He's gone back into speech mode, well practised and slightly stilted.

He gets to his feet, puts his hat back on, pulling it down over his sweaty forehead.

'After all, money isn't everything,' he says in conclusion, attempting a smile. 'Needless to say, I and many others around here hope you share that view, Laura.'

She watches the rear lights of his car disappear among the trees. It's obvious that someone sent him here. Persuaded him to drag himself away from a cosy Saturday evening at home. Someone who makes him nervous.

Maybe even frightens him.

The question is – who?

19

Winter 1987

The holiday village was full of subdued voices. Hedda's, Ulf Jensen's, Iben's two half-brothers'. They had gathered around Ulf's pickup truck, and Laura had opened the frosted bathroom window a fraction so that she could eavesdrop without being caught.

Not another one, her aunt had said when they found the horrific sheep's carcase about an hour ago. Laura had asked what she meant, but Hedda had simply told her to stay in her room. She had sounded stressed in a way that Laura had never heard before.

Hedda had made a phone call from her studio, then hurried over to the boathouse. A few minutes later Jack's car had driven away, and shortly after that the Jensens had arrived.

'Why the hell did you get the police involved?' Ulf demanded. Laura could just see him through the opening.

'Because this is the third incident in a month. It's not just kids messing about.'

'And what do you think the police are going to do? Station surveillance teams out on the marsh?'

'Well, keeping quiet about it hasn't worked, has it? Whoever killed that sheep is sick in the head. I have to think about Laura.'

At the sound of her own name, Laura gave a start and leaned closer to the window.

'. . . someone trying to get at me,' Ulf said. 'Some envious bastard who's too much of a coward to have a go at me personally, so he's attacking my animals instead. Costing me thousands. Sooner or later me and the boys will catch up with him.'

'This was different. Someone had poured paraffin all over the poor animal and set fire to it, possibly while it was still alive.'

Silence.

'Set fire to it . . .' Christian Jensen said. 'So do you think it's connected to the other fires?'

'If so he must be one sick fucker,' Fredrik joined in. He carried on talking, waving his arms around, but his words were drowned out by the sound of an approaching car.

A dark blue Saab with a large antenna on the roof pulled up. Two men got out, one short and broad-shouldered with an underbite that made him resemble a bulldog, the other well over six feet tall, with a boxer's nose and a shaven head. They were both wearing leather jackets, and although Laura immediately realised they were police officers, they scared her.

'Sandberg,' said the tall man. 'This is my colleague Holm. Where was the animal found?'

'This way,' Hedda said, and the group disappeared from view.

Laura crept into the living room and saw them heading off towards Alkärret. She stood at the window, not knowing what to do. Staying in her room like a little kid just felt stupid.

She spotted a movement among the trees, a hooded figure. When the person emerged and paused by the police car, Laura could see that it was Milla. Without really knowing why she pulled on her boots and jacket and went out to join her. Milla gave her a brief nod.

'Plain-clothes cops,' Milla said, kicking one of the Saab's tyres. 'You can tell by the antenna and the extra rear-view mirror. What are they doing here?'

Laura told her about the dead sheep.

'Someone set fire to it? Seriously? Fuck's sake!'

'Aunt Hedda said it wasn't the first time.'

'What?' Milla's eyes were shining.

'No. Ulf Jensen thinks it's someone who's envious of him.'

'That's crap.'

'Why?'

'Envious people talk about you behind your back. Scratch your car door, stick chewing gum in your hair. But to kill a sheep, hang it from a tree then set fire to it – that's not envy.'

'So what is it then?'

'Hatred, probably. Or love. Love makes people do weird things.'

Laura looked down, making patterns in the snow with her feet.

'I was going to make some coffee,' Milla said. 'Would you like a cup?'

Number six looked exactly the same as Laura remembered it. Fifty square metres, pine-panelled walls and ceiling, vinyl flooring which Jack had fitted in all the cabins last year. And yet the place felt completely different.

First of all, there was the smell. Perfume, hairspray, reminding her of her mother's bathroom. The kind of things she rarely encountered out here.

During the high season Laura usually helped out with cleaning the cabins. Most were done at changeover, but if guests were staying for longer than a week, an ongoing service was provided. Laura would volunteer for those jobs; there was something exciting about moving around among the visitors' stuff, trying to get to know them through their habits and possessions. She knew things about them that their families might not know – which books they read, which pills were in their bathroom cabinet. Which little secrets they kept hidden at the back of their underwear drawer or under the mattress. She enjoyed matching what she knew about the guest with their behaviour out and about in the holiday village. Who was lying, who was pretending. Milla's cabin made her feel the same kind of excitement. It aroused her curiosity, her desire to find out more.

'Take a seat.' Milla pointed to the sofa with its back to the kitchenette. 'I'll put the kettle on.'

The coffee table was strewn with magazines – *OK!*, *Frida*, *Starlet*, and at least ten cigarette packets. A large ashtray attracted Laura's attention. All the cabins had an ashtray made by Hedda. Not exactly works of art, but the summer visitors often thought they were sweet, and sometimes bought them to take home as a souvenir. The one on Milla's table, however, was made of glass, with JOHN SILVER written on one side. It looked as if it belonged in a restaurant rather than in a rustic cabin. Where had Milla got it from, and why had she brought it here? She didn't have an answer to that. And why were all the cigarette packets different brands?

'You do drink coffee?' Milla put down two mugs and a jar of Nescafé.

'Of course.' Laura had no idea why she was lying.

She looked at Milla, tried to read her. There was plenty to work on: the pink streaks in her hair, the plastic bracelets, the earrings, the ripped jeans. And yet it was unexpectedly difficult to draw any clear conclusions.

'Why do you come here?' Milla asked, interrupting her train of thought. 'Jack told me you've got a pool and everything where you live. Sunshine, palm trees, your very own housekeeper. Why come to this dump every holiday?'

Under normal circumstances the answer would have been simple: because all her friends were here. Everyone she cared about. Loved. But after yesterday that explanation no longer felt right.

'I've spent every summer and Christmas holiday with Aunt Hedda ever since I was little. You could say it's a tradition.'

'OK.'

Milla looked searchingly at Laura, as if she didn't really buy that.

'And what about you? What are you doing here?' Laura countered.

Milla pulled a face.

'I needed to get away. Kjell, my foster father, got a bit too friendly, if you know what I mean.'

She picked up a packet of Prince, tapped out a cigarette and lit it.

'He sat a bit too close to me on the sofa when we were watching TV, wanted me to rest my head on his knee. "Just happened"' – Milla held the cigarette in the corner of her mouth as she drew quotation marks in the air – 'to come into my room when I'd had a shower. In the end he said he was in love with me. Wanted us to run away together.'

She took a deep drag.

'So what did you do then?'

Milla's brutal honesty surprised Laura, but at the same time she felt privileged that Milla had chosen to confide in her.

'I called social services, of course, and asked to change families. Your aunt offered, so here I am. But only temporarily. I'll be eighteen in January, and then I'm out of here.'

'Where will you go?'

Milla blew a smoke ring at the ceiling.

'Copenhagen, Berlin, London. Or maybe somewhere warmer. Anywhere's better than fucking Sweden. My passport's already in my suitcase. That slimy bastard Kjell signed my passport application. The stupid idiot really believed we were going to run away together.'

Milla leaned forward.

'Can you keep a secret? You have to promise not to tell anyone!'

Laura nodded, realised she was holding her breath.

'The passport wasn't the only thing I got from Kjell. He gave me what you might call travelling expenses too.'

'How come?'

Milla smiled. 'I promised to say we just didn't get along, rather than telling social services what he'd done. They would have reported him to the police.'

'So he paid you to keep quiet?'

'Exactly.'

Milla looked very pleased with herself. She got up to fetch the boiling water.

Laura didn't really know what to say. Milla's story was unpleasant, but she was pleased to have been given a piece of the puzzle that told her something about the girl. A piece Milla presumably didn't give to just anyone.

Milla filled their cups, replaced the pan on the hob and sat down on the sofa once more.

'You're pretty,' she said. 'I can do your makeup if you like. Make you look a bit older – like your best friend, the one with the funny name.'

'Iben? We're not best friends.'

'No? Peter said you were. That the whole gang had more or less grown up together.'

Laura stared down at the table.

'A boy,' Milla said. 'It has to be a boy. That's the only thing girls fall out about so fast. You're both in love with the same person. Not Peter, he's too much of a clown. And Tomas is too weird. Which leaves Jack, the guy with the guitar.'

Laura clamped her lips together.

Milla shook her head, amused and annoyed at the same time.

'I told you about slimeball Kjell,' she said.

Laura hesitated for a few seconds. Milla was a stranger, someone she didn't really know. Then again, she was also the only person who was interested in Laura. Who wasn't preoccupied with her own secrets. Who treated her like an adult.

'It's all Iben's fault,' Laura muttered.

20

In the dream Hedda is sitting at the far end of the pontoon with a cigarette in her hand. It is a summer's evening, the water is dark and still, shining like a mirror. Hedda has her back to Laura, her eyes are fixed on the lamp on Johnny Miller's boathouse on the other side of the lake. Somewhere far away a bird calls, a plaintive, melancholy cry.

Laura really wants to run and throw herself into her aunt's arms, tell her how much she's missed her. But in the dream she is the grown-up Laura, the Laura who is angry with Hedda. Who doesn't talk about her feelings, but locks them away in little boxes and dulls them with pills.

Hedda takes a long drag on her cigarette. It is one of the ones she rolls herself, it smells of magic herbs. The glow flickers in the darkness.

The pontoon bobs beneath Laura's feet. She looks down at the grey, split wood. Catches a glimpse of the black water below.

When she looks up again, everything has changed. The trees have lost their leaves and the lake is partially frozen. Hedda's long hair is grey, her back is bent, and two fingers are missing from the hand holding the cigarette.

'I knew you'd come,' Hedda says without turning her head. 'She told me.'

'Who told you?'

Hedda points out across the lake. 'Who do you think?' She takes a final drag and tosses the butt into the water. The glowing tip draws an arc in the darkness before it is extinguished.

'Do you really think I'd fall off my own pontoon?' Hedda says.

'No.'

The bird calls again, its melancholy cry filling the air.

'A black swan. You know what that means?'

'That nothing is impossible,' Laura replies. 'Not even the impossible.'

Hedda turns and smiles sadly.

'I'm glad you were listening, my princess.'

The soft voice makes Laura choke up. Her eyes fill with tears, but she still can't move.

The swan calls once more, but the sound is different now, more like the crows' warning cries.

There is a movement out in the lake, a wave surging towards the pontoon, turning into a black pillar of water looming over Hedda.

Laura opens her mouth to warn her, but before she can make a sound the pillar has metamorphosed into a young woman with long blue-black hair. She is the nymph from Laura's painting, yet at the same time she is someone much more familiar.

As Laura says Iben's name, the beautiful young woman changes into a horrific, blackened creature with empty eye sockets. It stinks of soot, charred hair and burned flesh. The creature flings its claw-like arms around Hedda, digs its long nails deep into her chest before dragging her down into the dark water with an ear-splitting shriek.

Laura sits up, breathes in sharply. The nymph's shriek lingers in her mind, and her pyjamas are soaked with sweat. She is shivering, chilled to the bone, and she has to stand in the shower for over fifteen minutes to warm up. The nightmare refuses to let go.

This is her punishment for being careless with her happy pills. Not that they make her happy.

She orders breakfast from room service. Puts her pyjamas in one of the hotel's plastic laundry bags.

Hedda has been buried, Håkansson will take care of both George and the sale of the holiday village. She doesn't really care who buys it – the council or the castle, it makes no difference to her.

She has completed her task, and she can put all this behind her with a clear conscience.

So what is it that is still nagging away at her?

Why can't she accept the most logical explanation? That a seventy-two-year-old woman with a weak heart who'd been smoking a joint slipped in the darkness on an icy pontoon, and fell into the water.

Is it because a part of her still sees Hedda and the lake through the eyes of a child? Believes the tales she told about nymphs and black swans, and that the lake cannot harm anyone who trusts it.

Or is she just looking for an excuse? A reason to stay, to wait a little longer for someone who obviously isn't coming?

On the way down to the car park, she goes over the timeline.

Hedda suffers a heart attack in September. As soon as she recovers, she defies the doctor's orders and continues to put her damaged heart under strain with a daily sauna and swim. She doesn't stop until 12 November. That's when the major change in her behaviour occurs. According to Kjell Green, that was just before she received the offers on Gärdsnäset.

Maybe Hedda simply decided to take better care of herself so that she'd be able to enjoy the money. However, something else happens at around the same time. Something which suggests that Hedda had other plans.

Laura drives out of the car park, then pulls over and calls Håkansson. He answers almost right away and doesn't sound at all annoyed about being disturbed on a Sunday.

'You told me that Hedda contacted you fairly recently, saying that she wanted to make a will. When exactly was that?'

She hears him flicking through what is presumably a paper diary. Do people still use those?

'She came to my office on 12 November.'

'Did she say why she wanted to make a will?'

'No, but I knew she'd been ill.'

He doesn't ask why she's wondering, which she appreciates.

'Did Hedda tell you she'd had offers for Gärdsnäset? That she was thinking of selling?'

Håkansson hesitates.

'As I recall it did come up in the conversation, but Hedda had considered selling a couple of times in the past, so I didn't take it too seriously – particularly as Gärdsnäset was mentioned in the will.'

'So on 12 November, she hadn't settled on a purchaser or made a firm decision to sell?'

'That was certainly my perception.'

'But now we've had two offers, right? One from the council and one from Vintersjöholm.'

'Correct. I can send you the paperwork tomorrow if you like.'

'But we haven't had an offer from Iben's father? He asked me about Gärdsnäset at the funeral. He seemed to believe that everything was more or less done and dusted.'

'Ulf Jensen? No, he hasn't made an offer. And to be honest, I don't think that's on the cards.'

Håkansson clears his throat, as if he's said something he regrets. 'I'm afraid I have to go, but I'll speak to you tomorrow morning when you're back in Stockholm.'

He ends the call so quickly that Laura doesn't have the chance to say goodbye.

She continues her journey, returning to the timeline. At some point in early November, Hedda receives two offers that are sufficiently appealing to make her consider selling. But on 12 November, the day she makes a will that includes Gärdsnäset, she also stops swimming – as if she'd made a decision, possibly to hold onto the place. Because as Håkansson has just pointed out, you don't bequeath an asset you're intending to sell.

A week later, Hedda is found dead next to her own pontoon.

Laura scrolls down to Peter's phone number.

'A quick question,' she says once the pleasantries are out of the way. 'Have you been feeding George, or do you know of anyone else who is?'

'No. To be honest, I didn't think about the cat until you mentioned her at the funeral. I was relieved to hear she hadn't starved to death. Why do you ask?'

Laura wonders whether to tell him about the cigarette butts in the forest, the offers, and the fact that Hedda's will coincides with the last date in the bathing book, but decides against it, mainly because she wants more time to think it all over. Clarify her suspicions in her own mind before she shares them with anyone else.

'Someone's fed her. There were empty cat food tins by the front door.'

'Right. No, I've no idea who that could be.'

They both fall silent. Laura knows she ought to hang up, but she doesn't.

'Are you OK?' Peter asks.

'I don't actually know,' she answers truthfully. 'Maybe I'm just trying to process the fact that Hedda's dead. That I'm not a child anymore.'

'I understand,' he says gently. 'Even though I didn't have any contact with her, she's always kind of been there.'

Another silence. Laura still doesn't want to end the call. Not yet. She decides to ask the question that's been on her mind ever since she saw him in the church. Something she's wondered about for a long time.

'What happened to Tomas after the fire? After we told the police he'd started it?'

She can almost hear Peter's discomfort.

'He was sent to a reform school, as they were called back in the day. Then he was in and out of various institutions.'

'Did you keep in touch with him?'

'No.'

The answer is brusque, and comes a little too quickly.

'I'm guessing that you read the police investigation into the fire.'

He sighs. 'I did. It didn't make for pleasant reading. After we made our statements, the police went in really hard on Tomas. Much too hard, I'd say. We'd never get away with that kind of interrogation now, but the fact is that Tomas confessed quite early on. They also found a bottle of paraffin in the bushes with his fingerprints on it, so we have nothing to feel guilty about, neither you nor I.'

She can tell that he's tried to convince himself of that many times. As has she.

'Did anyone help Tomas? Defend him?'

For a moment she thinks Peter's hung up, but then she hears his voice again.

'No one. Not even his father.'

Laura reaches the turning for Gärdsnäset just under half an hour later. She has no idea what she's doing here, but she can't go back to Stockholm. Not yet, not until she finds answers to at least some of the questions swirling around in her mind.

As she approaches Hedda's house she sees a movement among the trees. A slim figure in dark clothing and a motorcycle helmet is running away.

Laura slams on the brakes, jumps out of the car and gives chase.

'Stop!'

The figure is trying to put on a backpack, and the distance between them is shrinking. Running after a stranger through the forest isn't something Laura would normally consider, but anger gives her strength, and her quarry is small and skinny.

The intruder rounds the corner of one of the dilapidated cabins and disappears from view. A second later, Laura hears the roar of an engine. She too races around the corner and sees the figure on a motocross bike, about to ride off. Summoning up a sudden burst of speed, she reaches out for the half-open backpack. The engine races, snow and leaves spurt up around the back wheel as the bike tries to gain purchase on the treacherous ground. Laura touches the backpack, the rider turns and sees how close she is. A moment of confusion, the back wheel skids sideways, the rider struggles to maintain balance, then the wheel hits a fallen branch and the bike crashes to the ground in a cloud of exhaust fumes. The engine coughs and stops. The rider has been thrown off and is lying face down, trying to move even though all the breath has been knocked out of his or her body.

Two tins of cat food have fallen out of the backpack.

Laura drags the intruder upright.

'What the hell do you think you're doing?'

The rider removes the helmet, with some difficulty. She is a young woman with a defiant expression and cropped, coal-black hair. She has two rings in one eyebrow.

Laura immediately recognises her from the school photograph at the police station.

This is Elsa, Peter's daughter.

21

Winter 1987

'There – what do you think?'

Milla screwed the cap on the mascara and stepped aside so that Laura could see herself in the bathroom mirror. Laura couldn't help inhaling sharply.

She'd tried putting on makeup on the few occasions when she thought her mother wouldn't catch her, of course, but this was on another level.

The person gazing back at her looked so grown up. So . . . beautiful. She turned her head, admiring her face from different angles.

'It'll be even better if you let me fix your hair and clothes.'

Laura still couldn't stop staring at her reflection.

'Jack won't be able to take his eyes off you, I swear. But we need an occasion to show you off. Do they have discos in this dump?'

'Sometimes, at the leisure centre – but they're usually for under-sixteens.'

'OK, so how about a party?'

Laura shook her head. 'We don't really go to parties. Peter and Tomas are never invited, Jack's too old, and I'm not at school here, so I hardly know anybody in the village.'

'But Iben's invited?'

Laura shrugged. 'I suppose so, but she doesn't go.'

'Why not?'

'I've no idea. Maybe she doesn't like parties. Or maybe . . . maybe her dad won't let her go.'

'Oh, so her dad's one of those. What does he think about the situation with Jack, then?'

Laura thought about what Kent Rask had said in the car.

'I assume he doesn't know.'

Milla's voice took on a different tone.

'So they're keeping it quiet because of Daddy.'

Laura had told her about Iben's betrayal. Milla had confided that the same thing had happened to her a year or so ago with one of her friends, and she knew exactly how Laura was feeling. However, the new tone made Laura think she'd said too much. Revealed details she should have kept to herself.

She quickly changed the subject.

'What kind of errands do Peter and Tomas do for you?' She'd been wondering ever since she met Peter outside Wohlin's.

Milla looked at her for a few seconds. 'Do you really want to know? Seriously?'

Laura nodded. This was another piece of the puzzle that would tell her something about Milla, possibly something important.

'OK, let's go and sit down. I need a smoke.'

Milla returned to the sofa, tapped out a fresh cigarette. Laura sank down on the armchair opposite, watched as Milla lit the cigarette with a large gold-coloured lighter.

'Tomas and Peter get into cottages that are closed up for the winter,' Milla said, blowing smoke out of the corner of her mouth. 'They bring me fags and booze. They're getting really good at it.'

Laura was taken aback. 'You mean they break in?'

'No, no. Almost everyone hides a key. It's hanging from a nail tucked away somewhere, or it's in a biscuit tin in the woodshed. If you unlock the door with a key, that doesn't count as breaking in. It's more like visiting without asking for permission.'

Laura sat there open-mouthed, trying to digest what she'd just heard.

'Your turn,' Milla said brusquely.

'What?'

'Its two-one to me. Your turn to tell a secret. Something nobody else knows about you.'

Laura wasn't sure what to say. The secret Milla had just shared was huge, and even though it worried her, it also excited her. Milla trusted her.

'Sometimes . . .' she began. 'No, forget it.'

'Go on,' Milla urged.

'Sometimes I look at people. Mainly the other girls in school. I look at their clothes and their stuff, listen to the way they talk. Try to get to know them from a distance . . .'

'What do you mean?'

'I try to work out things about them. What kind of music or books they like, whether or not their parents have money. What they don't want anyone else to know.'

'Just by looking at them?'

Laura realised how stupid the whole thing sounded. How desperate she must seem, spying on her fellow students in an attempt to make friends.

'I have to go,' she said, getting to her feet.

Milla walked back with her. Hedda, Iben's father and half-brothers and the two police officers were talking at the foot of the boathouse steps. There was still no sign of Jack.

'Do you know either of the cops?' Milla asked.

Laura shook her head.

'OK.' Milla took Laura by the arm, made her stop by the police car. 'Tell me something about one of them.'

'Like what?'

'Anything at all.'

Laura swallowed. The men were standing ten metres away. Their leather jackets and dark-coloured trousers were almost identical – a kind of uniform that revealed nothing, but she really wanted to show Milla what she could do.

She glanced inside the car. There was a bag on the back seat, and she could see something sticking up out of it. She shaded her eyes with her hand to get a closer look.

'One of them is going to visit someone in hospital.'

'What makes you think that?'

'There's a bunch of flowers on the back seat, and a bag with a women's magazine in it. And there's a bulge in the bag that could be a bunch of grapes. Flowers, grapes, magazine – exactly the kind of thing you'd take to someone in hospital. A woman,' she clarified.

Milla peered into the car, then looked at Laura. Without a word she flipped down her hood and set off towards the little group.

Laura wasn't sure what to do. She tried not to look at Milla, but she couldn't help herself. In seconds Milla had completely changed her facial expression and body language. She was nodding and smiling at the two police officers, brushing against the arm of one of them, tilting her head to one side. Even her voice had altered. As if by magic, the Milla Laura had just been talking to had disappeared and been replaced by a different person. She was wearing the same clothes and had the same pink streaks in her hair, but she was still completely transformed. The five men were smiling at her. The only person who didn't seem entirely amused was Hedda.

After a while Milla turned and came back to Laura. On the way she flipped up her hood, and in that one movement became herself again.

'You were right.'

'What?' Laura was too bewildered to grasp what Milla meant.

'The flowers, the magazine. The big guy's wife is in hospital. He's going to visit her as soon as they're done here. That's seriously cool, Laura.'

Laura flushed at the unexpected praise.

'So what do you know about me?' Milla challenged her.

Laura had been thinking about that for quite a while, trying to put together the pieces of the puzzle. Milla's cabin, her clothes and possessions. The story of her foster family, the revelation about Peter and Tomas. The information she had seemed to be sprawling in all directions, but after what had just happened with the police officers, she had realised what the pattern was. Or rather – that there was no pattern.

'You're good at disguising yourself,' she said. 'Playing a role to get people to do what you want.'

22

Laura helps Elsa to brush off the snow and the leaves, and to pick up the bike and prop it against a tree. It's heavy, at least one size too big for its owner.

'My name's Laura. I saw your photo in your dad's office.'

Elsa refused to meet her eyes.

'Dad doesn't want me to ride the bike,' she mumbles. 'He's threatened to sell it, even though Grandad gave it to me. Since my mum's accident, he worries about everything. That's why I ran. People like to tell tales.'

Laura nods slowly.

'I'm sorry for your loss. It must be tough.'

Elsa looks up. Her eyes are black.

'My mum was sick in the head. Do you know what really happened?'

'No.'

'She was out with her boyfriend – or maybe I should say lover. He was driving way too fast. He came off the road and went straight into a tree. The car burst into flames. Whoosh!' She waves her hand to illustrate a sudden blaze. 'No survivors.'

'How terrible!' Laura shudders.

'It was my dad who really suffered. Mum and I didn't have much contact with each other. She had an apartment in Helsingborg; she only turned up in Vedarp when she needed someone to make a fuss of her, or she felt like playing Mummy for a couple of days.'

Elsa's directness surprises Laura, and arouses her curiosity.

'And how did your dad react?'

Elsa snorts.

'He's way too nice. He let her come and go as she liked, consoled her when the latest boyfriend dumped her, helped her feel better when she'd partied too hard.' She touches the tip of her nose to underline what she means. 'She treated him like shit.'

There is a brief silence, and Laura decides to change the subject.

'You're the one who's been feeding George, I assume.'

Elsa nods. 'I didn't want the poor little thing to starve to death. Now Hedda's not here anymore . . .' She pauses, looks genuinely upset for the first time.

'So how did you know Hedda?'

'I ride my bike up there in the forest.' She points in the direction of the main road. 'There's hardly ever anyone around, no one to tell my dad. One day last summer, my chain broke. Hedda came along when I was messing with it – she nearly scared me to death.' A grimace that might be a smile. 'We wheeled the bike to the holiday village and she helped me to fix it. From then on I used to stop and have coffee with her whenever I came here.'

The grimace turns into a proper smile.

'She could be a bit difficult, but I really liked her. And I liked the cat. My mum was allergic, so I was never allowed a pet of my own.'

'Same here,' Laura says. 'George was my substitute cat. Not the same George, of course. All Hedda's cats were called George.'

'Yes, she told me that. I looked after George when Hedda was in hospital in the autumn.'

Elsa looks around. There is a large glade in front of them, with the lake beyond. Over by the shore a small iron cross is sticking up above the thin covering of snow.

'That's where Iben Jensen died, isn't it?' Elsa says.

Laura nods. Her brain has already conjured up the dance hall that once stood in the glade. The flames, the heat, the smells, the noise. Her scar comes to life.

'My school's named after her,' Elsa goes on. 'All her trophies and medals are in a display cabinet by the main entrance.'

Laura makes a non-committal sound, trying to block the images in her memory.

'My dad was injured in the fire – he suffered burns to one leg, although you can hardly see it now. Mum sent him to a plastic surgeon before they got married. Hedda lost two fingers. Were you hurt?'

They could just as easily be chatting about the weather. Laura makes an effort to maintain her composure. The scar is burning so fiercely that the droplets of sweat must be turning to steam.

'I have a scar on my back.'

Oddly enough, the words ease the pain a little.

'And you haven't had plastic surgery to remove it?'

Laura shakes her head.

'I carry a virus – nothing infectious,' she quickly adds. 'But anything that has a traumatic effect on the body could activate it – like an operation. Or a pregnancy,' she hears herself say.

'So you don't have any children?'

'No.'

Laura takes a deep breath. Decides to tell the truth.

'Just over two years ago I was expecting a little girl, but she died before she was born.'

'Because of the virus?'

'The doctors couldn't be sure, but I think so. Anyway, she died in the womb, with no explanation.'

'That's awful!' Elsa tilts her head to one side. 'What was her name?'

'Andreas wanted to call her Saga.'

'And you?'

'I wanted to wait until she arrived.'

Because you knew the winter fire could take her, a voice whispers in Laura's head.

Elsa can see that she's uncomfortable. She takes Laura's arm.

'Come on, let's go back to the house. George must be hungry.'

They're sitting on the porch while George tucks into the food Elsa has brought.

Laura's shirt is still damp, but the scar has stopped burning, and a strange sense of relief is spreading through her body.

'Does your dad ever talk about the fire?' she asks.

Elsa strokes George's back, and the cat rubs her head against Elsa's hand before going into the house.

'No. It was my mum who told me about his leg.'

'Do you know if he's still in touch with any of the others who were there? Tomas Rask, for example?'

She is thinking of Peter's abrupt answer to her question.

Elsa frowns, takes a lighter out of her pocket.

'I know he speaks to Tomas on the phone occasionally, and it's nothing to do with his job. Dad has a work tone of voice and a personal one,' she clarifies. 'Almost all his calls are to do with work, but with Tomas it's almost like when he used to talk to Mum. That's why I've noticed it.'

Laura leans forward.

'When did you last hear them talking?'

Elsa plays distractedly with the lighter, flicking the wheel back and forth to create sparks.

'I don't remember, but Dad's phone was on the kitchen table this morning, and I saw he had a text message from Tomas.'

Laura tries not to sound too interested.

'Did you see what it said?'

Elsa looks up, apparently untroubled by Laura's questions. In fact, she seems faintly amused.

'He wanted to know if he and Dad were meeting up this evening.'

23

Winter 1987

Hedda hardly mentioned the dead sheep, the conversation with Ulf Jensen or the fires for the rest of the day. Instead, she chatted away as if everything was perfectly normal. She admired Laura's makeup, said how pleased she was that Laura and Milla were getting along. Laura understood perfectly; Hedda wanted them to have a lovely Christmas together, without any unpleasantness like fires or dead animals. Laura actually liked the fact that Hedda was making such an effort.

And in any case, she'd already uncovered enough secrets. About Peter and Tomas. And about Milla, her new ... new what?

Friend?

After dinner they washed up together, with George rubbing against their legs as Hedda scraped the leftovers into one of the cat's dishes.

'The sauna's heating up,' she said. 'I thought it was high time we took a winter dip – what do you think?'

'Great idea!'

They waited until it was fully dark and the stars appeared in the sky. Changed outside the sauna, then ran out onto the pontoon with their towels over their shoulders. Someone, probably

Jack, had cleared the snow from the pontoon, but Laura tiptoed along to avoid the cold wood. Hedda went down two rungs of the ladder and threw herself into the icy water. Laura stayed put. She knew she'd made a rookie error. The heat of the sauna was already leaving her body, and in seconds she would be shivering. But it was so lovely standing here gazing at the stars, the moon, the ice and the black water. She'd seen this sight so many times before, and for a little while it was actually possible to convince herself that nothing had changed. She dropped the towel and clambered onto the ladder. The metal was freezing cold to her hands and feet.

'Exactly zero degrees,' Hedda said, holding up the thermometer that was tied to the ladder. 'Don't hesitate, just jump in, Princess!'

Laura filled her lungs with air. Closed her eyes. Jumped.

Afterwards they walked back to the house together with that wonderful mixture of warmth and cold prickling their skin.

'What shall we do tomorrow?'

Laura glanced up at the top floor of the boathouse. The lights were on, and Jack's car was back.

'Don't know.'

Hedda had obviously noticed the glance. She stopped at the bottom of the steps.

'Shall we see if Jack would like to join us for a cup of hot chocolate?'

'OK.'

Laura tried not to sound too keen. Part of her didn't want to see Jack, another part wanted nothing more.

They climbed the steps and Hedda tapped gently on Jack's front door. They heard noises from inside, but no one came. She knocked again, harder this time. The curtain at the window moved, then the door opened. Jack was in his underpants and T-shirt, and looked as if he'd just woken up.

'Were you asleep?'

'Yes.'

He stood in the doorway, deliberately filling the narrow space. Laura stood on tiptoe to try and see over his shoulder, but the light had been switched off.

'We wondered if you'd like a hot chocolate?'

'Thanks, but not tonight. I'm really tired.'

He smiled uncomfortably. The atmosphere changed. Hedda could feel it too.

'No problem – goodnight then.'

'Goodnight.'

Jack closed the door and Laura heard the key turn in the lock.

There was something in his apartment that he didn't want them to see. Something or someone. The realisation made her jealousy flare up, and the pain in her stomach came back. She wondered whether to say anything to Hedda, but couldn't make up her mind.

They lingered at the top of the steps for a few moments. The view from up here was so beautiful – the white blanket of snow embracing the lake, the black water reflecting the lights.

In the distance they heard the sound of sirens, rising and falling tones coming closer and closer until they stopped abruptly.

'Can you smell smoke?' Hedda said.

Laura stopped brooding about Jack and sniffed the night air.

'I think so.'

Beyond the trees, over towards the village, they saw a flickering glow in the sky. The smell of smoke grew stronger.

Another siren, then another.

'Let's get you inside,' Hedda said, putting her arm around Laura.

24

Laura waves Elsa off as she makes her way along the bumpy track. There's something about the young woman that she really likes.

She hasn't talked to anyone about her little girl for a long time. No, that's wrong – she hasn't talked to anyone except Andreas, but he just wants to go over the same things again and again, getting nowhere. He more or less accuses her of not caring, because she never visits the grave. And her mother doesn't mention it, pretends it hasn't happened, as she does with everything that might be unpleasant.

Laura understands why Elsa and Hedda liked each other. They're very similar – direct, unafraid, honest. And maybe they can both hold a grudge.

She thinks about all the letters she wrote to Hedda. The replies she never received. Then again, she's not here to bury herself in old disappointments, but to find answers. And she's already found one – she now knows who's been feeding George. A small victory.

However, she's also been left with more questions.

Peter clearly lied to her about Tomas, just as she suspected. Has he lied about anything else? About the details surrounding Hedda's death?

The little greenhouse is behind the toolshed. Double glazing and a sheltered, south-facing position have provided the cannabis plants inside with optimum growing conditions. Peter was telling the truth about that; she can't verify the rest, but she has no difficulty in picturing Hedda smoking an evening joint out on the pontoon.

She needs to go back a few steps, back to the time around 12 November. That was when something happened, something that made Hedda change her mind about selling Gärdsnäset.

But what?

She goes back into the house. Selling the home she'd lived in for almost fifty years must have been a huge step for Hedda, requiring a great deal of thought. There were two offers – a generous one from the castle, and a lower one from the council. Hedda had never reached that kind of decision lightly.

Then she abruptly changed her mind. Rejected the money, the chance of a more comfortable life.

Laura suddenly remembers the planning board.

Hedda wanted to see everything laid out in front of her before she reached any major decision. She would stick lots of photographs, sketches and objects on a big whiteboard. Sometimes Laura and Iben were allowed to help by cutting pictures out of magazines, or adding their own drawings until the board was completely covered.

A mood board, long before the concept was invented. Eventually, when he was old enough, Jack would complement the board with more practical contributions such as designs, colour samples, possible timelines and shopping lists, converting Hedda's vision into reality. He never tried to change her, though. First the board, then the decision. No shortcuts.

You can't decide on something you can't see.

Had Hedda still thought that way? Wanted to see the alternatives set out in front of her so that she could weigh up the pros and cons? It was certainly worth investigating.

Laura switches on the lights, pulls on her gloves and rummages among the chaos, but she can't find the board. George sticks close by her side, as if she's wondering what Laura is up to. After a while Laura begins to wonder the same thing.

Hedda had probably changed her approach. Moved from a board to something simpler, like a good old-fashioned notepad for example.

The problem is finding a pad in the middle of all this. However, it looks as if Hedda didn't actually use much of the house, so the kitchen seems like a good place to start.

The table is cluttered with junk mail, catalogues and envelopes with windows. On top of one of the piles is a spiral-bound notebook and a pen. Laura opens the notebook; it's empty. Nothing, not even a doodle. However, along the binding are small scraps of paper, left behind when pages have been torn out.

So where are the notes? Has someone been in and taken them, someone who wanted to remove evidence?

It takes about ten seconds before her brain leaves TV crime-series territory and returns to normal logic.

For a start, it would have been a lot easier for the mysterious intruder to take the whole book rather than ripping out pages. And evidence . . . of what?

What does she actually suspect? That Hedda was murdered?

What solid evidence is that suspicion based on?

A towel in the water, a bathing book that wasn't filled in. Last night's nightmare.

She goes out onto the porch, hoping the cold winter air will clear her head. She needs to stop this, whatever it is.

She hears a sound from the forest, the loud crack of a branch. She gives a start, peers into the darkness to try and make out the source, but the exterior light above her head makes the darkness among the trees even more compact.

She looks up. The crows aren't particularly agitated, so there's probably a natural explanation for the sound. A deer, maybe. Still she lingers for a while, attempts to pinpoint the spot where the unidentified smoker must have stood, but all is quiet and peaceful.

She goes back into the house, turns off the lights in the bedroom and studio. Stands in front of the sofa. Hedda sat here, day after day, night after night, all alone. Stared at the TV, smoked and drank her way to three heart attacks.

Laura perches cautiously on the arm of the sofa.

Why is she still incapable of seeing Hedda through the eyes of an adult, in spite of a wealth of evidence? Why can't she accept the most logical explanation?

Hedda was an old woman who tumbled off her own pontoon. A woman who couldn't bring herself to sell this dump to the highest bidder, whose only sensible thought was to make a will, presumably because she'd realised that her heart wouldn't last much longer.

She'll go back to the hotel in a while, wash off the dust and dirt from this house. Then she'll swim a few lengths, order room service and go to bed. Get an early start in the morning so that she can fit in lunch with Steph and a few hours' work at the office. Return to her everyday life.

As she gets to her feet she notices the picture at the front of a dusty stack propped against the wall behind the TV. She recognises it.

That particular picture of the lake early on a summer morning used to hang in the main cabin. Veils of mist hover above the surface of the water, and beyond them the silhouette of the ridge is just visible. As a child, its contours made Laura think of a sleeping giant, but as an adult she realises there's something else about the work that appeals to her – an air of melancholy, reinforced by the solitary lamp on Miller's boathouse, shining at the exact point where land meets water.

She moves closer. It's the best thing Hedda has ever done. The lake at dawn, the mist, the sparkling water, the outline of the ridge and that lonely, yearning light on the other side.

She is reaching out for the painting when she notices something. It's in a stack of five, but the other four are covered in a thick layer of dust. This one, however, is hardly dusty at all, which means it's recently been cleaned. Or moved.

Laura picks it up. Her fingers touch something on the reverse. She turns it over, lays it on top of the pile. A piece of white canvas has been stapled to the back.

The first thing that draws her attention is the black swan's feather right at the top. It must be her feather, which means Hedda found the cigar box containing her childish treasures.

Roughly in the middle of the canvas two documents have been attached. Two offers for Gärdsnäset, one from Kjell Green and the council, the other from Vintersjöholm Development, signed by Heinz Norell, Project Leader. A whole host of other papers have been stuck around the offers. Cuttings of old newspaper articles with familiar headlines: TRAGEDY AT VINTERSJÖN, ARSON COST YOUNG WOMAN HER LIFE, ARSONIST SENT TO YOUTH OFFENDERS' INSTITUTION. Right at the bottom is a page torn out of a notebook, with three lines in Hedda's handwriting.

Laura is holding her breath.

Make will, followed by a neat tick.

Call Laura, followed by a question mark.

Finally, five words in capitals:

ASK TOMAS ABOUT IBEN'S SECRET!

25

Winter 1987

The following morning a grey, foul-smelling fog hung over the lake, just as it had done on her first morning here. Smoke, Laura was sure of it.

It was after ten when she knocked on Jack's door. He opened it right away, looking considerably more relaxed than the previous evening.

'Morning, Princess – tea?'

'Please.'

Laura took the opportunity to glance around while he clattered about in the kitchenette. Everything looked the same as it always did. The bed was neatly made, the floor clean. Jack liked to keep the place neat and tidy. She was pleased to see that the car magazine she'd given him at the airport was on his bedside table.

'That business in Alkärret yesterday was terrible,' she said.

He didn't answer, pretended to be preoccupied with the tea. She waited until he sat down opposite her. She had two questions for him. She opted to go for the easiest one first.

'So what's actually going on here? The fires, the dead sheep?'

Jack took a sip of his tea.

'It started in the autumn,' he said quietly. 'A couple of small fires that nobody really took much notice of. Litter bins, that kind of thing. But then the fires became bigger and more frequent.

Hunting towers, outhouses, empty cottages. People are nervous. And Jensen's sheep . . . Three in a month.'

Laura thought back to what she'd heard of the conversation in the yard the previous day.

'Ulf Jensen suspects someone, doesn't he?'

It took a few seconds before she managed to interpret Jack's expression. She gasped.

'You? He thinks you killed his sheep?'

Jack stared into his cup.

'But why? Why would he think that?'

Milla's words came into her mind – that killing the sheep was about hatred. Or love.

'Iben,' she said in a small voice.

'Ulf doesn't like us hanging out together,' Jack said. 'He's had a go at Hedda about it several times, and the other day her brothers made it very clear to me.'

He pulled up his T-shirt to reveal a huge bruise. Laura's stomach contracted into a hard knot.

'So Ulf thinks you're killing his sheep to show you're not scared of him?' she managed to say.

'Something like that.' Jack shrugged. 'I guess he blames me for the other fires too. He's crazy . . .'

He placed a hand on her arm, exactly as Iben had done the other day.

'We didn't mean to hurt you. It just happened. After you left in the summer . . .'

He fell silent. The knot in Laura's stomach tightened. She wiped away a tear, then another.

'Are you in love with her?'

Jack looked tortured. He slowly removed his hand.

'You don't understand . . .'

'So explain it to me! Explain what's changed from last summer!'

Jack shook his head.

'I can't. I'm sorry, but I just can't, Princess.'

'Don't call me that – I'm not a child!'

The apartment felt cramped, the air suffocating. Laura leaped up and headed for the door, fighting back the tears.

She ran down the stairs and into Hedda's house. Threw herself on the bed and buried her face in the pillows. Sobbed and sobbed, her whole body shaking.

After a while Hedda came in, sat down on the bed and gently stroked her hair.

'Oh, sweetheart,' she whispered. 'Sometimes living really hurts.'

26

We can't choose our parents, Princess. Just as we can't choose our children.

Ensligheten, the place where Tomas grew up, is actually on the GPS map. Laura thinks she's only been there once, with Hedda and Jack. She can't remember why – did she wait in the car?

The morning sky is grey and overcast, the yard one great big frozen pool of mud. A battered Opel is parked to the side. There is no snow on the roof, which means the car is used regularly, and that someone is probably at home. Two scruffy dogs come racing out of the barn, barking loudly and running around her car a couple of times before disappearing back where they came from.

The rotting roller-door has long since parted company with its mechanism, and is propped up against one wall of the barn. Inside are a couple of old cars that are apparently being used as dog kennels.

Laura parks as close to the house as possible, facing in the right direction so that she can get away quickly if necessary. The wind brings down a swirl of wet, loose snow from the roof of the barn. It stings her face, and she pulls on her hat and buttons her jacket right up to her chin.

The house was once green, but a combination of sun and dirt have turned the wood yellowish-grey. A huge tarpaulin has been fixed over the ridge, and next to the chimney she can see a rusty television aerial at such a drunken angle that it looks as if it might come crashing down at any moment. The concrete steps have been cleared of snow – just about. On the porch a case of beer is just visible beneath a lopsided plastic table.

The whole place gives Laura the creeps. She pauses at the front door, gathers her thoughts. She could have called Peter last night on her way back to the hotel. Told him about Hedda's board, but after giving the matter some thought, she'd decided not to.

Peter lied to her about Tomas. What is he trying to hide, and is there a connection with Hedda's interest in Tomas?

The only way to find out is to try to contact Tomas.

She knocks on the door. It takes several attempts before she sees a movement through the frosted glass.

'Yes?'

The old man who opens the door is wearing a filthy dressing gown and Crocs. His hair is thin, he's wearing thick glasses and is clean-shaven. Once upon a time he was getting on for two metres tall, but now his back is bent.

'Kent Rask?' she asks, although it can't really be anyone else.

'Whatdoyouwant?' He runs the four words together.

'I'm looking for Tomas.'

'He's not here.'

'Do you know where I can get hold of him?'

'Why?' The old man's eyes narrow. 'You remind me of someone.'

'I'm Laura Aulin – Hedda's niece.'

Kent Rask exposes a set of nicotine-stained teeth.

'Of course – little Laura. How's your rich daddy?'

'He's dead.'

'Is he indeed? And how much did you inherit?'

The smile makes him look like an ageing wolf. He throws the door wide open and steps back.

'I'm only kidding, Laura. Come on in. Don't stand out there in the cold.'

Laura hesitates, remembering how frightened of Kent she once was. She and everyone else. But that was thirty years ago, and he's well over seventy now.

'Thank you.'

She steps inside. The house is warm. She is prepared for the usual 'bachelor' odours, but all she can smell is fried bacon.

'Come in, come in.' He leads the way through the hall, beckoning her to follow.

The walls are adorned with hunting trophies – antlers with a white piece of skull bone still attached, screwed onto wooden plaques. Above the living-room door is the head of a wild boar, mouth open, glass eyes staring.

'Take a seat.'

Kent removes a pile of newspapers from one of the sofas. Otherwise the room is surprisingly clean and tidy. The TV is showing *Emmerdale* or some similar soap. An electric fire glows brightly in one corner. The old man seems to be almost as cold as she is.

Laura reluctantly unbuttons her jacket, perches on the edge of the sofa.

'Coffee?' He points to a thermos in the middle of the table.

'No thanks,' she replies, a little too quickly.

Kent sits down in the worn armchair by the fire.

'So – why does little Laura Aulin want to speak to my Tomas, if I might ask?'

She hesitates, then decides to tell the truth.

'I want to know if he's spoken to Hedda recently.'

'I thought Hedda was dead?' he says with a grin.

'Before she died,' Laura clarifies, unnecessarily.

Kent leans forward. His nose and cheeks are covered in a fine network of broken blood vessels.

'And what would Tomas and Hedda have been talking about that's interesting enough to bring you all the way out here?'

'Only he can answer that.'

The grin disappears. 'Tomas is in an institution. That's where he's spent most of his time over the past thirty years. He's not right in the head, you see.' He taps his temple with one finger. 'God knows I've tried to knock some sense into him, in every possible way. Sometimes to the point where my fists hurt.'

Laura bites her lip. Remembers Tomas and his refusal to make eye contact, the way he kind of slunk along by the walls. She and the others couldn't understand why he wouldn't take off his T-shirt or jumper and go swimming. It all makes sense now.

'But even if he's out, he's not stupid enough to turn up here,' the old man adds.

'Why not?'

A snort. 'Because of Ulf Jensen and his boys, of course. They've been here plenty of times asking for him. That's why I keep the shotgun ready.'

He turns to face the window and pulls back the curtain to reveal a shotgun leaning against the wall. Laura pretends she's not scared at all.

'Tomas was punished, but the rest of you got off lightly. Peter Larsson, running around playing at being a cop. The orphan boy and that trollop, whatever her name was, who took off as soon as they could. Hedda, who should have been keeping an eye on all of you. And then there's you, with your rich daddy and your slick lawyers.' A thread of saliva gets caught at one corner of his mouth. 'Tomas took all the blame. The cops decided it was him and no one else. That was the simplest way.'

He shakes his head.

'Thirty years, and still no one can really let it go. People spit at me in the village. I assume you know why?' His eyes darken. 'Because Ulf Jensen won't let anyone forget what happened. He even persuaded the council to rename the school, to make sure that future generations would learn what a fucking saint his daughter was.'

He leans back, fishes a snuff tin out of his pocket and inserts a large plug under his top lip. He must have stopped smoking.

'You know they were together? Saint Iben and Orphan Boy?'

'You mean Jack?'

The subject is still painful, and Laura wishes the old man hadn't brought it up.

He ignores her correction.

'Ulf Jensen couldn't stand the thought that his snow-white daughter was sleeping with a gypsy—'

'Jack wasn't a gypsy,' Laura interrupts him.

'No?' Another grin – she can see the plug of snuff beneath his lip. 'It doesn't really matter – nobody would have been good enough for Ulf Jensen's girl. In a way I think the hypocritical bastard is pleased about the fire. It gave him the chance to put his daughter on a pedestal. Nobody will ever be able to touch her. She'll stay young and pure for all eternity. A snow-white saint, just like St Lucia.'

Kent adjusts the plug of snuff with the tip of his tongue.

'Your aunt didn't like him – did you know that?'

Laura shakes her head. Her memories don't match the old man's assertion. Hedda and Ulf were always polite to each other. Which, in hindsight, seems a little odd. Hedda was never polite to anyone else.

'It's true,' Kent continues. 'That was one of the reasons why I liked Hedda. She could see straight through Ulf Jensen, all that holier-than-thou crap. The brave single father, bringing up three kids all by himself and turning them all into winners.' He leans forward again. 'The boys' mother died, that much is true. But the second wife – Iben's mother, the woman he imported from up north . . .' He taps his temple again, as he did when he was talking about Tomas. 'Sofia was an attractive woman, there's no doubt about that, but she wasn't right in the head. She tried to set fire to Källegården one night when Ulf was out.'

Laura suppresses a gasp.

'He got home just in time – I'd given him a lift. Another twenty minutes and we'd have been too late.'

'When was this?'

Kent frowns.

'It must have been '76 or '77. Ulf and I were doing some business together back then. Tomas was with us too – he was only five or six. I remember him and Iben sitting in the back seat of my car with their arms around each other while me and Ulf and the boys put out the fire.'

'And Iben's mother?'

'Sofia was dancing around the yard in her nightdress, laughing at the top of her voice. It must have gone on for at least a quarter of an hour before Ulf managed to shut her up.'

Kent licks his lips.

'Ulf told the kids it was an accident. Then he convinced them and everyone else who asked that Sofia had left them because she couldn't settle in Skåne, and had gone back up north. In fact, he'd had her admitted to St Maria's in Helsingborg.'

'What happened to her after that?'

'I've no idea. I never heard any more about her. People like Sofia and Tomas should be locked up forever.' He gives a contemptuous smile. 'Ulf gave me a hunting permit to say thank you for my help. I could hold onto it for as long as I kept my mouth shut. He never dared to withdraw it, not even when he started playing the big man and we fell out. I presume he didn't want anyone to find out that his little angel's mother was in the loony bin.'

He sits back.

'I've kept my promise all these years, but now I'm too old to hunt. Plus, Ulf wants to sell the permit to someone else. Rumour has it that he's running short of money.'

Kent winks at her, which irritates Laura. In fact, everything about this bitter old man infuriates her. Kent Rask used to beat his son instead of trying to help him. He accepted a hunting permit in return for keeping quiet about Sofia Jensen, and let Iben grow up believing that her mother had left her. The thought of young Iben and Tomas alone in the back seat of Kent's car while Källegården burned and Sofia danced around laughing makes her head pound.

Is this the secret Hedda was interested in?

'I think I'd better go.'

She gets to her feet, but Kent grabs her wrist.

'Why are you in such a hurry, little Laura? We haven't talked about your aunt yet. Hedda and I did quite a bit of business together.'

She remains motionless. The fingers digging into her wrist are rough, dirt ingrained in the cracks. The three dots are still visible between the thumb and forefinger, as is the uneven triangle on the back of his hand.

She ought to leave, right now. But she came here to find information, so she snatches her hand away and sits down again.

'What kind of business?' she asks as calmly as she can manage. Tries not to look at the shotgun.

'Forest business.' Kent places his index finger on his lips. The nail is long, with a black edging of snuff. 'In the Eighties I did a little home distilling. It was very lucrative; there weren't many state-owned off-licences around. Your aunt was one of my best customers.'

He digs out the plug of snuff with his finger, transfers it to the coffee cup in front of him, then wipes the finger on his dressing gown. Laura feels sick.

'Hedda sold the moonshine on to the summer visitors in the holiday village, of course.'

Kent says this as if it's common knowledge, then realises that Laura is surprised.

'Didn't you know? I thought you helped out. Orphan Boy often came here to collect Hedda's orders.'

Laura doesn't reply. She really hates that nickname.

'Anyway. Once Hedda got the dance hall going, plus the boat and all the rest of it, she had lots of new thirsty customers. My equipment was working overtime.'

He savours the memory for a few seconds before continuing.

'We had a couple of really good summers, until Ulf Jensen started interfering. Said he didn't want his daughter anywhere near booze or illegal activities. He threatened to call the police. I can't understand why Hedda didn't tell him to go to hell – half the police force were buying from us, and Hedda wasn't exactly scared of confrontation. But this time she gave in. Ended our association.'

'When was this?'

Laura can't look at the old man's lips, where the remains of the snuff still linger.

'Autumn '87. I remember because it was the same year as the fire.'

Laura makes an effort to match what she's just heard with her own memories.

'You gave me a lift in your car that winter,' she says. 'You said you had to pick up something for my aunt. We came off the road.'

'Oh, you remember that!' Kent says with a laugh. 'Yes, Hedda had paid in advance for a delivery. After Ulf threatened her, she asked for her money back. I stalled for a while, hoped she'd change her mind. But I repaid her a few days before the fire.'

'You were going to fetch the money that night?'

Kent nods. 'You ran away like a frightened little rabbit. What did you think I was going to do? Rape you?'

Laura clenches her jaw. She remembers Ulf Jensen turning up, how the two men nearly got into a fight.

'You must have been furious with Ulf. You'd already fallen out, and now he'd lost you your best customer.'

'Furious isn't the half of it. That self-righteous fucker cost me thousands of kronor.'

'So what did you do about it?'

Kent grins at her once more.

'Wouldn't you like to know?'

Another image comes into her mind: the blackened cadaver of a sheep, hanging from a tree while the crows peck at its brain.

She's about to accuse him when he struggles to his feet. She hears barking in the distance – not the sound of the guard dogs that met Laura when she arrived, but a shriller, more anxious sound.

'Can you smell smoke?'

27

Winter 1987

I t was afternoon when Laura woke up, but she was still tired. She felt drained of both strength and emotion.

There was nothing left of everything she had longed for since the summer. All that remained was betrayal – and lies.

A gentle tap on her door, then her aunt said: 'You have a visitor.'

Laura wiped her red, puffy eyes with the back of her hand. 'OK.'

Peter stuck his head around the door. 'Can I come in?'

She nodded, hiding her disappointment that he wasn't Jack.

'How are you feeling?' he said, sitting down on her desk chair.

'Like shit,' she mumbled. 'This whole winter is shit. Everyone's lying to me, or keeping secrets. Hedda, Iben and Jack, even you and Tomas.'

Peter's face flushed red. In a strange way, that made her feel better.

'I know what the two of you have been doing,' she went on. 'Breaking into summer cottages and stealing stuff for Milla. How the fuck did you come up with that idea?'

'It was Tomas. He wanted to impress Milla. He mows the lawns for some of the summer visitors, so he knows where they keep their spare keys. He said we could just walk in and take what we wanted.'

'And you didn't object? You're just as bewitched by Milla as he is. You look like two lovesick puppies whenever you're anywhere near her.'

The knot in her stomach loosened slightly; unleashing her anger on Peter was helping.

'I'm just trying to keep an eye on Tomas,' he said. 'Make sure he doesn't do anything really stupid.'

'Like what? Is there anything more stupid than breaking into cottages when the owners can easily work out that Tomas knows where the keys are?'

'There are worse things. Much worse. And much more dangerous.'

Peter looked away.

Words echoed inside Laura's head. *There seems to be a pyromaniac on the loose.*

She inhaled sharply.

'You think Tomas is responsible for starting the fires?'

He still couldn't meet her gaze.

'We have to tell Hedda!'

Peter got to his feet. 'No, we don't! We can't do that to Tomas.'

'Why not? He needs help.'

'I don't know for sure that it's him, but if a rumour starts, then he's going to get the blame. Don't you remember what it was like when we were little? Tomas confessed as soon as an adult looked at him – whether he'd done anything or not.'

He came and sat beside her on the bed.

'If the police question Tomas he'll confess – you know that.'

Laura nodded slowly. Peter was right.

'So what do we do?'

'Like I said, I'm keeping an eye on him. We can't do anything until we're certain. Don't say a word to anyone about this. Promise me, Laura!'

28

Kent Rask stumbles into the hallway with Laura close behind him. The old man is right; the smell of smoke is getting stronger.

He flings open the door. 'No!' he shouts, hurrying down the steps. He runs across the yard as best he can, accompanied by the two dogs. Laura remains standing just outside the door, incapable of moving.

A wall of thick dark grey smoke is pouring out of the barn, spreading across the yard and making it increasingly difficult to see. The air is filled with the stench of burning wood and straw, which makes Laura's knees give way.

She grabs the handrail to stop herself from falling, sinks down on the top step, gasping for air. Her heart is racing, the scar is crawling all over her back. Her brain is full of messages, all telling her to flee, run, escape. Get as far away from the fire as possible.

Kent is doing the opposite, heading for the barn with his Crocs flapping against his heels, his dressing gown fluttering behind him like a cape, exposing his half-naked body.

The dogs run ahead, still barking.

She sees them all disappear into the cloud of smoke. Realises in spite of her panic that he's never going to be able to put out the fire on his own, and after a few seconds she manages to make her shaking hands take out her phone and key in the emergency number.

'There's a fire,' she says. 'At Ensligheten outside Vedarp.'

The call handler on the other end of the line is unnaturally calm, asking lots of questions that Laura answers in monosyllables. Kent has been inside the barn for more than a minute now.

One of the dogs emerges, its belly almost touching the ground, tail tucked between its legs. There is no sign of Kent.

The call handler is still talking, but Laura has stopped listening.

The smoke thickens, she can hear the flames crackling, an uneven staccato sound as the fire tries to consume the damp wood. Still no sign of Kent. The dog is running around in circles at the bottom of the steps; it doesn't know what to do with itself.

The scar heats up the cold sweat, making Laura's skin boil.

'Ambulance,' she mumbles into the phone. 'Send an ambulance too.'

She hangs up, drags herself to her feet. Her brain is still yelling at her to get away. She staggers over to her car, opens the driver's door and collapses on the seat. The feeling of safety the car always gives her allows her head to clear a little. Her only escape route lies through the smoke. She will have to drive virtually blind, hoping she doesn't crash into something and end up right next to the barn.

She starts the engine, puts the car in Drive. Her fingers are clamped to the wheel. She can see only a metre or so in front of her. Kent's car is parked somewhere up ahead. She has to avoid it, while at the same time keeping away from the burning barn.

Just as she is about to depress the accelerator, she senses a movement in the smoke. Kent comes stumbling out with another dog jumping around his legs. His thin hair is standing on end, his face is streaked with soot and tears, and the bottom of his dressing gown is singed.

His pockets are bulging, and he is clutching something dark-coloured to his chest. She opens the car door, and as he sinks down by her left front wheel she sees what he's risked his life for. Five scruffy little puppies.

Less than an hour later, the fire is under control. Eight men from the part-time fire service are still working to make sure the site is safe, but the thick, suffocating smoke has dispersed, leaving only faint wisps finding their way out between the blackened planks and cracked roof tiles.

'So is this you keeping a low profile?'

Peter sits down beside Laura on the steps. She is wrapped in a blanket thanks to the paramedics, and her legs are shaking from the adrenaline rush. She is desperate to get away; the only reason she's still here is that her car is boxed in by the fire service.

The back doors of the ambulance are open, and Kent Rask is lying inside on a bed with an oxygen mask over his face.

'Would you like to tell me what you're doing here?' Peter goes on.

Laura decides to be honest – more or less.

'I wanted to ask Kent if he'd heard from Tomas.'

'And had he?'

She shakes her head.

'He claims that Tomas never comes here, because he's afraid of the Jensen family. However, I'm pretty sure it's down to him.'

She points to Kent, who is still holding the runt of the litter, gently stroking its head.

'Can you believe he risked his life for a few puppies, yet he beat Tomas black and blue just because he was different?'

Peter doesn't answer. There is a streak of soot down the side of his face, and without thinking Laura reaches out and wipes it away. Her touch makes him jump, but he doesn't stop her. She realises what she's doing and rubs her hand on her thigh, feeling a stab of revulsion.

'Did you see how the fire started?'

Laura shakes her head. 'It was already well under way when we came out. I helped Kent back into the house while we waited for the fire service. What have they said?'

'That it was probably deliberate. You can smell petrol in there, but fortunately the straw was so damp that the whole place didn't go up.'

'Who would want to burn down the old man's barn?' Laura asks, trying not to look at the sooty mark on her jeans.

'Well, Kent Rask isn't exactly short of enemies. Did he say anything to you?'

'No, he could hardly speak. But he keeps a shotgun in the living room. He told me it was because of the Jensens, but I don't know if that's true. He's certainly scared of someone.'

Peter nods.

Inside the ambulance the paramedics seem to be arguing with Kent. Judging by the body language, they want to take him to hospital, but he's having none of it. After a while one of the paramedics calls to Laura.

'He refuses to leave until he's spoken to you.'

She stands up, makes her way shakily to the ambulance with Peter following behind.

Kent's eyes are glassy, and he looks exhausted. He lifts the mask.

'She wrote to him,' he says hoarsely. 'Hedda. She wrote letters to Tomas all through the years. That was a kind thing to do.'

Peter leans forward to hear better, but the old man sees the movement and glares at him. He beckons to Laura to come closer.

'I'm pretty sure he wrote back,' Kent whispers in her ear. 'Hedda never threw anything away, so those letters must be at Gärdsnäset somewhere . . .'

'What did he say?' Peter asks when the ambulance has gone.

'He was worried about the dogs.'

She knows that Peter isn't telling the truth about Tomas – plus he was first on the scene today. He arrived a few minutes before the firefighters, just as he did when Hedda was found dead.

What does that mean?

Maybe nothing, except that he happened to be working on both occasions. She can feel his eyes on her, but refuses to meet them.

'I need to conduct a formal witness interview with you,' he says. 'Tomorrow will be fine, when everything's calmed down. Shall we say two o'clock at the police station?'

He makes it sound like a question, even though it isn't. And it might be her imagination, but there is a sharpness in his tone, as if he's worked out that she's lying to him.

Peter offers her a lift back to the hotel, but she declines. As she arrives at her destination the last of the adrenaline finally leaves her body, and shock sets in with full force.

After what feels like only moments she is sitting on the floor of the shower with hot water cascading over her body. Her pulse is racing, the scar on her back is on fire and she is shaking with cold.

She is exhausted. Her brain keeps replaying what happened. The smoke, the smell, Kent Rask risking his life for his dogs. Then the blue flashing lights, the sirens.

She keeps blowing her nose until she's got rid of all the black snot that's imbued with the burning smell. Drags herself to her feet and washes her body and her hair until all the little bottles provided by the hotel are empty.

When she's finished she pushes her clothes into the laundry bag and places it in the corridor along with her shoes and jacket. Still the smell of burning won't go away. It seems to be forcing its way in around the edges of the door.

She calls reception, asks them to come and collect her clothes immediately. That doesn't help either. The smell has established itself in the room; it is hiding in the carpet, the sheets, the curtains.

In the end she has no choice but to attack the window. Using the iron she finds in the wardrobe, she smashes the lock on the security chain and flings the window wide open. She stands there in her bathrobe with wet hair, taking deep breaths of the cold winter air until both her heart and her scar finally calm down.

29

Winter 1987

Hedda made them a late lunch, then persuaded Laura to come out for a walk. She would have preferred to stay in her room. Crawl into bed and pull the covers over her head. But Hedda was having none of it.

'Come on, let's go!'

They headed west along the shore, in the direction of the village rather than Alkärret. The wind was blowing off the lake, and out in the centre that wide-open, dark eye looked back at them.

'Jack cares about you,' Hedda said after a while. 'More than you think.'

'In that case he's got a funny way of showing it.' Laura could feel the anger bubbling up in her chest. 'Why didn't you say something? Iben's father has spoken to you about them, said he didn't want them seeing each other.'

'To be honest, I didn't really listen. Ulf Jensen has some strange ideas, particularly when it comes to Iben. After you left she carried on coming here for dinner some evenings. At first I think it was because she missed you – and probably because she wanted to get away from Källegården. Find some peace and quiet.'

Hedda tucked her arm through Laura's.

'I liked having her here, mainly because it reminded me of you. As time went on, she and Jack started ending the evening up in the boathouse. I could hear them singing and playing. And then . . .'

She stopped, chewed her lower lip.

'And then what?'

Laura tried not to sound too aggressive, but she couldn't help herself.

'Something happened. Just a couple of weeks before you were due back.'

'What?'

Hedda looked worried.

'I don't actually know, but I noticed that Jack was . . . troubled.'

Laura turned her head away. It wasn't difficult to work out what had happened, or why Jack had been plagued by a guilty conscience. She was determined not to cry.

They continued past the closed-up dance hall. In the summer it was the liveliest place in the holiday village, but in the winter it looked pretty rundown. The domed roof was covered in snow, and all the windows were boarded up with big sheets of plywood.

'The first time you fall in love can be agonising,' Hedda said. 'All those feelings you've never experienced before – love, longing, anger, sometimes even hatred.'

She stopped again, turned to face Laura and gently put a hand under her chin.

'It's easy to go too far. To say and do things you later regret – do you know what I mean?'

Laura nodded reluctantly.

'You and Jack and Iben have been friends for a long time,' Hedda went on. 'Regardless of what's gone on, you care about one another, and none of you would hurt the others deliberately. Try to remember that, even when things are at their worst, OK?'

'OK.'

Hedda put her arm around Laura's shoulders and drew her close, then pointed out across the ice.

'I've always loved this lake, ever since the summer when your grandfather brought me and your father here for the first time. I was about your age.' She squeezed Laura a little tighter. 'We stayed at Gärdsnäset for a week. We went sailing and fishing. It was one of the best weeks of my life.'

Hedda smiled to herself.

'You see, my first love was also painful.' Her voice had taken on a melancholy tone. 'I was twenty-one when your grandfather died. Old enough to be able to make my own decisions. Your father and I inherited quite a bit of money. Jacob used his share to start a business. As you know, he was a lot more sensible than me. I had other plans . . .'

'Like what?'

Hedda had never really talked about her life before Gärdsnäset.

'Travelling, partying – all kinds of fun. I lived in Berlin for a while, Australia, the south of France. I was young, attractive, and I had money. Life was fantastic.'

'So what happened?'

Hedda shrugged. 'I fell in love.'

'Who with?'

'A guy with a guitar. Talk about a cliché.' She laughed. 'He was a few years older than me, and so good-looking. For a few enchanted months I thought he was the one.'

'But he wasn't?'

'No. Prince Charming turned out to be married – a detail he'd forgotten to mention. I was furious, and I did something really stupid.'

She looked down at the snow, kicked a lump of ice out of the way.

'What did you do?'

'We had a fight. He'd . . . We'd both been drinking and taking God knows what. I was high, drunk, jealous and angry. Not a good combination. In the end I hit him over the head with a bottle. Walked away and left him lying there in a pool of blood.'

'Did he die?' Laura gasped.

'Fortunately not. The neighbours had already called the police. They broke the door down and found him. I was arrested on suspicion of serious assault.'

Hedda was still kicking at the snow, her expression showing how difficult she was finding this conversation.

'Your father came to my rescue. He flew to France the very next day, organised a good lawyer, sorted me out and made sure I was more or less drug-free for the trial. I got away with four months in jail.'

'What happened after that?' Laura said eventually. Hedda's face softened.

'When I got out, your father helped me to buy Gärdsnäset. You could say it became my salvation. Without Jacob I wouldn't be here today.'

A gust of wind from the lake sent a little cloud of loose snow whirling up around them.

'Why did you never get married?' Laura asked.

Hedda shrugged, gazed out across the lake.

'I guess you could say I'd been burned. By life, and love.'

*

They walked slowly back to the house, arm in arm. Laura glanced at her aunt from time to time. She'd never really known Hedda's story, and now she did, she saw her through different eyes.

'What do you do if someone you care about is doing something dangerous?' she asked after a while.

Hedda looked at her. 'What do you mean by dangerous?'

'Something that might be illegal. And if I tell on them, it will just make things so much worse.'

'Is it someone I know?'

Laura swallowed. Shook her head. 'One of the girls in school.'

Hedda frowned. 'The best approach is to try and talk to the person concerned.'

'But what if they don't want you to get involved?'

'Then you just have to try to explain that you're getting involved because you care about them, not because you wish them any harm. Tell them that's what friends do.'

Laura nodded slowly. It would have been such a relief to unburden herself, to tell Hedda what Tomas and Peter were up to before the situation got worse. But Milla had shared a confidence with her. They'd exchanged secrets. Plus, she'd made a promise to Peter.

'Are you absolutely certain it isn't someone I know?' Hedda asked.

Laura shook her head again, looked away.

'Like I said – it's a girl in school.'

30

When Laura opens her eyes it is already Monday morning. Her mouth is dry as it always is when she's taken a double dose of her medication. Her teeth are aching in spite of the mouth guard. She orders breakfast from room service, even though she's not really hungry.

Three missed calls on her phone, two from Andreas last night, one from Steph this morning. She sends the same text message to both of them. She can't face talking to anyone right now.

Sorry, things are taking a bit longer than expected.

Steph replies almost immediately.

Are you OK?

Laura summarises the previous day in her head. Kent Rask, the fire, her own delayed collapse. No, she is fucking far from fucking OK, as Steph might have put it. But she can't say that; Steph would probably get the first flight down here.

Absolutely, she writes instead. Adds a couple of suitable emojis.

She tries to gather her thoughts. What is stopping her from simply turning her back on all this, getting in the car and driving home as planned?

Nothing.

So why doesn't she do it?

Her phone starts buzzing. She's pretty sure it's Steph, in which case she won't answer. In fact, it's the office, calling about yet another of Marcus's cock-ups. She listens for thirty seconds, then makes a decision. It's high time her little brother came out of her blind spot. Or rather, it's time she forced him out.

'I'm busy,' she says. 'I'll send you a number where you can reach Marcus.'

She ends the call then sends the office her mother's mobile number, plus the landline at the villa in Spain, then switches off her phone.

The man in the ironmonger's in Vedarp is just over fifty and well built. She doesn't recognise him, wonders if he's related to Sven-Erik who used to run the shop. Maybe he's his son? Too much time has passed for her to see any resemblance.

'A skip?' the man says as he adds up her purchases. 'Let me think . . . my brother-in-law can probably help you out. Would you be paying cash?'

'Absolutely. I just want the stuff gone.'

While she packs the car with cleaning products, rubber gloves, buckets and plastic sacks, the ironmonger makes a call, then comes out to join her.

'You're in luck – he can deliver the skip this afternoon. What's the address?'

'Gärdsnäset. The old holiday village.'

He lets out a long whistle.

'I thought so – you're Hedda Aulin's niece, the one from Stockholm.'

'I am. Laura Aulin.'

'You were there when the dance hall caught fire. You, Peter Larsson, Tomas Rask and the other two. The foster kids, whatever they were called.'

Laura doesn't bother to supply Jack and Milla's names.

'I used to train with Ulf Jensen,' the ironmonger goes on. 'Shot put and hammer, alongside Fredrik, his youngest son. Ulf was the best coach I've ever had. He still remembers my results whenever we bump into each other. Fredrik and Christian were good, they were nearly always in the top ten when they competed, but Iben was the real star. Who knows how far she could have gone?'

His expression hardens.

'I heard you were out at Kent Rask's place yesterday when the fire started.'

'I was – what about it?'

He leans closer. His breath smells of coffee.

'You know, some people around here think Tomas Rask wasn't the only guilty party back in the day. They believe that more of you were involved. You turn up for the funeral, and there's another fire. After three decades. Strange, wouldn't you say?'

Laura swallows hard, searches for something to say.

'You're going to sell Gärdsnäset to the council as agreed?'

The question and the sudden change of subject take her by surprise.

'After all, that's the least you can do for the village. Not to mention poor Ulf Jensen. I'm sure a few hundred thousand here or there doesn't make much difference to you – you've got plenty of money.'

He pats the roof of her car as if to show that he knows exactly how much it costs.

'The last thing those of us who live here need is an influx of rich bastards driving up house prices and not paying their local taxes. And we don't need construction companies who employ Polish builders and don't buy locally.'

He pats the car again. Gives her a chilly smile.

'But I'm sure you'll make the right decision, Laura Aulin. Let's hope so, anyway.'

Back at Gärdsnäset Laura starts by putting on the overalls, protective head covering, mask and wellingtons she bought earlier. She flings open all the windows in Hedda's house, then goes down to the shore for a while in the hope that the cross-draughts will disperse the worst of the odours. George follows her like a dog, glancing up at her from time to time as if she's trying to work out what on earth Laura is doing.

It is cloudy and grey, and only a few degrees below zero. A faint mist lingers among the trees, and the ice on the lake is tightening its grip on the black eye in the centre.

The nightmare. The nymph that was also Iben, rising from the lake to sink her claws into Hedda. Even though it was only a dream and she doesn't believe in trolls or fairies, it won't let go. And then there are the words Hedda wrote on her board: *Ask Tomas about Iben's secret.*

What secret, and how was it connected to the sale of Gärdsnäset?

The conversation with the ironmonger has supplied her with more pieces of the puzzle. It is clear that people in the village have an opinion about the sale. Did they pass on that opinion to Hedda? More than likely.

So where does Ulf Jensen come into the picture? Is he the one who sent Kjell Green?

She remembers what Kent Rask told her about Ulf and about Iben's mother.

Kent hated the Jensens, yet at the same time he was so scared of them that he kept a shotgun at the ready in his living room.

And the fire in the barn showed that he had good reason to be afraid.

But why was the fire started yesterday, during the brief period when she happened to be visiting Kent? Surely it couldn't be a coincidence.

Who was responsible for the fire, and why? Was the intention to frighten Kent Rask, or Laura? Or both?

She kicks out at the snow in frustration, then leans back against a tree trunk. Too many questions.

Kent Rask said that Hedda and Tomas wrote to each other, which means that at least some of the answers ought to be somewhere in the house. Searching for letters means digging through three decades of dirt and crap – not exactly her idea of a good time. George seems to realise that she needs support, and keeps rubbing around Laura's legs.

The nasal buzz of an engine interrupts her train of thought. George obviously recognises the sound. She slips away through the trees and hurries around the corner of the house to greet the visitor. Laura follows more slowly and sees Elsa sitting astride her motocross bike.

'What are you doing?' the young woman asks when she's removed her helmet.

'Cleaning,' Laura replies, which is at least partly true.

Elsa climbs off her bike and props it against a tree.

'Cool. Do you want some help?'

They begin by clearing a passageway straight through the house, from the front door to the room Hedda used as her office and studio.

In spite of the fact that she is more or less covered from head to toe in protective clothing, Laura has to make a real effort to ignore the little voice in her ear, telling her how many different micro-organisms there are per cubic metre of air, or the potentially fatal consequences of sustaining even the tiniest scratch from one of the dusty corners lurking all over the house.

However, Elsa sets about the task with such enthusiasm that Laura has no choice but to steel herself and get on with it. By the time the skip arrives, they've made good progress.

The truck driver is a sullen individual who appears to be as kindly disposed to Laura as the ironmonger was, but Elsa jollies him along, and he ends up helping them to carry out two of the old fridges, a bed and a rusty sink unit that are blocking the way into the living room.

When the driver has left, they decide to take a break. They brush the snow off the top step and sit down on two faded garden chairs with a can of Coca-Cola Zero each and a packet of cinnamon buns to share.

'Shouldn't you be in school?'

'Christmas holidays.'

'Come on, Elsa – it's not even Lucia yet.'

'Are you going to tell my dad?'

'That depends on how well you clean.'

Elsa tries not to smile, but fails.

'You had a little gang when you were kids, didn't you?'

'Mmm. Your dad used to call us the Goonies. Like in the film,' Laura adds, realising from Elsa's expression that her generation are probably not interested in comedies from the Eighties.

'What was she like?' Elsa asks after a pause.

'Who?'

'Iben Jensen. Dad never wants to talk about her. Was she as amazing as everyone says?'

'She was smart – really smart. Top marks in everything . . .'

Elsa waves a dismissive hand.

'I already know all that. Tell me something else, something nobody knows.'

Laura thinks for a moment.

'Iben was very competitive. She always had to win – she got really angry if she didn't. She'd even get mad playing Uno.'

Elsa looks slightly more interested.

'That must have been annoying.'

Laura shrugs. 'We all have our hang-ups.'

'Did you ever fall out?'

'I guess so.'

'What about?'

Laura tosses the question straight back at her.

'What do you and your friends usually fall out about?'

'What makes you think I have a lot of friends?' Elsa stands up, makes a point of looking at her phone. 'I have to go home. I might stop by tomorrow.'

'Fine.'

Laura stays where she is while Elsa puts on her helmet, kick-starts the bike and disappears.

It feels a little sad to be left alone, not least because twilight is falling. On the other hand, it suits her very well. She doesn't want curious teenage eyes watching her when she's searching for Tomas's letters.

The studio/office is probably the best place to start. She removes the cardboard boxes containing the accounts for the holiday village, a couple of old lamps and a broken chair, but the room still feels cluttered. The shelves are crammed with more boxes, folders and piles of papers, and the floor space is filled by three ill-matched filing cabinets, a large desk and a lathe. Oil paintings of various sizes are stacked against the walls; some are finished, some are not. Most are in the naïve style using bright colours, and they're really not very good. Nowhere near the same class as the one Hedda has been using as a noticeboard.

Laura goes over to the desk, flicks through some of the papers. Most are old, and seem to be related to the accounts. Dust whirls around the room, and for what must be the fiftieth time she presses her fingers against her mouth to make sure the mask is as tight-fitting as possible.

But maybe the dust can help her.

She moves to the bookshelves and looks closely at the layer of dust that covers everything like a grey mat. On the top middle shelf there are six shoeboxes with a much thinner coating of dust. She lifts them down, places them on the desk.

The first contains slides, the next photographs. She picks up a couple. Hedda when she was young, at a pavement café somewhere with palm trees in the background. She is surrounded by happy, smiling people, raising their glasses in a toast to the photographer. From a purely statistical point of view, at least half of them must be dead by now, just like Hedda. She hears Steph's voice in her head:

What a little ray of sunshine you are, Laura!

The next box is full of bundles of postcards and letters. She tips them out onto the desk, immediately recognises the handwriting in the thickest bundle.

Her own.

She skims through some of the correspondence. The tone is so childish. Steph would call it needy.

Dear Hedda, I can't wait to see you. I'll be there soon. What are you doing? What are the others doing?

The same *dear* Hedda who saved all these letters suddenly stopped writing to her.

Laura is slightly ashamed of herself. The whole thing was her fault, after all. If she hadn't done what she did, Iben would have lived, had a family of her own. Maybe Laura and Jack would have found their way back to each other, maybe Peter and Tomas's lives would have been different, maybe . . .

She puts down her old letters, turns to the postcards. The first one makes her heart leap.

I've arrived in Hamburg. Don't worry, everything's fine.

Happy Christmas, by the way.

Jack

The card is dated 21 December 1987. A week after the fire. Five days after he kissed her goodbye at the hospital.

There are five postcards from Jack in total, all with equally brief messages, sent at intervals of a few months. First a couple from Hamburg, then one from Munich. All saying the same thing: I'm fine, don't worry. No contact details. No address, no post box number, no phone number.

The last two were sent from Berlin in 1989. The final one is dated in October, less than a month before the wall came down. This time there is an addition that makes her heart leap again.

I hope you've heard from Princess, and that she's doing OK.

Jack was thinking about her. Almost two years after the fire, he was still thinking about her.

She tries to focus, move on, but an irritating sliver of happiness remains.

At the bottom of the box she finds letters from her father. The handwriting is clear and plain, the tone matter-of-fact. They're mostly about money, shares from Laura's grandfather, a property they inherited that Jacob has sold.

He ends the letters to his sister with *Yours sincerely*, which doesn't surprise her. More surprising is the discovery of a couple of letters from her mother in the same bundle. They deal with practical details – Laura's term dates, planning for summers and winters at Gärdsnäset. The tone is polite, nothing more.

One single letter is tucked down the side of the box. The envelope is stamped 1995, which makes it considerably more recent than the rest. The handwriting is rounded, almost childish.

Dear Hedda,

Thank you for your letters.

I often think about what happened. Sometimes I see her face before me. No one was meant to get hurt. But things didn't turn out the way we expected.

Tomas Rask

She reads the letter several times, trying to interpret the clipped sentences. Tomas seems to be admitting that he was behind the fire. That he has regrets. It's somehow reassuring, but the last sentence leaves her shaken.

Things didn't turn out the way we expected.

We? Who else was involved? What had Tomas and this other person expected?

Her thoughts are interrupted by the sound of a phone ringing. Automatically she reaches for her mobile, then remembers that she turned it off because she wanted to be left in peace, plus there's hardly any coverage out here.

The ringing continues; it's coming from the living room. On the floor between the sofa and the wall she tracks down a dusty old push-button phone.

She picks up the receiver. 'Hello?'

'Laura? It's Ulf Jensen. I heard you were still at Gärdsnäset.'

'Yes, I'm staying a few more days.'

She tries to work out who told him – presumably, the ironmonger or his brother-in-law.

'Do you need any help? Christian and Fredrik would be happy to come over.'

'Thanks, I can manage.'

'You only have to give us a call, you know that. Neighbours help each other out.'

'Thank you . . .'

'By the way, I was wondering if you'd like to join us at Källegården for dinner this evening?'

Her first instinct is to say no, come up with an excuse, but there are so many questions whirling around in her mind. Who set fire to Kent Rask's barn, who were the 'we' in Tomas's letter? And what did Hedda mean by Iben's secret? The best place to find out is probably Iben's home.

'That would be lovely,' she says.

31

Winter 1987

'Here.'

Milla lit a cigarette, then pushed the ashtray across the coffee table before sinking back against the sofa cushions.

Laura had mastered the art of lighting her cigarette, maintaining a film-star air of cool and taking something that resembled a drag. In fact, she simply held the smoke in her mouth for a few seconds before blowing it out. Milla could probably see right through her, but didn't say anything. That was one of the things Laura liked about Milla – she didn't judge.

'I've been thinking about this business with Jack and Iben,' Milla said.

'Yes?'

Laura sat up a little straighter. The knot in her stomach made its presence felt, as it always did when the subject was raised. They'd talked about Jack and Iben quite a bit over the past few days. Milla was a good listener – something else Laura liked about her.

'Iben knew you were keen on Jack. She knew you'd kissed down on the pontoon in the summer.'

'Mmm.' Laura took another fake drag.

'And she still got together with him. She didn't care how you felt, she exploited the fact that you weren't here. Your best friend.'

'Mmm.' The knot hardened.

'I've seen the way Jack looks at you,' Milla went on. 'He might be with Iben, but it's obvious he still thinks about you.'

'Is it?' Laura tried not to sound too eager.

Milla clapped her hands.

'I know! Let's arrange a party, make sure Jack and Iben are there. I'll do your makeup and your hair, and you can borrow some of my clothes. You'll look gorgeous, I promise. Like Baby at the end of *Dirty Dancing*. Jack will realise he's chosen the wrong girl.'

'Do you think so?'

'Absolutely!'

Milla stubbed out her cigarette in the big glass ashtray.

'Tomas and Peter will help – we're all on your side. What do you say?'

The thought was exciting, but a part of her still wanted to say no. She and Iben were friends, in spite of everything. Or rather – *had been* friends. Because just as Milla had pointed out, it was Iben who'd destroyed everything. Iben who had sacrificed their friendship to get what she wanted. To win . . .

'When?' Laura asked.

Milla grinned at her. 'Thirteenth of December – Lucia.'

32

The driveway leading up to Källegården looks more or less the same as Laura remembers it: a narrow dirt track lined with old willow trees, all leaning away from the wind at the same angle.

A sign next to the postboxes informs passers-by that wood, Christmas trees and fireworks are for sale. Behind it is a bigger sign, hanging askew.

JENSEN & SONS CONSTRUCTION LTD

Laura realises she's nervous. Ulf surely hasn't invited her in order to fling accusations at her, but there's still something unpleasant about approaching the place.

Källegården has two yards. The first is surrounded by stables, a barn and a storage shed for machinery. The second is higher, and is encircled by a stream that turns it into an island. The buildings all have the same yellow-rendered façades, but the garage is considerably newer than the farmhouse itself, which has stepped gables.

The snow has been cleared from the drive and both yards. In front of the farmhouse stands a Christmas tree almost as big as the one by the church down in the village.

She looks for the sports facility that Ulf once built for Iben and her brothers, but the running track, discus circle and long-jump pit have been replaced by a dense plantation of Christmas trees.

As always, the change of temperature makes her shiver as she gets out of the car.

Before she reaches the house, the front door is flung open and Ulf steps out. He is beaming, and looks much brighter than he did at the funeral.

'Laura – welcome!' He takes her hand in both of his. 'It's so good to see you here again.'

'Thanks for inviting me,' she says, glancing at the huge red-and-white painting on the wall.

She recalls the story of the Jensen family coat of arms that was 'found' when Ulf renovated the façade, but she's never thought about what it represents until now. A shield-shaped Danish flag, divided into quarters containing a knight's helmet, a wild boar, a sword, and three flames.

She shivers once again, but this time it's nothing to do with the cold.

'Come on in and have a drink. Can I take your jacket?'

Laura is given a cup of mulled wine to warm her fingers while Ulf shows her around.

She recognises the classic wallpaper, the old muskets and swords on the walls, the aerial photograph of Källegården hanging in the hallway. She also remembers the heavy furniture in dark wood, and the slightly creepy paintings of long dead relatives. She's not so sure about the smell. Maybe she's mixing it up with the way her grandmother's house in Djurholm smelled. Or possibly a museum somewhere.

There are framed photographs of Iben and her brothers on just about every flat surface. Laura avoids looking at them. One wall is reserved for diplomas and awards. *His Majesty the King's*

Medal for Special Merit – that one is right at the top, followed by *Skåne Sport Honorary Award, Sports Coach of the Year,* and a dozen or so diplomas of lesser prestige.

After a while Iben's brothers appear. Christian is the nicer of the two. He chats away happily, introduces his wife, an almost transparent woman whose name Laura instantly forgets. Their three children politely say hello before settling down to gaze at their screens.

'In our day we only had fifteen minutes of children's programmes on TV,' Christian says. 'Makes you wonder how we survived!'

From the ongoing conversation Laura learns that younger brother Fredrik is divorced. His children live with their mother, while he has moved back to Källegården. Fredrik doesn't say much. He mostly stares at the floor, avoiding eye contact with Laura as he did at the funeral. No doubt he remembers their previous encounter. She certainly does.

Fredrik is powerfully built. The shirt he's wearing is too small, the collar too tight, which makes the rolls of fat at the back of his neck look even thicker. He has a fresh-looking bandage around his meaty left hand.

Christian sees that Laura has noticed. He grabs his brother's hand and holds it up in the air.

'Fireworks,' he says. 'Fredrik was showing off in front of the kids and he burned himself. What an idiot – fifty years old and he still can't act responsibly.'

Fredrik snatches his hand away and mumbles something unintelligible.

As they head for the dining room, Laura's phone rings. It's Peter. She slips into the hallway to talk privately. He's annoyed, not surprisingly.

'You were supposed to be at the police station at two o'clock for your witness interview. Ring any bells?'

She swears to herself. 'I'm so sorry, I completely forgot.' She hates those words, hates them even more when she's the one saying them. 'I can come in first thing tomorrow if you like?'

The apology and the offer seem to mollify him.

'Nine o'clock.'

'Have you found out any more about the fire?'

'We're still waiting for forensics, but it was probably arson.'

A brief silence. Laura thinks about Kent Rask's comments on the Jensens, about the fresh burn on Fredrik's hand. Should she say something? Peter gets there first.

'I wanted to ask you . . .' He hesitates. His voice has softened. 'If you're not doing anything this evening, would you like to join me for something to eat?'

'That's so kind of you, but I'm already at a dinner.'

'Where?'

'Källegården.'

'I see. In other words, you're still keeping a low profile.'

'Ulf called and invited me here.'

'And why do you think he did that? To be nice?' A snort of derision. 'Ulf Jensen never does anything without an ulterior motive. You can tell me what it is when I see you tomorrow. Nine o'clock at the station. Have a nice evening.'

He ends the call abruptly, which annoys her. Peter has absolutely no right to dictate what she can and can't do. She'd like to call him back and make that clear, but the others are already taking their seats around the table.

On the dining-room wall there is a large portrait photograph of Iben at the age of fifteen. She wears her dark hair loose, and is gazing straight into the lens. Laura tries not to look at it, but it's impossible. Time and time again it draws her in, until she has memorised every last detail. The determined expression, the colours of her clothes, even the way the wallpaper nearest the frame has a yellowish tone.

In spite of the photograph, dinner is more pleasant than Laura had expected. The food is good, and Christian and his wife do their best to make sure she is enjoying herself. They ask about Stockholm and her job, treat her like an honoured guest. Ulf also asks the odd question now and again.

Fredrik, on the other hand, speaks in monosyllables and still won't look at her.

Ulf taps his knife against his glass.

'Dear Laura,' he begins. 'As I said before, it's so good to see you at Källegården again. I've always regarded you as my second daughter, in a way. You and Iben ...' He breaks off, his eyes shining with unshed tears. 'You were like sisters.'

Christian's wife reaches out and pats her father-in-law on the arm.

'I remember it like yesterday – the two of you up in Iben's room, with you trying to teach her to speak Swedish without a Skåne accent...'

He relates the entire anecdote, and Laura adopts a suitable expression. Her memory of the incident is quite different from Ulf's. Nor does she remember spending time here as a child. On the contrary, Iben never wanted to meet up here. However, she doesn't say anything; she simply nods.

'Your aunt and I had a number of conversations about the future of Gärdsnäset,' Ulf goes on. 'It took a long time before Hedda decided to sell, mainly because she didn't want the land to go to someone who was only interested in making money from it.'

Laura doesn't react. Peter's warning is ringing in her ears.

'Hedda wanted the land to be used for something good,' Ulf continues. 'She was so pleased when I told her that the council wanted to build a sports facility out there. Several different training grounds with both Astroturf and real grass. A new, modern sports hall to replace the old one, equipped for a whole range of activities.'

He pauses.

'Both Hedda and I agreed that Iben would have loved the idea. It would be a wonderful way to honour her memory.'

A single tear trickles down his cheek.

'Excuse me.'

Ulf gets to his feet and leaves the room, followed by Christian's wife. No one says a word. Laura can feel Iben's eyes burning into her from the photograph.

'I . . .' She clears her throat. 'I'll talk to Håkansson tomorrow.'

Christian exchanges a glance with his brother, then he nods and smiles warmly at Laura.

Laura waits until they've had dessert. As they move into the living room, she excuses herself and slips away to the bathroom. By this time she's kept the mask in place for almost two hours, and is exhausted. She splashes her face with cold water, then sits down on the toilet and rests her head on her knees.

She should never have come here. Not to Källegården, not to Gärdsnäset, not to Vintersjön.

She takes out her phone. She needs to call Steph, to hear her voice, tell her she'll be home soon, think about and talk about things that have nothing to do with fires or huge photographs of dead friends.

But suddenly she realises something, and almost swears out loud. *Scheming bastards!*

Coffee, tea and cake have been set out in the living room. She sees Fredrik pour himself a large whisky, then one for his father before starting to cut slices of cake for his nephews and nieces.

Laura goes over to the fireplace. Above it hangs an oil painting of a stern-looking elderly gentleman wearing a curly seventeenth-century wig. She gently lifts one corner of the frame and inspects the wallpaper behind. It's just as she thought.

'There you go.' Christian hands her a cup of tea. They remain standing in front of the portrait.

'Who's that?' she asks.

'To be honest, I don't remember. We could ask my father, but there's a risk we'd get a fifteen-minute history lesson.' He smiles in a way that is presumably meant to be conspiratorial.

'It probably looked better in the dining room.'

Christian's smile fades. 'How did . . .'

'The wallpaper. The photograph in there has a yellow line all the way round it. This –' she lifts the frame again – 'covers the yellow area and a good bit more. I'm guessing you swapped it with Iben's photo so that I'd be looking at her all the way through dinner. You were trying to manipulate me.'

Christian nods, his face red with what appears to be genuine embarrassment.

'I take full responsibility – it was a stupid idea. But I'm desperate.'

'Why?'

He leans closer, lowers his voice. Everyone else is busy with coffee and cake.

'We're on the verge of bankruptcy – the company, the farm, the whole lot. Fredrik and my father made some foolish invest-ments a few years ago, put everything into building a golf course. But then the costs soared out of control and we ran out of capital. We're up to our necks in debt.'

He falls silent, seems worried that the others might have overheard.

'I've done my best to try and clean up after them,' he says even more quietly. 'Christmas tree sales, strawberry picking, fireworks, hunting trips – anything that brings in a bit of extra money. The Gärdsnäset project is our only lifeline. The council have already promised us the building contract.'

'Can they do that? Doesn't that kind of thing have to go out to tender?'

'My father's done a lot for the council and the community over the years – nobody would dare give the contract to anyone else. Particularly because it's Gärdsnäset.'

'And what if the land is sold to Vintersjöholm Castle instead?'

Christian spreads his arms wide in despair.

'Then we'll have to leave Källegården after six generations. That will finish my father.'

Laura glances over at Ulf. He is sitting in an armchair with one of his grandchildren on his lap. When he feels her eyes on him, he looks up at her and smiles in a way that is impossible to interpret.

33

Winter 1987

Laura, Milla, Tomas and Peter met at Wohlin's and secured the same table that Laura and Iben had chosen less than a week ago.

'We've got problems,' Tomas said.

Laura was surprised that he was taking the lead. He usually stayed in the background, avoided eye contact, but in Milla's company he was different. More self-confident, less anxious. Tougher.

Peter, on the other hand, kept shuffling uncomfortably and looking over at Laura.

'What kind of problems?' Milla snapped. 'As I said, we need stuff for the party. More booze, a tape player, something to eat. You said you could fix it.'

Tomas nodded. 'I know a place. The owners come to stay from time to time throughout the year, so there should be food in the fridge and freezer, plus plenty of wine and beer.'

'So what's the problem?'

'We don't know where they hide the key.'

'And?'

Peter cleared his throat.

'It was different with the other summer cottages. No one noticed we'd been there – who the fuck remembers how many bottles of booze they left behind last summer? But if we break in, smash a window or something in a place the owners come back to at regular intervals' – he spread his hands wide – 'they're bound to call the police. Then there's this business with the fires . . .'

His eyes flicked sideways to Tomas for a second.

'What about the fires?' Milla said.

'The police might link them with the break-in.'

'Why would they do that?'

Peter couldn't come up with a good answer. He gazed pleadingly at Laura, who came to his rescue.

'Not much happens around here,' she said quickly. 'Two incidents at around the same time . . . If the police make the connection they'll put in more effort, and the risk of being caught increases – isn't that what you mean?'

Peter nodded, gave her a grateful smile.

'OK.' Milla drummed her fingers on the table. 'In that case we'll just have to be more careful. Me and Laura will come with you. I'll keep a lookout for the owners, and Laura can help you search for the key. She's good at finding things out about people.'

Peter opened his mouth, but before he could protest she heard a voice say, 'Fine.'

Only when she saw his surprised reaction did she realise the voice was hers.

34

Laura pauses by the car. There is snow in the air, and her head is spinning. The Jensens are on the verge of bankruptcy. That explains Håkansson's cryptic comment when she asked about the offers, and the ironmonger's overtly threatening insistence that she ought to sell Gärdsnäset to the council for Ulf's sake. Hedda had held the family's fate in her hands, and she could have saved or destroyed them with one single decision.

Did that decision have anything to do with her death? The fact that she'd written about Iben on her board shows that the family had been on her mind – but in what way?

'Laura!'

She turns and sees Fredrik coming towards her. He offers her a cigarette, but she shakes her head.

'I don't smoke.'

He smiles and lights a cigarette.

'Me neither.' The smile broadens. 'Dad once caught Christian and me having a secret fag. He made us do fifty laps of the running track as a punishment.'

'I know.'

His expression is hard to read.

'I assume Iben told you. Did she also tell you how he found out?'

Laura shakes her head.

'Because she made sure he knew. Iben was Daddy's little girl. Christian and I always came second. Or rather: Iben came first, then nothing, then Källegården, then the sports club and then, a long way down, Christian and me.'

He takes a deep drag and blows out the smoke. Laura can't stop staring at the bandage on his hand.

'I went to see Kent Rask yesterday,' she says.

'So I heard. How was old Kent? I believe he had a few problems with his barn.'

Fredrik grins again.

'He told me about Sofia, Iben's mother.'

The smile disappears. 'Did he now.'

'Do you know what became of her?'

A shrug.

'Dead. At least that's what people say. She took off when we were little.'

'Is it true that she tried to burn down Källegården? That she was admitted to a mental hospital?'

Fredrik looks taken aback. He stares at her for a few seconds, then bursts into scornful laughter.

'It seems as if you'll believe anything.' He takes another drag. 'Sofia wasn't from around here. She was never happy at Källegården, so when Iben was six she packed her bags and left. There was nothing more to it. The only person I know who's been locked up in the loony bin is Kent Rask's pyromaniac son. Talk about crazy . . . Did he tell you what happened to Tomas?'

Laura doesn't reply, but Fredrik interprets her silence correctly.

'He carried on setting fire to things. He almost burned down an entire psychiatric wing when he was in St Sigfrid's in Växjö. Ask your friend Peter if you don't believe me.' He shakes his head. 'But it wasn't that particular nutjob I wanted to talk about. You're busy out at Gärdsnäset. Going through Hedda's stuff.'

'And?'

'You've even got yourself a little helper – the girl on the motocross bike. She seems to be as weird as her father.'

Laura is trying to work out where he's going, but without success. He moves a little closer.

'Do you know if your aunt heard anything from him afterwards? Orphan Boy?'

'Jack?'

The question surprises her.

'Who else? Have you heard from him?'

She thinks about the postcards from Germany. About the smoker in the forest.

'Why do you ask?'

She doesn't really expect an answer, but Fredrik surprises her again.

'He stole something from us, back then. After the fire . . .'

'What?'

'Almost a hundred thousand in cash. Money Dad couldn't keep in the bank, for . . . business reasons. Very useful if you wanted to flee the country.'

'How do you know it was Jack?'

Her question is a little too quick, and she can see she's angered him.

'Because Dad had hidden it in a safe place. Not even Christian and I knew where it was. But Iben knew about the money and the hiding place. She must have told Orphan Boy. They were very close, those two. A little too close, wouldn't you say?'

The grin is back.

Much to her annoyance, Laura feels herself blushing.

'Hedda always defended that kid, almost as if he were her own flesh and blood.' Fredrik shakes his head. 'But Dad was right – he recognised his type right from the start. A fucking gyppo.'

He points to Laura, the cigarette pinched between finger and thumb.

'The little fucker didn't just steal our money. He got into Iben's bedroom too, stole the jewellery her mother had left her. Stole from a dead girl, for fuck's sake! If I ever get hold of Jack Olsson, he'll pay dearly for that, I can promise you.'

He drops the cigarette butt in the snow, grinds it beneath his heel. Steps forward until he's so close that she can smell the whisky on his breath.

'Now be a good girl and sell Gärdsnäset to the council. It's no good hanging onto that old dump. It's nothing but a fire hazard.'

He winks at her, then turns and walks back to the house.

Laura waits until he's gone, then bends down and picks up the squashed butt.

A Prince Red.

It begins to snow as she crosses the bridge to the lower yard. The wind has increased, and by the time she reaches the main road it is snowing so hard that her windscreen wipers have to work at full speed.

Her mind is racing, and her body begins to remember all the physical exertions of the day. At the turning for Gärdsnäset, she pulls over. The snow on the carriageway is getting thicker and thicker with the help of the wind. The motorway will be even worse, and she could well get stuck or end up in a jam because of an accident between here and the hotel. She makes a decision and heads for Gärdsnäset instead.

George is pleased to see her – but then the cat is probably glad of any company. Laura switches on as many lamps as she can, then goes into Hedda's studio and fetches the box of postcards from Jack. She takes them into her room and closes the door on the chaos in the rest of the house before settling down on her bed to read through them again.

She's never really thought about how Jack could afford to leave the country. Presumably she just assumed that Hedda had helped him somehow. But maybe the truth is completely different.

They're after me. I have to get away from here!

For all these years she's believed that Jack was so frightened that night at the hospital because Ulf Jensen and his sons blamed him for Iben's death. Not because he was a thief.

And why didn't Jack just settle for the money? Why did he steal Sofia's jewellery?

Then there's the unpleasant memory of Fredrik Jensen's threat. Was that his own idea, a more robust version of his brother's attempt at psychological warfare and Ulf Jensen's perfectly judged tears?

Had they put the same pressure on Hedda, and if so, what had the Jensens been prepared to do if they got wind of the fact that Hedda had decided to sell to someone other than the council? A decision that meant they would lose Källegården . . .

Is Fredrik the person who's been watching her, standing out there among the trees and smoking, trying to work out what her own plans for Gärdsnäset might be? On the other hand, Prince Red is a very popular brand of cigarettes. It could have been someone else. She doesn't want to let go of that thought.

It could have been someone else.

*

She dreams about Källegården. It is night, all the lights are out, and the only illumination comes from the big Christmas tree in the yard. The snow lies thick and heavy on the farmhouse roof. She moves slowly towards the front door, floating above the ground rather than walking. Above the door, the three flames in the Jensen family crest are flickering. Then she is inside, drifting through the silent rooms.

Iben's photograph hangs above the open fireplace, but present and past merge, and without knowing why Laura senses that she is not the only intruder. She turns, glimpses a shadow in the hallway. Someone has broken in with the intention of stealing a treasure.

She opens her mouth to call out, but no sound emerges. Instead, she finds herself transported to the upper floor. She is sitting at the dressing table in Iben's room. The top drawer is open and empty.

She hears a movement behind her, turns around.

Jack is standing in the doorway. He is holding a fabric bag that looks heavy.

'Why do you think she left it behind?' he says. 'If Sofia really did leave her family, why did she leave her jewellery? Wouldn't you have taken your jewellery with you if you were running away?'

She stares at him, still incapable of saying a word. She thinks she hears the sound of car doors slamming in the yard, then the faint sound of sirens.

She manages to speak. 'You have to get away! They're coming!'

The next moment she is far out on the frozen lake, only metres away from the black eye. Hedda is standing beside her. She is both the Hedda Laura remembers, and the old woman in the pine coffin. Her eyes shine, reflecting the glow of the lamp on Miller's boathouse.

'There's a spring down there,' she says. 'Water seeps out from underground and keeps the eye open.'

She takes Laura's hand. Two of her fingers are no more than pink stumps.

'No one escapes the winter fire. Not even you and me, my princess.'

Laura hears the sirens again, closer this time. Blue flames flare up from the ice around them, forming a wall of heat and cold.

Her clothes catch fire, her hair, her skin. She screams as the ice gives way beneath her and she plunges down into the black water.

And one for the nymph who lives down below.

Laura sits up in bed and draws a shuddering breath. Her pyjamas and sheets are soaked with sweat, the scar on her back is throbbing. She'd expected the nightmare. Her medication is in her hotel room, and over the past few days she has been careless with the dosage.

However, it isn't the dream that has woken her. She heard a noise, she's sure of it. A familiar, creaking sound, like an old wooden staircase. She jumps out of bed, runs through the house, flings the front door wide open.

The snow is still coming down heavily, she can hardly see the boathouse, and yet she's certain he's there. She takes a couple of steps out onto the porch, thinks she sees something, a shadowy figure moving among the trees. Or is she still dreaming?

'Jack!' she calls out into the falling snow. 'Jack, wait!'

A gust of wind blows snow into her face and she raises her hand to protect her eyes.

When she lowers it, the figure has gone.

'We'll go down to the bathing area beyond the cottage. Leave the mopeds there and walk across the ice. That means we'll be able to get in at the back without anyone seeing us from the road. Milla's with me, Laura with Peter.'

Once again Tomas was showing a side of himself that Laura had never seen before. From time to time he would glance at Milla, needing a little nod of encouragement.

The summer cottage he'd picked out was kind of remote, surrounded by trees and facing away from the lake. To be honest, summer cottage was a misnomer. The house was well equipped for winter, with an open fire and a chimney. The snow was regularly cleared from the drive, presumably by one of the Jensen family.

Laura tried not to think about Iben, but it was hard. They hadn't spoken to each other since the argument at Wohlin's. Jack was keeping out of Laura's way too. He was either out in his car, or shut away in the boathouse. He didn't even come down to join them for dinner as he always used to.

Hedda did her best to make excuses for him, but it was obvious that she too found the situation difficult. The atmosphere at the dinner table was strained.

Iben hadn't only taken Jack from her and splintered her family; she'd also managed to poison the place Laura loved the most.

They parked the mopeds where Tomas had suggested. Laura took off her helmet and hung it on the handlebars. The sensible part of her wanted to ask Peter if they were really going to go through with this. If the two of them shouldn't try to call the whole thing off before it was too late, but something made her hold back. A tingling feeling that grew stronger and stronger. It was both appealing and unpleasant. She knew Peter was experiencing the same thing; she'd felt it when she was sitting behind him with her arms wrapped around his waist, and now she could see it in his eyes.

'Shall we go?' he said, pointing to the others, who were leading the way. 'The Goonies on an adventure.'

Dusk was falling. The ice was covered in a thick layer of snow, which the wind was moving around into small drifts. In some places it had exposed patches of black ice.

'Do you think she can see us?' Laura whispered.

'Who?'

'The nymph, of course.'

They both burst into nervous giggles, which made Tomas turn around.

'Shut up!' he hissed crossly. 'No talking!'

They kept walking as darkness drew in. The wind whipped up little flurries of sharp snow into their faces, and quickly obliterated their footprints. Laura was glad they didn't have to go any further out onto the lake. It would be very easy to lose your bearings if you didn't have the shoreline to follow, and the black eye was out there waiting. Ice-cold, deep water that never froze.

Milla waited for Laura, took her arm and slowed her down. Peter raised an eyebrow, but Milla waved him on.

'You know he's in love with you, don't you?' she said.

'Who?' Laura tried to play dumb.

'Peter, of course. Unfortunately for him you're not interested, as I've already explained to him.'

'Why?'

Milla shrugged. 'It's true, isn't it? Or are you ready to give up on Jack?'

Laura set off again without answering.

'I thought not,' Milla said with a laugh. 'But don't worry – Jack won't be able to take his eyes off you at the Lucia party.'

After about five minutes they reached the jetty belonging to the house – three pairs of concrete posts supporting the walkway, about a metre above the ice.

Tomas continued to take the lead.

'OK, as I said I don't know where they hide the spare key – or if there is one. It's not in the shed where they keep the lawn-mower, anyway.' He pointed to a low wooden building in one corner of the garden. 'I've brought this just in case,' he went on, producing a hammer from his jacket pocket.

'We'll let Laura take a look around first,' Milla said. 'She's good at working people out.'

Laura swallowed. Her plan had been to do a circuit of the house, then say she hadn't found anything. Get them all to head back to Gärdsnäset without having done anything illegal.

However, Tomas's hammer changed the situation.

Using a key to enter the house without permission was one thing, a bit like when she'd cleaned the cabins last summer and had taken the opportunity to poke around among the visitors' possessions. Breaking a window was another matter, a proper break-in that was bound to be discovered and reported to the police.

Milla patted her on the back.

'It's all down to you now.'

Laura swallowed again. Out of the corner of her eye she saw Peter shifting uneasily from one foot to the other.

There was a carport at the front, and a small wooden structure with a roof, just big enough for the bins.

'I've already checked in there,' Tomas said. 'I felt behind all the beams and pillars you can reach from the ground. I did the same with the house.'

It was clear that he had no faith in Laura's ability. She had only minutes before he lost patience and insisted on using the hammer. Maybe he was right, maybe there was no hidden key – but she wasn't prepared to give up before she'd even started.

So, not the carport or the shed. Where did that leave? The jetty? No, nobody would be stupid enough to hide a key near the water, One slip and it would be gone.

She walked around the house, peered in through the windows. The walls looked as if they'd been painted recently, possibly in the summer, and the kitchen couldn't be very old. These people looked after their property.

'Are there tools in the shed?'

'Yes.'

'Old or new?'

'Mainly old.'

'Anything electrical? A drill? A chainsaw?'

'No, only hammers and nails and a few garden tools. Why do you ask?'

Laura nodded to herself. So the owners weren't into DIY, yet the inside of the house looked freshly renovated. Therefore, they regularly employed skilled tradesmen, which meant there should be a key somewhere. In a hiding place that was relatively easy to explain to a tradesman over the phone. The conclusion gave her a fresh burst of energy.

'How's it going?' Milla asked. She too was beginning to sound impatient.

'Give me a minute.'

Laura positioned herself by the front door. On the right was a WELCOME sign with a white goose and the flag of Skåne. Just above the sign was a little half-moon-shaped mark in the façade, where something had scraped against the wood not once but many, many times. She reached out and felt the wood, then the sign. Noticed that there was a screw missing. Her excitement was rising.

The sign was only attached at one side. It could be pushed up, covering the mark on the wood and revealing a metal pipe inserted in the wall.

She pushed her fingers inside and drew out a key.

36

Everyone's afraid at some point, Princess. Anyone who says differently is lying. Everyone has something they fear.

Laura is woken by loud knocking. It takes a few seconds before she remembers where she is, and what happened during the night.

Did she really see someone out there in the forest, or was it all a part of her dream?

The knocking comes again. She pulls on her jacket, pushes her feet into her shoes.

Peter is standing on the top step. Behind him she sees a liveried police car and two uniformed officers.

'What time is it? Have I missed the meeting?'

Peter shakes his head. 'Can I come in?'

She moves back. 'Of course, but the place is still a tip.'

She glances at Hedda's planning board; to her relief she's turned it around so that only the painting can be seen.

Peter waves to his colleagues and follows her inside.

'Do you have any coffee?'

'I'm sure there's some in there.' She points to the kitchen. Her head still feels heavy, her mind slow.

She sits down on a stool she scrubbed yesterday, hears Peter rummaging around in the other room. Through the window she sees one of the officers walking around the boathouse.

After a while Peter reappears with two cups of instant coffee and hands one to her.

'I don't drink coffee,' she says, but he stands there holding out the cup, so she takes it and forces down a couple of sips. The coffee is lukewarm and tastes bitter.

'We've just come from Källegården,' Peter says. 'There was a fire out there last night.'

Laura gives a start. 'Was anyone hurt?'

'Fortunately not.'

Peter falls silent as if he's expecting her to say something, but her brain is preoccupied.

'Where was the fire?' she asks eventually. At least it's a sensible question.

'In an accommodation block behind the stables. Polish immigrant workers live there in the summer, but in the winter it's empty. Thank goodness.'

He gazes at her pensively, then takes his notebook out of his pocket.

'What time did you leave Källegården?'

'About ten thirty. When did the fire start?'

'Fredrik discovered it just after midnight and woke his father. They called the emergency services, then Christian, before tackling the blaze as best they could. Did you see anyone as you drove away?'

Laura shakes her head.

'No, it was snowing heavily. It was hard even to see the road.'

Peter makes a note. 'Why did you come here instead of going back to your hotel?'

'As I said, it was snowing heavily. I was tired, and I didn't want to risk getting stuck in a drift or in a jam on the motorway.'

He makes another note. His expression is tense, almost grim.

Maybe it's down to the coffee, but her brain finally wakes up.

'Am I suspected of something?'

'We're talking to everyone who was in the area.'

'That doesn't answer my question.'

Peter meets her gaze.

'This is the second fire in two days. You were there on both occasions.'

'I left Källegården an hour and a half before the fire broke out. Ask Fredrik – he saw me drive away.'

'I've already spoken to him. He claimed you were angry.'

'What?'

'He said you talked about fires, brought up Tomas and Jack.'

'He was the one who brought up Jack! And if anyone was angry it was Fredrik – he more or less threatened me. Told me I ought to sell Gärdsnäset to the council, that the whole place was a fire hazard.'

Peter makes yet another note.

'You don't believe me,' Laura says.

He doesn't answer, he just keeps writing, which infuriates her. She's about to challenge him when there's a knock on the door and one of the uniformed officers appears.

'We've found something,' he informs Peter.

They head for the boathouse. Nobody has told Laura to stay away, so she follows them. The door of Jack's apartment is open, surprisingly. Didn't she lock it when she was up here the other day?

The familiar creaking of the wooden steps takes her mind back to the events of last night.

The three men are standing in one corner of the room. On the floor is a red petrol can and a well-filled plastic bag that definitely wasn't here on her previous visit.

'Insulating material and petrol,' she hears one of the officers say to Peter. 'All you need to start a fire.'

'Those aren't mine!' she blurts out. 'I heard someone on the steps last night. I saw someone running away.'

Peter exchanges a glance with his colleagues, then turns to face her.

'I'm afraid you'll have to accompany us to the station, Laura.'

They drive to the station in Ängelholm, not the little one in Vedarp. Peter mumbles something about bigger cases being handled from here, but Laura is lost in her own thoughts.

Someone is clearly trying to frame her for the fires at Kent Rask's place and at Källegården. But who, and why? How is everything connected – the fires, Hedda's death, the sale of Gärdsnäset?

Those questions will have to wait, because right now she has a more practical problem to resolve. She is going to be questioned – quite possibly regarded as a suspect – and she ought to contact the legal practice that the company uses. However, if she does that there's a significant risk that her mother will find out what's going on, followed by Marcus, Andreas and finally Steph. The last thing she wants is for any of them to turn up, so she decides to call Håkansson instead.

The interview room measures only ten metres square and has neither windows nor anything on the walls. In the middle of the floor is a pale wooden table with a tape recorder and four chairs. In two of the corners, just below the ceiling, are small cameras that are impossible to ignore.

Håkansson is there in fifteen minutes. He looks worried, says it's years since he dealt with criminal law, he'd be happy to recommend someone else. Laura waves away his misgivings.

'What are you going to say to them?' he asks.

'What do you mean?'

'What's your version of events?'

'My version . . . You mean the truth?'

He doesn't answer.

'You don't seriously believe . . . ?' she begins.

Håkansson holds up his hand.

'Of course not. I'd just like to know what you're intending to say to the police.'

'That I have nothing to do with the fires, and that I haven't a clue where the petrol can and the bag of insulating material came from.'

'Good.' Håkansson nods, although his expression says something else entirely.

After another fifteen minutes or so Peter enters the room, accompanied by an older officer, a tall, powerfully built man aged about sixty-five, with a shaven head.

'This is the head of the crime team,' Peter says. He avoids looking her in the eye.

The man holds out his hand.

'Laura.' He gives a wry smile that makes his boxer's nose look even more crooked. 'Do you remember me? It's been a while.'

Laura can't bring herself to return his smile. Her brain has seized up, and she is fifteen years old again.

'Bengt Sandberg,' the newcomer introduces himself to Håkansson. 'You could say that Laura and I are old acquaintances.'

37
Winter 1987

The house smelled of paint and IKEA furniture. Laura locked the door from the inside then reached for the light switch, but Peter stopped her and handed her a torch.

'Only use it if you have to.'

Tomas shrugged off his empty backpack and he and Peter started opening the kitchen cupboards, working methodically from right to left. It was obvious that they'd done this many times before.

'Come with me!' Milla took Laura by the hand and led her further into the house.

The largest bedroom overlooked the driveway. Two single beds with a bedside cabinet in between.

Milla pulled out the drawers in the dressing table one by one. Laura went over to the beds. There were two books on the cabinet: *The Democratic Terrorist* by Jan Guillou, and JD Salinger's *The Catcher in the Rye*. The painting on the wall above was attractive, depicting what she assumed was the view from a ridge, with the bright autumn colours of the forest down below.

'Check this out!'

Milla was holding up a narrow object that she dug out of the bottom drawer. Laura could just make out black metal with a handle at one end.

'What is it?'

'A spring baton. A guy I used to know had one.'

She slashed it through the air and it made a whining noise. The movement made Laura feel ill at ease.

'This can easily smash someone's kneecaps. Maybe you'd like to borrow it? Teach Iben a lesson?'

Milla held out the baton. Laura didn't know what to say. Before she could come up with a response, Milla laughed. 'Just joking!'

She unzipped her jacket and tucked the weapon inside.

A bright light filled the room, quickly growing stronger. Laura looked out of the window to see a car heading up the drive.

'Someone's coming!' Milla shouted to the others.

Laura was frozen to the spot. She'd seen the car before; it was the same dark blue Saab that had been parked in the yard at Gärdsnäset. It stopped and the lights went out. The doors opened and two men in leather jackets climbed out, one shaven-headed and powerfully built, the other short and broad-shouldered.

'Cops,' Milla hissed, grabbing her arms. 'Let's go!'

Laura and Milla raced out of the back door heading for the ice, with Tomas and Peter some distance behind them. They'd just reached the end of the jetty when the exterior lights were switched on and the garden was bathed in light.

'In here!'

Milla dragged Laura into the darkness underneath the jetty. They pressed themselves as far back into the shadows as they could, waiting for Tomas and Peter to join them. The light extended a good way over the ice, but there was no sign of the boys. They must have found another hiding place.

Laura was having difficulty breathing. She could already imagine Hedda's disappointment, her father's anger. Her mother would say that Laura had brought shame on the family, she would never be allowed to go to Gärdsnäset again . . .

Milla peered up between the planks.

'Ssh, they're coming!' She huddled close to Laura in the darkest corner. Laura's mouth was as dry as dust, her bladder so full that she had to clamp her knees and thighs together to prevent an accident.

She heard voices approaching.

'They're bound to see our footprints!' she whispered, utterly panic-stricken. 'They'll know we've come this way and hidden under here!'

'It's too windy,' Milla hissed.

The voices came closer and closer. Snow began to drift down between the planks as the two men walked out onto the jetty.

'Nice place your cousin's got here,' said the one with the boxer's nose.

'Yes, these lakeside properties don't come onto the market very often. It certainly wasn't cheap, and Göran's spent a fortune doing it up.'

'What does he do?'

'Fuck knows – something involving stocks and shares.'

The footsteps paused directly above the girls. They could see the soles of the men's shoes through the gaps. Laura felt as if her bladder was about to burst.

The shorter officer cleared his throat. 'Shall we make a move, Bengt?'

As the men walked away Laura let go of Milla and fumbled with her jeans and knickers. Just as she squatted down the lights went out. The relief almost made her weep.

*

After about five minutes they crawled out from under the jetty. Everywhere was dark and silent.

'What's happened to the boys?'

The door of the shed opened slowly and Tomas emerged, followed by Peter, who closed the door carefully before joining them.

'Let's get out of here.'

Tomas kept going, straight down to the ice. His backpack looked well filled. Milla set off after him, but Laura waited for Peter. His body language had changed. As he drew closer, she became aware of something else. Peter smelled of petrol.

'What happened in there?' she said quietly when they reached the ice.

'Tomas decided to have some fun. Picked up a can of petrol and started splashing it around inside the shed. Said he was going to burn the whole place down if we got caught. I had to tear the lighter out of his hands. Fuck knows what would have happened if I hadn't.'

Laura looked at Tomas, leading the way with Milla. Saw them talking to each other, just as she and Peter were doing.

'Tomas isn't well,' Peter said. 'Milla's playing games with him. If nobody stops this, something terrible is going to happen.'

38

'At approximately what time did you see an unknown person in the forest last night?'

'About two o'clock,' Laura says for the third time.

Peter has already dealt with all the obvious questions, returned to them wrapped in new speculations. Now he's on the third round.

'Why did Kent Rask feel threatened by the Jensen family?'

'They were after Tomas.'

'Still? After all these years?'

'That's what Kent said.'

Peter is mixing things up, jumping from questions about the fires to the events in the holiday village instead of sticking to the timeline as he did during the first two rounds. It comes across as slightly unprofessional, but in fact it's a skilfully delivered interrogation technique that she herself sometimes uses when interviewing candidates. Lies are easier to remember in a certain context, and if she was lying she would have started to find it difficult to keep a handle on what she had and hadn't said.

But Laura hasn't lied. She's just omitted a couple of details. Hedda's board. Tomas's letters.

No one was meant to get hurt.

But things didn't turn out the way we *expected.*

'When were you last in the apartment above the boathouse?'

'On Friday.'

'What did you do there?'

'Poked around, relived old memories.'

Peter gives her a long look.

'Did you lock the door when you left?'

'I don't remember. Maybe not – there was nothing in there that was worth keeping under lock and key.'

'The petrol can and the bag of insulating material?'

'As I said before, they weren't there on Friday. I've never seen or touched them.'

She's irritated now, and can't be bothered to hide it. The situation is absurd to say the least. Thirty years ago they were in a similar room, at the hospital. She and Peter and the lawyer from Stockholm, facing Bengt Sandberg. The difference now is that she and Peter are on opposite sides of the table.

She tries in vain to avoid looking at the man sitting in the corner, watching them. Sandberg hasn't really changed, which isn't surprising. He was already an adult when they last met.

He ought to be nearing retirement age, but he doesn't have the air of a man who's simply serving his time until he reaches sixty-five. His eyes are sharp, his body toned. He is wearing a short-sleeved shirt in the middle of winter; a long white scar is visible on one forearm. On his left hand is a large signet ring, but no wedding ring. Laura thinks back to their first encounter in Hedda's yard, the flowers and magazines in the car that she pointed out to Milla in a stupid attempt to impress her. Sandberg's wife was in hospital then, so maybe he's a widower – or divorced. Married to the job, like her. She feels his eyes on her. Sandberg frightened the life out of her when she was fifteen, and reluctantly she has to admit that he's having much the same effect on her now, even though she's forty-five.

Peter has finished going through the questions for the third time. Judging by his body language, there won't be a fourth. Håkansson shuffles on his chair beside her.

Sandberg gets to his feet in a surprisingly smooth movement. He comes to the side of the table and leans forward, over Peter as much as over her. She can smell his aftershave.

'Has anything else happened, Laura?' he asks. 'Something you've come across in the last few days that you haven't told us?'

His eyes bore into hers.

She glances at Peter. Is he the one Tomas was referring to in his letter? Is it Peter who makes up 'we'? Thanks to Elsa, she knows they're in touch.

'Thirty years, Laura,' Sandberg continues. 'You were more talkative back then. So was Larsson here, come to think of it.'

He moves behind Peter and places his big hands on Peter's shoulders. Peter stares down at the table. Laura would like to do the same, but forces herself to meet Sandberg's gaze.

'Tomas Rask confessed as soon as he heard you'd named him. His best friends.'

Peter's lips have gone white.

'There hasn't been a single incidence of arson around Vintersjön in thirty years,' Sandberg goes on. 'But Laura Aulin turns up, and suddenly we have two in as many days. We can live with Kent Rask's barn, to be honest. An old curmudgeon like him has probably brought it on himself – several times over. But when someone attacks a pillar of the community like Ulf Jensen, that rings alarm bells. I've had both the chief of police and the governor of the county on the phone, which is why I'd like to be aware of the progress of the investigation. Plus, of course, it's given me the chance to catch up with a couple of old friends.'

He releases his grip on Peter's shoulders.

'So. Tomas Rask has made a career as an arsonist. Do we know if he's still detained at the taxpayers' expense?'

'He's been out for about a year,' Peter says.

'Last known address?'

'He's registered just outside Skövde, at a sheltered accommodation complex for people with . . . problems. But according to the staff, no one's seen him for a month or so.'

'Which means that theoretically it could be our old friend Tomas Rask who's sneaking around in the forest. Could it have been him you saw at Gärdsnäset?'

'Maybe . . .'

Laura tries to recall the figure she thought she saw among the trees, but instead Kent Rask pops into her mind. *Tomas isn't right in the head. God knows I've tried to knock some sense into him, in every possible way. Sometimes to the point where my fists hurt.*

Sandberg picks up on her thoughts.

'What was the relationship between father and son like?'

'Tomas hated his father,' Peter says quietly.

'In that case he definitely has a motive for trying to burn down the old man's barn,' Sandberg states. 'What about the Jensens? Does Tomas have any reason to hold a grudge against them?'

He pulls out a chair and sits down between Laura and Peter.

'If that is the case, then there's another question we have to ask ourselves: why now? Why is Rask running around starting fires in this area again after almost exactly thirty years? What's the trigger?'

Laura doesn't know if she's expected to answer. Sandberg is talking to her and Peter as if they're all on the same side. Presumably it's some kind of trick, a way of lulling one of them into a false sense of security. But which one?

Sandberg turns to her.

'You were in the vicinity of both fires, and if you're telling the truth, then it seems as if the perpetrator – or someone else – has made an attempt to frame you.'

He leans across the table.

'Maybe . . .' he says slowly, 'all this is about you, somehow?'

Laura agrees to provide fingerprints and a DNA sample for comparison with the petrol can and the bag of insulating material. Håkansson tells her that she is under no obligation to do so, but she has nothing to hide. She's also convinced that a refusal would make her look even more suspicious in Sandberg's eyes.

She'd hoped that Peter would drive her back to Gärdsnäset, giving her the opportunity to ask him about Tomas, perhaps hint that she knows they've been in touch. However, as soon as the interview is over he disappears into the depths of the police station, and she has to ask Håkansson for a lift.

Back at Hedda's house she opens the front door and pauses for a moment. The smell is less overpowering now – or maybe she's just getting used to it. She turns and looks over at the boathouse, then the forest where she thought she saw someone last night. Sandberg might be unpleasant, but he made an important point: the fires do seem to be connected to her.

Or is there another explanation? Could they be linked to Gärdsnäset, to Hedda?

She goes inside, takes off her coat, says hello to George and feeds her. Turns over the painting to reveal Hedda's improvised noticeboard.

She still has no idea of what Hedda was actually doing, why she'd put up the newspaper cuttings about the fire, why she'd frozen the sale, why the black feather was there, what she'd meant about Tomas and Iben's secret.

But she can't shake off the feeling that the answers lie somewhere in this house.

She thinks back to the words Kent Rask whispered in her ear: *Hedda never threw anything away, so those letters must be at Gärdsnäset somewhere . . .*

Laura goes into Hedda's studio and takes down the remaining shoeboxes. They all contain photographs – no more letters or postcards from either Tomas or Jack.

She returns to the living room and the noticeboard.

Kent Rask said that Tomas and Hedda wrote to each other, but so far she's found only the letter written in 1994, in which Tomas seemed to indicate that he hadn't acted alone.

Didn't he write back to Hedda the rest of the time, or are there more letters in a different place? That's possible, of course.

The note about Tomas and Iben is right at the bottom, which means that it was the last thing Hedda added, probably in early November. If she'd written to Tomas and asked him about the secret at the same time, then his reply wouldn't be in an old shoebox. But if she had heard from him, then why wasn't the task crossed off the list and the letter pinned up on the noticeboard?

She is struck by a thought.

It was the postman who found Hedda in the water. He'd driven out here to deliver her mail, got worried when the door was unlocked and the house was empty. But what had he done with the mail?

Laura goes to the front door. There's more room now, since she and Elsa have cleared away the worst of the mess. Beneath the hallstand there is a half-full rubbish bag. She tips out the contents. Newspapers from five years ago, junk mail, campaign material from the 2014 election. Among it all there is a white envelope, the address written in a rounded, almost childish hand. It's Tomas's writing.

She slits open the envelope, her pulse racing.

Dear Hedda,

Thank you for your letters. I haven't written back for a long time. I'm very sorry.

You asked me about Iben's secret. I swore I'd never reveal it, but what does that matter now? And I know that you'd never tell anyone.

Iben hated her father.

Hated Ulf Jensen more than anyone or anything.

But most of all she was afraid of him.

39

Winter 1987

The phone rang out so slowly that Laura felt as if she could hear her own heartbeat echoing down the line.

'Källegården, Christian speaking.'

'Hi, it's Laura – is Iben there?'

She was aware of the nervousness in her voice. Christian either didn't notice, or didn't care.

'Ibeeen! Phone!'

A thud as the receiver hit the table. Then footsteps walking away, followed by others approaching.

Laura pressed Hedda's office phone closer to her ear. Milla gave her an encouraging nod.

'Hello?'

'Hi, it's Laura.'

'Hi!'

Iben sounded wary, but pleased. At least Laura thought so. Oddly enough, it made her feel a little tearful.

'I . . . I've missed you.'

There was a brief silence.

'Have you?' Iben said in a small voice.

Laura swallowed, tried to force out the sentence she'd practised, but to no avail. Milla elbowed her in the side.

'I'm sorry we fell out.'

'Me too.'

A soft warmth spread through Laura's chest, a warmth that made her want to forget the whole thing. The party, Tomas and Peter, Milla's plan. She just wanted life to go back to the way it used to be.

'Jack's sorry too. We really didn't mean to hurt you, Laura.'

The warmth was gone just as quickly as it had come.

We really didn't mean to hurt you.

We REALLY didn't mean . . .

She realised that Milla was watching her. Made a huge effort to pull herself together.

'We were thinking of having a Lucia party,' she said, involuntarily grimacing as she spoke. 'Tomas, Peter, Milla and me. It would be great if you could come. Both of you . . .'

She had to pause, take a deep breath before she could finish.

'You can tell your dad that you and I are going to the cinema if you want.'

'Sounds fantastic. Where are you having the party?'

'At the dance hall.'

40

Laura is still clutching Tomas's letter in her hand. The words reverberated inside her head, over and over again. *Iben hated her father. Hated her father. Hated her father. More than anyone or anything.*

The dusty air in the living room runs out, and she gropes her way to the front door. Just as she is about to open it, she registers the crows' warning cries; the birds are going crazy. She holds back, peers outside. A huge, shiny SUV with a company logo is slowly driving through the holiday village.

She returns to the living room, pins the letter to the notice-board, then turns the board over.

The black feather falls off and drifts across the room. She props the board against the wall, checks that it looks like a painting and nothing more, then scoops up the feather on her way back to the door.

The driver is a man in a thick winter overcoat with an army cap pulled right down to his eyebrows. Laura opens the door before he has time to set foot on the bottom step. He looks surprised, but quickly recovers his equilibrium.

'Laura?' he says, smiling as if they know each other.

'Yes . . . ?'

She tries to place him. He's about fifty and looks as if he's in good shape. The eyes behind the glasses are brown, and a greying, well-trimmed beard covers his cheeks. Adventure-magazine-handsome, as Steph would say.

'Heinz Norell. I'm the project leader for Vintersjöholm Development – we own the castle.'

Laura nods. She recognises the name from the offer on Hedda's board.

The crows are still making a hell of a noise, flapping their wings, occasionally hurling themselves off the branches on short, anxious flights between the trees.

'May I come in? I can hardly hear myself think out here.'

Laura hesitates, and Norell seems to understand why.

'Don't worry about the mess. Your aunt invited me in for coffee a couple of times.'

Laura reluctantly steps aside.

'I see you're busy sorting the place out. And you've made a discovery.'

It takes a moment for Laura to realise that he means the black feather, which is still in her hand.

'This was mine when I was little,' she says.

'Childhood memories. So you grew up here?'

She can hear a slight accent now.

'I came here every Christmas and every summer until I was fifteen.'

The crows are gradually calming down.

'Gärdsnäset is very beautiful,' Norell says. 'The fact is' – he gives a little laugh – 'I probably shouldn't say this, given that we've made an offer for the land, but I've worked on construction projects on virtually every continent, and Gärdsnäset and Vintersjön is one of the loveliest places I've ever been. I hope that won't make you push up the price.'

He smiles again, and Laura can't help doing the same. There's something about Heinz Norell that makes him instantly likeable.

'Anyway, I'm sorry to disturb you,' he goes on. 'I just wanted to call in to introduce myself and offer my condolences. I liked your aunt.'

Laura waits for him to say that Hedda was special, but he doesn't.

He laughs and shakes his head.

'The first time I came out here she threatened me with a golf club, but then she realised I was German. She'd spent a few years living in Berlin when she was young, so we had a certain amount in common.'

Laura thinks about the photographs in the box. 'Your Swedish is excellent.'

'Thank you. My mother was Swedish.'

She waits for him to expand on this, but instead he takes a brochure out of his pocket.

'I wanted to show you our plans for Gärdsnäset. Hedda really liked them, and of course I hope you will too. Take a look and call me if you have any questions. My phone number's on the back.'

He turns and opens the door. The crows strike up their warning cries as soon as he sets foot outside.

'Those birds clearly don't like Germans,' he says. 'Nice to meet you, Laura. I hope to see you again soon.'

He gets into the car and waves to her before driving off. The crows settle down, glaring at her with their peppercorn eyes as they exchange sceptical little noises.

She stands in the doorway for a moment with the brochure in one hand and the black feather in the other. Stares at them, then puts them down. She needs some fresh air. She puts on her jacket and boots and sets off at a brisk pace along the shore of the lake towards the village.

After a couple of hundred metres she switches on her phone; there is a faint signal.

Her inbox is full of missed calls – Steph, Andreas, even her mother. Several voice and text messages, all basically saying the same thing: *Call us!*

But she has enough to do, and what would she say? That she's dug so deep into her past that she's found something horrible? Something that might even be worth murdering for?

She makes do with a text message to Steph.

Everything fine, home soon.

Peter answers after the fifth ring.

'Hi, Laura – has something happened?'

Laura takes a deep breath. She might as well take the bull by the horns.

'What do you know about Iben and her father?'

'Sorry?'

'Did you know that Ulf treated Iben badly? That she hated him?'

'Where did you hear that?'

A counter-question instead of an answer. Laura has experienced this many times in her work; it's a classic trick to avoid talking about something unpleasant.

'So you do know something.'

Silence. She thinks she hears his office chair squeak, then he sighs.

'There's an old note. I came across it when I was reading through the investigation.'

'Go on.'

'An anonymous caller claimed that Iben was having a bad time at Källegården.'

'In what way?'

'There are no further details.'

'So what did the police do?'

'Nothing. The call came in on 11 December 1987. Two days—'

'Before Iben died.'

'Yes.' Peter sighs again. 'As I'm sure you'll understand, the anonymous call wasn't followed up. Ulf had just lost his daughter, so why add to his torture? Besides, there were plenty of people who had a grudge against Ulf, or were envious of his family's successes. Tall poppy syndrome, or *Jantelagen* as we say in Sweden. So the note was hidden right at the back of the file.'

Laura's brain is working overtime.

'Any information about the caller? Was it a man or a woman?'

'That's not clear. If I remember correctly, the person who took the call said the voice was difficult to hear, possibly because the mouthpiece had been covered.'

'Can I have a copy of the note?'

'Of course, but tell me what's going on.'

Laura hesitates. She still doesn't know if Peter is somehow involved in whatever is happening, but at the same time she needs his help.

'Hedda and Tomas used to write to each other. He told her that Iben hated Ulf more than anything or anyone, but also that she was afraid of him. Why was that, do you think?'

Silence once more.

'Tomas isn't very well,' Peter says quietly.

'So I keep hearing, but do you think he could have misunderstood something like that? He and Iben had been friends since they were little.'

She sees the two six-year-olds in the back seat of Kent Rask's car, clinging to each other as the fire rages at Källegården and Sofia Jensen dances around the yard.

'Maybe not . . .'

Peter doesn't sound entirely convinced.

'We need to talk to Tomas,' Laura says firmly.

'Why?' Peter is wary now.

'Don't you want to know the truth? Ulf Jensen has been playing the martyr for thirty years. Everyone feels sorry for him. They've even renamed the school in his honour. What if it's all built on a lie? And besides . . .'

She pauses, takes another deep breath.

'If Tomas is right, then Ulf could be guilty of a serious crime. Isn't it your job to put away people like that?'

This time the silence goes on for so long that she thinks he's hung up, but eventually he speaks.

'I'll see what I can do.'

The call ends and Laura stops dead. She's reached the glade near the spot where Elsa came off her bike the other day. Right in the middle, where the dance hall once stood, the little iron cross is sticking up out of the snow. Beside it there is an object that must have been put there very recently. As she moves closer, she sees what it is. A burned-out grave lantern.

41

Winter 1987

Laura was sitting on one of Milla's kitchen chairs. The table in front of them was littered with makeup and hair products. Milla had made her put on something that resembled a bathing cap, and was busy teasing strands of hairs through holes in the rubber with a crochet hook.

'Hedda was here this morning,' she said.

'Oh yes?'

Milla studied her closely. Their faces were only inches apart.

'She said I have to move.'

'What? Where to?'

'She's sorted out a place for me in Värmland.'

Milla was still watching Laura's expression as her fingers worked with the hook.

'But why?'

'She didn't say. She was pretty short with me. Said I had two days to pack – a car will come and pick me up the day after tomorrow, for fuck's sake!'

The hook dug into Laura's scalp and she winced in pain.

'Someone must have ratted on me,' Milla went on. 'That's the only possible explanation.'

She pushed the hook through the next hole, even harder this time. Laura bit her lip.

'I'm sure you know who it was,' Milla said.

Laura tried to shake her head, but Milla seized her face between both hands and leaned forward so that the tips of their noses were almost touching.

'No,' Laura managed to say. 'Hedda hasn't said anything to me, I swear.'

'Who's she seen? Who's she spoken to?'

'I don't know – let go of me!'

Milla turned away and started fiddling with a bottle, then she smeared something cold and chemical-smelling over the cap.

'Who do you think she'd listen to?'

Her voice was gentler now, but the anger was still there beneath the surface.

'I don't know,' Laura said again.

Milla's eyes narrowed.

'Maybe Iben told her about the break-ins.' She didn't wait for a response. 'If so, how did she find out about them?'

Laura swallowed. The chemicals brought tears to her eyes.

'Tomas?' she suggested. She had no idea why.

'Tomas would never talk.'

'No . . .' Laura tried to stay calm. 'But he's changed a lot. He and Iben have known each other since they were little. If she noticed something and asked him straight out, he wouldn't be able to lie. He always owns up, even to things he hasn't done.'

Milla nodded slowly, her expression softening.

'Well done, my little master detective. No wonder I like you.'

She spread more of the chemicals over the cap; this time the movement felt more like a caress.

'As soon as Jack sees you tonight, he's going to forget all about Iben. And then I'm going to make sure that pious little bitch gets exactly what she deserves.'

42

L aura has run out of food, and has to drive over to Vedarp to do some shopping. On the way she tries to recall Ulf Jensen and Iben together, searching for details, hints, things she'd missed that will back up what Tomas wrote in his letter. Admittedly she was only a child at first and then a young woman, but she was already pretty good at reading people. At least that's what she'd thought, until she found Tomas's letter.

She remembers that Ulf was always hard on Iben during training sessions, and insisted that she needed to achieve top grades in her academic subjects. He wanted to know exactly where she was going, and almost always came to pick her up in the evenings, even from Gärdsnäset, which was only a short cycle ride from home. What did that prove? Nothing, except that Ulf was committed to his daughter and took good care of her. Laura had actually felt a little envious. Of course, Ulf could have been a completely different person behind the closed doors of Källegården. Was that why Iben never wanted to meet up at home?

She had always seemed a little subdued when she was with her father. So had her half-brothers, come to think of it. But didn't that apply to most children who had a parent like Ulf Jensen?

And how did Ulf's grief fit into the picture? Was he a despairing father mourning a beloved daughter, or was there something more behind it? She thought about what Kent Rask had said – that Iben's death had given Ulf the chance to put her on a pedestal, that she would remain young and pure forever.

The thought is so unpleasant that a shiver runs down Laura's spine, in spite of the warmth inside the car.

There is another explanation, of course. Tomas could simply have been suffering from delusion. After all, the poor guy had spent most of his life in various institutions. Or – if you preferred a conspiracy theory – the whole thing was a deliberate lie, a kind of counter-attack on the Jensen family who, according to Tomas's father, were still after him.

However, that doesn't explain the anonymous caller who contacted the police two days *before* Iben's death.

So what was the truth? Maybe that was what Hedda had been trying to establish.

Laura parks behind the supermarket, pulls her hat well down over her forehead and goes in. She nods and smiles politely as she passes a couple in their sixties who, judging by their red shirts, seem to be running the place. She feels their eyes on her for some time, and she hears them whispering behind her back.

When she's halfway round she realises she should have used a trolley instead of a basket, but she manages to make it to the checkout.

Two of the tills are open, and she joins the shortest queue. When it's Laura's turn, the woman she encountered on the way in places a sign on the conveyor belt: CHECKOUT CLOSED.

Laura looks around. There's no one behind her, but in the other queue there are two pensioners, trolleys piled high.

'Can't you just put me through?' she asks.

'No, sorry. You'll have to go over to the other side.'

The woman demonstratively slams the till shut, then turns her back on Laura with a sniff.

Laura is so taken aback that she can't think of anything to say. Instead, she obediently moves across to the other queue. When it's her turn, the man on the till glares at her.

'Is that it?' he snaps when he's scanned her goods.

'Yes.'

Laura enters her pin number, and the man presses a key. The card reader beeps angrily.

TRANSACTION FAILED, the display states.

'Try again!'

She repeats the procedure, with the same result.

'You'll have to try again.'

This time she presses the buttons more slowly, watching the man's movements. He hits the key before she's even entered the fourth digit. The angry beep is repeated.

'You don't have another card?' His tone is overtly unpleasant.

'No, but you could try leaving the keys alone until I'm done,' Laura replies as calmly as possible.

He gives her a filthy look. 'Try again.'

This time it works.

She packs her purchases into a paper bag. A short distance away the woman is chatting to a couple of other customers. Laura can't hear what they're saying, but once again she feels their eyes on the back of her neck as she leaves the store.

When she reaches her car, she understands what's going on.

Sell up and fuck off! someone has scratched into the driver's door.

She puts down the bag and leans closer. The scratches are so deep that in some places she can see the exposed metal. A key, probably. Someone who wanted to cause trouble and frighten her. Unfortunately, they've succeeded on both counts.

She straightens up and looks around. There are only a few lights in the car park, and several vehicles nearby that would have hidden the perpetrator from view. She catches a movement in her peripheral vision and turns to see a small figure in a thick padded jacket coming towards her.

'Hi!'

It's Elsa, with her hands pushed deep in her pockets. She's wearing a cap with earflaps that covers half her face.

'Hi,' Laura says, staring at her damaged car once more. Elsa joins her.

'Fuck! Did you see who did it?'

'No – I was in the shop, but I could tell there was something going on.'

Elsa nods.

'It's the fires. Everyone's heard that you were taken in for questioning. There are all kinds of rumours flying around. Frightened people do stupid things.'

Laura looks at her.

'How do you know that?'

'I heard my dad say it on the phone.'

'Who was he talking to?'

'No idea.'

They stand in silence for a few seconds.

'He likes you.'

'Who?' It's a ridiculous question, but the word is out of her mouth before Laura can stop it.

'My dad, of course.'

'What makes you say that?'

'His face kind of lights up when he talks about you.'

'Does it?'

So Peter talks about her.

'He was in love with you when you were young, wasn't he?'

'You'll have to ask him that.'

Elsa shakes her head.

'No point. Like I said, he never talks about the old days. I've asked him about the fire and Iben Jensen loads of times, but he always changes the subject.'

'And Tomas Rask?'

'Same there, but I've checked his phone. It's not exactly difficult. He used to use Mum's birthday as the code, but now he's changed it to mine.'

Elsa pauses deliberately, well aware that Laura is keen to hear what she has to say.

Laura gives in. 'And?'

'Dad and Tomas have called each other at least ten times over the past few days. The last time was yesterday evening.'

Laura drives Elsa home. She and Peter live in a large, slightly ostentatious two-storey property with a view over the lake. Bright lights illuminate both house and garden. Combined with the tall wrought-iron fence, the place looks more like an ambassador's residence than a family home.

'Nice,' Laura says.

'It's Mum's really. Her father bought it for her when she and Dad got married. I think we ought to move, but Dad doesn't want to. This is my mum's style, not mine and Dad's, if you know what I mean.'

Laura nods.

'Do you want to come in?'

'Another time, thanks.'

*

During the drive back to Gärdsnäset, Laura goes over what she's just learned.

Peter didn't tell Sandberg that he was in touch with Tomas. But why so many calls, and why now?

The answer comes to her as she turns off the main road. Tomas is in the area, and Peter knows where.

She sees a glint of metal up ahead, and as she approaches her usual parking spot, she is surprised to discover another vehicle there. A white pickup truck with the words JENSEN & SONS CONSTRUCTION LTD on one side.

She stays in the car with the engine running, headlights fixed on the pickup. The driver gets out and raises his hand in a friendly wave. Christian Jensen. To her relief he appears to be alone. She lowers the side window.

'I was just about to leave when I saw your lights,' he says. 'Have you got time for a quick chat?'

He points to the house and Laura tries to remember if she turned Hedda's noticeboard around before she left. She can't let Christian see it.

'The place looks like a bomb site,' she says apologetically. 'We can talk here.'

Christian seems surprised, but he walks around the car and gets into the passenger seat.

'Terrible business with the fire,' Laura says, mainly because he's probably expecting her to comment.

'Yes ...' He clears his throat. 'Obviously we're not accusing you of anything, Laura. I want you to know that.'

'OK.'

The scratches on her car door suggest that someone else has a different view.

'But that's not why I'm here.' Christian shuffles in his seat. 'You remember what we talked about the other day? The debts, the risk that we could lose Källegården.'

She nods.

'There was one thing I didn't tell you.'

'Oh?'

'Dad has cancer. The prognosis isn't good.'

'I'm sorry to hear that.'

Christian nods slowly. 'That's another reason why we need the construction contract for Gärdsnäset. Dad's dreamed of building a new sports facility for thirty years. We want to give him that opportunity, as a final victory. We might even name it after Iben.'

He pauses, clears his throat again. Laura doesn't know what to say. Tomas's words are echoing in her head.

'Anyway,' Christian goes on. 'I heard you'd spoken to Kjell Green from the council. Their bid is four hundred thousand less than Vintersjöholm's.'

He is stating a fact, not asking a question.

'Hedda told us that back in the autumn,' he adds when he sees Laura's raised eyebrows. 'So Fredrik and I made her an offer. We've tucked away a certain amount of money over the years – Christmas trees, wood, various bits and pieces. We can't use it to pay off the loan – the bank would ask too many questions, plus it's nowhere near enough. But . . . two hundred thousand in cash is the equivalent of over three hundred thousand through what you might call official channels. That makes the two bids almost the same. Maybe that will help you to decide?'

He smiles, but he still looks uncomfortable.

'And that's the offer you made Hedda?'

He nods.

'What did she say?'

'Hedda was no stranger to forest business.'

'So what happened? Why didn't she sign on the dotted line?'

'I don't know. Everybody thought the matter was settled, but suddenly Hedda started putting it off. And then . . .'

'And then she died.'

Laura can't help thinking about Tomas's letter again. She has to try to broach the subject.

'Your father . . .' she begins. 'He and Iben were very close.'

'Very.'

Laura doesn't quite know how to continue.

'Too close?' she says eventually.

Christian frowns. 'What do you mean by that?'

'I heard a rumour. There was an anonymous call . . .'

She expects anger, but Christian just looks weary.

'That fucking phone call has haunted us for thirty years. We first heard about it a few days after the fire. The chief of police and my dad were good friends, so he promised to see that the information about the call never came out, but knowing it existed was enough, somehow. The thought that someone could make up something so terrible about our family.' He sighs. 'Dad could be very hard, and God knows he demanded a lot from us, but he did it with the best of intentions. He had the same attitude as a sports coach. That was why we won everything that was going. Do you know that Vedarp athletics club has had five competitors at national level because of him? Five – from a village with a population of four thousand. People came from all over north-western Skåne to train with Ulf Jensen.'

He pauses, shakes his head.

'There were those who didn't understand his methods, mainly parents whose kids couldn't take the pressure. A lot of crap has been talked about my father over the years, but who-ever made that anonymous call takes the biscuit.'

He turns to face her.

'The four of us were a close family, maybe closer than a lot of others because we didn't have a mother. The idea that my father would have done something to my sister is just ridiculous. And besides . . .' He looks her in the eye. 'You and Iben were best friends. Did she ever say anything to you? Did she ever even hint that things weren't OK at home?'

'No.'

'There you go. The person who made that call was an evil fucker with a sick mind, but because Iben died, his allegation remains unchallenged.'

Christian glances at his watch.

'Sorry – it's getting late and I promised to be home for din-ner. Think about our offer and give me a call. Here's my mobile number.'

He places a business card on the dashboard and gets out of the car, then changes his mind and sticks his head back in.

'One more thing.'

'What?'

'Don't mention that phone call to Fredrik. He goes crazy whenever it comes up, and as you might recall, he isn't quite as cool-headed as you and I are.'

Laura watches him drive away.

. . . *his allegation remains unchallenged.*

According to Peter, the officer who took the call hadn't been able to tell whether it was a man or a woman. It could have been a slip of the tongue on Christian's part, but the more Laura thinks about it, the more likely it seems that Christian knew who he was talking about – or at least had his suspicions. She thinks back to the conversation with Fredrik at Källegården, how he'd asked about Jack, told her the story of the break-in, the missing money and jewellery. What if there were more reasons for the Jensens to hate Jack?

That would also explain why Jack has stayed away for all these years, why he didn't even dare to show up at Hedda's funeral.

On a sudden impulse she takes her torch out of the glove compartment, gets out of the car and follows the path along the shoreline. Long before she reaches the iron cross, she sees a little dot of light among the trees. The flickering flame of a grave lantern.

43

Winter 1987

Laura looked at herself in Milla's bathroom mirror for at least the tenth time. The person staring out at her had backcombed hair with blonde streaks. Dark blusher highlighted her cheekbones, and eyeshadow, eyeliner and mascara brought out her eyes. Her lipstick was pink and glossy. No longer a little princess, but a young woman.

She glanced at her watch: exactly seven o'clock. The party was starting, but Milla had told her to wait in the cabin. She and Peter and Tomas would take care of all the preparations.

She went into Milla's bedroom. A packed suitcase stood by the wall, while another lay open on the bed. Milla had picked out some of her own clothes for Laura to wear. High-waisted stonewashed jeans, a wide belt and a Bardot top. Finally, wedges; she'd needed a little practice to be able to walk in them.

Laura had mixed feelings about Milla's departure from Gärdsnäset. They'd become allies, but at the same time Milla was obviously no good for Tomas. And then there was that vague, unpleasant feeling that you never quite knew where you were with her, that she could turn her back on you at any moment. It was as if she were playing a game in which Tomas, Peter and Laura were merely counters.

She heard footsteps, then the door opened and Milla came in, wearing her hoodie as usual. She might have had a bit more makeup on.

'OK,' she said. 'Showtime!'

The dance hall looked pretty good. The air inside was warm and smelled of fan heaters, cigarette smoke and food. Peter and Tomas had moved the tarpaulin-covered stacks of outdoor furniture and other summer equipment to one side, leaving a space roughly in the middle of the dance floor. A long table was laid with plastic cups and serviettes that they must have found in one of the boxes, and they'd hung up the coloured lights that had been used in the main cabin on the night she'd arrived.

On another table the boys had rigged up a couple of hotplates and set out the sausages and bread they'd stolen the other day, along with several bottles of wine and spirits that must also have been nicked from somewhere. The boom box, which looked new, was playing 'Soul Deep' by Roxette.

Jack, Peter, Iben and Tomas were sitting at the table, and Peter was busy pouring wine into glasses.

'There she is,' he said a little too loudly as Laura and Milla arrived.

Milla stopped just inside the door and let Laura go on alone. Everyone was staring at her, and for a moment she considered changing her mind and running back home to Hedda. Instead, she straightened her shoulders and calmly walked up to the table. One foot in front of the other, as Milla had taught her.

Jack's eyes grew bigger as she came closer – but not only his. Peter was staring too, as was Tomas, and even Iben. Wide-eyed, open-mouthed, almost exactly as she'd imagined it.

Laura pulled out a chair and sat down next to Jack.

'What do I have to do to get a drink around here?' she said to Peter.

The evening went better than she'd dared to hope. Jack seemed to have fallen completely under her spell, as had Peter.

Iben was clearly irritated, while Tomas said nothing, as usual. Milla wandered around looking pleased with herself – or full of anticipation for what was to come?

Peter topped up Laura's glass yet again, and she felt the dance hall begin to spin very slowly. Jack took out his cigarettes and tapped out a Prince Red. Laura raised an eyebrow; that was all it took for him to offer her one. She placed it between her lips in the cool way that Milla had shown her, then leaned in towards him, placed her hand on his and gazed into his eyes as he lit the cigarette.

Jack's cheeks flushed red. Laura's confidence grew, and the warmth of the wine spread through her body. This was the best night ever.

Someone tugged roughly at her arm.

'I want to talk to you,' Iben hissed. 'Put your jacket on!'

Laura followed her outside, walking slowly so that Iben would be forced to wait for her, but also to avoid falling over. The wedge heels and the wine weren't a good combination, and she promised herself that she wouldn't drink any more this evening.

They stopped beneath the light. The ice shone white, the moon was reflected in the black eye out in the lake.

'What the fuck are you doing?' Iben snapped.

'Sorry?'

'Me and Jack are together, and yet you're coming on to him.'

'What do you mean?'

Laura pretended to be surprised, but realised that the wine was making her overact.

'Oh, please!'

'You knew I was in love with Jack, but you still got together with him, without a word to me. Your best friend.'

'We . . . we thought all that was sorted. We thought you were OK with it.'

There was that word again. We. As if Iben and Jack belonged together and had been talking about her.

'I'm not fucking OK with anything,' Laura informed her. 'I've known Jack longer than you. There's always been something special between us, but you jumped in when I wasn't around.'

Iben snorted.

'You don't live here – you're just a tourist. Someone who turns up in the holidays and does fun stuff. Who gets pampered and mollycoddled like a spoiled princess. And now you're sulking because you can't have something – or someone – you want.'

'That's rich coming from you, Wonder Woman! With your sporting records and your top grades. Iben Jensen, who never fails at anything. You're just a bad loser. That's one thing your daddy hasn't taught you.'

Iben moved a step closer and clenched her fists. Her face was red, her eyes burning in a way Laura had never seen before. Laura recoiled involuntarily, tripped over her own feet in those ridiculous heels and landed on her bottom in a snowdrift. Before she could get up, Iben grabbed her by the hair.

'Ow!' Laura whimpered, trying to prise Iben's fingers away.

'Don't talk about my dad!' Iben yelled. 'You know nothing!'

Laura's eyes filled with tears. She struggled to free herself, but Iben was too strong.

'Let go of her!'

Milla had appeared out of nowhere, and was standing there with one hand behind her back.

Iben turned around.

'Let go!'

Milla produced the baton she'd stolen from the cottage.

'You think you're so fucking cool,' Iben muttered. 'But Tomas has told me what you're doing, making him and Peter run your errands. And now you've dragged Laura into it as well!'

She straightened up and took a step towards Milla.

'Go on, then. Hit me if you dare.'

The two girls were of equal height, but Laura was in no doubt about who was the stronger. Milla raised the baton, but Iben wasn't afraid. She laughed in Milla's face.

'At least Hedda's finally realised what you are – a psychopath.' The scorn in her voice was unmistakable. 'Have a lovely time in Värmland!'

Iben walked away and went back inside. Laura scrambled to her feet and brushed the snow off her bottom. Her cheeks were burning.

Milla slowly lowered the baton. Stared after Iben.

'We have to do something about her,' she said.

The telephone kiosk was behind the main cabin, a plastic bubble attached to the wall, surrounding a green metal box. Laura inserted a one-krona coin, hesitated briefly when she heard the dialling tone.

'Do it,' Milla whispered. 'Iben's in there with Jack. Fuck knows what she's saying about you.'

The dial felt ice-cold to Laura's index finger, and made a rattling noise every time she let go of it. The phone rang out, once, twice, three times, four times. She was about to hang up when she heard a click.

'Jensen.' It was Fredrik's voice.

'Iben isn't at the cinema.' Laura tried to cover the receiver with her hand, like they did in the movies. 'She's at the dance hall at Gärdsnäset with Jack Olsson. Orphan Boy!'

44

Why did you never get married, Aunt Hedda?
Because I'm too difficult. People like me live alone.

Laura heats the water for tea in the grubby microwave, then stands by the window gazing out across the lake. It's about half an hour before daybreak, and Johnny Miller's lamp is glowing as always. Johnny Miller, Peter's father-in-law.

She remembers how people thought he was crazy, spending so much money to live all alone on the northern side of the lake, behind his high walls.

Maybe that was why she and Iben made up the story of the troll? Fantasised about rowing across the water and stealing his treasure, buying Vintersjöholm Castle and living happily ever after. Two princesses, no princes.

Now she's the only one left. Alone with her questions. But one of them at least seems to have been answered. Everything points to the fact that it was Christian who lit the grave lantern in the forest. At first, she thought it was a lovely gesture from a big brother to his little sister, but then she remembers the trick with the photograph at Källegården. She is finding it difficult to shake off the feeling that the Jensens are still trying to manipulate her.

At exactly eight o'clock she calls Ola at the office from Hedda's landline. Stops him as soon as he starts reeling off a list of problems.

'Marcus will have to take care of that. You have spoken to him?'

'I have . . .'

Ola's tone of voice tells her everything she needs to know: Marcus isn't at all happy about being held accountable.

She tries not to smile, but it's impossible.

'I need your help,' she says. 'Can you check out the finances of a company called Jensen & Sons Construction from Vedarp in Skåne?'

'No problem – can I ask why?'

'It's to do with a piece of land I've inherited down here.'

'OK.'

She hears the rasp of his pen.

'Anything else?'

'Yes . . .' She hesitates, then makes up her mind. 'Can you also check out Vintersjöholm Development?'

'Absolutely.'

'Good. Don't call my mobile, the coverage isn't great. I'll contact you later.'

'OK.'

She hears the motocross bike as she puts down the phone. She feels both irritated and pleased. She wanted to carry on digging through Hedda's things, but at the same time there's nothing wrong with some company. And she likes Elsa.

She turns Hedda's noticeboard around, makes sure it looks like a perfectly innocent painting before she lets the young woman in.

'I thought you might like some breakfast!'

Elsa holds up a paper bag of fresh pastries.

After breakfast they focus on the task in hand, carrying out rubbish bags full of junk mail, cardboard, newspapers and magazines, and bills that are long out of date. Then they move on to empty bottles, plastic containers and broken furniture. Elsa eventually manages to free up the record player in one corner, and much to their surprise, it works. Elsa blows the dust off the record on the turntable and reads the label.

'It's one of Grandad's,' she says, sounding both startled and proud. She puts it on; the music is discordant rock, which isn't Laura's style at all. But she doesn't say anything to Elsa.

When Laura returns after what must be her twentieth trip to the skip, she finds Elsa sitting on the sofa. On the coffee table in front of her are the photographs from Hedda's shoeboxes.

'Is this you and Dad?' Laura and Peter must be eight or nine years old, screwing up their eyes at the sun and the photographer. 'It's obvious he was in love with you even then.'

Elsa puts down the picture, selects another.

'And this is Iben Jensen. There's a photo of her in school.' She moves on so quickly that Laura hardly sees it. 'But who's this? There are lots of pictures of him.'

Jack, standing on the roof of one of the cabins holding a hammer. He is bare-chested and tanned.

'That's Jack,' Laura says, keeping her tone as neutral as possible.

'He's fit. Were you together?'

Laura shakes her head.

'Was he with someone else?'

She avoids the question. Sits down beside Elsa, rummages through the photos. She finds several more of Jack, usually with a paintbrush or a hammer in his hand. Always smiling at the camera, with a glint in those blue eyes she once loved.

Elsa carries on looking for pictures of her dad, while Laura is absorbed in a pile of considerably older images.

Hedda as a young woman, from various places around the world. Hedda on the roof of a dusty jeep, with the savannah in the background. Riding a camel in a red desert. Holding a koala in her arms.

Sometimes other people are there, dressed for an adventure or a party. One of the faces catches Laura's attention: a blond, dark-eyed young man with a beard. She finds more pictures of him. In one he has his arm around Hedda, in another she is kissing him on the cheek. In spite of the fact that these pictures are at least forty-five years old, and the colours have faded, there is no mistaking their love. Why does he seem so familiar?

Laura imagines him as he might look today, with a grey beard. It's not difficult. She knows exactly who he is; she met him only the other day. She remembers something Hedda told her a long time ago, about someone she was in love with – a relationship that didn't end well.

A guy with a guitar.

She quickly gathers up the photos before Elsa catches sight of them and takes them into the studio.

From the window she can see the whole lake – and Miller's house, far away on the northern shore.

Johnny Miller, Elsa's maternal grandfather, the troll on the other side of the water. He's the guy with the guitar, the man Hedda once loved. The man for whose sake she did something crazy and ended up in jail.

Suddenly, it's as if several pieces of the puzzle fall into place. The binoculars on the kitchen windowsill. Johnny Miller's appearance at the funeral. Hedda, sitting by herself at the end of the pontoon on summer evenings. The melancholy painting that doubles as a noticeboard, the painting that features that solitary, yearning lamp on Johnny Miller's boathouse. The music coming from the record player.

She shuffles through the pile and finds more pictures of Hedda and Johnny. Happy pictures of two people who love each other.

A couple of the photos have stuck together, and when Laura eases them apart she finds a flat object that she immediately recognises.

A plastic ID bracelet, the kind you're given in hospital. It was once white, but now it's yellowed with age. Hedda's name is at the top, followed by a series of numbers, then three words that take Laura's breath away.

ÄNGELHOLM MATERNITY UNIT.

Laura manages to get rid of Elsa before lunch, making the excuse that she has a couple of errands to take care of. Elsa is disappointed, but she accepts the lie. Laura hasn't exactly been good company. The bracelet has occupied all her thoughts, and she's barely answered when spoken to.

It can only mean one thing, and there's someone who can confirm her suspicions. She picks up the receiver and dials the long Spanish number.

'Hi, Mum, it's me.'

The reproaches rain down on her immediately.

'Why have you given out our contact details? The office is calling every five minutes – poor Marcus hasn't had any peace!'

Laura doesn't answer the question, but allows herself a little smile.

'We were starting to think you'd had some kind of break-down. Why aren't you answering your phone?'

'I'm fine, Mum.'

A brief pause. The rustle of a cigarette packet.

'Are you at home?'

Laura is a fraction too slow with her response, which gives her mother time to work out what's going on.

'Tell me you're not still in that dump.'

'There are a few things I need to sort out.'

'Like what? Taking all Hedda's empty bottles to the recycling centre?'

Laura is taken aback.

'How did you know that Hedda drank? Who told you?'

Silence, the click of a cigarette lighter. A weary exhalation, then a quick change to martyr-mode.

'Is that why you're ringing, to cross-examine me? Even though I've been worrying about you for days?'

Laura doesn't take the bait.

'Hedda had problems for as long as I knew her,' her mother continues. 'Spirits, marijuana, more serious stuff when she was young.'

'And you still let me stay with her?'

'That was your father's idea. If it had been up to me, you'd never have set foot in that ghastly holiday village. Hedda ruined your life—'

Her mother breaks off, takes an irritated drag on her cigarette. Laura decides to change the subject, ask the question which is the real reason why she called.

'Did Hedda ever have a child of her own?'

'Why do you ask?'

The counter-question comes immediately.

'I found an old maternity unit bracelet among her things. I know she ended up in jail in France for attacking her boyfriend, and I know Dad helped her. I think she was pregnant when she came back to Sweden, and maybe Dad bought Gärdsnäset for her so that she'd have somewhere to go.'

She pauses, waits for a response. For a few seconds all she can hear is her mother's breathing.

'Hedda knew exactly how to manipulate Jacob's feelings, and he walked straight into her trap every single time. Cleaned up after her, got her back on her feet.'

Laura had expected a denial, or at least some kind of delaying tactic.

'So I was right? Hedda fell pregnant?'

'Yes.'

'What happened to the baby?'

Her mother blows out more smoke, or maybe it's another sigh.

'Hedda was in no state to look after a child, so your father helped her to have it adopted, as discreetly as possible.'

'When was this?'

'I don't really remember – it's such a long time ago.'

That's a lie, but it doesn't matter. Laura's already worked it out.

'Nineteen sixty-nine?' she says, writing down the number on the pad in front of her and drawing circles around it. She's on the fourth loop when her mother answers.

'Possibly.'

She sounds tired, almost defeated.

After the call Laura sits down on the sofa and places the pad on the table. She stares at the ringed date.

1969 – Hedda moves to Gärdsnäset. Gives birth to a child in Ängelholm Maternity Unit. Laura's father helps her to have the baby adopted.

She leaves a couple of lines blank, then writes down another date.

1979 – Hedda's got her life in order, and ten-year-old Jack Olsson arrives at Gärdsnäset. He has finally found a place where he is loved.

Laura looks for more photographs of Jack, finds one of him sitting with a guitar resting on his knees. Her heart is beating so hard that it hurts.

A guy with a guitar.

45

Winter 1987

I ben and Jack were standing in a corner of the dance hall. The music from the boom box drowned out their voices, but one look at their body language told Laura that they were quarrelling. Tomas was pouring vodka into a glass. Peter was still sitting at the table. His face lit up as soon as he saw Laura, but he became serious again when he realised she was upset.

'What's happened?'

Before Laura could answer, Iben and Jack came towards them. Iben's expression had softened, and the burning gaze from before was gone. Jack looked grim.

'Can I talk to you?' Iben said.

Laura hesitated, glanced around to see where Milla was. But Iben's tone was conciliatory rather than aggressive – and Jack was watching for Laura's reaction.

'OK.'

Iben gently took her hand and drew her behind a pile of chairs, out of sight of the others.

'I'm so sorry. I don't know what came over me. You're my best friend, I didn't mean to . . . Please forgive me!'

Iben let out a sob and hid her face in her hands. Laura didn't know what to think. A few minutes ago Iben had been furious, ready to punch her in the face. Now she was crying.

'It's all right,' she said, awkwardly patting Iben's hand.

But Iben flung her arms around Laura's neck, weeping so that her whole body was shaking. Laura's tears began to flow too, and the hard knot that she'd had in her stomach ever since that first evening began to dissolve.

'I'm sorry too,' she murmured in Iben's ear. 'Sorry, sorry, sorry.'

Suddenly they heard angry voices, followed by some kind of fracas. Iben and Laura ran outside.

Ulf Jensen's truck was parked in the yard, with the engine running and the headlights full on. In the middle of the beam Jack was fighting with Iben's half-brother Fredrik, swinging his fists wildly. Fredrik was stronger, and clearly used to this sort of encounter. He effortlessly parried a blow with his left hand, and punched Jack in the midriff with his right. Jack's knees gave way. Fredrik grabbed hold of his collar, held him up and hit him again. And again.

'No!' Iben and Laura yelled almost simultaneously.

They rushed over, but Christian, Iben's other half-brother, had crept forward in the darkness and held his sister back.

Laura hammered at the back of Fredrik's neck with both fists. It was like punching a wall. She moved to the side and raised her hand with the intention of scratching at his eyes, but he struck her hard across the face. She staggered backwards. Her lips were burning, they felt warm and sticky.

In her peripheral vision she saw Fredrik release his grip and let Jack fall. Iben and Christian were yelling at each other as Iben struggled to free herself. Peter came running and jumped on Fredrik's back, but Fredrik merely shook himself, took hold of Peter's arm and hurled him to the ground.

Jack managed to get to his knees, but before he could regain his balance, Fredrik was on him again. This time the blow struck his face. The sound of the impact was horrible, and Jack fell backwards.

Iben and Laura both screamed. Laura spotted Tomas, leaning against the wall. She staggered over to him, trying to lick the blood from her lips.

'Help!' she sobbed. 'Fredrik's going to kill him!'

But Tomas didn't move. His eyes were wide open, his face was chalk-white, his jaws were grinding.

Jack had rolled himself into a ball.

'You fucking gyppo!' Fredrik yelled at him. 'We told you what would happen if you went anywhere near her!'

He drew back his foot and kicked Jack as hard as he could.

'Stop it!' Iben was still trying to free herself, but Christian had her hands locked in an iron grip and had pushed her up against the truck. Tomas was still paralysed. Laura suddenly saw Milla only a metre or so away, watching the drama unfold. She was holding the baton.

Laura stumbled over to her. 'Do something!'

Milla looked at her in surprise.

'Why? This is what you wanted.'

Laura shook her head frantically.

'No, not this, not . . .'

Milla's lips curled in a scornful smile.

'Oh, come on. You must have realised what would happen when you made that call?'

Fredrik delivered another vicious kick, and Laura heard Jack let out a groan of pain. Her mouth was filled with the taste of iron, and tears scalded her cheeks and throat.

Milla continued to watch, a smile playing on her lips. Laura's chest felt as if it was on fire. Without thinking she snatched the baton out of Milla's hand and raced across the yard, swinging it high above her head. The blow struck Fredrick on the shoulder, making him stagger to one side.

'You little bitch!'

Laura saw the sinews in his neck contract, saw his fists clench and unclench. She raised the baton again. They were less than a metre apart, and she had to act fast before he hurled himself at her.

He lowered his chin, took a step forward. In the same moment Laura heard a hissing noise behind her, and a thick stream of white foam hit Fredrik full in the face, sending him reeling.

Peter moved forward, holding the big fire extinguisher that usually hung on the wall in the dance hall. He depressed the lever again and gave Fredrik another blast.

Fredrik tottered away, covering his face with his hands and bellowing in pain. Peter followed him and continued to spray him with the contents of the extinguisher until Fredrik collapsed in a snowdrift. Laura dropped to her knees beside Jack. He was covered in blood and whimpering quietly.

Peter pointed the extinguisher at Christian, who was still struggling to hold onto Iben.

'Let go of her!'

Christian hesitated. He looked over at Fredrik, who was lying on his belly feverishly rubbing snow into his eyes.

'Let go of her, or I'll blind you!' Peter shouted.

Christian released his sister and held up his hands.

'OK, OK. Calm down, Larsson, for fuck's sake!'

Iben ran over to Laura and Jack. Christian dragged Fredrik into the truck and slowly reversed out of the yard.

After a while Jack was able to get to his feet. A wound above one temple was bleeding heavily, and Peter gave him a scarf to press against it.

They went back inside in silence, sank down on the chairs and avoided meeting one another's eyes.

'The Goonies win the day,' Peter murmured, but not even he managed to raise a smile.

Tomas and Milla poured vodka into plastic cups and passed them along.

'Drink,' Milla said. 'It'll help with the shock.'

Nobody questioned her.

Laura wanted to explain what had happened – it was her fault that the brothers had turned up, Milla had persuaded her to call them. Instead, she just sat there and obediently drank from her plastic cup, like the others. The alcohol seared her throat, made her cough. Milla stared at her with something approaching contempt.

'Another round!' Milla waved to Tomas, who topped up their cups. They carried on drinking, still without saying anything. Jack kept the scarf pressed to his head, but couldn't stop the bleeding.

Milla switched on the boom box.

'Let's get this party back on track!'

She nodded to Tomas, who refilled the cups yet again. Laura leaned back, resting her head on a stack of furniture behind her. The adrenaline rush had subsided, the vodka was mixing with the wine she'd drunk earlier, and her body felt heavy. She closed her eyes.

'*Skål!*' she heard Tomas say.

Then a scraping noise as someone got up from the table, the volume increased and the music swallowed her thoughts.

Laura woke to find someone putting an arm around her. Instinctively she turned and leaned against what must be Jack's shoulder. She felt a hand on her cheek, then someone pressing his lips to hers. She opened her eyes and realised Peter was trying to kiss her.

'What are you doing?' She pushed him away and stood up.

'I thought you wanted to.' Peter looked both embarrassed and hurt.

Laura tried to clear the fog in her head. They were alone in the room.

'How long was I asleep?'

'Three-quarters of an hour, maybe a bit more.'

'Where are the others?'

'Tomas is pissed – I think he's outside throwing up. Milla and Iben have taken Jack off to clean him up.'

He waved in the direction of the area behind the stage where there was a toilet.

'What, together?'

Laura found this hard to imagine, but Peter nodded.

'Milla offered. She's training to be a nurse.'

Laura wondered whether to join them, then decided she needed some fresh air.

'Wait!' Peter took a deep breath. 'Listen, I like you. That's why . . .'

Without waiting for him to finish, Laura headed for the exit. She pushed down the handle, but the door opened only a centimetre or so. She tried again with the same result.

'Someone's dropped the bar on the outside.'

Peter got to his feet. 'They probably wanted to make sure we were left in peace.' She didn't return his smile, and he quickly adjusted his expression. 'I'll go round and open it. You stay here.'

He disappeared, and Laura went and sat down. The vodka bottle was empty. She put her elbows on the table and rested her head in her hands. All she wanted to do was to run home to Hedda, throw herself in her arms and tell her everything that had happened over the past few days. Confess what she'd done and ask Hedda to help her fix things.

Five minutes through the forest and she'd be home. The thought made her feel better. She closed her eyes.

'Fire!'

Peter's voice made her jump. He came stumbling towards her between the piles of furniture, mouth and eyes wide with fear.

Behind him a wall of flames was climbing to the ceiling, a living creature devouring everything in its path.

46

They hammer on the door until their hands are numb. The smoke makes their airways contract, tears pour down their cheeks, they can hardly see. They can feel the heat on their backs. And then there's the noise, a deep bass tone reverberating against their eardrums, getting louder and louder.

They continue to hammer on the door. Peter tries to shout, but all that comes out of his mouth is a harsh, dry cough.

Laura knows what happens next. A flash of light, a blast wave that knocks her off her feet. The smell of burning clothes, skin, hair. The realisation that this is the end – that at any moment now she will be dead.

Far away she hears a crash as the door opens. Then screams, her own, another person's. Someone picks her up, carries her over their shoulder with almost superhuman strength. Runs faster and faster, first across the snow and then across the ice, out towards the black eye while the skin on Laura's back bubbles and boils like lava.

She sees the water coming closer. Manages to take a deep breath. The cold slices through her body, slowly extinguishes the lava on her back. She kicks out, trying to reach the surface but getting nowhere.

Something is grasping her foot. She opens her eyes, stares down into the darkness, kicks out again to free herself. Instead, the grip tightens and she is dragged down and down, away from the surface. Somehow, she is able to make out what is holding onto her: a pale female hand with nails like talons. She sees a face, beautiful and terrifying at the same time.

'You are mine now, Laura,' the nymph whispers through sharp, pointed fish-teeth. 'Mine forever.'

She wakes up drenched in sweat with her heart racing. Sits up so abruptly that she frightens George, who jumps down off the bed.

'It was only a nightmare,' she murmurs, picking up the cat and cuddling her.

She hasn't had that particular dream for twenty years, except for one occasion two years ago when she lost her daughter. She sees the little body in her mind's eye, remembers the brief time she held her in her arms. So small, so beautiful. And yet all that remains of her is a tiny sleep suit, a piece of paper with hand- and footprints, and a flannel rabbit in a box hidden away in a storage unit in a cellar.

Andreas's phone goes straight to voicemail, which is hardly surprising – it's three o'clock in the morning. 'Hi, it's me,' she says after the beep. Immediately regrets it and ends the call. Steph is right, she and Andreas are divorced. It's high time she stopped leaning on him.

She puts George on the floor, slips on her shoes and goes into the kitchen. Then out through the front door and down to the shore.

Laura's last memory of Gärdsnäset was being carried towards an ambulance on a stretcher. Even though it was only a fragment it felt incredibly detailed, seared onto her retina.

The blue lights, the people in uniform who seemed to be moving in slow motion. The glow from the burning dance hall that extended far into the trees, lengthening the shadows. The cold that had settled deep inside her, making her teeth chatter. And the all-pervasive stench of charred flesh.

Hedda was by her side, squeezing her hand. She was soaked to the skin, with ice crystals in her hair. One sleeve of her jacket was gone, the hand below it burned black. And yet she refused to leave Laura, repeating her name over and over again to keep her awake.

Laura, Laura. Please don't go to sleep.

Two shadowy figures in the forest. A spotlight swept across, revealing them for an instant: Milla's ripped jeans and hoodie, Jack's ashen face. Their backs as they turned and ran.

'That's Ulf Jensen's car,' she heard someone say as the ambulance doors were slammed shut.

Her next memory was from the hospital. A mask over her mouth, hospital clothes, thin walls through which she could hear voices.

First, the lawyer who'd come down from Stockholm:

'The body was found this morning. Such a tragedy. Apparently, the girl's father has had a complete breakdown.'

Then her mother and father:

'Have you seen the burns on her back? She's going to be scarred for life! This is your fault, Hedda!'

'Calm down, Madeleine. Flinging accusations around is no help at all. We need to concentrate on the practicalities. What happens next, Adolphson?'

The lawyer again:

'I've spoken to Peter Larsson's parents, and to Detective Inspector Sandberg. The Rask boy is currently the main suspect, both for this fire and the others. Sandberg and I have arranged to hold a joint interview here at the hospital. It's important that we agree on a version of events.'

Hedda's voice, angry and despairing:

'What do you mean, a version? Iben was Laura's best friend. They were all friends.'

The next memory was a day or so later. Her wheelchair was pushed into a room where Peter, Adolphson and the police officer with the boxer's nose were sitting at a table – all in scrubs because of the risk of infection.

'So who do you think did it?' Sandberg asked with a smile.

'Tomas,' Peter replied, glancing at her with more than a hint of embarrassment.

After a second she nodded.

Next memory: she was back in her room. It was night-time, half the lights in the corridor were out. Jack was sitting by her bed, white-faced with fear in his eyes.

They're after me. I have to get away from here!

He leaned forward, kissed her so tenderly that next morning she thought the whole thing had been no more than a dream. Then she saw the photograph on the bedside table – all the gang together in one last happy moment.

Don't forget us, Princess!

And then it was all over. Dad flew her home to Hong Kong on a chartered medical transport plane. She wasn't even allowed to say goodbye to Hedda. It was only later, when there were no letters from Hedda, that she understood why. Hedda was angry, not only with her parents but also with her. Maybe Milla had told her about the phone call as an act of revenge for being sent away, or maybe Hedda had worked it out for herself. Whatever the explanation, the fact remained: if Laura hadn't called Källegården, if she hadn't told on Jack and Iben, the fire would never have started. Iben would still be alive and Jack wouldn't have had to run away.

In Hong Kong she was admitted to St Paul's – the best care money could buy, as her father said. Her mother spent hours talking to the doctors about skin transplants and therapy, about how to erase all traces of Vintersjön as quickly as possible.

The scars, the memories, the people.

What none of them knew was that the nymph had sent something with her that night. A virus hidden among her nerve endings, a winter fire that burned both hot and cold at the same time, a fire that would never, ever let her forget what had happened.

Laura fills her lungs with the cold night air and exhales up towards the sky as she stands there on the shore.

Far out across the ice, the black eye stares back at her.

47

The dirt track on the northern side of the lake is narrow and climbs the slope of the ridge, higher and higher until Laura can only just glimpse the ice cover down below.

Dense deciduous forest lines the track, straight trunks and bare branches highlighted against the grey winter sky. The snow cover between the trees looks deeper than on the southern side.

At one point Laura meets another vehicle and is forced to move so far onto the verge that the car begins to tilt alarmingly. The other driver – a man in his fifties wearing a baseball cap and sunglasses – barely acknowledges her.

The turning for Johnny Miller's house is marked by a red-and-yellow traffic sign and a notice with the words: PRIVATE PROPERTY. The track winds its way down the slope, straightening out only when it reaches a high wall with a sturdy iron gate. There is a CCTV camera on one gatepost. The large house is at the very end of a headland, surrounded by water just like Hedda's home across the lake.

There is an entryphone by the gate, and Laura presses the button. No answer. She goes over everything one more time. Hedda's relationship with Johnny Miller could easily be a red herring. There was nothing on Hedda's noticeboard to suggest that Miller had anything to do with the situation.

She tries to recall Hedda's expression when she found out that Laura was in love with Jack, but that he and Iben were together. Had she seemed relieved? She should have been, because if Laura is right, then she and Jack are cousins.

Did Jack know? Laura doesn't think so – or at least, not who his father was. But what happens if Jack really is Hedda's biological son? That means Gärdsnäset is his, which makes it impossible for her to sell the place without talking to him.

Is that really why she's here? To find a cast-iron reason for starting to search for him in earnest? Or does she believe that Hedda's forty-five-year love affair has something to do with her death? Good questions. Unfortunately, she isn't anywhere near having the answers. Not yet.

A huge skein of geese flies over the lake, fifty or sixty birds in a perfect V-formation on their way to the sea. Their mournful cries echo across the water.

She presses the button again.

'Hello?' says a hoarse male voice.

'Hi, I'm looking for Johnny Miller.'

'What's it about?'

'My name is Laura Aulin. You knew my aunt – Hedda Aulin over at Gärdsnäset.'

Silence. For a moment Laura thinks the man has hung up, but then the gate slowly begins to open.

The two-storey white house is impressive. The tower at one end goes all the way from the ground to a considerable height above the roof.

Johnny Miller opens the door himself. He looks the same as before, with a big bushy beard and dark glasses.

'Come on in.'

He shows her into a gigantic living room at the back. Down by the jetty she sees the boathouse. She thinks about the lamp that burns there every night, year after year. The lamp in Hedda's painting.

'Coffee?'

'I'd prefer tea, if you don't mind.'

He disappears, giving her the chance to explore. Gold and platinum discs are displayed on the walls, along with photographs and framed concert posters – Budokan, Whiskey a Go Go, Madison Square Garden. There are five different guitars, plus a grand piano. The room smells faintly of chesterfield furniture, along with something else that can't be blown away by throwing the windows wide open, something she has been aware of in Hedda's house and even in her own newly built apartment: loneliness.

Thanks to Wikipedia, she knows that Johnny Miller's real name is John Mellgren. He was born in 1945, and his glory days were from the early Seventies until the late Eighties. He stepped back from life in the public eye in 1994. He has lived in Ireland and Cyprus for tax reasons, and Elsa's mother Victoria was his only child, born to his second wife.

Johnny reappears with a tray, which he places on the coffee table. He moves some books and magazines out of the way.

'Sorry about the mess – I don't often get visitors.'

Laura sits down in an armchair and takes the cup of tea he offers her.

'So, Laura Aulin, what do you want with me?'

He pours himself a coffee and sits down on the sofa opposite her.

'The last time I saw you was in the churchyard at Hedda's funeral,' she begins. 'The big wreath on the coffin – that was from you, wasn't it?'

He adds sugar to his coffee, his expression neutral.

'I've seen her old photos. You knew each other in the Sixties.'

He slowly sips his drink, showing no sign of joining in with the conversation. Laura decides on more drastic measures.

'She hit you over the head with a bottle. I'm assuming you deserved it.'

His coffee goes down the wrong way and he starts coughing so violently that she almost leaps up to thump him on the back.

'You're definitely Hedda's niece,' he mutters when his colour has returned to normal. 'You act like her and you look like her.'

He takes a tentative sip; his expression has softened slightly.

'Hedda and I met at a party in Paris. I was used to getting any girl I wanted, which looking back was pretty arrogant of me. But Hedda put me in my place right away. I fell in love with her that same night.' He smiles to himself. 'We were together for about six months. She came on tour with me. I adored her; I was much more deeply in love with her than she was with me.'

'Why did it end?'

He shrugs.

'Too much partying. Booze, drugs. We were young and stupid. Especially me.'

'And you forgot to tell her you were already married.'

He sighs heavily.

'It was a drunken Vegas wedding with a girl I barely knew. It was over within a month, but neither of us had filed for divorce.'

'So Hedda hit you over the head with a bottle.'

He nods. 'She had a hell of a temper, your aunt. And we were both high and drunk. It wasn't her fault.'

'What happened next?'

'Her brother showed up. Made sure she got the shortest possible sentence, then took her home to Sweden.'

'That was my father. And what did you do?'

He pulls a face.

'I kept a low profile. My manager thought it was for the best. I hid away in a recording studio in LA, but to be honest I didn't get much done.'

'You didn't stay in touch?'

'I wrote to her, but she didn't reply, so in the end I came here to find her. She threw me out, said she never wanted to see me again.'

'But you didn't give up?'

He shakes his head.

'I bought this plot and built the house, hoping she'd change her mind.'

'She didn't.'

Another shake of the head. The sorrow in his eyes is unmistakable.

'So you remarried and had a daughter?'

'Yes. I'm sure Peter's told you about Victoria's car accident.'

'I've heard both his version and Elsa's.'

'Poor Peter. He worshipped Victoria, he still won't say a word against her. But Elsa's a smart kid.' He gives a wry smile. 'Maybe it's a terrible thing to say about your own child, but Victoria was a very selfish person who always put her own needs first, even before Elsa's. It was my fault – I gave her whatever she wanted. I thought that was how to be a good parent.'

'Why did she marry Peter? Surely she had her choice of men – why go for a boy from the local village?'

'He was stable, and he was good at his job. He was in the murder squad back then; I guess she thought it was exciting, like a TV crime show. But she soon grew tired of him. Wealth provides no protection against unhappiness, as I'm sure you know.'

He pauses, finishes off his coffee.

'Did Hedda ever talk about me?'

'Not that I can remember. We drifted apart after—'

'The fire. Yes, Peter told me all about it. Such a tragedy. I know the Jensen girl's father; I've donated money to the sports club over the years. He seems like a good guy. We both know what it's like to lose a daughter.'

Laura takes a deep breath. She isn't sure how far to go, but the sadness in Johnny's eyes helps her to decide.

'Hedda had a child shortly after she moved here. My father helped her to have it adopted, but when the boy was ten he came back. He grew up at Gärdsnäset, presumably without knowing that Hedda was his biological mother. After the fire he left, just like me.'

Johnny has gone pale.

'The boy's name was Jack,' Laura went on. 'And I'm pretty sure he's your and Hedda's love child.'

Johnny sits in silence for a minute or so, eyes shining.

'I'm afraid I'll have to ask you to leave,' he says, sounding exhausted.

Back in the car Laura discovers that her phone is once again full of missed calls. Four are from Andreas, and further down the list she sees both her mother's and Steph's numbers.

It's her own fault. Things had just settled down, but the middle-of-the-night call to Andreas and the interrogation of her mother have set the whole circus going again.

She switches off the phone and tosses it on the passenger seat. Looks up at the big house. For years and years the lonely old man inside has kept a lamp lit for Hedda. Put his life on the back burner, hoping in vain that she would come back to him.

She starts the car; can't help feeling relieved when the gate closes behind her and she drives away from Johnny Miller's gloomy home.

On the way to Gärdsnäset she meets a dark-coloured Volvo and thinks the driver is gesturing at her, but she can't make out who it is. In her rear-view mirror she sees the car do a U-turn and set off after her, with blue-and-red lights flashing on the radiator grille.

A police car. She slows down, pulls over onto the verge and stops. The driver gets out and comes up to her side window. It's Peter.

'I've been trying to call you, but you're not answering your phone.'

'No. Work is onto me all the time, so I keep it switched off.'

'OK – well, I checked the notes on that anonymous call. Back then there was an exchange that put callers through to a different station if there was no one on duty locally, and this one ended up with the neighbouring district of Nedanås instead of Vedarp. So I contacted them.'

'What did they say?'

'It turns out that the colleague who dealt with the report in 1987 was a real stickler for procedure. Henry Morell – he actually became Chief of Police eventually. Anyway . . .'

Peter reaches into his inside pocket and brings out an old cassette tape.

'Morell recorded parts of the conversation. The tape has been in their archive all these years; no doubt it's as dry as dust, which means there's a risk it will break if we put it in an ordinary cassette player. However, there's a sound technician that we sometimes use. He lives half an hour from here – are you up for a little Goonies adventure?'

*

They take his car and leave hers at Gärdsnäset.

'I heard you met Elsa,' he says. 'She told me someone scratched your car. You ought to report it to the police.'

'Do you think you're likely to make any arrests?'

He snorts, a mixture of laughter and resignation.

'I like Elsa,' Laura goes on. 'She's a cool girl.'

Peter looks pleased. 'She had a tough time after Victoria's death.'

'In what way?'

'Unauthorised absences from school, poor results, difficulty in making friends. She says she prefers to be by herself. She thinks I don't know she goes whizzing around in the forest on her motocross bike.' He shakes his head. 'I really ought to lock it away.'

They sit in silence for a little while.

'There's something I've been wondering,' Laura says. 'About the fire at the dance hall. And what happened afterwards.'

'Go on.'

'Milla and Iben took Jack to the toilet behind the stage to clean him up, but then Iben was alone when the fire started. Why?'

'According to interviews with both Milla and Jack, he was bleeding heavily and they couldn't stop it. Milla had a first aid kit in her cabin, so he went off with her.'

'Just the two of them? Without Iben?'

'Iben needed the toilet – she said she'd follow them over. Apparently, she was badly shaken after the incident with her brothers, so maybe she was afraid to leave the dance hall. Milla hinted as much when she was questioned.'

'Which way did they leave?'

'Through the back door – that was the quickest route from where they were.'

'Weren't you heading the same way?'

'Yes, but the fire spread so fast that I couldn't get through.'

'Did you see Tomas?'

He shakes his head, without taking his eyes off the road.

'Did they ever find out who dropped the bar on the outside of the main door?'

'In his confession Tomas said he lit the fire then ran out through the back – he didn't mention the main door. But later, when Sandberg pressed him, Tomas changed his statement and said he was the one who'd dropped the bar. But he never explained why.'

'And what do you think? Was it him?'

Peter doesn't answer. Instead, he points to a house up ahead. A small sign tells them that this is HELLREC STUDIOS.

'Here we are.'

The sound technician is called Lelle. He's about sixty years old, with thick glasses and thinning hair. His studio is in the garage, and is considerably more impressive than the modest exterior would suggest. He has a huge array of technical kit, including a mixer desk along one wall, linked to three monitors.

He works on the cassette for a while, explains which method he is using to ensure that the fragile spool won't break when it's stretched in the tape player. Laura listens with half an ear. She is busy trying to picture Jack in Milla's cabin, Milla playing the nursemaid, bandaging the wound on his head. Why did Milla do that? Did she feel guilty about the fight?

'There you go,' Lelle says. 'I've made a digital copy of the recording. The sound quality is pretty poor, but I'll try to improve it. I'll send you copies when I'm done.'

He moves the mouse and a scraping noise can be heard from the speakers, a thud followed by a deep voice speaking in a broad Skåne accent.

'I'm sorry, could you please repeat that?'

Laura assumes this must be the police officer, who's just switched on his tape recorder.

A thick, subdued voice speaks, then a rasping sound as something hits the microphone.

'... Källegården ... his daughter.'

'Sorry, it's a bit difficult to hear you,' says the police officer.

'Källegården. Near Vedarp. Ulf Jensen. He's messing with his daughter.'

The voice is still unclear. It sounds like a young man, and Laura tries to compare it with her memories of Jack's voice.

'It sounds as if the caller has covered the mouthpiece,' Lelle explains. He moves the mouse again, makes some adjustments.

'What do you mean, messing with his daughter?'

'He forces her to sleep in his bed. He does things to her, terrible things.'

The voice is slightly clearer now. Is she hearing Jack for the first time since 1987? She leans in closer to the speaker, and Peter does the same. There is a mechanical click, and the call ends abruptly.

Lelle replays the last part and manages to enhance the click.

'A phone box,' he says with absolute certainty. 'The old green metal type, if you remember those.'

'There were only two in Vedarp,' Peter says. 'One in the village square ...'

'And one behind the main cabin at Gärdsnäset,' Laura chips in. She pictures Jack standing there, dialling the number for the police, covering the mouthpiece with a scarf.

Lelle goes back to the beginning of the recording, makes one or two further adjustments. This time the caller's voice is clearer; the muffled effect is almost gone.

'He forces her to sleep in his bed. He does things to her. Terrible things.'

Laura inhales sharply. Admittedly the voice is deep, as if the caller is making a huge effort to disguise it, but now it's clear that it belongs to a young woman.

She turns to Peter. 'That's . . . That's Iben's voice.'

48

They remain silent in the car for a long time, both of them trying to process what they've just heard and what it means.

'She sounded terrified,' Laura says eventually as they approach the outskirts of Vedarp.

Peter doesn't reply; he just stares straight ahead at the dark road. Without warning he pulls into a lay-by and stops. Turns to face her.

'What exactly are you doing?'

'What do you mean?'

'First, you showed up to organise the funeral and the sale of Gärdsnäset. You were about to leave, then you moved into Hedda's house and started digging up the past.'

The question is entirely logical; she's been expecting it for a while. In fact, she's surprised it's taken this long. She has to tell him the truth. She explains about the two offers, and Hedda's noticeboard. Strangely enough, she feels a sense of relief.

Peter glares at her as if he's trying to decide whether she's making the whole thing up, so she goes on. Tells him about the dinner at Källegården, the Jensen family's financial difficulties, and finally the letter Tomas sent to Hedda.

'And you think all this is somehow connected to Hedda's death?'

Laura nods.

'Why didn't you say anything to me earlier? When you asked about Iben and Ulf?'

'Because . . .'

She hesitates, giving him time to work out the answer for himself.

'You didn't trust me?'

She thought he'd be angry; instead he looks amused.

'But now you don't think I'm involved in . . . whatever this is?'

'No.'

That's not entirely true. She hasn't forgotten that 'we' in Tomas's first letter. She knows that Peter is in touch with Tomas, and that he's keeping it from her. But he doesn't know that she knows, which gives her the upper hand.

'Good. Because what we're saying now is that we suspect Iben's father of a very serious crime. Ulf Jensen, known and respected by the entire community. Ulf Jensen, who was given a medal by the King.'

He falls silent, the amused expression no longer in evidence.

'Poor Iben . . .' Laura shivers in spite of the warmth inside the car. 'She was desperate enough to make an anonymous call to the police. It was a cry for help, and no one came. Not the police, not social services – no one.'

Peter shakes his head. 'She never said anything to you?'

'No. I've gone over the old memories time and time again. How about you?'

'Not a word – or maybe I was just too young and stupid to understand. Ulf was always around, coming to pick her up, wanting to know exactly where she was.'

'Do you think the brothers knew?'

'Maybe, maybe not, but after what Christian said to you yesterday, they seem pretty keen to keep the lid on it.'

'Are you going to question them?'

'No.'

'Why not?'

He sighs.

'Well, for one thing the statute of limitations for that particular crime is long gone, and for another the accuser is dead.'

'I thought the statute of limitations never ran out on certain crimes.'

'Correct – but that's when we're dealing with murder.'

Laura thinks for a few seconds.

'What if it was murder?' She sees his expression and quickly goes on. 'What if Iben's death is linked to that phone call to the police? Maybe someone wanted to shut her up. You have to admit that there are question marks surrounding the fire. Iben was all alone behind the stage. Someone could have come in and murdered her, then set fire to the dance hall to conceal their crime.'

She holds up one hand to prevent him from interrupting.

'Just before Hedda's death, she was thinking about both the fire and Iben. She delayed the sale of Gärdsnäset while she looked for answers, but she died before she found them. Then as soon as I showed up and started asking questions, there were two fires in the local area. Someone has even tried to frame me for arson, and made people suspect me – presumably so that I'll sell up and disappear as soon as possible.'

She waits for Peter's objections, but he doesn't say a word. He starts the car and pulls out of the lay-by.

'Where are we going?'

'To see an old friend,' he informs her in a voice that doesn't invite discussion.

After a mile or so he leaves the main road and turns onto a narrow dirt track that slowly climbs the northern ridge. For a few minutes Laura is convinced that they're heading for Johnny Miller's house, and wonders whether to reveal her recent visit and the reason behind it. However, Peter keeps going, following the winding track deeper and deeper into the darkness.

She sees a white sign with the symbol for walking routes. The whole gang used to cycle out here in the summer to enjoy a barbecue at one of the old campsites.

Peter drives past the sign and onto a logging track. The forest changes character, from deciduous to coniferous trees. The track is actually little more than two wheel ruts in the snow, and Peter tries to keep his speed up in order to avoid getting stuck. They should have taken her car instead; her four-wheel drive tank would have easily coped with this. She ought to ask who they're going to visit, but Peter is fully focused on the task in hand. Plus, she thinks she knows the answer.

They reach a small plateau and Peter parks next to another car, a rusty VW Golf with no snow on the roof or bonnet.

The air is cold and clear. From up here you can see the entire lake, the lights of Vedarp and Johnny Miller's place. On the far side is a little dot of light that must be the exterior lamp on Hedda's house. Diagonally down to the left, on the eastern shore, are the towers of Vintersjöholm Castle. The ice covers most of the lake, but the black eye glimmers out in the middle. The eye that never blinks, never freezes over, because it is kept open by an underwater spring. Laura shudders, wraps her scarf more tightly around her neck.

Peter points in among the trees. 'This way.'

They follow a path for a few minutes before they spot a welcoming glow. As they get closer Laura realises that it is coming from an old workman's hut, partly covered in undergrowth.

Peter knocks on the door. Someone is moving around inside, and Laura feels her pulse rate increase. The door is opened by a powerfully built man with bushy hair and an equally bushy beard. For a moment she thinks it's Jack, but then reality catches up with her.

'Hi, Tomas,' she says. 'It's been a while.'

49

They sit down at the table inside the hut. Tomas makes coffee, and Laura takes a sip out of politeness. The place is surprisingly clean and tidy, with a faint smell of damp and smoke. It is sparsely furnished, with only a camp bed in addition to the table and chairs. She presumes the other door leads to a toilet. There is a small wood-burning stove in the corner. She can just see the flames – enough to make her feel ill at ease.

'This is where Kent used to make his moonshine,' Tomas informs her.

His voice is nothing like the way she remembers it. Instead, it is rough and deep – the voice of a middle-aged man, not a teenager. The same applies to his appearance. To be honest, she wouldn't have recognised him if they'd bumped into each other under different circumstances.

'The power comes from the electricity box up the road,' Tomas continues. 'And there's a stream behind the house. That's all you need. Peter brings me food. He takes care of me, makes sure I'm OK.'

Peter looks uncomfortable. Laura waits for him to say something, ask a question, but he doesn't. Eventually she has no choice but to do it herself.

'I believe you and Hedda wrote to each other?'

'Yes – well, it was mostly her. I'm not good at replying.'

'You told her something about Iben's father.'

Tomas nods slowly. 'I'd promised never to say anything to anyone, but Hedda's letter made me happy, so I thought I owed her that.'

'When was this?'

'Not long ago – maybe a month or so? I collect my mail from a postbox in Ängelholm.'

'Did she say why she was asking?'

'I think Iben had tried to tell Hedda at some point, then changed her mind. Something about Ulf, which Hedda didn't really understand. She wrote that she'd been turning it over in her mind for years, and wondered what I knew. So I told her.'

'Did you have any further contact after that?'

Tomas shakes his head. He reminds her of a large, unhappy bear.

'No. Peter called and told me that Hedda was dead.'

'How . . . ?' Peter clears his throat. 'When did you find out about Iben and her father?'

'We must have been eleven or twelve. She said she slept in Ulf's bed, and she told me other things too. Things I don't want to say out loud.'

Tomas looks down at the floor, the muscles around his eyes twitching.

'Do you think her brothers knew?' Peter asks.

Tomas snorts derisively. The air in the hut feels sticky.

'They lived in the same house – of course they knew. Christian and Fredrik have always been Ulf's obedient little lapdogs.'

'Did Iben try to talk to anyone apart from Hedda?'

'I don't think so. She was terrified of Ulf, terrified of what he'd do to her if she told anyone.'

Laura looks at Peter, sees that he's thinking the same as her. The phone call they've just listened to.

'But I tried to do something,' Tomas goes on.

'What?'

Silence.

'What did you try to do?' Peter says.

Tomas places his big hands on the table and studies them closely. It's obvious that he doesn't want to discuss the matter any further.

'What actually happened that night at the dance hall?' Laura asks gently.

Tomas looks up. 'I lit a fire. I used to enjoy lighting fires back then.'

He falls silent, plucks at the sleeve of his jumper.

'Why?'

'It feels nice. Something inside me . . . eases.'

'You dropped the bar on the door,' Laura says. 'Locked us in.'

'No!' Tomas shakes his head. 'I didn't lock anyone in! The fire spread much faster than I'd expected. I never meant for anyone to get hurt. I never meant for her to die. Not like that . . .'

We decided, Laura thinks. She holds her breath; is Tomas trying to catch Peter's eye?

No, he's looking down at the table again.

'In your interview with the police—' she begins, but Tomas holds up his hand.

'I don't want to talk about that night anymore.'

He reverts to plucking at his sleeve. There is a patch of pink, bubbly skin on his wrist, and Laura realises what the plucking is about. The scar on her back begins to crawl.

'You burned yourself,' she says. 'You burned yourself too.'

Tomas glances up. Something flickers in his eyes. Laura takes a deep breath, stands up and takes off her jacket. Undoes the top

309

buttons of her shirt, turns her back on the two men and slips down the shirt so that her scar is visible.

'Jesus,' Tomas whispers.

Laura adjusts her clothing before turning around again. Tomas has tears in his eyes, Peter's face is ashen.

'I'm so sorry, Laura.' Tomas's voice is thick with emotion. 'It was never meant to be like this. I didn't really want to do it, it was like a favour—'

He breaks off, looks away.

'A favour for whom?'

Peter's question comes like the crack of a whip. Tomas recoils.

'No one,' he mutters. 'Forget I said anything.'

Laura goes and sits down beside him. Places her hand on his arm.

'Who asked you to start the fire, Tomas? Was it Milla?'

He glances up at her, the muscles around his eyes twitching frantically now. Without a word he stands up, grabs his jacket, opens the door and walks out. Laura and Peter look at each other. After a few seconds they push back their chairs and follow him.

'Tomas!' Peter yells into the darkness. 'Tomas!'

But all they can hear is the wind soughing in the trees.

50

Peter carefully manoeuvres the car back along the narrow logging track. Laura doesn't want to distract him.

'Haven't you asked Tomas about that night before?' she says eventually.

'No. I never wanted to. Or dared to. What if he'd said he was innocent, that Sandberg had pressured him into confessing? You and I accused him . . .'

Peter doesn't go on. There's no need.

'Do you think he's lying?'

'No. He seemed very upset when he saw your . . . your . . .'

'Injuries,' Laura supplies, realising she doesn't have a problem talking about her scar. 'I don't think he was lying either.'

They fall silent. The car tilts slightly on the slippery surface, but Peter skilfully keeps it on the track.

'I'll come back up tomorrow,' he says after a while. 'Tomas just needs time to get himself together.'

'Did he start the fires at his father's place and at Källegården?'

'Why would he do that?'

'Because he's a pyromaniac. Because he hates both his father and Ulf Jensen.'

'Tomas hasn't been in trouble for years. He's behaved himself, followed his treatment plans.'

'You don't have to protect him, Peter. He admitted that he was the one who started the fire at the dance hall. You – or we – didn't accuse him of something he hadn't done.'

Peter doesn't answer; he keeps his eyes fixed on the route ahead. The headlights light up the snow-covered ground on either side of the track, but in among the trees it is pitch-black. Way down below them, the ice on the lake glimmers. Laura decides to change the subject.

'Did Tomas mention Milla when he was interviewed by the police?'

'No. Sandberg asked him on several different occasions whether anyone else was involved – Tomas denied it every time.'

'And Milla? What did she say?'

Peter glances at her for a second.

'She and Jack told the same story. They'd gone to Milla's cabin so that she could put a dressing on his head injury. They heard noises and went back to the dance hall, but it was already in flames. The fire service arrived shortly afterwards.'

'And then?'

'She left only a couple of days later. Hedda had found her a new place somewhere – I can't remember where.'

'Värmland. She was furious. Do you know what became of her?'

Peter shakes his head. 'I can run a database search tomorrow.'

'Good idea. Do you think Milla was involved in the fire? Was she the one Tomas meant?'

'I've no idea. Tomas lives in a fantasy world to a certain extent. He's on some pretty strong medication. On the other hand . . .'

He falls silent as he negotiates a bank of snow to access the wider track.

'We know how manipulative Milla could be. She talked me and Tomas into doing those break-ins. She could wind people around her little finger.'

Including me, Laura thinks, but she doesn't say anything.

'I'm sure she could have persuaded Tomas to set fire to the dance hall if she'd wanted to,' Peter goes on. 'But why would she do that?'

'Iben knew about the break-ins, and Milla got the idea that Iben had told Hedda, and that was why she was being moved to Värmland. She was very angry with Iben.'

'Fuck.' Peter's grip tightens on the wheel.

'Milla, Iben and Jack were together just before the fire broke out. According to Jack's and Milla's statements, Iben was supposed to follow them to Milla's cabin. If Milla had wanted revenge on Iben, that means she must have met Tomas on her way out of the dance hall, but that isn't mentioned in any of their statements. Both Jack and Milla said they didn't see anyone on their way to the cabin.'

'She could have spoken to Tomas earlier.'

'True, but don't forget that Tomas and Iben had known each other since they were little. She even told him what Ulf was doing to her. Tomas, not you or anyone else. That's how close they were.'

The last sentence is like a knife in Laura's heart.

'Tomas adored Iben,' Peter continues. 'He would never have agreed to do anything that would harm her. No chance.'

'And yet he did,' Laura says quietly.

Peter doesn't reply, but his silence implies agreement.

'It was me, by the way,' he says after a moment. 'I was the one who told Hedda. I felt as if everything was spiralling out of control, so I called Hedda and explained what had been going on.'

'Did you tell her I was mixed up in it?'

'No, and she didn't ask – but I think she worked it out. She certainly moved fast to get Milla relocated.'

They reach the village, pass the church, the sign for the Iben Jensen School.

'When did they rename the school?'

'A few years ago, when Ulf stepped down from his post as chair of the council. It was a kind of leaving present.'

'Did nobody object? Nobody think it was strange to name a school after a dead girl?'

'Not as far as I know. If anyone felt like that, I guess they kept their opinions to themselves.'

'Because people are scared of Ulf?'

'Not scared exactly.' Peter turns onto Gärdsnäsvägen. 'Ulf has coached generations of kids in athletics. Led them in competitions, on training camps and trips. Most of them are grown up now, and they feel a strong loyalty to Ulf.'

Laura thinks about the reception she got in the ironmonger's and the ICA store – and about the scratches on her car. But something is still bothering her about Tomas. How unfamiliar he looked.

'Do you think we'd recognise her?'

'Who?'

'Milla. Do you think we'd recognise her if she showed up?'

'I've no idea. People change a lot from their teenage years to adulthood.'

'Even if it's someone you knew really well?'

He frowns. 'Are we talking about Milla, or somebody else?'

Laura's cheeks flush red. 'Jack. I've got a feeling he's back – I don't really know why.'

'Have you kept in touch?'

Laura shakes her head, registering a sharpness in Peter's tone of voice. 'The last trace of him is a postcard to Hedda, sent from Berlin in 1989.'

Peter doesn't say another word until they reach Hedda's house. He gets out of the car and walks her to the door.

'By the way, would you like to have dinner with me and Elsa tomorrow evening? She wanted me to ask you,' he adds hastily.

'That would be lovely,' Laura says. 'But only because Elsa wants me to come.'

It is Peter's turn to blush. The tension from a little while ago is gone, replaced by something else. Something warm and soft that Laura likes.

They are standing opposite each other on the porch. Without really knowing why, she leans forward and kisses him on the cheek. She stays where she is while he jumps in the car. Just as he's about to drive off, he lowers the side window.

'I think you might be right.'

'Sorry?'

'I met an old classmate from the police academy on a course a couple of years ago. He'd put on twenty kilos, lost half his hair and was wearing glasses. We were really good friends at one point, but I hadn't a clue who he was. It was pretty embarrassing when we shook hands. And you didn't recognise me in church the other day, even though I've done nothing but age thirty years. So if Milla or anyone else turned up with a different name and appearance, there's a strong possibility that neither you nor I would recognise them.'

51

She switches on all the lights in the house. In spite of her and Elsa's efforts the place is still a terrible mess, but Laura consoles herself with the thought that at least it looks better than when they started. Plus, it no longer bothers her as much. She takes out her phone, plays the sound file Lelle gave her. Hearing Iben's voice is so uncomfortable that she involuntarily hunches her shoulders.

Källegården. Near Vedarp. Ulf Jensen. He's messing with his daughter.

So this is Iben's terrible secret. A secret Tomas has kept for over thirty years.

Poor Tomas in his hideaway in the forest, and Peter who has done his best to protect him all these years, because of a guilty conscience. Peter, who stubbornly insists that Tomas is not behind the fires at Ensligheten and Källegården, even though all the indications suggest that he is.

She tries to go over everything that has been said between them, but it's all too much. She decides to go out and get some fresh air, clear her mind. She pulls on her jacket and boots and takes her cup of tea with her. George accompanies her, leaping around in the snow like an excited puppy.

'Stupid cat,' she murmurs.

George looks up and tilts her head to one side. When they reach the pontoon, the cat stops and looks at her again as if to say: this far and no further. She disappears into the darkness like a grey speckled shadow.

Laura goes right to the end of the pontoon and stands by the ladder. The ice has formed a thin covering at the bottom, and is well on the way to winning the battle against the slight current that has kept the water open.

She gazes across at the northern shore, the yearning lamp on Miller's boathouse, the silhouette of the ridge, all the way to the castle.

Was Jack out there somewhere, having changed so much that she didn't recognise him? Or is the whole thing just a fantasy, wishful thinking based on an unhappy teenage love affair? If she'd sat down and carried out a risk assessment the way she did at work, dealing with facts and not emotions, the result would have been a given. The likelihood of Jack being anywhere near Vintersjön is so low that it's almost non-existent.

And yet she can't get it out of her mind, in spite of everything she's found out, in spite of the fact that she and Jack are actually cousins. She will never be able to share this with Steph. The cousin-jokes would come thick and fast, and Steph would bombard her with video clips of unfortunate banjo-playing hare-lipped souls in dungarees.

She smiles to herself, realises that she misses Steph's dark sense of humour. She sips her tea and looks over at the castle, remembering how she and Iben dreamed of stealing the troll's treasure and buying Vintersjöholm. Steph would have liked that story.

So what now? Ulf Jensen's abuse of his daughter is beyond the statute of limitations, and Tomas has admitted that he was behind the dance hall fire, even though he hinted that Milla talked him into it.

Laura can see the black water through the thin crust of ice. Images of Hedda's dead body come into her mind. Was it Iben's secret that cost her her life? If so, the main suspects are Ulf Jensen and his two sons, either together or acting on their own initiative.

Hedda was on the trail of the secret, and if she'd found out the truth she would probably have refused to sell Gärdsnäset to the local council. She would have let Ulf lose his beloved family farm. She might even have revealed everything, dragged his good name through the mud.

The Jensens would go a long way to stop that from happening.

But how far? And how big is the secret? Does it stop at abuse, or is there something even worse?

She tries to recall the fight outside the dance hall, Fredrik beating up Jack, Iben screaming at Christian to try and get him to let go of her.

What if Iben had yelled something about Ulf, threatened to tell everyone what had been going on? How would Christian and Fredrik have dealt with that?

Could one of them have returned later in the evening and seized the opportunity when Iben was separated from the others? It's not impossible. Iben was young and strong, and she was only a few metres from the back door. Nobody had been able to explain why she didn't get out of the dance hall – but what if she was already unconscious, or even dead, when the fire broke out?

Could the 'we' Tomas had mentioned in his letter – the 'we' that had almost slipped out an hour or so ago – could he have been referring to Iben's brothers? Tomas certainly seemed to loathe the two of them as much as he hated Ulf, but during the fight he'd been paralysed with fear. Had they threatened him, forced him to start the fire so they'd have a scapegoat?

A faint glow high up on the ridge catches her eye. At first she thinks it's the lights of a car, but then she realises it's getting bigger and brighter.

The scar on her back begins to move, writhing faster and faster as she grasps where the glow is coming from.

She is sweating now, shivering with the cold at the same time, and yet she can't make herself go indoors. Instead, she stands there on the pontoon staring at the dark slope of the ridge on the other side of the lake, where Tomas Rask's hideaway is in flames.

52

She is dreaming about the dance hall again. The minutes before the fire. She can see herself sitting at the table, sleeping. Peter beside her, clumsily edging closer. Then the perspective shifts. She is in the area behind the stage, the wall plastered with pictures of the dance band who played here last summer. The big mirror that covers another wall, the sagging sofa against the third. The toilet door, with the lock showing red.

There is someone else here, someone she senses but can't see. She looks around, thinks she glimpses a movement in the mirror.

The lock changes to green with a click. The handle is pushed down, and for a second she's convinced that the Iben from her nightmares is behind the door.

Instead, it's a different Iben who emerges, the Iben who is her best friend, the Iben she taught to speak with a Stockholm accent, the Iben who would never let anyone come between them.

'Laura,' she says, her face lighting up. 'There you are!'

They fling their arms around each other, Laura hugs Iben as tightly as she can. Presses her cheek to Iben's, realises she's crying. She wants to own up, tell Iben that she was the one who called her brothers, but she can't do it.

Iben holds her at arm's length, with sorrow in her eyes.

'You know my secret.'

'Yes,' Laura sobs.

Iben nods slowly. 'I think everyone suspected. But no one dared to say anything. They were all afraid . . .'

Something behind Laura's back makes Iben stiffen. Her expression changes from sorrow to fear.

'No,' she whispers. 'No!'

Laura turns, sees movements in the mirror once again, shadowy figures with blurred outlines, growing bigger and clearer.

Christian and Fredrik on either side of Ulf, with no compassion in their eyes. Behind them the gloomy façade of Källegården, the flames on the coat of arms flickering slowly.

I have always regarded you as my second daughter. You and our little Iben . . . Ulf whispers, and the hairs stand up on the back of Laura's neck.

Källegården. Near Vedarp. Ulf Jensen. He's messing with his daughter, says Iben's terrified voice on the phone.

The picture changes. Tomas, messing with some boxes next to one of the walls of the dance hall. Flames shoot up around his hands, set fire to his jacket before greedily licking at the dry wood.

The final figure in the mirror is also familiar.

Aunt Hedda outside her house, raising a hand in greeting.

You're my little princess. You always will be.

The perspective shifts again.

Laura is at the very end of the pontoon, the scar on her back wriggling like a burning snake. On the other side of the lake Miller's lamp is flashing, and above it the forest is in flames.

A sandwich for father, a sandwich for mother, sing two high, girlish voices.

And one for the nymph who lives down below, the creature standing behind Laura murmurs through rows of sharp fish-teeth in a charred face.

The nymph wraps her arms around Laura and digs her claw-like fingers so deep into her breast that the pain slices right through her dream. Then the nymph drags her down into the cold black water.

George wakes her by jumping up onto her chest, then padding around until Laura pushes her away and sits up. Outside the crows are making an enormous racket, and in the middle of it all Laura thinks she hears a car door slam.

She gets out of bed, pulls on her jacket over her pyjamas. It's gone ten o'clock, and her head feels heavy.

George must be hungry. She nearly trips Laura up in the living room, so Laura picks her up and carries her. The car from the castle is parked outside the window.

There's a knock on the door. Laura opens it to see two people standing there – Heinz Norell, and a woman in a fur coat, earmuffs and huge sunglasses. It takes her half a second to place the woman, but her brain needs more time to process the realisation.

'Steph?'

'Oh, so you're still alive,' Steph says with a smile. 'Even if you have stopped answering your phone.'

She lowers her sunglasses to the tip of her perfect nose and looks Laura up and down. The hair standing on end, the jacket over the pyjamas, the cat in her arms.

'My God, Laura. What have these country bumpkins done to you?'

Laura mumbles something and puts down George, who immediately shoots off through the door.

'What are you doing here?'

'Andreas and your mother are both convinced that you've had some kind of breakdown, so I offered to drive down and rescue you. Not a day too soon, if you ask me.' Steph wrinkles her nose. 'When did you last take a shower?'

Laura hesitates, and Steph holds up her hand.

'Never mind – we'll sort you out. I'll wait outside – the smell in there is getting into my clothes.'

She pulls a face, steps down from the porch and digs a vape pen out of her bag. Heinz Norell winks at Laura.

'Best if we do as we're told,' he whispers. 'Would you like me to come in and give you a hand?'

Laura makes a huge effort not to look at the noticeboard just metres away.

'No thanks. Give me five minutes.'

She packs the few things she's brought with her, then puts some food in George's bowl. The cat dashes in as soon as Laura places it on the floor.

She's still trying to process the fact that Steph is here – with Heinz Norell from the castle. But the nightmare is still messing with her mind, along with everything that happened yesterday. The tape recording, the fire, the blue lights that eventually appeared high up on the ridge. Peter, who isn't answering his phone even though she's called him at least five times from Hedda's landline.

Outside the smell of smoke still lingers in the air. Heinz puts her bag in the boot of the shiny car with the Vintersjöholm logo on the side. Steph seems to have been for a walk around the property; she stops next to Laura's car, where the salt from the roads has already turned the deepest scratches red with rust.

Sell up and fuck off! she reads. 'So, cat lady – you didn't think it was a good idea to take that advice?'

Heinz holds the car doors open, first for Laura and then Steph before jumping in the driver's seat.

'Where are we going?' Laura asks.

'To the castle, of course – where else?' Steph replies, tapping away on her phone.

'But . . . how . . .?'

Laura's brain still isn't functioning properly.

Steph finishes her message and lowers the phone, her expression more serious now.

'Your mother managed to scare Andreas to the point where he was about to come here himself. Apparently, your brother has had enough of the firm, they've had enough of him, and for different reasons everyone is worried because you're not answering your phone.' She leans back and smiles. 'With a little skilful diplomacy I managed to knock that idea on the head. It seemed to me that whatever you were going through, the last thing you needed was your ex-husband trailing around after you. In return I had to promise to come and find you. The things I do for you, Laura.'

Steph winks at her over the top of her sunglasses.

'Things became a little more straightforward when your mother told me where you'd gone. You'd never actually mentioned Vintersjön, and to be honest I hadn't asked. I kind of lost interest when you started talking about some backwater in Skåne.'

The car reaches the main road and heads east towards the castle.

'I've had some business dealings with Pontus von Thurn, who owns Vintersjöholm,' Steph goes on. 'He and Erica were more than happy to help, so here I am!' She waves her phone in the air. 'I've just reassured everybody that you're safe and well, but I won't send them any pictures of you until later this afternoon when you've tidied yourself up. Anyway, enough of all that. Tell me what the hell is going on!'

Laura catches Heinz Norell's curious gaze in the rear-view mirror.

'Later,' she murmurs.

She's been along the avenue leading to Vintersjöholm a few times with Hedda, but she'd forgotten how impressive it is. Five metres wide, dead straight, lined with huge oak trees, it stretches for almost a kilometre before ending in front of a huge arch. Heinz presses a button on the dashboard, which opens the black wrought-iron gates leading into the park.

The castle itself is in the French Renaissance style, a large main building with a black metal roof and a tower at each end. The lawns and neatly clipped hedges are covered in snow. There are a couple of Portakabins to one side.

Laura's room is on the second floor. It has heavy velvet curtains and a carpet so soft that it absorbs the sound of her footsteps.

'We're having lunch with our hosts at twelve thirty,' Steph informs her. 'The bathroom is in there.' She points to a door at the far end. 'I'll be back in half an hour, and I want all the details. By the way, there are some clean clothes in the wardrobe. I called in at your apartment. You do know you don't have to wear trouser suits and cashmere cardigans all the time, don't you?'

Steph smiles and leaves before Laura has time to think of a response.

She looks out of the tall windows at the park, a couple of hundred metres of trees and snow-covered grass. She assumes the low buildings by the jetty are a sauna and a boathouse. One is surrounded by scaffolding, the roof protected by a tarpaulin, but no work seems to be going on.

Across the ice is the southern shore. She can just see the roof of Hedda's dilapidated house. The contrast couldn't be greater.

The bathroom is the same size as the living room at Gärdsnä-set, a paradise of brass and Italian marble, warm towels that are at least an inch thick. Laura takes a long shower, closing her eyes and enjoying the heat flowing through her body. At the same time she feels as if she's waking from a trance. The last few days have been unreal, almost dreamlike. The idea that she – who can hardly bear to shake anyone's hand because of the risk of germs – has actually eaten and slept in Hedda's horrible house is incomprehensible. It's as if that was a completely different Laura from the person she usually is.

Steph wasn't joking about the clothes. Two of her jackets, cardigans and pairs of trousers are hanging in the wardrobe, along with beautifully ironed white shirts. One of the drawers contains underwear. Admittedly she did once give Steph a spare key to her apartment, but she'd never envisaged it being used in this way. Steph has been in her home without Laura there, touched her possessions, rooted around among her clothes, maybe even learned things about her that Laura would prefer to keep to herself. And yet . . . All she needed was a decent hot shower and a couple of luxury towels to revert to her normal, repressed self.

Steph has launched an entire rescue operation, driven over six hundred kilometres, pulled countless strings – for the simple reason that she cares about Laura. That's the feeling Laura ought to cherish, instead of giving in to her need to be in control.

There is a full-length mirror inside the wardrobe door. She positions herself in front of it, lets the towel fall below her shoulders. Goes through yesterday evening's meeting yet again. Herself, Peter and Tomas. Three old friends, all scarred by the fire. They carry visible and invisible scars.

She wonders what happened to Tomas. Did he set fire to the hut himself, and if so, why? She decides to try Peter again. She searches for her mobile, but can't find it.

She gets dressed, dries her hair in the bathroom. Revels in the feeling of being clean.

She's just finished when there's a knock on the door and Steph walks straight in.

'Now that's more like it,' she says with a big smile. 'How about a quick drink before lunch so you can fill me in on what the hell you've been up to over the past week? You can start by telling me whether Prince Charming showed up. No, wait! Judging by the cat lady look you were sporting until half an hour ago, I'd bet a hundred dollars that he didn't.'

Laura has had the chance to think about how much she's prepared to share with Steph. She sticks to the basics. Gärdsnäset was in a much worse state than she'd expected, Hedda had been a hoarder, and Laura wanted to clear the house before she sold up. She mentions in passing that she's met up with one or two old friends, but doesn't go into detail.

'And what about the scratches on your car door? The natives seem hostile.'

Laura can't help smiling at Steph's choice of phrase, which seems very much at odds with their current environment.

'There are strong opinions about who I should sell Gärdsnäset to,' she says.

They go down a staircase, turn right and enter a drawing room that smells of paint. The furniture is heavy, the walls are covered with flock wallpaper and paintings of English hunting scenes. Red jackets, horses with heads that are a fraction too small, packs of almost identical dogs.

Steph goes straight to the drinks trolley and pours them both a generous whisky.

'This is the good stuff. The one they offer visitors is in the main room.'

They both sink down on leather armchairs.

'So,' Steph says. 'Prince Charming didn't turn up, and your inheritance looks like the set of a horror film. And instead of heading back to civilisation as soon as possible, you decided to stay and clear out your aunt's house. My shrink would have plenty to say about that – like for example that you're running away from something else. Work, family, grief . . .'

The last word hits home, embeds itself in Laura's flesh like a thorn.

There is a knock on the door.

'Heinz – come and join us!'

Steph raises her glass, but Norell shakes his head.

'It's too early for me, plus I'm working. I just wanted to return this.'

He holds up Laura's phone.

'It was on the floor in the car.'

The screen is black. It reacts only when Laura presses the button on the side. Did she really switch it off? She can't remember.

'See you later,' Heinz says and leaves the room, with a long look and an over-the-shoulder smile at Laura.

'Fit, wouldn't you say?' Steph comments. 'And single. Well, kind of.'

'How do you know that? Do you know each other?'

'Heinz is a skilled project leader – one of the best I've worked with. He and Erica have been friends since they were young; I think they were at school together in Switzerland or something.'

Steph leans forward and lowers her voice.

'I think Erica is sleeping with Heinz, and that Pontus knows about it. A gentleman's agreement, so to speak. Maybe you could help me find out for sure? Use your special skills?'

Laura shuffles uncomfortably.

'Do you know that Vintersjöholm has made an offer on Gärdsnäset?'

'Yes, Heinz told me.' Steph pulls a face that's hard to interpret. 'But there's no pressure on that front. You're here as my friend, nothing else. No hidden agenda, OK?'

Laura takes another sip of her whisky, feeling the warmth spread through her body. She's pleased to see Steph, and realises how much she's missed her.

Steph looks at her small and extremely expensive wristwatch. 'So – time for lunch with our hosts. Don't look so worried, Laura – you'll like them, I promise!'

Steph turns out to be right. The von Thurns are a very pleasant couple. Pontus is a cheerful, slightly overweight man in his early sixties, so full of energy that he finds it difficult to sit still. He holds forth with passion about the history of the castle and the renovation projects they've undertaken and are planning for the future, then switches his focus to Laura at precisely the right moment. He seems genuinely interested in both her work and her background.

Erica is fifteen years younger, about the same age as Laura. She is beautiful in that strained way that suggests too many surgical interventions. She is tanned even though it's the middle of winter, and the diamond in her wedding ring is one of the biggest Laura has ever seen.

At first Laura gets the impression that Erica is a cooler, dark-haired version of Steph, but as lunch progresses she proves herself to be both intelligent and amusing in a more subtle way than her husband. Sometimes, when he is on the point of immersing himself too deeply in some anecdote, she pats him gently on the arm, which immediately makes him break off or let someone else speak.

Her Swedish is very good, but like Heinz Norell she has a faint accent which comes through occasionally. German, with a hint of French – hardly surprising if she grew up in Switzerland.

From time to time Laura notices that Erica is watching her – not with any hostility, but with curiosity.

Heinz joins them for coffee. The wine has enabled Laura to relax, and she can't help observing him discreetly.

She'd already established that he is good-looking in a weather-beaten way, and there's something about that warm smile. At first she found it irritating, but now it seems increasingly attractive.

Heinz, Erica and Pontus chat like old friends, but Laura can't see any signs of a closer relationship between the lady of the castle and the project leader. On the other hand, the absence of such signs could simply mean that the two of them are behaving with the utmost discretion.

'Have you had time to look at the brochure I gave you?' Heinz asks her. 'About what we'd like to do with Gärdsnäset?'

The question takes her by surprise. She tries to catch Steph's eye, but it is Erica von Thurn who steps in.

'Laura is our guest, Heinz,' she says tersely. 'She's not here to talk business.'

Heinz looks embarrassed. 'My apologies, Laura.'

'No problem.'

'We really love Vintersjön,' Erica says. 'It reminds me of my childhood home in Switzerland. Or north-eastern USA. It must have been wonderful to grow up here.'

Laura nods. 'I was really only here in the summer and Christmas holidays, but it was fantastic.'

'When was your last visit?'

'Almost exactly thirty years ago.'

'So the winter of 1987?'

Laura nods slowly. Erica holds up her hands as the realisation hits her.

'Oh, how stupid of me! I didn't mean to bring up . . .'

'Bring up what?'

Heinz leans forward, curiosity written all over his face.

Erica gives Laura an apologetic look.

'The Lucia fire,' she says slowly. 'In the winter of 1987. A young woman lost her life over at Gärdsnäset. But let's talk about something else.'

Laura feels everyone's eyes on her. She has avoided this subject all her life. Never told anyone, but maybe it's time. Time to free herself from the past at long last.

'It's fine,' she says. 'It was a long time ago, and there's not much to tell. We had a party in the dance hall, which was closed for the winter. A fire started, and one person died.'

'Who?' Pontus asks.

'Her name was Iben Jensen,' Laura says slowly. 'She was my best friend.'

Steph's eyes are shining with unshed tears, and Laura can't help loving her for that. Pontus looks troubled. His wife and Heinz Norell share the same expression: sympathy, on the surface at least. But there's something else just beneath the surface. A feeling Laura can't quite put her finger on – a feeling she doesn't like.

53

After lunch, Laura and Steph go for a walk in the park. Laura talks about that Lucia night in 1987 without holding back on any of the details this time, not even the most painful ones. The phone call, the fight, the fire. How her aunt carried her across the ice and plunged her into the water. The winter fire she took with her, which many years later probably killed her and Andreas's little girl. She tells Steph about the sleep suit and the tiny hand- and footprints that she keeps hidden down in the cellar. She brings Steph up to speed with everything that's happened over the past few days. The only thing she keeps to herself is the discovery about Hedda, Johnny Miller and Jack, mainly because she thinks it doesn't belong with all the rest, but maybe also because she wants to hang on to one secret.

'What a story!' Steph looks floored by Laura's revelations. 'That poor girl! Well, poor all of you.'

They walk on in silence for a minute or two.

'Why have you never told me this before?' Steph asks quietly.

'Because I was ashamed.'

'But it wasn't your fault. You didn't start the fire.'

'If I hadn't called Iben's brothers and said she was seeing Jack, then none of the rest of it would have happened.'

'You can't know that. Tomas clearly isn't well – nor that other girl. What was her name?'

'Milla.'

Steph counts Milla's 'qualities' off on her fingers.

'Manipulative, a pathological liar, lack of empathy. A textbook psychopath.'

Laura has never analysed Milla like that, but Steph undeniably has a point.

'So what are you going to do with the holiday village and all the rest of it?' Steph wants to know.

'As I said, both the council and Vintersjöholm have made offers. There's a lot of money involved.'

'Whose bid is the highest?'

'Your friends Pontus and Erica are offering four hundred thousand more.'

Steph raises an eyebrow.

'So why are you hesitating? The council's bid involves Iben's father, an evil bastard who abused his own daughter. Sell the dump to Pontus and Erica and be done with it.'

'It's not that simple.'

'No?' Steph looks sceptical. 'I really don't like being on the same side as your mother but she's right – your aunt's death seems to have stirred up a lot of old crap. Family feuds, incest, arson . . . But instead of doing what any sensible person would do – sell up and get the hell out of Dodge – you stay around. Carry on poking around in the mud and slime even though you've had more than one warning, and all this clearly isn't good for you.'

Her tone becomes serious.

'This isn't about your childhood sweetheart any longer, the Prince Charming you keep hoping will show up; this is about you, Laura. Do you really want to get dragged down into this mess?'

She leaves the question hanging for a few seconds, then goes on:

'Your aunt didn't contact you once in thirty years. Nor did Prince Charming. Ask Erica and Pontus to name a road or something after Hedda, then you'll be quits. Go and meet someone who cares about you. You deserve it, Laura. You deserve to be happy, whether you believe that or not.'

'I'll think about it,' Laura says eventually.

'Good.' Steph puts an arm around her. 'How about wrapping everything up over the next couple of days, then we can return to civilisation? All this nature is making me nervous. I need to see tarmac, inhale exhaust fumes.'

Laura has almost forgotten that she promised to have dinner with Peter and Elsa. Steph isn't happy about being abandoned, and for a moment Laura considers cancelling, but then she thinks about Elsa. She likes the girl, or the young woman – whatever she is. She likes Peter too, so she explains to Steph that this is a farewell dinner, which improves her mood a little.

Laura's car is still at Gärdsnäset, but Steph solves the problem with a quick phone call.

'Heinz will take you to Peter's and pick you up, so we can carry on drinking wine. He offered before I'd finished speaking.'

Heinz Norell's car is waiting outside the main entrance five minutes before the agreed time, which Laura appreciates. They make small talk on the way into the village, mainly about the weather.

He is obviously still embarrassed about his faux pas during lunch, and tries hard to make up for it. He asks polite questions, but stays well away from anything that could possibly relate to business.

She directs him to Peter's house and he stops right by the door.

'Do you have any more of those brochures?' she asks as she's about to get out of the car.

'Sorry?'

'About the Vintersjön project? I left the one you gave me at Gärdsnäset and I haven't had time to look at it yet.'

For a moment he looks confused, then his face breaks into a broad smile.

'Of course.'

He opens the glove compartment and hands her another copy. She tucks it into her inside pocket as she walks towards Peter's front door.

'Hi, Laura – come in!'

Elsa opens the door before Laura can ring the bell. She looks delighted to see her, and unexpectedly gives Laura a big hug. She frowns when she sees the car.

The entrance hall is generous, with a shiny marble floor and a chandelier. The walls are painted in a coral shade that is a little too brash. Elsa notices Laura's expression.

'The décor was down to Mum. As I said before, it's not really my style, or Dad's.'

Peter emerges from the kitchen, wearing a leather apron and with his shirt sleeves rolled up. He looks very professional. And handsome, Laura has to admit. His eyes are sparkling in a way that appeals to her.

'Welcome to our home, Laura.'

She kisses him on the cheek, lingers a fraction longer than last time. She blames the wine she's been drinking with Steph.

'Whose is the car?' Elsa asks.

'A friend's.'

'From Vintersjöholm?'

Laura nods, sees Peter frown.

Dinner is very enjoyable. Peter turns out to be an excellent cook, and Elsa is good company. The wines Peter has selected contribute to the positive atmosphere. They talk about all kinds of things – TV series, politics, which educational path Elsa should follow come the autumn.

'What did you do?' Elsa wonders.

'We lived in Hong Kong, so I went to a private school. You can't really compare it with the Swedish system.'

'What was your favourite subject?'

'Behavioural science.'

Elsa's face lights up.

'My first choice is sociology. Maybe you can help me with my homework.'

Peter's cheeks flush red.

'Maybe,' Laura murmurs.

As they clear the table she finally gets the chance to have a quiet conversation with him.

'I saw the fire all the way from Gärdsnäset,' she almost whispers. 'Is Tomas OK?'

Peter looks worried.

'I don't know, to be honest. He's not answering his phone, but according to the fire service the hut was empty. And his car is gone.'

'Have you told anyone that he was living there?'

Peter shakes his head, then gives a meaningful nod in the direction of Elsa, who is on her way into the kitchen.

They have coffee in the living room at the back of the house. The garden is lit up, just like the front. A sun terrace, a pool, various exotic plants – all beneath a thin covering of snow. Whoever designed this garden invested a great deal of time and money. Laura assumes it was Elsa's mother. At the same time she realises she hasn't been swimming for quite a while, and that she misses it.

'So have you decided what to do with Gärdsnäset?' Peter asks.

'I think I'm going to sell.'

'Why?'

Elsa's question is instant.

'Because Laura doesn't have the time to take care of a run-down holiday village,' Peter explains.

'Why not?'

Laura and Peter exchange a glance.

'Because I have a job and a family in Stockholm.'

Elsa's mouth becomes a thin, straight line. For a second she reminds Laura of someone she knows, but the moment passes. Elsa gets to her feet.

'Excuse me,' she says, but her body language and tone are anything but polite. She marches out of the room.

'Teenagers. You can't win,' Peter says with an apologetic smile. 'So who are you going to sell to? The castle?'

'I can't see any other option. The council would give the building project to Ulf Jensen, and as far as I'm concerned he and his fucking family farm can go up in smoke.'

She immediately regrets the clumsy choice of words.

'Sorry, I didn't mean . . .'

Peter waves a dismissive hand.

'I understand. But what if the council agreed to go with a different construction company? How would you feel about that?'

'That's hardly likely. You said yourself that—'

'But if they did,' he persists. 'If Ulf Jensen was out of the picture. Would you consider selling to the council then?'

She shrugs. 'Possibly.'

She reads his body language, his eager expression, the keen interest in his voice. This is more than a hypothetical discussion.

'Why do you ask?'

'Because I might be able to persuade someone to pull a few strings.'

Before she can ask him what he means, Elsa reappears. Her face is bright red and she slams something down on the coffee table in front of them.

'Are these your plans for Gärdsnäset, Laura? A mini fucking Torekov where only the rich can afford to live?'

It's the brochure Heinz Norell gave her, the one that was in her pocket.

'Hedda would have hated the idea!' Elsa snaps. 'She loved the lake, she wanted as many people as possible to be able to enjoy it. You're only thinking of the money!'

Laura's about to explain that Hedda was also considering selling to the castle, but Peter gets in first.

'That's enough, Elsa!' he shouts. 'Apologise to Laura immediately!'

Elsa lifts her chin defiantly, struggling to hold back the tears.

'Fuck you!'

She turns and runs out of the room, leaving the brochure open on the table. Pictures of row upon row of houses made of concrete, steel and glass, each with a private jetty where enormous yachts are moored.

VINTERSJÖ PARK, says the heading across the double-page spread. *A PLACE WHERE ONLY THE BEST IS GOOD ENOUGH.*

The evening never really recovers after that. Laura and Peter have coffee and a brandy and try to talk about something else, but Elsa's anger lingers in the air between them. After about half an hour Laura texts Heinz and asks him to come and pick her up.

Peter walks her to the door. He hands her the brochure with an apologetic smile.

'Elsa means well, but she's young. She thinks everything is black and white.'

'Like we did?'

He takes a deep breath.

'Sometimes I wish I could go back in time. Experience it all again. The summers out at Gärdsnäset, you and me, Hedda, George, Jack, Iben, Tomas. The holidaymakers, the dances. All that happiness we had before—'

He breaks off.

'Before it was taken away from us,' Laura says before she can stop herself. They stand in silence for a few seconds, until the beam of Heinz Norell's headlights sweeps across the front door.

'Don't sign right away, Laura,' Peter says. 'Give it a day or two.'

He holds her gaze, refuses to let her go until she gives him a nod of agreement.

Heinz makes more polite conversation on the way back, continuing to prove that he is both pleasant and intelligent.

'Which part of Germany did you say you were from?' Laura asks as they turn into the avenue leading to the castle.

'I've lived all over the place, but I was born and raised in Hamburg.'

The name rings a bell, but before she has time to marshal her thoughts, they have reached the main entrance.

'By the way, Erica wonders if you'd join her for a nightcap up in the library.'

That's the last thing Laura wants. She's tired and a little tipsy, but she realises she doesn't have a choice. Heinz holds the door open for her.

'I hope to see you tomorrow.'

The library is situated in one of the towers and has a fantastic view. The moon is shining on the ice, shimmering in the black eye in the middle of the lake. There are bookshelves from floor to ceiling, with a couple of ladders that run along tracks to access the higher shelves.

The lighting is subdued; there is a candelabra with ten flickering candles in one window. The fire in one corner is burning so brightly that someone must have put on more logs very recently. There is a clear crack running down the chimney breast above the mantelpiece.

The risk assessment part of her brain that has been quiet for several days springs to life, weighing up the combination of an open fire, a cracked chimney breast and tons of old, bone-dry paper over and over again until her palms begin to sweat.

Erica von Thurn is sitting in a wing-back armchair by the window. She gets to her feet as Laura comes in.

'Laura – how kind of you to keep me company.' She pours a glass of red wine from the carafe on the table and hands it to Laura. 'Come and sit down.' She points to the armchair closest to the fire. Laura hesitates, then sits down. The heat is nice, yet alarming.

'Did you have a pleasant evening with your . . . friend?'

The dim lighting and the flickering flames create shadows that make it difficult to read Erica's expression.

Laura takes a sip of her wine. 'I did.'

'I wanted to apologise for earlier,' Erica says. 'My curiosity got the upper hand – obviously I had no right to bring up that ... tragedy from your past. I really do hope you can forgive me.'

'Of course.'

One of the logs gives a loud crack and Laura jumps. A drop of sweat trickles down the back of her neck and continues its way along her scar. The shadows from the fire play with the perfect proportions of Erica's face.

'Stephanie tells me you like to swim.'

Laura nods. The red wine seems to have reached her brain.

'We have a pool house, recently completed. You're welcome to use it tomorrow if you like.'

'Thank you.' Laura realises that something more is expected of her. 'And thank you for letting me stay here.'

Erica waves her hand.

'It's a pleasure. Stephanie's friends are our friends, and besides – we're neighbours.'

She raises her glass and Laura mirrors the gesture. Her head suddenly feels too heavy for her shoulders.

'Vintersjöholm is the apple of Pontus's eye,' she hears Erica continue. 'He loves the castle. Personally, I prefer the lake.'

Erica waves her glass in the direction of the window. 'This area really does have a fascinating history. You know the castle burned down? Several times, actually.'

Laura nods, she can't stop glancing at the open fire.

'Gärdsnäset is a wonderful place,' Erica goes on quietly. 'It must have been amazing to grow up there.'

Laura's head is getting heavier and heavier, while the sweat-snakes on her back are multiplying.

Erica leans closer, her face distorted by the shadows. It looks like a mask.

'We're having a little party here the day after tomorrow. Pontus and I would be delighted if you'd join us.' Her teeth are chalk-white, perfect porcelain veneers. 'You're welcome to invite your friend, if you like.'

Laura nods. Her mouth is as dry as dust, her eyes dart between the dancing flames and Erica's face. She's seen all this before, she's sure of it.

Or maybe it was a dream. Erica's voice drifts away.

'. . . a party to celebrate Lucia.'

The word makes Laura give a start. Is it the tenth already?

How has the time passed so quickly? She takes another sip of her wine, notices that the glass has magically emptied.

Erica quickly tops it up. 'Listen, I know we're not supposed to be discussing business.'

Her face reminds Laura of the nymph in her nightmares.

'I just want you to know that Pontus and I are prepared to increase our offer on Gärdsnäset. Have you had time to look at the brochure, by the way?'

She produces yet another brochure, identical to the one Elsa slammed down on the coffee table just over an hour ago.

'If you like,' Erica continues eagerly, 'and this is just an idea – but if you like, we could reserve a house for you. Here, in the best position.'

She points to a plan of the proposed development, but Laura can't take her eyes off the fire. The flames are so high now that they are reaching into the room, eagerly seeking out the bookshelves. The crack in the chimney breast has widened, it's getting bigger by the second. Sweat is pouring down her back, irritating and scalding her scar.

She can see the closest books beginning to curl and smoke in the heat, she can smell burning paper. The first book catches fire with a puff, and is immediately followed by several more.

The flames lick the shelves, consuming more and more books and racing towards the ceiling.

Erica's voice echoes through the room, but Laura can't hear what she's saying because the fire is roaring now. The crack opens wide, lets out a stream of liquid fire that flows across the floor. She wants to stand up, scream, run for the door, but instead she sits there as if she's turned to stone while Erica goes on talking, apparently oblivious to the danger.

A door opens, and Laura hears Steph's voice.

'Laura! I thought you'd gone to bed ages ago.'

Steph places a hand on her shoulder, ice-cold against the heat of her skin. In a second the fire is back where it belongs, the crack in the chimney breast is barely visible. The books and shelves are untouched.

'You must be exhausted, you poor thing,' Steph says, helping Laura to her feet. She glares at Erica. 'Come on, let's get you to your room.'

54

Laura is woken by her phone. Someone has put it on charge on the desk, and obviously switched it from silent. She might have done it herself last night; she can't be sure.

'Hi, it's Peter. Thanks for last night.'

'No, thank you.'

She's not sure how to go on. Her head is still woolly.

'Have you got time to come down to the council offices?'

'When?' She looks at her watch. Ten thirty.

'About two o'clock? I think we might have a solution to your dilemma over the sale of Gärdsnäset.'

She hesitates, tries to replay the previous day's events in her mind, but without much success.

'OK. See you later.'

Vintersjöholm's pool house is a separate building four minutes' walk from the castle itself.

It looks brand new, but there is no lock on the main door, tiles are still stacked in one corner, and several wall lights are missing. Just like the rest of the castle, Laura has the feeling that nothing is quite finished, and yet there is no sign of any workmen.

There is one changing room. Unlike her own specially made swimsuit, the one she's borrowed doesn't cover the scar on her back, but then she's not expecting company.

She slides down into the water, enjoying the sensation of weightlessness for a few seconds before she begins to swim. As always, swimming slows her thoughts to the point where she can pin them down, sort and categorise them.

What actually happened in the library last night? Was it just the wine and exhaustion taking their toll, making her see things that weren't there? If so, did it start in the car during her conversation with Heinz Norell? And why has she promised to meet Peter to discuss Gärdsnäset?

Is this really about Elsa? Is it because she sees herself in the girl, and can't bear to disappoint her?

She covers fifty lengths of the pool without coming up with any answers. Only when she gets out of the water does she notice the discreet CCTV camera up in one corner. She drapes her towel around her shoulders and instinctively turns away as she heads for the changing room.

Steph, Pontus and Erica have gone to a meeting, but the woman who serves Laura's lunch hands over an envelope. It contains a car key and a note from Steph.

Go and buy a dress - we're going to a party tomorrow night. No trouser suits allowed!

The council offices in Vedarp are housed in a building from the late Sixties that resembles a shoebox. Yellow brick, white metal trim, Advent candle bridges in every other window.

She gives her name at reception, and after five minutes Peter appears with the little man who came to visit her on the day of Hedda's funeral.

'Kjell Green,' he introduces himself, as if he doesn't expect anyone to remember his name.

They go into a small meeting room and Green makes a point of closing the door. He offers coffee and water, but both Laura and Peter refuse. In spite of the events at the end of yesterday evening, she realises she's pleased to see Peter again.

'So,' Green begins tentatively. 'As I understand it there are certain' – he glances at Peter – 'reservations with regard to our choice of construction company in the proposed Gärdsnäset development. Am I correct?'

Peter nods before Laura has time to speak.

'As the council doesn't yet own the land, no agreement is in place,' Green continues. 'No promises have been made, no guarantees offered—'

'Laura wants to be certain that you won't give the contract to Ulf Jensen,' Peter interrupts.

'Yes, you mentioned that.' Green looks troubled. 'As I said before, this is an important project for the future of our community, and of course we're ready to discuss any—'

'No discussion,' Laura says. 'I want the council to guarantee that the contract won't go to Ulf Jensen or either of his sons. If you can do that, then we have a deal.'

Green shuffles uncomfortably.

'It's not that simple. This type of project is governed by the law on public procurement. We have to go with the bid that gives the taxpayers the best value for their money.'

He clears his throat, leans towards Laura while giving Peter a nervous sideways glance.

'So we can't put anything in writing, if you take my meaning. That would involve breaking the law.'

'But off the record, the council is in agreement?' Peter says.

Green hesitates, then gives a brief nod.

'So you expect me to sell and trust you to keep your word?' Laura says.

It's Peter, not Green, who answers.

'It's in no one's interest to con you, Laura. We all want something good to come from Gärdsnäset, and I can assure you I'll be watching the council like a hawk.'

They leave together.

'Do you have time for a coffee?' Laura points to the espresso bar where Wohlin's once stood.

'I'm afraid not – I have to work. Sandberg is hassling me about the fires.'

She feels disappointed. 'Anything new on Tomas?'

Peter shakes his head.

'He's done this before, taken off and stayed away. One summer he went camping in Norway, didn't get in touch for months. Our visit stirred up a lot of stuff.'

Laura looks around at the snow and slush. It's not exactly camping weather, but she decides to drop the subject.

'How's Elsa?'

'What can I say? She's a teenager . . . But she'll be pleased that you're selling to the council.'

'I haven't made up my mind yet.'

'You soon will, though?'

'I will.' As he turns away she adds on an impulse: 'There's a Lucia party at the castle tomorrow.'

She notices that he dislikes the word as much as she does, and quickly goes on: 'I wondered if you'd like to come with me?'

The anxious expression is replaced by a smile.

'I'd love to.'

*

ANDERS DE LA MOTTE

She says goodbye to Peter and considers following Steph's instructions and going to look for some kind of party dress. She needs a cup of tea first, so she goes into the espresso bar, navigates her way through the range of teas advertised – easily resists the unappetising cakes on offer – and sits down at what used to be her favourite table in the window.

While she's waiting for her tea to cool down she looks around, searching for traces of Wohlin's, but there is nothing left.

She drinks slowly, tries to gather her thoughts.

She still has no proof whatsoever that Hedda's death was anything other than an accident. As far as the noticeboard is concerned, she has at least managed to find out what Iben's terrible secret was. She's also pretty sure, in spite of Peter's reservations, that it was Tomas who started the fires at both Ensligheten and Källegården. The fact that he set fire to his own hideaway reinforces her suspicions.

So what's left?

She still doesn't know who the mysterious smoker watching Hedda's house is, nor who planted the petrol can and the insulating material in Jack's old apartment.

And then of course there's the big question: who asked Tomas to start the fire in the dance hall? Who did he mean when he wrote 'we' in his letter?

Was it Milla – still the most logical answer – or could it have been one of Iben's brothers?

Laura is so absorbed in the puzzle that she doesn't notice someone come into the café. She doesn't look up until that person is standing right next to her table. She inhales sharply as she meets Ulf Jensen's gaze.

'So, little Laura. I hear you've been out and about. Talked to the council, laid down certain conditions.'

He pulls out a chair and sits down opposite her.

'I thought we were good friends, you and I,' he goes on. 'I almost regarded you as a daughter. And then you go behind my back with Peter Larsson, that little cuckold who couldn't even keep his own wife in order.'

His false teeth look like gravestones in his face. The smile infuriates her. So do his words.

'And what about you?' she says. 'Could you keep Sofia in order? Because I heard that she set fire to the farm because she didn't want to live with you.'

The comment has a greater effect than she'd expected. Ulf's expression darkens, his jaw tightens – but he doesn't take the bait.

'Do you really believe,' he says after a few seconds, 'that the council would use another contractor? After all I've done for this community? All the medals, all the newspaper articles. Not to mention all the terraces and conservatories the boys have built, all the kitchens and bathrooms we've renovated.' He lets out a bark of laughter. 'There isn't a single councillor who hasn't slipped me an envelope stuffed with cash for a job done. They owe me, all of them. So do you, Laura!'

He clenches his fist, then points a gnarled index finger at her.

'You and the others cost my little Iben her life. The least you can do is help me to save the farm where she grew up.'

'You mean the farm where you abused her?'

The words just come out, without passing through her brain.

Ulf's lips are white. He clenches both fists, and for a moment she thinks he's going to attack her.

'I loved Iben,' he hisses when he's regained the power of speech. 'I loved her more than life itself, and I won't let anyone say anything different – do you hear me?'

Saliva sprays across the table.

Laura calmly picks up her phone, searches for the sound file Lelle gave her. She is looking forward to throwing Iben's words in his lying, hypocritical fucking face. But she can't find it. It takes her a little while to work out why.

The file is gone.

Ulf slowly gets to his feet, looking a little more self-assured.

'Now be a good girl and sign that contract with the council,' he says, making an effort to remain calm. 'As I said, it's the least you can do for me and our little Iben. And do it soon, before something bad happens.'

55

Laura remains at the table, trying to make sense of what just happened. The fact that someone in the council offices told Ulf Jensen about the meeting with Kjell Green is bad enough, along with the fact that he's just threatened her. But the disappearance of the file containing Iben's terrible cry for help can have only one explanation.

A very unpleasant explanation.

During the past twenty-four hours, someone has deleted it from her phone.

Which leads to three questions: when, who, and most important of all – why?

There have been several occasions since the visit to the sound studio when she hasn't exactly kept an eye on her phone. She dropped it in Heinz Norell's car when Steph came to pick her up, it was in her jacket pocket when she was at Peter's, and then there was last night – she doesn't even remember how she got to bed, or if she was the one who put the phone on charge.

Plenty of opportunities, all possible answers to the question of when.

The phone is locked, of course, but anyone could have watched her when she unlocked it and memorised the code. Or simply taken it before it was locked.

If she moves on to who, the list is equally long: Heinz Norell, Elsa and Peter Larsson, Erica von Thurn. But why would Peter delete a sound file he'd helped her to access? On the other hand, he hadn't known it was Iben's voice on the tape until they'd listened to it together. Elsa can't really be a suspect, even though she did poke around in Laura's pockets.

After a little thought she realises that it's not possible to exclude an unknown person. She swam for almost an hour this morning, leaving her phone in the unlocked cupboard in the changing room at the pool house.

Which leaves the third question: why?

Why would someone want to delete the file in which Iben accuses her father of abuse, from beyond the grave?

In order to protect Ulf Jensen – that seems the most likely explanation, making him, Christian and Fredrik the main suspects.

But Peter still has the original tape, and a digital copy of his own on a USB stick.

She calls him, says she's accidentally deleted the file and asks about his copy.

'Everything's at the office, but I'm not in Vedarp at the moment. Can it wait until tomorrow? Or this evening at least?'

He sounds stressed, and she reluctantly agrees.

She thinks back to Steph's note and decides to head for the nearest shopping centre and look for a dress.

During the drive she goes over what Ulf Jensen said – that he has such a hold over so many of the local councillors that they will never give anyone else the contract for Gärdsnäset. If that's true, and she has no reason to doubt it, then she will just have to sell to the castle and let Erica, Pontus and Heinz transform Gärdsnäset into a rich man's enclave. Elsa will never speak to her again. Why does she care about that? Why does she care what a teenage girl and possibly her father might think of her?

Another good question, which doesn't have a good answer.

Or does it? She likes Elsa, recognises something of herself in the girl – that's all there is to it.

So she can't sell to the council because of Ulf Jensen, and she can't sell to the castle if she wants to continue to have a relationship with Peter and Elsa.

Where does that leave her?

There is a third option, of course: to hang onto Gärdsnäset for the time being, until she can come up with a solution to the problem.

On the way back to the castle she decides to call in and check that George has enough food. A small part of her actually misses the warmth of that little furry body, and the reassuring sound of purring at the foot of the bed.

It's dark by the time she reaches the holiday village. The remains of the archway and the dilapidated snow-covered cabins look even sadder than they did a few days ago, if that were possible.

Her car is still parked next to Hedda's house where she left it, but as she approaches she sees something written in large letters on one side.

Sell up and fuck off!

She slams on the brakes. Her initial impulse is to turn the car around and drive away, but instead she gets out, leaving the engine running and the lights on. Some of the crows croak a warning, as if they sense her unease, know that something horrible has happened.

The words are written using some kind of dark red, sticky substance that has trickled down the car doors before the frost stopped it.

She edges closer. There is a dark bundle on the windscreen. A familiar stench turns her stomach. Hair, soot, burned flesh.

She stops by the bonnet, stares at the bundle, glimpses a bare tail, speckled grey charred fur, glassy eyes staring blankly at her.

'George!'

She collapses behind the nearest tree trunk and throws up onto the snow.

Laura weeps for the first time in two years. She sits on the porch with her head resting on her arms and sobs, her whole body shaking. It's as if something has burst inside her. Things she has stowed in plastic boxes with the lid firmly on, locked away deep in the cellar, have escaped. Hit her hard like a punch in the stomach, left her incapable of doing anything but crying. George, Iben, Hedda, Jack, Peter and Tomas.

But most of all she is weeping for her little girl. Her and Andreas's beautiful daughter. The life that could have been.

Somewhere in the distance she hears Hedda's phone ringing, but she doesn't have the strength to get up and answer it. She simply sits there crying until her body is stiff with cold and she has no more tears. Even then she can't move.

She hears the angry sound of an engine, sees the beam of a single headlight bobbing through the trees.

Elsa.

Laura forces herself to stand up, scoops snow in her hands and rubs it all over her face as she staggers down the steps. The ice crystals chafe her skin, make her wake up. She can't let Elsa see what's on the car.

She switches off the engine of the borrowed car, which kills the lights, then she runs along the track to intercept Elsa.

'Hi,' the girl says as she takes off her helmet. Her voice is subdued, but as soon as she sees Laura's face, she knows something is wrong. 'What's happened?'

'There's been a break-in.' Laura's voice falters on the lie. 'We mustn't go any closer in case there are traces left behind. Is your dad home?'

Elsa shakes her head. 'No, but I can call him if you like. He always answers when it's me, but I'll have to go back to the main road to find a signal.'

Peter arrives fifteen minutes later. He's already far from calm when he gets out of the car, and it takes Laura a few seconds to realise this isn't about his daughter sitting on a motocross bike that she's too young to ride on the roads. She really wants to throw herself into his arms, but she has to keep the mask in place for Elsa's sake. She quietly tells him what's happened.

Peter goes over to look at the car and George's charred body, then he makes a couple of calls.

'There's something else,' he tells Laura when he's done. 'There's been a break-in at my office. The place has been trashed. A scene-of-crime team are working on it now.'

He lowers his voice and leans closer. 'The cassette tape and the digital recording of Iben's voice are gone.'

56

I t's only seven in the morning and the castle is silent as Laura picks up her towel and heads for the pool house.

She didn't dream last night, at least not as far as she remembers, which surprises her. Maybe her brain is so overloaded with terrible images that it needs to rest.

The weather is milder, the temperature is around freezing and the air is damp. Laura swims fifty lengths, trying to clear her mind.

She told Peter about the unpleasant encounter with Ulf Jensen. Like her, Peter believes that Ulf is the main suspect, both for stealing the recordings and killing poor George.

If the recording of Iben's voice came out, not even Ulf's contacts would be able to save him or his farm. But how did the Jensens know that the recording existed? Until the other day, there was nothing but a brief note about an anonymous phone call, buried deep in a thirty-year-old police investigation.

There were only three people who knew about the tape: Peter, herself and the sound technician. That professional studio in Lelle's garage must have cost a fortune. Unless of course it was a case of cash in hand. 'Forest business' with a local builder.

All it would have taken was a phone call to Källegården, a brief summary of the contents of the tape and where the copies were. Fredrik could easily have taken care of the rest. Accessed her phone while she was swimming, broken into Peter's office.

He doesn't seem the type who'd have a problem with that kind of thing. Or killing and setting fire to a poor defenceless cat.

She sees a movement at the side of the pool and stops when she reaches the end of her length.

Steph and Erica von Thurn are lying on loungers, both wearing bathrobes and holding paper cups.

Laura stays in the water. Her robe is on the table between the two women, and walking past them would mean exposing her back.

'Well done!' Steph yells. 'Erica and I were so inspired by you that we decided to keep you company.'

Laura nods, remains where she is.

'Come on out – Erica's made breakfast smoothies!'

Steph holds up a third cup. Laura has no choice but to get out. She tries to keep her back turned away as she grabs her robe, but it proves impossible.

'Oh my goodness,' Erica says. 'Is that the scar from the fire?'

'Mmm.'

Laura does her best to let her tone and body language show that she really doesn't want to talk about it, but Erica isn't the type of person to pick up on discreet signals. Or she doesn't care.

'Why haven't you had plastic surgery?'

'Because Laura has an intolerance to anaesthetic,' Steph says quickly.

'Oh, I see.' Erica seems to buy the lie.

'Is everything OK?' Steph says, changing the subject. 'We didn't have the chance to chat yesterday.'

'I had an early night,' Laura says. Steph tilts her head to one side, as she always does when she doesn't believe her friend.

Laura decides to tell them what happened to George, if only to avoid more intrusive questions about the fire.

'Oh my God, poor cat,' Steph murmurs. 'And the police don't know who did it?'

'No – not yet, anyway.'

'It sounds like a madman.' Erica's eyes are huge, the smile lingering at the corners of her mouth betraying both distress and fascination. 'But you don't need to worry – you're safe here. We have CCTV cameras and alarms. And there will be lots of people around tonight.'

Laura maintains her composure with some difficulty. She'd forgotten all about the Lucia party, but she can't back out now. She's a guest, and going back to Gärdsnäset isn't an option. Plus, she's already invited Peter.

'There's a really nice group coming; they already have a summer place in Torekov, but they're starting to find it a bit too . . . lowbrow, if you know what I mean?'

Erica stops herself.

'I promise we won't be talking business, Laura. At least not much. We won't try to influence your decision, but of course Pontus and I would be delighted if you chose to sell to us.'

Laura takes a sip of her smoothie. Steph looks uncomfortable, mouths 'sorry' at her when Erica turns away.

Steph slips into Laura's room shortly before the guests are due to arrive. Inspects the dress Laura bought, decides her shoes don't cut it and lends her a pair of her own.

'I'm sorry about this morning,' she says. 'Erica can be a bit too direct sometimes. Must be the German genes.' Her expression grows serious. 'I know I shouldn't get involved in this business of selling your inheritance, but Erica's right. Whoever did that to the cat and your car is one sick individual. Then there are the fires and the damage to your car the other day . . .'

Steph comes and sits beside her on the bed.

'Why don't you just sell up to Pontus and Erica as we discussed, and walk away from this whole mess?' She pulls a face. 'You can't seriously be thinking of selling to the council, letting that . . . paedophile and his cat-killing sons get the contract.'

Laura has asked herself the same logical question several times, and yet she doesn't have a satisfactory answer. She thinks of Peter, Elsa, Hedda, Johnny Miller . . .

'Jack,' Steph says. 'That's who this is all about, isn't it? You still haven't given up on the idea that Prince Charming might show up.'

Her tone is sympathetic, which bothers Laura more than if it had been teasing. Steph takes her hand, looks Laura in the eye in a way that is difficult to ignore.

'Thirty years have passed, Laura. Thirty years when Jack or your aunt could have got in touch. But neither of them did – not a phone call, not even a fucking postcard. You don't owe them anything. Isn't it time to let go?'

Laura looks away. Steph is right. As long as she clings to Gärdsnäset that is a little flicker of hope. But what is she hoping for? A happy ending?

Do happy endings even exist?

57

The drive leading up to the castle is lined with burning torches. Fir branches have been laid out in the courtyard and along the steps by the main entrance.

Peter arrives dead on seven o'clock. He has brought a bottle of wine, which judging by Pontus von Thurn's expression is more than decent, and he is wearing a dinner jacket that is well tailored but clearly not new.

He has surprised Laura. She'd underestimated him, been worried that he might show himself up in company. Instead, she's the one who's embarrassed.

'Not bad,' Steph whispers in her ear after Laura has introduced Peter to her. 'And yet he's not Prince Charming . . .'

After a couple of minutes Steph already has him wrapped around her little finger. She chats away in exaggerated Swenglish, jokes with him as if they were old friends, touches his elbow at regular intervals. Laura is used to this performance and usually finds it quite entertaining, but this evening it is irritating her for some reason.

Steph guides them up to the balcony above the big staircase.

'Best spot for people watching,' she says.

Down below the guests are pouring in, dressed to impress. They hand over furs and overcoats, carrying with them a blend of perfume and cigar smoke that drifts all the way up the steps.

'Who are these people?' Peter asks.

He's talking to Laura, but it's Steph who answers.

'Money in various shapes and sizes,' she says. She points to a group who have just arrived and are greeting Pontus loudly and enthusiastically. Men in their sixties with female companions at least twenty years younger.

'Those are Pontus's old friends. All on wife and family number two – three, in some cases. Old money, boarding school, a touch of inbreeding and all that kind of thing . . .'

She points to another group – younger, more bored.

'And they're the new economy. IT, Bitcoin, streaming, you name it. Snotty kids with more money than they can spend. Both ends of the spectrum have that problem in common, and Erica and Pontus are very good at relieving them of significant sums and doing something sensible with it, something that brings pleasure to a lot more people. That's one of the reasons why I like the von Thurns.'

She gives Laura a long, meaningful look, then tucks her arm beneath Peter's.

'I need another drink,' she says. 'Would you mind escorting me to the bar? Laura tells me that Johnny Miller is your father-in-law. I'm a huge fan . . .'

Laura stays where she is, studying the activity down below. Time and time again her eyes are drawn to Erica, who is skilfully working the room, making a point of speaking to everyone and making them feel welcome. She seems to change depending on who she's with, speaking fluent German with a foreign guest, exchanging cheeky banter with Pontus's male friends, saying something that makes the younger gang burst out laughing.

There is no doubt that Erica is good at handling people. Maybe even manipulating them. Was that what she was trying to do in the library the other evening? On the other hand, Steph insists that Erica and Pontus are good people.

She continues to observe her hostess. Her movements, her expressions. The way she switches between playing beautiful and slightly dumb, to as sharp as a razor blade.

Someone touches her arm and she turns around.

'I've been looking for you,' says Heinz Norell, handing her a fresh glass of champagne with that cryptic smile of his. 'What do you think of our little gathering?'

'Nice.'

She regrets the word, but can't think of anything better.

Heinz moves a fraction closer than is comfortable; the balustrade means she can't move away. He smells good – cigars, aftershave.

'What's happened to your companion?'

'Steph took him off to the bar.'

'Ah.' His smile grows wider. 'Caught in Stephanie's web. So I have you to myself for a few minutes.'

Laura has no idea what she's expected to say. There's something attractive about Heinz, something slightly dangerous.

'You look very beautiful this evening.'

'Thank you.'

'How about meeting some of the other guests?'

He holds out his arm, and after a brief hesitation she takes it.

As they walk down the stairs, she notices several men in the room looking at her in a way she isn't used to. She begins to wish she hadn't chosen a dress and Steph's high-heeled shoes instead of her usual attire, but after a while she begins to relax, thanks to the champagne and Heinz's company.

They wander around the whole room, but none of the guests makes much of an impression.

Just as she starts wondering where Peter and Steph have got to, the lighting is dimmed and the sound of beautiful singing can be heard. A procession of ten young girls in white dresses each with a wreath of candles on her head moves through the drawing room, followed by two boys looking distinctly uncomfortable in their 'star boy' costumes. They gather in the hallway and sing some of the traditional songs associated with the feast of Lucia. Their voices are lovely, but Laura hardly hears them. Her eyes are fixed on the young woman representing St Lucia. She is sixteen or seventeen years old, with long dark hair. Tall candles flicker in the wreath on her head.

The flames make Laura very uneasy.

The feeling remains after the procession has left. Even the guests' warm applause doesn't drive it away. Cold sweat breaks out on her back, meeting the heat of her scar.

'Laura?'

She glances up, realises that Heinz has said something she missed. He seems worried.

'Are you OK? You've gone very pale.'

She nods. 'I just need something to eat.'

He accompanies her to the table and it turns out they're sitting next to each other, which is hardly a coincidence – nor is the fact that Steph has Peter beside her. She suspects that Steph has planned the whole thing, that Heinz is another one of her little matchmaking projects. In which case she has to admit reluctantly that it's one of her more successful ideas. Heinz Norell is good company, and he's intelligent. He reads books, has a sound grasp of current affairs, and also asks her questions that suggest he's genuinely interested in her life.

'Stephanie tells me you're dangerous,' he says when they've finished the main course. 'She says you can read people, reveal secrets they'd prefer to hide.'

Laura glances at Steph, wishes she'd kept quiet about that particular skill.

'I love Sherlock Holmes – have done ever since I was a little boy. I love the way he looks at people's clothes and immediately works out where they've come from.'

He lifts his chin, puts on an English accent:

'You, sir, work for a lord whose finances are in a poor state. You took the 11.32 train to Paddington this morning, and had scones for breakfast.'

Laura can't help laughing.

'Is that the kind of thing you do?'

She shakes her head.

'As I said, my work involves screening. The people I interview are smart, they know what's at stake, and they make every effort to show their best side. My job is to try and see behind the façade, compare what they say with their behaviour, search for things that don't quite match.'

'Such as?'

Laura takes another sip of red wine. It's her second glass, and after the champagne and the white wine that accompanied the first course, she is feeling a little tipsy. It's not like her at all, but she's enjoying herself – which is unexpected.

'Such as your name, for example. Your surname is Norell, but you said your mother was Swedish and your father was German. Why don't you have your father's surname?'

Heinz pulls a face.

'Nothing dramatic. My parents weren't married. I grew up mainly with my mother. Is that all, Miss Holmes?'

He looks disappointed, so Laura decides to dig deeper. She observes him closely, his face, his hands, the smile that never really leaves his lips. His dark eyes.

'You wear coloured contact lenses,' she says.

To be honest she isn't completely certain, but there is a faint discrepancy between his eyes and his general colouring – his skin, his pale eyebrows, the neatly trimmed beard.

He is clearly taken aback, but then that confident smile returns, accompanied by an impressed whistle.

'Busted!' he says. 'Caught out in one of the worst sins – well done!'

'Which sin is that?'

'Vanity, of course. I have an eye defect known as coloboma. The pupil in my right eye appears to spill over the iris. I noticed from an early age that certain people found it unpleasant, and avoided looking me in the eye. Coloured contact lenses solved the problem. I've worn them since my late teens.'

'So your eyes are actually blue?'

'Yes. Unfortunately that's the shade that shows up coloboma particularly well. So I live in disguise. Hardly anyone knows my dark secret, or rather my pale blue secret, but you exposed it. Bravo, Miss Holmes.'

After coffee Laura finally gets the chance to catch up with Peter.

'Are you having a good time?'

'Absolutely. Steph is charming. By now I know more or less everything about you.'

'Like what?'

'That you keep the company going more or less single-handed, in spite of a manipulative mother, a freeloading younger brother and an ex-husband who refuses to let go. That you haven't had a holiday for years.'

'I see.'

The description is so accurate that she can't help blushing and smiling at the same time.

'Steph said something about germophobia, but after seeing you rummaging around at Gärdsnäset, I told her you must have got over it.'

Laura grabs a drink from the tray of a passing waiter. She thinks she recognises him as one of the star boys from earlier.

'The fact is I'm taking some time off right now. I've dragged my brother Marcus out of the blind spot and made him do some work.'

She makes a gesture to illustrate what she means, and spills some of her drink. Peter catches both the glass and her hand. Holds onto her hand.

'I'm glad you invited me,' he says.

Laura empties her glass, then gives in to a sudden impulse.

'I think Iben was murdered,' she says. 'I think someone wanted to stop her from revealing what was going on at Källegården. And I think Hedda was murdered for the same reason.'

She sees Peter's smile fade. At first, she doesn't understand why – not until he lets go of her hand.

'Sorry, I didn't mean . . . I'm glad you're here. Very glad.'

Peter turns away.

'We're missing the dancing,' he says tersely.

58

Laura was expecting a live band, but instead there's a DJ. A dozen couples are already dancing in front of the stage. The women's jewellery sparkles by the light of the crystal chandeliers, and at one side of the room a bartender is busy mixing cocktails. Laura tries to find a way of convincing Peter that she didn't invite him here to talk about the fire or Iben, but before she comes up with anything Heinz appears out of nowhere.

'Excuse me,' he says to Peter. 'I'd like to ask my table companion to dance.'

Peter gives a brief nod and heads over to the bar, where Steph is holding court.

Laura doesn't really like dancing. She's never understood the appeal of pressing her body against that of a sweaty stranger in what is essentially a prolonged embrace, following a series of predetermined movements. Nor does she like the sensation of someone else's hand on her back.

Needless to say, however, her mother forced her to learn how to deliver some basic moves, at least.

Heinz steers them to a part of the room where the music allows them to talk to each other.

'So is he your boyfriend?' He nods in the direction of Peter, who has just sat down next to Steph.

'An old friend.'

'From your childhood?'

She can feel the warmth of his hand through her dress, on the scar, turns a fraction to try to shift it, but instead Heinz draws her closer.

'You're a very special woman, Laura.'

The expression brings her up short. She's heard it a number of times over the past week, always to describe Hedda.

'You deserve someone who realises how special you are,' he murmurs in her ear, pulling her even closer.

She looks at Peter, sees him watching them. Feels Heinz's lips brushing against her skin.

'Why don't we get out of here for a while, just you and me?'

Before she can answer, the music stops and Erica von Thurn takes over the microphone.

'Dear friends – how lovely to see you all here. My darling Pontus has been working on the renovation of the castle for several years, and it's high time we celebrated his achievements!'

She blows her husband a kiss, and Laura think she sees a flash of irritation cross Heinz's face.

'If you could make your way out onto the terrace, I have a little surprise for Pontus. Don't worry about the cold – there are blankets, and plenty of champagne!'

The glass doors are flung open. Outside there are a dozen or so fire baskets burning brightly, and the waiters and waitresses are ready with trays laden with glasses.

Heinz takes Laura's hand and leads her towards the doors. She looks for Peter, but there's no sign of him. The flames in the fire baskets are high, and she stays as far away from them as possible. Heinz wraps a blanket around her shoulders and passes her a glass of champagne. The girl holding the tray is the one who represented St Lucia earlier. Laura tries to avoid looking at her.

Roughly a hundred metres away on the snow-covered lawn halfway between the castle and the lake, two figures wearing head torches are moving back and forth. Laura can just make out some kind of frame that has been set up, presumably for a firework display.

Erica leads her husband to the balustrade.

'Darling Pontus,' she declaims. 'I know how much you love the castle and its history. You like to tell the story of its inauguration in 1712, when an overenthusiastic and intense canon salute set fire to the roof.'

'Seventeen thirteen!' Pontus shouts, making everyone laugh.

'Whatever,' Erica responds. 'I would like to offer you your very own little salute – hopefully a less dangerous one. *Skål*, my love.'

She clinks glasses with her husband, then picks up a torch from the balustrade and flashes the beam twice in the direction of the lawn. Seconds later the sky explodes in a huge firework display. Laura is standing right next to the von Thurns; she sees Pontus's eyes shining, sees Erica tuck her arm beneath his. At the same moment she feels Heinz's hand on her hip, then it slides further down.

She moves it away, but as soon as she lets go, the hand is back. This time the grip is tighter, more determined.

She turns to face him, receives a teasing smile in response. He says something, but the noise of the fireworks and the oohs and aahs of the audience drown out his voice.

He puts his arm around her, pulls her close, presses his lips to hers.

She pushes him away, but he simply makes another attempt. Everyone is gazing up at the sky, so no one notices anything amiss.

He grabs her wrist tightly – it hurts.

Laura puts down her glass and tries to free herself, but he seizes her other hand too. He looks amused, as if they're playing a game. The explosions overhead turn into a rattling bombardment. Flashes of bright colours are reflected in Heinz's eyes, the shadows making his face look eerie. She twists her hands around towards his thumbs, yanks hard and manages to escape his grasp. His smile stiffens, his expression hardens. At that moment the firework display comes to an end, and the guests on the terrace break into spontaneous applause, cheers and whistling. Laura quickly steps to one side so that there are people between her and Heinz, then looks around for Peter once more.

Suddenly there is a loud, piercing scream that silences everyone. All eyes turn to the lawn and the two pyrotechnics experts, but they are looking in the direction of the lake. The door of the boathouse has opened and someone staggers out, the clothing on its upper body on fire. Huge flames come shooting out of the doorway.

Laura's legs almost give way; she holds onto the stone balustrade to stop herself from collapsing. The burning figure throws itself down onto the snow and rolls over and over, dousing the flames.

The two men on the lawn run towards the boathouse, but a sudden flash of light stops them in their tracks. It is followed by an explosion and a heat wave that makes Laura instinctively cover her face with her arms. When she looks up, the boathouse is ablaze. The person in the snow is on their feet, limping towards the edge of the forest before disappearing among the trees.

Laura's pulse is racing, the scar on her back wriggling and jumping so wildly that she thinks she can feel the blanket over her shoulders moving. She turns away, sinks down, leaning against the balustrade. The glow of the fire lights up the people around her. Steph is close by, next to Erica and Pontus. Her mouth is open, her expression one of shock. Pontus looks the same. His wife, however, appears to be neither shocked nor afraid. Instead, her face betrays excitement, fascination.

Someone grabs Laura's arm and pulls her to her feet. She thinks it must be Heinz, gathers her strength to push him away yet again, but it's Peter. Any trace of anger is gone.

'Come on!' he says, gently placing his arm around her waist. He steers her through the crowd, past terrified guests. The girl who represented St Lucia is right by the door, rigid with shock. The fire is reflected in her eyes, and for a second she reminds Laura of Iben.

Peter quickly guides Laura through the castle and out to his car in the car park. He settles her in the passenger seat, starts the engine, turns up the heat and wraps the blanket more securely around her. Then he spends a minute or so on his phone before getting in and driving off.

'Sandberg and his team are on their way,' he says. 'They'll want to interview all the witnesses at the scene, but he's happy for us to leave, given our ... history. There's nothing to be gained by making either you or me experience that whole circus all over again. I've told them which way the suspect went; it shouldn't be too difficult for them to track him down.'

Laura doesn't have the strength to answer; she merely nods.

At the end of the long avenue they meet a police car and three fire engines, followed by an ambulance. By this stage the temperature inside the car is well over twenty degrees, but Laura is still shivering. Memories flicker past her mind's eye, both old and new, in a cycle that is played over and over again, always with the same image: the burning figure screaming as it staggers out of the boathouse.

'Do you think it was Tomas?' she asks as they approach the village.

Peter doesn't answer, but she can see from the set of his jaw that he has come to the same conclusion.

'Why would he do that?' she says.

He shakes his head. 'I've no idea. If it was him, of course. There are others who have a problem with the owners of the castle . . .'

He pauses for a few seconds – long enough for her to work out what he's going to say.

'. . . and with you.'

'The Jensens. Do you really think they're that desperate?'

'Ulf Jensen is used to getting what he wants, and the farm is at risk. Then there's his family name, his reputation . . .'

Laura thinks about Fredrik again, the bandage on his hand, which according to Christian was due to a mishap with a firework. Fredrik was also the one who discovered the fire at the Jensens' farm. She pictures him with burning clothes, throwing himself down on the snow outside the boathouse.

'Anyway, we should soon know,' Peter goes on. 'Whoever it was can't have got far.'

He turns onto his drive, presses a button on the instrument panel that opens both the gate and the garage door. As the headlights illuminate the inside of the garage, he brakes sharply.

'What's wrong?' Laura asks, but he doesn't reply. All the colour has drained from his face.

It takes a few seconds for her to realise what he's seen. Or to be more accurate – what he hasn't seen. Something that ought to be there, but isn't. A motocross bike that is slightly too big for a fifteen-year-old girl.

59

Peter leaps out of the car with Laura right behind him. He flings open the front door of the house, calling Elsa's name over and over again. There is no response.

His hands are shaking so much that he drops his phone at Laura's feet, and she has to help him call the number. The signal echoes through the silent, empty house. Twice, three times, four times. Then the call cuts off without going to voicemail.

'Shit, shit, shit,' Peter mutters, before trying again.

The signal rings out twice before the call is ended.

On the third attempt, voicemail kicks in immediately.

Laura places her hand gently on Peter's arm without saying anything. He looks up at her, his eyes filled with despair.

'It wasn't her,' Laura assures him as firmly as she can. 'It wasn't Elsa that we saw.'

'How can you know that?'

'I just do, OK?'

The scar on her back has stopped burning. She is calm, decisive in a way that she doesn't recognise.

'But what the fuck is she doing out? At night? And why isn't she answering her phone?'

'My phone has been playing up like that for almost two weeks. She's bound to be out at Gärdsnäset. There's hardly any coverage there. I'll drive, you keep trying.'

She holds out her hand for the car key. Peter stares at her for a few seconds, then nods and passes it over.

The car is easy to drive; it takes her only a couple of minutes to get used to it, even though she's wearing a big pair of boots she dug out of the closet in Peter's hallway. She feels stone-cold sober, but knows that she isn't. She silences the risk calculator in her brain by telling it that this is an emergency, and that Peter is barely capable of making a phone call, let alone driving a car. She shoots through Vedarp going as fast as she dares. The village is deserted. The temperature has climbed a little higher. She tries to peer over towards the eastern side of the lake where the glow of the fire ought to be clearly visible, but a damp mist rising from the ice obscures the view.

Peter keeps calling, but is put through to voicemail each time. Laura can hear him swearing quietly to himself.

His phone rings, which makes them both jump.

'Sandberg,' he murmurs before answering. After a brief conversation, he ends the call.

'No sign of the suspect. They've just brought in a dog, but they're at least thirty to forty minutes behind. The trail leads south alongside the lake. In the direction of Gärdsnäset.'

Laura puts her foot down as they approach the turning for the holiday village, skidding as she takes the bend.

'Look!' Peter calls out.

The tyre tracks of a motorbike are clearly visible in the thin layer of wet snow on the road.

'Faster!'

The car bounces over the potholes as they follow the narrow tyre tracks through the archway, up to the yard in front of Hedda's house. They continue past the steps leading up to the boathouse, then along the path towards Alkärret.

Laura doesn't even slow down. Low-growing bushes scrape the windows, the car bounces into a deep hole, then another, then comes up just in time for a thick tree branch to rip off the left wing mirror.

Peter hardly seems to notice. He points ahead into the darkness, where something is reflecting the lights of the car.

'There!'

The headlights pick out an overturned motocross bike. Laura slams on the brakes, just managing to avoid a rock sticking up in the middle of the path.

Peter is already out of the car. He slips and falls, which gives Laura the chance to catch up with him. The bike is on its side, wheels in the air, as if someone has tossed it aside. Beyond it, next to the stone wall and at the bottom of the steep steps leading across to Alkärret, a dark figure is lying on the ground. Laura inhales sharply, but then another figure detaches itself from the shadows.

'Elsa!' Peter and Laura shout simultaneously.

The girl's face is chalk-white, she has blood and soot on her clothes and she is clutching her mobile phone.

'I've tried to ring, over and over again. He needs help!'

As Peter wraps his arms around his daughter, Laura hurries over to the person on the ground. She is met by a disgusting, familiar stench that makes her stomach contract.

The man is barely conscious. Most of his hair and beard are gone, the skin on his head and face is pink and blistering.

'Laura . . .' he croaks through burned lips. He reaches up to her; astonishingly, his hand is undamaged. She takes it, crouches down beside him.

'Oh, Tomas,' she says, tears pouring down her cheeks. 'What have you done?'

He looks at her with pleading eyes.

'I did what she asked me to do . . .'

'Who?'

Tomas shakes his head. His eyelids are growing heavy, while the skin on his face seems to be living a life of its own.

Out of the corner of her eye Laura sees Peter clamber up onto the wall to try and get a signal.

'Who asked you, Tomas?' she whispers close to the spot where his right ear used to be.

'The nymph,' he whispers back, before slowly closing his eyes.

60

Peter has settled Elsa in the back seat of the car, switched on the heater and wrapped her in the blanket Laura brought with her from the castle.

Meanwhile, Laura is standing a few metres away with Sandberg. The ambulance took Tomas away a few minutes ago, blue lights flashing; his injuries are serious. On the ground where he lay are several empty plastic bags that contained needles, electrodes and intubation tubes.

'You're like some kind of reverse moth,' Sandberg says. 'Flames are drawn to you instead of the other way round.' He laughs at his own joke. 'Anyway, let's hope that's the last of the fires. Poor bastard.'

The final two words sound surprisingly sympathetic.

'What was Larsson's girl doing out here?'

'Riding her motocross bike.'

'In the middle of the night?'

The calmness Laura felt earlier is still with her.

'Apparently, she goes out when Peter isn't home.'

'Why here?'

'Plenty of space, no nosy neighbours to call the police or tell her dad.'

Sandberg seems to accept the explanation.

'We'll need to talk to her, of course, but it can wait until tomorrow. Tomas Rask is going nowhere. Did he say anything to you?'

'He wasn't making much sense, but he mumbled that some-one had asked him to start the fire.'

'Who?' Sandberg leans forward, interested.

'The nymph.'

'The nymph?'

His eyes narrow.

'That's what he said.'

'And what do you think he meant by that?'

'I've no idea.' She shrugs. 'As soon as I've worked it out, I promise I'll be in touch.'

She meets his gaze, and for a few moments they stand there in the semi-darkness, glaring at each other. Then Sandberg lets out a snort, turns on his heel and marches towards his car, mut-tering something she can't quite hear.

Peter winds down the window. Elsa's head is resting on his shoulder; she seems to have fallen asleep.

'What did Sandberg say?'

'That the interview with Elsa could wait – Tomas isn't going anywhere.'

'OK, good. In that case we'll go home. You're very welcome to stay the night with us if you like. In the guest room,' he adds unnecessarily.

Laura thinks about the castle, the smell of smoke. She looks at Elsa.

'Yes please,' she says.

She follows them in her own car. One of the scene-of-crime officers, or maybe it was Peter, has kindly washed off the blood, but the usual feeling of safety the car gives her is no longer there. She can still see poor George, and Tomas's badly burned body. How did he manage to drag himself all the way to Gärdsnäset? And why?

She thinks she knows the answer to the second question. He was frightened and hurt, so he made for a place that he associated with security.

Peter carries Elsa up to her room, giving Laura the chance to speak to Steph, who has called several times, and explain what's happened.

'I'm so sorry you've been dragged into all this, Steph.'

'No problem – I'll survive.'

She sounds composed, but it's clear that even Steph has been affected by tonight's events.

'How are things at the castle?'

'The fire is out, but there are still plenty of firefighters running around. Not quite as hunky as in the movies, unfortunately.'

Laura can't help smiling. 'And how are Erica and Pontus bearing up?'

'Pontus is in shock. He was on oxygen for a while, which sent Erica into hysterics. She kept screaming that he was going to die and all kinds of other crap, but Heinz managed to calm her down. Most of the guests have either gone back to their rooms, or are helping me polish off Pontus's second-best whisky in the drawing room.'

'I'm spending the night here. Peter has a spare room.'

'Good call – things are crazy around here. Sleep well and I'll speak to you tomorrow. Say hi to Peter from me – I kind of liked him.'

The guest room is in the basement. There is plenty of space for a double bed and a giant TV, and it has its own bathroom. Everything is so well designed that it feels like a hotel.

'There are towels, a toothbrush and toothpaste in the bathroom cabinet,' Peter informs her. He has taken off his jacket, undone his bow tie and unbuttoned his shirt. He is lean and fit, with an impressive six-pack. She finds this unexpectedly attractive.

'By the way,' he goes on, 'I meant to tell you earlier – I ran a search on Milla and called a guy I know in social services, who checked their archive. Apparently, she never showed up at her new placement in Värmland.'

'That doesn't really surprise me – she really didn't want to go there. So what happened?'

'She was listed as missing for a month or so, but as soon as she turned eighteen that no longer applied. I've searched every database, but she doesn't appear anywhere after that. The tax office transferred her to the "non-existent" register at the beginning of the 1990s, and that's that.'

'She did talk about moving overseas,' Laura says. 'She had her passport ready, and she'd been putting some money aside.' She considers telling him how Milla acquired her savings, but decides it can wait until tomorrow.

They stand there for a few seconds, as if each is waiting for a signal from the other, then the moment is gone.

'Goodnight,' Peter says.

'Goodnight.'

61

Laura sleeps fitfully, dreams of the boathouse in flames, Tomas's whispered words.

She asked me to do it, he says, stretching out a hand with pink, bubbling skin and pointing over her shoulder, just as Iben did in her previous nightmare.

When Laura looks around, she sees a line of women standing behind her.

Peter's wife in her white wedding dress, and an older woman that she knows, the way you do only in dreams, must be Iben's mother, Sofia.

Milla, with her hood up. Then two faces Laura hadn't expected to see.

Erica von Thurn with her intense, fascinated gaze, and beside her the Lucia-girl who resembled Iben, the fire still dancing in her eyes.

Before she can work out what they're doing in her dream, she wakes up needing to pee. She pads into the bathroom. The house is dark and silent.

It's five to seven and she's slept for only a few hours, but she can't get back to sleep. After tossing and turning for a little while, she decides she might as well get up.

She puts on her clothes. Her dress is crumpled, her high-heeled shoes are up in the hallway where she kicked them off and changed into boots. Her tights are laddered.

She checks her phone, discovers an email she missed yesterday. It's from Ola in the office.

Hi, Laura,

You never called back about that check you asked me to run, so I'm emailing you instead. Jensen & Sons are on the verge of bankruptcy. They've been on their knees for years, and have acquired enormous debts. There's a property listed as part of the company, Källegården 12:1, which is mortgaged to the hilt.

Vintersjöholm Development isn't exactly stable either. A huge amount of money has been spent on renovating a castle, Vintersjöholm 1:1, over the past few years, with no actual income.

At the moment there are two cases with a debt collection agency – tradesmen who haven't been paid for work done on the castle. There is some money in the bank, so to speak, but if they don't get a decent injection of cash very soon, they're heading in the same direction as Jensen & Sons.

Give me a call if you want any more info.

Laura sits on the bed, staring at her phone. She already knew that the Jensens were in trouble. Vintersjöholm, however, is another matter. Then again, her whole visit, including the Lucia party, has been peppered with little clues that the castle's finances are not as good as Erica and Pontus would like to pretend. So how can they offer almost four hundred thousand more than the council for Gärdsnäset? Erica even said that they were prepared to raise their bid.

If the von Thurns had money to spare, then surely they would have spent it on finishing off the renovations to Pontus's beloved castle instead of buying more land that won't provide an income for years. So where is the money coming from?

She emails Ola asking him to find out if there are any other investors involved in Vintersjöholm Development.

Then she switches on the light and tiptoes into the corridor. The stairs are on the left, but instead she heads to the right, feeling the same tingle of excitement as she did when she was cleaning the cabins in the holiday village as a teenager. Moving around someone else's house, almost as if she were invisible. Crossing the line, doing something that wasn't allowed, yet with the perfect excuse.

The smell of detergent is getting stronger. The laundry room is on the right – two washing machines, two tumble dryers, plus a mangle and the kind of professional iron that she's only seen in a dry cleaner's.

At least ten identical white shirts are hanging on a rail, along with the same number in pale blue. Peter seems to like an organised, orderly life, as she does.

She continues along the corridor, passing a home gym that must measure some twenty-five square metres, with mirrors along one wall. In the middle of the room is a martial arts training dummy on a black base. The dummy's head is battered, as if someone has given it a beating every day for several years.

At the end of the corridor there is a closed door. Laura expects it to be locked, but to her surprise it opens easily. The light switch is just inside.

She sees rows of cheap pine IKEA shelves. On some are neatly labelled boxes: CHRISTMAS, EASTER, MIDSUMMER. But most of the shelves are empty, as if someone recently had a clear-out.

She realises that the room reminds her of her own basement storage unit. The place where she keeps painful memories in a box with the lid firmly on, under lock and key.

There is a strong smell of paint and glue. A large desk is covered with a green felt cloth, and in the middle is a model ship. She moves closer. It's a pirate ship, and on the deck are seven small figures dressed in fairly modern clothes that don't match the period. It takes Laura a few seconds to work out what she's looking at.

One-eyed Willy's ship, with the whole Goonies gang on deck. Mikey, Mouth, Data, Chunk, Brandon, and the girls – Andy and Stef. She can't help smiling. She must have seen the film a dozen times, along with Peter, Tomas, Jack and Iben – all watching the pirate copy that Peter's uncle had somehow acquired.

Happy days, long before disaster struck.

The ship must have taken hundreds of hours to build and paint, and yet Peter keeps it here, down in the basement.

She moves over to the shelves lining the walls, where more models are displayed. Most are planes, like the one in Peter's office, but one particular model attracts her attention.

It's a car that has crashed into a tree. The front has crumpled into a U-shape, and one of the passengers, a blonde woman, has gone straight through the windscreen and is sprawled over the bonnet. There is blood on her pale dress. Laura bends down to take a closer look. A man is sitting in the driver's seat. His head is crushed, his facial features barely distinguishable, and in one place the skull is grinning through. Small yellow flames have sprung up around the petrol tank, and even though they're plastic and not remotely dangerous, she breaks out into a sweat.

The model represents Peter's wife and her lover.

Laura straightens up. She has a horrible feeling that she's intruded into something extremely private, something she definitely shouldn't have seen.

She steps back and is about to leave the room when she catches sight of a model on another table.

She recognises this one right away. The domed roof, the boarded-up windows. The tall, straight trees. The ice extending into the distance. It's the dance hall at Gärdsnäset. Fascinated, she goes over and lifts off the roof. The inside of the hall is an almost exact replica of her own memories. The stacked-up furniture, the tables, the folding chairs, the tape player, the bottles of booze they stole when they broke into the cottage. A drop of sweat trickles down her spine.

Two figures are sitting at the small table. The boy is leaning forward, as if he's trying to kiss the red-haired girl. She, on the other hand, is leaning back, rejecting his approach. Maybe it's her imagination, but Laura thinks she can see the distaste on the girl's face.

She is the girl, Peter is the boy.

She shudders.

But there are more figures inside the dance hall. In one corner behind the piles of furniture a boy is slumped, with little plastic flames all around his hands. She doesn't need to look any closer to know that this is Tomas.

Iben is there too, looking in the mirror in the toilet behind the stage. Her dark hair is pulled back in a tight ponytail.

Outside among the trees, two figures are standing side by side, watching. One has a large dressing on his forehead, the other's hood is pulled up.

'The moment before the catastrophe,' she murmurs to herself. She reaches out and gently touches Jack with her fingertips.

'What the hell are you doing?'

Laura spins around. She was so absorbed in the model that she didn't hear Peter coming. He is wearing his dressing gown and slippers and would look quite sweet if it weren't for the expression on his face. Pure rage.

'You have no right to snoop around in here!' he shouts. Laura instinctively holds up her hands.

'I wasn't snooping.'

This is clearly a lie, and Peter knows it.

'Get out!' he yells. 'Get out of my house!'

His face is white with fury, his fists opening and closing. Laura thinks about the training dummy in the gym, the fact that someone has delivered thousands of blows to its face. Someone filled with pent-up anger. Years and years of humiliations and hurt feelings.

She lowers her hands.

'I'm so sorry, Peter. You're right, it was wrong of me. I'll leave immediately.'

She quickly walks past him and heads for the door without looking at him. Suppresses a sudden urge to run towards the staircase.

Peter doesn't follow her. He stays where he is, and as she is about to set off up the stairs she thinks she hears him let out a sob.

62

Gärdsnäset is silent and peaceful once more. All that remains of last night's drama is a series of tyre tracks criss-crossing the yard. The temperature has risen, making the mist thicken over the lake and hiding the black eye in the middle.

It is beginning to grow light, and some of the crows who are early risers greet her with raucous cries.

She unlocks the door, switches on the lights and is met by the familiar smell of dust, dirt and loneliness. She almost calls out to George, but stops herself at the last minute. The George dynasty at Gärdsnäset is over. The thought makes her sad.

She makes tea and sits down at the kitchen table, trying to process the events of last night and this morning.

It's obvious that Peter is just as much of a mess as she is. He deals with his grief by methodically recreating key moments from his life. The car crash and the dance hall were already finished, but he was still working on the ship. A happier project than the others. Does that mean anything? She hopes so, for Peter's sake. And Elsa's.

She decides to call him from Hedda's phone to apologise once again for overstepping the mark, but when she picks up the receiver, there is no dial tone. Presumably the phone bill was in one of the envelopes Hedda decided to ignore. Or maybe all the dust she and Elsa have churned up has made the old phone breathe its last.

Mobile coverage is as patchy as ever, so she makes do with a text. Sits and stares at the screen while her phone slowly sends the message.

So what now? Is she going to sell to the castle? Let Pontus and Erica turn the lake into a playground for their rich friends? Or trust the council to keep their lukewarm promise not to employ Ulf Jensen and his sons?

She takes a sip of her tea, contemplates Hedda's noticeboard. Her aunt struggled with exactly the same dilemma; that was why she set everything out in one place. To give her an overview.

The contracts, the letter from Tomas, the notes someone destroyed. The black feather from a *cygne noir*, which Laura has put back in its place at the top of the board. It must have symbolised Iben's secret, the unbelievable, terrible thing that had gone on right in front of them. Ulf Jensen had abused his daughter for years without anyone noticing. And since then he has played the grieving father for thirty years; he even persuaded the council to rename the school in honour of his victim.

The thought enrages her. She can't sell to the council, can't risk helping Ulf Jensen in any way. At the same time, selling to the castle doesn't feel right either.

And several mysteries still remain.

It seems likely that Tomas was behind the fires. He didn't exactly lack motive: he loathed his father, he loved Iben, and he knew what Ulf had done to her. Maybe he was the one who'd killed those sheep over at Alkärret all those years ago, a silent way of hitting back. But why would he try to frame her for the fires?

Tomas wasn't a planner; he did as he was told.

So who was the nymph who had persuaded Tomas to start fires wherever Laura had been?

Who planted the petrol can and the insulating material in the boathouse?

Who killed George?

And what about Hedda's death? Was it because of the Jensen family's secrets that she died out there in the cold water, or was there another reason? One that Laura hadn't yet worked out?

Who is behind the von Thurns' bid for Gärdsnäset, since they clearly don't have the funds themselves?

There are several people in the area who have money and a possible interest – Johnny Miller, for example. But why hide behind Vintersjöholm Development?

Laura sits down and tips out Hedda's old photographs on the coffee table in front of her. For want of a better idea, she decides to sort them into piles.

Hedda and Johnny Miller, along with pictures of their love child Jack Olsson, who wasn't Prince Charming but was in fact her cousin.

Another pile for pictures of herself and Hedda, a third for the Goonies gang.

She finds two photos stuck together, and carefully separates them. Jack and Milla by his car – standing at little too close to each other? They both left the area at about the same time, and they are both listed as no longer resident in Sweden.

And yet it has never occurred to her that they might have gone away together. Not until now.

The realisation makes her go cold all over. She replays all the memories she can dredge up of Jack and Milla – gestures, tone of voice, words. One memory grows clearer and clearer. She is sitting by her window, watching a female figure among the trees. A figure who ran from Jack's apartment towards cabin number six.

Can it be true? Did Jack and Milla fool them all? She doesn't want to believe it.

But if it's true, what does that mean?

She stares at the photograph. She hasn't seen Milla's face for thirty years. It looks the same as she remembers it – but somehow it doesn't. She screws up her eyes, tries to imagine that face thirty years older. After cosmetic surgery, maybe.

She hears the sound of a car engine and glances out of the window to see Ulf Jensen's white pickup truck pull up in the yard, accompanied by the crows' cacophony of warning cries.

She considers locking the door, but all the lights are on and her car is parked outside. Instead, she picks up her phone and sends a quick text to Peter and Steph.

Am at Gärdsnäset. Jensens are here, please come!

She presses send, watches the little symbol slowly move sideways, then slips the phone into her pocket. She looks out of the window again; Fredrik has Christian with him, which makes her feel a little better.

She definitely doesn't want them in the house, so she puts on her jacket and meets them on the porch.

'Hi, Laura,' Christian says. 'We heard what happened last night and we just wanted to check that everything is OK out here.'

'Everything's fine, thank you.'

She stays where she is, making it clear that she's not inviting the brothers in. The crows are still making an enormous racket, flapping their wings and hurling themselves out of the trees on short forays.

'So Tomas Rask really was back in the area,' Christian goes on.

'Yes.'

'The fucker got what he deserved at last,' Fredrik says with a scornful smile. 'It's high time he paid for what he did to Iben.'

'You mean as opposed to what your father did to her?'

Laura regrets the comment immediately, but it's too late. Fredrik leaps up the steps and grabs her.

'What the fuck are you talking about, you little bitch?'

His strong fingers dig into her upper arm.

'Fredrik,' Christian says warningly, but he does nothing to stop his brother. Fredrik pushes his face close to hers. The crows crank up the volume.

'Say that again,' he hisses, emitting a fine spray of saliva. 'Say that again if you dare!'

Laura tries to remain calm, but it's impossible not to be afraid. Fredrik is built like a bull, a vein is throbbing at his temple and his teeth are bared as if he's about to bite her.

'We've brought some papers with us – and a big bag of cash that will be yours as soon as you sign on the dotted line, like a good girl.'

'And if I refuse?' She makes a huge effort to sound confident.

Fredrik grins, exchanges a glance with his brother.

'What Fredrik is trying to explain is that we'd very much like you to sign,' Christian says, joining his brother on the porch. 'I've already told you what a difficult position we're in, and to be perfectly honest, it's the least you can do. Fredrik recognised your voice. It was you who phoned Källegården that night, you who set the wheels in motion. If it hadn't been for you, Iben might still be alive today.'

Laura has thought the same thing a thousand times, but still his words hit her like a punch to the stomach.

'I . . .' she begins, but she can't look either of them in the eye.

Christian produces a rolled-up document from his inside pocket.

'So how about we go inside and get this sorted once and for all, little Laura? In a nice, friendly way. After all, Hedda promised to sell to us back in the autumn, before that bitch from the castle turned up and put ideas in her head.'

He moves behind her, opens the door wide with a welcoming gesture.

'By the way,' he adds, 'didn't you used to have a cat? Fredrik said he'd seen you making a fuss of it. You seemed very fond of the poor little thing.'

Out of the corner of her eye she sees Fredrik grinning broadly.

Suddenly, she is incandescent with rage, and that rage gives her courage.

'You know what, Christian? You can take your fucking papers and shove them up your arse. Or even better, shove them up your incestuous paedophile of a father's arse. You and Freddie here must have made a hell of an effort not to see what he was doing to your sister. Or maybe he had a go at you too? Is that why you're still so scared of him? Slinking along by the walls like terrified—'

The blow comes so fast that she doesn't have time to defend herself. Christian punches her in the face so hard that her head jerks back; there is a loud, whining sound in her ears, mingled with the warning cries of the crows and the sound of black flapping wings as they take off from the treetops.

'Fucking bitch,' Christian hisses, raising his hand again. 'Hold onto her, Fredrik. It's time she got what she deserves . . .'

Fredrik locks her arms from behind. Laura tries to break free, but she has no chance. She aims a kick at Christian's crotch, but there is no strength in it. She closes her eyes, waits for the next blow.

Instead, a car comes racing into the yard, stopping Christian in his tracks. Laura hopes it's Peter, but instead the vehicle has the Vintersjöholm logo on the side. It screeches to a halt, the door flies open. Steph gets out and runs towards them. She is wearing a cap with earflaps, pulled well down over her forehead, and for some reason she is also wearing sunglasses. Her hands are pushed deep into the pockets of her oversized jacket. Fredrik alters his grip, but keeps hold of one of Laura's upper arms.

'Two big boys and one little girl,' Steph says acidly. 'Are you sure you can manage?'

'Stay out of this,' Fredrik snaps. 'We're just having a chat, aren't we, Laura?'

He squeezes her arm and she winces with the pain.

'They want me to sign the contract selling Gärdsnäset to the council,' she groans, still trying to twist free.

'Do they indeed,' Steph says, stopping at the bottom of the steps. She still has her hands in her pockets, as if she's out for a brisk walk in the forest. She turns her head towards Fredrik, then Christian.

'Didn't your daddy tell you that men don't hit girls?' she says quietly. 'Oh no, sorry. Your daddy abused them instead. By the way, was it all girls, or just the ones he was related to?'

Christian slowly moves down the steps.

'Get back in your fucking car and disappear,' he says.

Steph doesn't move a muscle.

Christian reaches out to grab her jacket. Steph takes one hand out of her pocket and pushes it into Christian's chest. There is a loud crack, like a whiplash but followed by an electrical rever-beration. Christian drops to the ground as if he's been felled by a hammer, lies in the slush with his arms and legs twitching uncontrollably.

Steph holds up an object that resembles an electric shaver with two prongs at one end. She presses a button, producing another crack and making a blue flame shoot out between the prongs.

'Let go of my friend,' she says quietly.

Fredrik doesn't react. His mouth is hanging open as if he can't work out what the hell is going on.

Steph crouches down, pushes the taser into Christian's crotch and fires again. He rolls up into a trembling ball.

'Didn't you hear me? Or would you like me to lobotomise your brother?'

She holds the taser an inch or two from Christian's temple.

Laura feels the grip on her arm loosen. She takes a couple of steps away from Fredrik, who remains standing there with his hands dangling by his sides, a confused expression on his face.

'Pick him up and fuck off,' Steph says. Her voice has a sharp-ness that Laura has never heard before.

Fredrik does as he's told. With some difficulty he manages to get his brother on his feet and drags him over to the truck. Christian can barely stand. He whimpers faintly as Fredrik bun-dles him into the passenger seat.

Fredrik starts the car and spins it around, revving the engine. Gives them the finger as he skids away along the slushy track with a screech of tyres.

Steph puts the taser back in her pocket.

'There you go,' she says. 'Now, how about a cup of coffee? Or preferably something stronger, if your aunt has anything along those lines tucked away.'

63

They are sitting at the kitchen table. Steph has laced their tea with the schnapps she managed to find in one of the kitchen cupboards. Laura shows her the noticeboard, tells her about her fresh discoveries, but once again she leaves out Hedda, Johnny Miller and Jack. She's still not sure why.

The schnapps makes her feel warm and slightly nauseous at the same time; she is also experiencing a strange sense of elation. It's good to share her thoughts at long last, to have someone who is one hundred per cent on her side.

'Where the hell did you get the taser?'

'I brought it back from the USA. To be honest, I nearly always carry it with me, just in case. If anyone asks I say it's a vibrator. Works every time.' She points to the noticeboard. 'So you think those two gorillas and their disgusting father murdered your aunt because she wouldn't sign?'

'Yes.'

After the events of the last few minutes that conclusion seems inescapable. Or maybe not.

Laura picks up the photograph of Milla and looks at it again. Finds the magnifying glass and once again tries to imagine her thirty years older, maybe after cosmetic surgery.

There's definitely a resemblance.

'What do you actually know about Erica von Thurn?' she asks. 'Apart from the fact that she's from Switzerland and is married to Pontus.'

'Not much . . . I know her through Pontus. As I said before, she and Heinz are old school friends, and I think she's probably sleeping with him. Why do you ask?'

Steph pulls off her cap and pushes her sunglasses up on top of her head.

Laura takes a deep breath.

'Because I think Erica could be Milla.'

Steph looks shocked.

'Milla? The girl who was involved in the fire? The psychopath?'

Laura nods.

'She's had cosmetic surgery, changed her hair colour. Her age and height fit, and her character. Milla was very good at transforming herself, becoming the person others wanted her to be. She also dreamed of travelling to Berlin. Germany, Switzerland – they're pretty close, and Erica's Swedish is suspiciously good for someone who learned it as an adult.'

She pursues her train of thought.

'And I thought of something else. Milla and Jack could have left together. His last postcard to Hedda was sent from Berlin. If Milla's back, then Jack could be here too.'

'Prince Charming? Are you saying he might be Heinz?'

'I thought so for a while, but then something happened at the party, during the firework display.'

'What?'

'He tried to kiss me, and it felt so wrong. Heinz isn't Jack.'

'So where is Jack?'

'I don't know. Still lying low, I guess.'

Steph leans back and takes a sip of her tea, her expression serious now.

'What does all that mean for this place? What about the sale?'

'I'm going to wait until I've got a clearer picture of everything. I've asked my office to do an in-depth check on everyone connected with Vintersjöholm Development. False identities are hard to maintain. If there's the tiniest crack, we'll find it. And we'll find out where the money is coming from that the von Thurns are planning to use to buy Gärdsnäset.'

Steph puts down her cup.

'Are you saying you're not going to sell?'

'Not until I know the truth.'

Laura picks up the magnifying glass again, holds it over Milla's face and follows the contours. The position of the eyes in relation to each other, the distance between the cheekbones, the height of the hairline.

'You have to sell,' Steph says.

Her voice sounds different. Laura looks up, realises that Steph hasn't spoken Swenglish for a long time. She has pushed her sunglasses so far up that they have stretched the skin of her forehead. Something clicks in Laura's mind. Steph, whom she feels she's known much longer than she actually has. Steph, who has always been slightly too blonde, slightly too loud, slightly too attractive. Steph, who speaks such exaggerated Swenglish that Laura has always suspected it was a game. A disguise so over-the-top that it can't possibly be a disguise.

A disguise. A mask.

Her heart leaps into her throat.

'It's you!' she gasps. 'You're Milla!'

Steph raises her eyebrows, remains motionless for a second, then relaxes into a cool smile.

64

We are who we are, my princess. For good or evil . . .

They are still sitting at the kitchen table. Neither of them has moved or said anything for several minutes.

Laura feels seasick, as if the whole world all around her is bobbing up and down, and she can't find a fixed point to anchor her gaze.

'Jack . . .' she says eventually. 'Where is he?'

Steph – who is actually Milla – leans back and takes another sip of her tea.

'Dead.'

Laura's stomach contracts into an ice-cold, solid lump.

'How? When?'

'An overdose, summer 2013. We were living in New York. He'd struggled with his addiction for a long time. He'd been in and out of various treatment facilities. For a while I thought he was going to make it; he was clean for years. But then he lost his way again.'

Laura can hardly breathe.

'Then I got the opportunity to move back to Sweden,' Steph goes on. 'Maybe I saw it as a sign, a chance to make another fresh start. The business community in Stockholm isn't that big; the fact that we bumped into each other was a coincidence. Well, nearly. I was curious about you. I wondered whether my disguise would fool you. After all, I'd spent almost thirty years honing it to perfection. I thought that if you didn't realise, then no one would. Our first meeting was meant to be a one-off. A test.'

Steph shrugs.

'But then I found that I liked you. I was pretty lonely; I hadn't yet built up a network of contacts in Sweden. You were in the middle of a divorce and needed someone to talk to.'

'The blind spot,' Laura murmurs.

'Sorry?'

'You moved into my blind spot while I was looking in a different direction. You stayed there the whole time, diagonally behind me so that I couldn't see you properly. Pretending to be my friend.'

Steph lowers her voice.

'There was no pretence, Laura. I was your friend. I *am* your friend.'

Laura shakes her head. She would really like to cover her ears with her hands, block out everything Steph is saying. Her head is full to the brim with memories, meetings, conversations, confidences they've shared. She feels as if her brain is about to explode, then it abruptly falls silent.

'Jack sometimes talked about you,' Steph says. 'I know he thought about you. Maybe that was another reason why I sought you out.'

'Jack was Hedda's son,' Laura snaps.

She doesn't really know why, perhaps she wants to show that she too has a secret to reveal – information Steph was unaware of concerning someone she cared about. It works. Steph looks shocked, which is a tiny, tiny consolation in the middle of all this.

'How do you know that?'

'I found a maternity unit bracelet among Hedda's things and worked out the dates. He was her and Johnny Miller's love child.'

'The troll who lived on the other side of the lake?'

'Yes. They met when they were young. Hedda fell pregnant and he dumped her, then he changed his mind and came after her. But by then it was too late – Hedda had already given Jack up.'

She runs out of breath; she has to pause, take deep breaths.

'When he was older she went looking for him and became his foster parent at Gärdsnäset.'

Steph still looks taken aback – and kind of upset.

'Do you think he knew?' Laura asks. 'That Hedda was his mother?'

Steph shakes her head.

'No. He cared about her, sent postcards so that she wouldn't worry.' She points to the noticeboard. 'But when we moved to the USA we decided that he should stop, so that our trail ended in Germany. I know it was hard for him.'

They both take a sip of their tea, which has grown cold.

'So you're one of the investors in Vintersjöholm Development?' Laura says quietly.

'The main investor.' Steph spreads her hands wide. 'I didn't want to say anything; I hoped everything would sort itself out. It still can.' She leans across the table. 'We can do this together, Laura. Sell to us and invest the money in the project.' Her tone is eager now. 'We can build something amazing. Name a road after Hedda.'

'And another after Iben?'

Steph gives a start.

'You do remember Iben, don't you?' Laura continues. 'The girl who burned to death because you asked Tomas to set fire to the dance hall? Because it was you who asked him, wasn't it? Just as you asked him to set fire to Kent Rask's barn and the accommodation block at Källegården, and to plant the petrol can in Jack's apartment. All to pressure me into selling.'

Steph doesn't answer, but there's no need. Laura knows she's right.

'I don't understand how you got him to do all that. After all, you'd only known each other for a few months before he burned down the dance hall. And why did he start the fire in the boathouse at Vintersjöholm last night?'

Steph looks away. Something in her expression and her body language has changed. It's as if the thought of Tomas bothers her.

'The boathouse was his own idea,' she mumbles. 'He did it to show that he was thinking of me.'

For a second something flickers behind the mask. Something familiar. And all at once there is another click in Laura's mind, considerably louder this time.

'The nymph,' Tomas whispers in her ear, his voice cracking. She looks up at Hedda's noticeboard. At the black swan's feather.

A present from the nymph, a *cygne noir*.

What does it mean, Aunt Hedda?

That nothing is impossible, my little princess. Not even the impossible.

Hedda was right. Because the impossible is sitting right in front of her.

'The troll on the other side of the lake,' Laura says slowly. 'Iben and I used to play that game when we were little. We fantasised about rowing across the water to steal his treasure so that we could live happily ever after. Because everything is so simple when you're a child, isn't it? All you need is some treasure, a castle and your best friend.'

Steph looks down at the floor.

'But Milla never played that game,' Laura goes on. 'She's never heard of the troll or his treasure.'

Steph raises her head, her eyes shining with tears. The colour is wrong, because she's wearing contact lenses. So is the skin tone and hair colour. Steph is fair-skinned and blonde.

And yet she is a black swan.

The impossible that is possible, in spite of everything. That makes the whole world shift on its axis, so that from this moment on nothing will ever be the same again.

'Iben,' Laura says. 'You can stop hiding now. I know it's you.'

65

'I presume this is all about your father.'

Laura is surprised at how calm she sounds. Her world has just imploded, everything she has believed for the past thirty years has been a lie. And yet her voice is steady, under control.

'You want revenge for what he did. You want to take Källegården away from him.'

'I don't want to take it away!' Steph's eyes flash with rage. 'I want to raze it to the ground. I don't want a single stone left standing of his beloved ancestral home. I want to plant fir trees everywhere until all that's left is a fucking Christmas tree plantation. And when the old man is on his deathbed, when the cancer has finally eaten its way through his black heart, I'm going to lean over him and tell him exactly who is responsible. The girl he's wept crocodile tears over for the past thirty years.'

She leans back. Her expression has changed again; it's much harder now.

'I tried to put it all behind me. Jack managed to persuade me to let go, move on. I studied hard, got myself some decent qualifications, a good job. Built up my CV, married a rich man, stashed away plenty of money. But now and again I couldn't help doing a little googling to see what was happening around Vintersjön. That was how I'd found out that they'd renamed the school after her. After me. As a way of honouring *him*!' Steph spits out the last word. 'That was when I decided I had to take my revenge, but it was a while before the right opportunity came up – the von Thurns bought the castle and started making plans for the area around the lake. At the same time, via a little discreet manipulation, I managed to get Jensen & Sons to invest in a golf course project which I then shut down. All that remained was to persuade Hedda to sell.'

'But she refused.'

'At first she wanted to sell to the council, but I called her one evening, disguised my voice, dropped a few hints about Källegården, told her that Tomas knew the truth. The thing is, I'd tried to tell Hedda what was going on a few days before the fire, but I just couldn't do it.'

She pauses, takes a deep breath.

'Anyway, Hedda contacted Tomas, just as I'd hoped. He'd always done what I asked him to do, ever since we were little, but it wasn't until he started killing Ulf's sheep that I realised there were no limits to what he was prepared to do for me.'

'Like lying about the fire? Or at least not giving away the fact that it was you who'd asked him to start it?'

Steph nods. 'Tomas loved me, and I loved him. He was the brother I should have had instead of those two apes.'

She gestures angrily in the direction of the yard, as if Christian and Fredrik were still out there.

'And yet you made sure he ended up in jail.'

'Not in jail. Tomas needed care, and that was what he got. Sooner or later he would have set fire to something else – a house, a school. People would have been killed or injured. He knew it too. Knew he needed to be locked up.'

It is Laura's turn to lean forward.

'So what actually happened that night?'

Steph shrugs.

'Milla and I took Jack into the toilet behind the stage. While we were in there, Milla said she knew what Ulf was doing to me – she'd had a foster father who did the same thing. At first I was shocked, then incredibly relieved. At last there was someone who understood what I was going through. I'd only just plucked up the courage to tell Jack.' She presses her lips together. 'But then Milla suggested we should use the information to blackmail Ulf, get money out of him and split it between us. A few thousand each – that's all my suffering was worth as far as she was concerned. When I refused, Milla said she'd do it off her own bat – she was leaving in a few days anyway. I realised what would happen. Ulf would know I'd told someone, and what he'd do to me afterwards didn't bear thinking about.'

She pauses, clears her throat.

'Both Jack and I begged her not to do it, but Milla just laughed at us. So we wrestled her to the floor, tried to shut her up, but she wouldn't stop laughing. She was crazy. Jack lost it completely. He grabbed her by the throat. And suddenly she went quiet . . .'

Steph takes another sip of cold tea.

'It was a pure accident, but of course we knew that we were completely fucked. After a few minutes I came up with a solution. Milla was about to turn eighteen, and already had a passport. We were about the same height, with the same colour hair and eyes. So we locked Milla's body in the toilet, I put on her hoodie, glasses and jewellery, and we sneaked back to her cabin and put a few streaks in my hair. Then I asked Tomas to start the fire.'

She catches Laura's eye, underlining the last sentence.

'The bar,' Laura says. 'Who dropped the bar?'

'Jack. He was afraid that one of you would open the door and see us heading for Milla's cabin, realise it was me and not Milla.

But then we forgot to tell Tomas to lift it up. No one was meant to get hurt, I swear. I stayed inside Milla's cabin, and the police officer who questioned me later that night just glanced at my passport to confirm my identity. Jack gave Milla – or rather me – an alibi, and as soon as Tomas had confessed and the police were no longer interested in Milla, we took off.'

'But first you broke into Källegården.'

Steph nods. 'We needed money and I knew where Dad' – she bites her lip – 'where Ulf hid the cash that didn't go through the books.'

'And you took your mother's jewellery.'

'Yes. Ulf tormented my mother. Drove her crazy and had her locked up in an asylum. I couldn't leave her jewellery with him.'

'And Jack?' Laura can't help asking.

'Jack loved me.' The answer comes a little too quickly; Steph seems to notice it herself. 'I understand now that he was Hedda's son. He'd inherited her appetite for drugs and booze. Did you know she used to run a moonshine ring with Kent Rask?'

'Yes, he told me.'

'No doubt he also told you that Ulf forced her to stop, but do you know why she agreed? Not because she was afraid of either Ulf or the police – she was terrified of you finding out. Or your parents. She didn't want them to stop you coming to visit. Her little princess.'

Hedda's words sound poisonous on Steph's lips.

'I decided early on that I was going to change. Not make do with pretending to be Milla for a while until we'd managed to get out of the country – I wanted to become a completely different person. Someone who'd never been anywhere near Vintersjön, never lived at Källegården and been subjected to Ulf's abuse. Someone who wasn't a victim.' Steph slowly shakes her head.

'Do you have any idea how much work it takes to reinvent yourself, change absolutely everything? Not only your appearance, speech, gestures, the way you move, but also the way you think. I did all of that, and yet it wasn't enough for Jack. Time doesn't heal all wounds.'

Her tone is bitter now.

'He never stopped pining for you. However much I changed, I was still damaged goods in Jack's eyes, and the woman who'd made him a murderer. I couldn't possibly compete with a perfect, snow-white little princess. So Jack sought refuge in the promised land of drugs, just like your aunt.'

She nods contemptuously in the direction of Hedda's sagging sofa.

'As time went on, the secrets poisoned our relationship almost as much as his addiction. I dumped him and married money a couple of times, as you already know. But Jack was my partner in crime, and I couldn't risk him returning to Sweden, so I took care of him. Made sure he got what he needed.'

'You mean the drugs he needed.'

Steph's enigmatic expression probably means yes.

'But then he decided to get clean, said he was going to sort out his life. I discovered that he'd been googling your name. It was only a matter of time before he got in touch, jeopardising everything I'd spent twenty-five years building up.'

Laura inhales sharply.

'So you killed him?'

'No. Jack decided to go for one last hit before he started his new life. I found him on the bathroom floor with the canula in his arm. He was fitting, foaming at the mouth.'

Laura tries not to picture him like that, but fails.

'You didn't bother calling an ambulance.'

'Jack wasn't himself anymore. You wouldn't have recognised him. He'd been using on and off for over twenty years. He had hepatitis, he was as thin as a rake. Believe me, it was for the best.'

Laura closes her eyes. Sees eighteen-year-old Jack. His smile, his eyes. The thought that he no longer exists is unbearable.

'It was you who deleted your voice from my phone,' she says.

Steph nods. 'It was easy. I've seen you enter the code a thousand times. I left the break-in at the police station to Tomas. I was a little worried about what that recording might lead to.'

'But why? Peter and I could have used it to nail Ulf.'

'A thirty-year-old recording of a dead girl's voice? The statute of limitations is up on all the crimes Ulf committed against me. And besides, I'm the one who's going to destroy Ulf. Destroy him completely, not with some kind of fucking half-measure that will end up with a shelved investigation.'

'And Hedda? What happened after Tomas told her about Ulf?'

'She agreed to sell to Vintersjöholm, just as I'd hoped – but then I made a mistake. I thought that if even you couldn't see through my disguise, then no one else would be able to. So I came down here with Heinz one day. By that time Hedda was in more or less the same state as the house. It was upsetting. She was once almost like a mother to me.'

She paused, shook her head.

'I'd underestimated Hedda; something during our meeting must have made her suspicious, because shortly after that she wrote to Tomas and asked him what he knew about me and Ulf. She started making excuses not to sign the contract, said she wanted to give the matter a little more thought. That was when I realised she'd seen right through me. I came back down and found her out on the pontoon.'

'You pushed her into the water,' Laura whispers.

'Hedda was never going to sell Gärdsnäset.'

'But you hoped you could manipulate me into doing so. After you'd killed Hedda.'

'I hadn't planned it. I tried to reason with her, make her understand, but she refused to listen.'

Steph looks away.

'Do you know what the worst thing was? She begged me to forgive her, because she hadn't understood what I was trying to tell her all those years ago, because she hadn't protected me from Ulf. She'd been too preoccupied with you to see what was happening to me.'

Steph's voice is pure steel, and Laura can't bear to listen to another word. She covers her eyes with her hands, tries not to think of Hedda's poor, damaged heart exploding in the cold water, but it's no good.

She hears the sound of a chair scraping across the floor. The rustle of a pocket.

She lowers her hands, is about to ask another question when a searing pain strikes her back. An electrical whiplash that makes the scar contract in pain, then wraps the whole world in merciful darkness.

66

As soon as Laura regains consciousness, she is aware that the house is on fire. She doesn't even need to register the smell, the heat, the crackling sound of the flames devouring all the flammable crap. Because she knows that this is the only logical conclusion for Steph. The only way she can win.

Steph, who has the same name as one of the two girls in the Goonies gang. It all seems so obvious now. The signs were there, but she didn't see them, even though it's her job. Because Steph was in her blind spot. Diagonally behind her, just out of sight.

Or maybe she just didn't want to look in that direction, because she wanted a friend. Was that it? Whatever the reason, she made the same mistake as everyone else, thinking only white swans existed. Everyone except Hedda.

She is lying on the floor in her old room. The smoke is already thick below the ceiling, gradually pressing down, and within a minute or so she will be forced to inhale it, deep into her lungs. Her body is still aching from the electric shock, the scar feels distorted, as if it has rolled itself into a ball at the top of her spine.

Her hands and feet are bound with ties made of sacking, which will burn up and leave no trace. A tragic accident in a house that was a serious fire hazard, that's how Steph has planned it all. But she's forgotten one thing. This is Laura's house, Laura's old bedroom. She wriggles over to the walk-in closet, then kneels with her back towards the door. Rips off the crumbling piece of foam rubber Hedda stuck there long ago to protect her shins, then moves the sacking tie up and down over the sharp corner as fast as she can.

The room is very warm now, it's becoming harder and harder to breathe, but she can't give up. She feels the fibres breaking, one by one. Her airway is constricted, she can't stop coughing.

More fibres give way and she tries to free her hands, but without success.

She hears a loud bang from the living room. The smoke is so dense that she can barely see the walls. The paint on the inside of the door is rapidly turning yellow, then brown. The door is about to catch fire.

Her wrists are hurting, she can feel blood on her palms. Her eyes are streaming, she can't breathe. With a muted sigh the door begins to burn, with thin, slender flames licking at the wood all the way to the top.

Laura bends right down to the floor, fills her lungs with comparatively clean air and jerks her hands apart as hard as she can. For a moment she's afraid she might have dislocated a shoulder, then the sacking finally gives up the ghost.

She pushes back the plastic matting to reveal the inspection hatch in the floor. She hears a crash behind her as part of the wall above the bed collapses. The last thing she sees before she dives head first through the hatch into the crawl space is the painting of the nymph being consumed by the flames.

Laura lands on her face and one hand. She draws up her legs and rolls away from the hatch, coughing and gasping for oxygen. The air is clearer down here, and after twenty seconds she is able to see and breathe more or less normally.

She can hear the roar of the fire right above her head, the old house screaming in pain as the flames devour it. It is almost completely dark in the crawl space, but she wriggles past the ventilation shaft towards the grille on the side of the house facing the lake. The fire is deafening now. Light flickers over her body, which means the flames are eating through the floorboards, threatening to trap her like a rat.

She turns over onto her back and presses her feet against the shaft. It comes away almost immediately, but the grille to which it was attached is a more challenging prospect. She begins to kick, heavy, rhythmic kicks with both feet, over and over again until she feels the screws gradually begin to loosen. There is a loud crack only a few metres behind her as the floor above comes crashing down, filling the crawl space with smoke. Laura holds her breath. Keeps on kicking rhythmically, just as she does when she's swimming. Steady, even movements, using as little oxygen as possible.

Her lungs protest but still she goes on kicking. She can feel the grille shifting, one millimetre at a time, until it finally drops out into the darkness.

She throws herself through the gap just as another section of the floor lands exactly where she was lying. She scrambles to her feet, tries to orientate herself.

She is standing at the furthest point of Gärdsnäset as the fire races through Hedda's house. In front of her there is a sheet of ice. The mist has thickened into a fog, visibility is down to between five and ten metres. The current flowing towards Alkärret where the ice is weaker cuts off the eastern route, which leaves her very little choice. She will have to walk straight out onto the lake so that she can then head west in the direction of the village, under the protection of the fog.

She takes a few tentative steps. The surface of the ice has become porous and grainy in the milder weather; pools of water have formed here and there.

She advances cautiously, her body still in pain from the electric shock, her lungs still not functioning as they should.

After about ten metres she stops and looks back. The house is ablaze, the roar of the fire drowning out any other sound, and yet she thinks she can hear an engine in the distance. A chugging, sputtering engine that could be a motocross bike. She listens harder, but the sound is gone as quickly as it came. The heat of the fire thins the fog and she sees a figure standing by the pontoon to her left, staring at the devastation. Iben.

Because that is her real name. Iben Jensen, who was once her best friend. Twice, in fact. Once as Iben and once as Steph.

Suddenly, Iben catches sight of Laura. She seems to be taken aback for a second, then she begins to run down the pontoon. Her movements are powerful, those of a trained athlete. About halfway along she jumps onto the ice, losing virtually none of her speed, and continues straight out across the lake.

Laura turns and runs as fast as she can, constantly glancing over her shoulder to see if the fog is giving her enough cover to change direction. But the warm air from the burning building drifts towards her, dispersing the fog. Iben is getting closer and closer, the taser in her hand.

Laura keeps heading north, towards the black eye that lies somewhere up ahead. Iben's footsteps continue to pound behind her. Then she hears another sound, like a woman singing. It takes Laura a few seconds to realise that it is coming from the ice, growing louder the further out she goes. She stops dead.

The veils of mist swirl up around her, revealing that she is no more than two metres from the edge of the ice and the black, ice-cold water.

The eye of the nymph, she thinks as she slowly turns around.

'Why couldn't you stay in the house?'

Iben is five metres away, the prongs of the taser pointing straight at Laura's chest.

'You don't have to do this, Iben.'

Laura raises her hands, but Iben moves forward, forcing her to step back.

The ice sings again, this time a more metallic tone that echoes across the lake. The fog forms dirty white walls, concealing both the holiday village and the fire.

Iben keeps coming. Laura glances over her shoulder. She is only a metre from the water now. She looks to the right and the left, but she knows that Iben is too fast; she can't escape.

She takes another step back. The ice gives a warning crack, ending in a strange dissonance.

'Wait!' Laura says, holding up her hands again. 'If you're not careful we'll both end up in the water.'

Iben stops, trying to work out if she's bluffing. The ice falls silent, and Iben begins to move again. Laura is only half a metre from the black water that has featured in all her nightmares.

Iben reduces the distance between them – three metres, two. She holds up the taser, ready to press the button.

'I'm sorry it has to end this way, Laura – but I have no choice. I can't let Ulf win.'

She takes aim at Laura's chest. Laura tenses her body, preparing herself for the shock, but instead of a whiplash she hears a deafening crack as the ice beneath them gives way, plunging them both into icy darkness.

The cold is so intense that Laura almost loses consciousness. It slices right through her, overloading her neural pathways. She can feel herself sinking as her sodden clothes drag her down, yet she can't move. She is paralysed by both the cold and fear. A part of her brain replays thirty years of nightmares, while another part remains strangely calm. It is somehow logical that it should end here, where it all began.

A sandwich for father, a sandwich for mother. And one for the nymph who lives down below.

She continues to sink. Opens her eyes, even though she knows she is in total darkness. Her lungs feel as if they are about to burst, her heartbeat is thumping against her eardrums and soon it will be over.

Soon there will be no more pain, no more sorrow. No box containing tiny hand- and footprints and traces of a life that could have been. No more winter fire. Maybe this is for the best. Her heart slows, on the point of giving up. Colours sparkle in the water around her, glowing lights that are only a hallucination. The lights come together to form faces, first Elsa's, then Peter's.

Something touches her foot. She gives a start, peers down into the gloom. Glimpses something white, a hand grasping her ankle. But it is not the nymph's claw-like grip, but an elderly woman's hand, two of the fingers no more than stumps.

The lake will hold you up, my princess, Hedda's voice whispers. *And we are right behind you. Me and your little girl. All the way home.*

She feels a slight pricking sensation exactly where the hand is holding her, an electrical impulse that travels up through her body and makes the scar on her back burst into flames. The warmth brings her muscles back to life. She doesn't want to die here. She doesn't want to be a victim. Not anymore. Laura kicks hard, and maybe there is a hand helping her upwards, or maybe it exists only in her oxygen-starved brain. It doesn't matter, because she is swimming towards life, swimming so fast that the water is singing in her ears, rejoicing as she breaks the surface. There is nothing to see, only bobbing ice floes and the fog swirling beneath the night sky.

She ought to crawl out onto the ice before the cold paralyses her again. Run towards the blue lights and voices on the shore.

Instead, she takes two deep breaths and dives back down.

Because she is not afraid – not of the darkness, nor the cold.

Inside her chest and across her back, the winter fire burns for the last time. A strong, clear flame that keeps her warm for long enough to find the person she is looking for and bring them back to the surface.

67

All that remains of Hedda's house is a charred skeleton. The foundations, the bottom half-metre of some of the walls. A blackened pillar that is part of the chimney breast.

Piles of burned crap everywhere. The remains of furniture, machinery, household items, all drenched in water. It all looks even more pathetic in the pale afternoon sunshine.

The snow around the house, even the ice closest to the shore has melted in the heat, leaving a circle of mud, puddles and trampled yellow grass.

The fire engines, police cars and the ambulance are long gone. The crows have returned to their trees, glaring anxiously and flapping their wings, but otherwise they are surprisingly quiet, as if the night's events have given them a fresh perspective on what danger really means.

Laura and Peter are standing side by side a short distance away from what used to be the porch. A piece of the handrail lies in the mud along with the remains of one or two of the steps; otherwise everything is gone. Elsa is stomping around in wellington boots, peering curiously at the mess.

Laura wants to tell her to be careful, but the impulse is nowhere near as strong as it used to be. Plus, she's tired, utterly exhausted by everything that has gone on.

'Jesus,' Peter mutters.

Without a word she moves closer to him, rests her head on his shoulder. He gives a slight start, then relaxes.

'So what happens now?' she says. 'To Iben . . .'

'Bengt Sandberg has taken over the case. He thought I was too close, and he's absolutely right. He's a good cop, deep down. Unnecessarily hard maybe, but he's good at what he does.'

'And Tomas?'

'The doctors say he'll probably survive.'

'Why do you think he did it? Went along with whatever she said, just like that?'

'Tomas has always loved Iben, ever since they were little.'

Laura pictures them at six years old, in the back of Kent Rask's car. Clinging to each other in terror as Källegården burns right outside the windows. The flames, the shouts, the smoke. Iben's mother dancing around them. That must have affected them for the rest of their lives, bound them together. She closes her eyes, pushes away the image.

Elsa knocks something over. The bang makes them jump, but she waves to show it's OK.

'I'm sorry if I scared you the other night,' Peter says. 'The models are a kind of therapy. A way of . . . I don't know . . . processing things.'

'I understand.'

'So what are you going to do?' Peter asks after a few seconds. 'About Gärdsnäset and . . .' he hesitates '. . . everything else?'

'I don't actually know.'

'You could stay.'

She's had the same thought herself, but however much she would like to, she can't.

'I have a company to run. A family that's dependent on me.'

Peter opens his mouth to say something. Part of her hopes he will, but he changes his mind. They stand there in silence for a little while as Elsa continues to rummage among the ruins.

'I've found something!' she shouts, holding up a black rectangle.

She brings it over, and Laura recognises it. A cigar box, so blackened that it is no longer possible to make out the word MONTECRISTO on the lid, but Laura knows exactly what it is. Her old treasure chest, the one she hid in the crawl space all those years ago.

Inside there are two bundles of letters. The heat has turned them yellowish brown, but the writing on the envelopes is still legible. Hedda's characteristic, careless, sprawling handwriting.

Princess Laura Aulin

128 Kotewall Road

Hong Kong

But the address has been crossed out in black ink. Three words have been added in sharper, more efficient writing that Laura also recognises.

Three words, that's all her mother wrote. The same three words on every single one of Hedda's letters.

Over and over again, without even opening the envelopes.

Return to sender.

The top letter is postmarked 23 December 1987. Ten days after the fire.

The next one is postmarked a week later, then another, and another.

She counts the letters, her eyes filled with tears.

Fifty-two – one a week for a whole year, in spite of the fact that they kept on coming back. Then five more, sent once a year a few days before her birthday. Her mother wouldn't even let a greetings card through.

Beneath both bundles there is one more letter. Her name is on the front, but this one has no address, no stamp, no postmark, no 'Return to sender' from her mother.

One final letter that was never sent.

She opens it.

Darling Laura, it begins.

I loved you from the moment I held you in my arms for the first time. Maybe even before that. My perfect little princess.

But I was afraid, afraid that someone like me wouldn't be able to protect something so small and fragile as you.

So I made a mistake. A mistake I've regretted all my life.

Hedda's letter continues, but a tiny object that was stuck between the pages falls into Laura's hand and makes her stop reading. A yellowing ID bracelet from the maternity unit at Ängelholm, almost identical to the one she found among Hedda's photographs, except that this is smaller, meant for a newborn.

Once again the world tilts on its axis and she almost falls to the ground.

'Are you OK?' Peter asks anxiously.

She doesn't answer. She simply holds the little plastic bracelet in her hand, staring at it as if she can't really grasp what it means. A bracelet that a midwife once placed around the wrist of Hedda's and Johnny Miller's love child.

The child Hedda gave away. The child that came back.

The child Hedda brought up, loved, risked her life for.

The child she was forced to part from for a second time. The child she never saw again.

Unstoppable tears pour down Laura's cheeks.

'What is it?' Peter says, putting his arm around her.

She shows him the bracelet. Scrawled across it in blue ink, in Hedda's sprawling handwriting, are four words.

Her name is Laura.

Epilogue 1

There are three people in the windowless visitors' room. The air is thick, hard to breathe. Bengt Sandberg, the police officer with the boxer's nose, is sitting in the corner with his arms folded. His chin is raised as if he's listening carefully. He is only a silent observer of this conversation.

A man and a woman are sitting at the table in the middle of the room.

The man is aged about seventy, but looks older. His face is grey, his skin almost transparent. His gaze is fixed on the woman opposite, but his eyes are empty. He can't really take in what he is seeing, which is hardly surprising. The woman he is staring at is a ghost. The dead walking again. Maybe she is the nymph, risen from the bottom of the lake? That's what some people are saying.

The woman is between forty and fifty, and she is wearing the green tracksuit required by the custody suite. No makeup, her hair tied back in a tight ponytail. Still blonde, but Sandberg can see her dark natural colour beginning to come through at the roots.

'I'm going to tell them everything,' the woman says to the old man. Her speech sounds awkward, as if she is speaking with an accent she hasn't used for many years. 'I wanted you to know that, just in case you manage to die before the trial is over.'

The woman leans across the table, her lips curling in a contemptuous smile.

'And when I'm done with you, Daddy dear, no one will be able to mention Ulf Jensen or Källegården without spitting afterwards. That will be your legacy, the only thing you leave behind. A bad taste in the mouth.'

The woman sits back, folding her arms and looking pleased with herself. The smile is simultaneously triumphant, angry and malicious.

But Sandberg sees something else in her eyes. A glimpse of a damaged, lonely little girl who has been let down by all those who should have protected her.

He feels a flicker in his chest, a sensation he can't explain. Without knowing why, he thinks of his own children and grandchildren.

And for the first time in his long career, Bengt Sandberg realises that he is actually looking forward to his retirement.

Epilogue 2

The winter that relented for a little while in December came back with a vengeance in January. Held the landscape in its icy grip until well into March, but at long last spring came to the lake. The light, the green shoots, the returning migrant birds.

The car is a Jaguar, so old that there are no seat belts in the back, which worries Laura slightly. Peter notices; he pats her knee gently and nods in the direction of Johnny Miller, who is at the wheel.

'He never drives faster than fifty. And we're not going far.'

Laura accepts the reassurance, but checks that Elsa has fastened her belt in the passenger seat. She and Johnny are chatting loudly about goodness knows what; Laura can't hear over the music coming from the speaker. It's one of Johnny's own songs. She's learned to like some of them. Peter leans over.

'So what did your brother say? Any issues?'

'No. Marcus and Mum were happy with the price the valuer suggested. We signed the contract, so it's all settled. The company is their problem now.'

'What are you going to do with all that money?'

She thinks about Gärdsnäset, the dilapidated cabins, Hedda's burned-down house, the old pontoon.

'Oh, I'm sure there's a bottomless pit somewhere that I can pour it into.'

She sees from Peter's smile that he understands. She likes it when he smiles. More than likes it.

She takes his hand and squeezes it. In the front seats Elsa and Johnny have started singing along.

The farm is ten minutes away.

Johnny shows them into the barn as if the place were his, but the farmer doesn't seem to mind.

'There,' Johnny says, pointing eagerly behind a hay bale.

The mother cat is lying on her side, with four grey tabby kittens tumbling around her.

'Do any of them fit the bill?'

Elsa bends down, carefully examines each kitten in turn. Settles on one that has taken itself off to the side and is washing its paws.

'This one,' she says, picking it up. The kitten immediately starts playing with the ties on her jacket.

'That's a female,' the farmer says.

'Excellent!' Elsa smiles and lifts the kitten above her head. 'Have I got it right, Aunt Laura?'

Laura nods and smiles. Feels a pleasant sensation begin to spread through her chest, as if the warmth of spring has reached her core. She takes Peter's hand again, squeezes it as tightly as she can.

Elsa lifts the kitten even higher until her arms are fully extended. A beam of spring sunshine finds its way through the wooden planks making up the walls of the barn, lighting up her face and making her eyes sparkle.

'Welcome back to our family, little George.'

Author's Note

Vedarp and Vintersjön are both fictional places. Like Tornaby in *Rites of Spring* and Reftinge in *End of Summer*, they are based on the area where I grew up in north-western Skåne, principally the communities of Bjuv, Åstorp and Ängelholm.

The thirteenth of December in Sweden is known as Lucia Day, or Saint Lucia's Day. A Christian feast day that can be traced back to the fourth century, it commemorates the martyr Lucia of Syracuse, who, according to legend, brought food to Christians hiding in Roman catacombs. She found her way by wearing a candlelit wreath on her head and today the custom includes 'Luciatåg' processions featuring a Lucia with a lit-up wreath, her handmaidens, and star boys who all wear white and decorative red ribbons. They sing the main Lucia song, 'Sankta Lucia', before Lucia and her helpers hand out treats, such as gingerbread biscuits and an S-shaped saffron bun called a 'Lussekatt'.

Keep reading for an exclusive extract from
the next book in the Seasons Quartet

Deeds of Autumn

Old sins cast a long shadow . . .

1990: It's a late summer's eve and five childhood friends have set up camp by their secret bathing spot, a closed quarry on one of southern Sweden's mountain ridges. The mood is effervescent, but under the surface tensions run deep. Though the evening is supposed to be a last farewell to their childhoods and each other, not everyone is ready to let go, or be left behind. When dawn breaks and the first autumn rain has subsided, a body is floating in the dark waters of the quarry. The police label it a tragic accident, but not everyone is convinced.

Today: For twenty-seven years, the accident remains an open wound in the community, a conflict waiting to catch fire. When the old chief of police is replaced by Anna Vesper, a newly arrived homicide detective from Stockholm, things start moving. Soon Anna is left with no choice but to ignore all warnings and reopen the case from that autumn in 1990. An autumn that few will admit to remembering, but nonetheless refuses to be forgotten.

Coming soon

Keep reading for an exclusive excerpt from
the next book in the Seasons Quartet

Deeds of Autumn

Old lies and a long shadow

Prologue
29 August 1990

The water began its journey in the darkness somewhere deep inside the ridge. It flowed from an underground spring with such force that it was pushed upwards, driving metre after metre through rock, mud and sediment. The ridge was over two hundred metres high, and without human assistance the water would have eventually lost its momentum, turned downwards, found its way out between the roots of the deciduous trees that covered the slopes and ended up as a stream in one of the steep ravines that sliced through the sides of the ridge. However, at the beginning of the twentieth century, a quarry was opened up high on the ridge. Diabase and amphibolite – hard, black varieties of rock well suited for gravestones.

The workers blasted and excavated eagerly, deeper and deeper, until the day the shaft crossed the path of the water, providing it with an easier route to the surface. And the water thanked them by gushing forth with a power no one could have imagined. Only six months later the pumps were shut down, the machinery was taken away and the quarry was abandoned.

As time went by, the place was all but forgotten. The water transformed the quarry into a small, deep pool, surrounded on three sides by steep, dark cliffs, and on the fourth by a sloping bank. The forest swallowed up the access road and the undergrowth reclaimed the area until all that remained were a few overgrown ruins of former workmen's huts, and a glade right next to the bank where the shards of rock were packed so tightly that no living thing could fight its way through.

The quarry wasn't rediscovered until the Sixties, when the logging machines required new routes. In spite of the fact that no one was allowed on site, the beautiful, hidden pool became a favourite place for the young people in the area to swim and sunbathe. It was a perfect spot to meet and do whatever they wanted, without the feeling of constantly being monitored. By that stage no one had any idea how deep the quarry was. Some claimed that the water must be at least twenty metres deep, others forty. Some even said the quarry was bottomless, although how that was possible was a complete mystery.

There were lots of rumours about what was hiding down there. Old cars, the proceeds of robberies, the remains of people who had disappeared long ago. Rumours that couldn't be verified, and therefore grew even more fantastical with each retelling. However, all those who had ever visited the quarry were agreed on two things: that the black water was so deep that even high summer in Skåne couldn't raise its temperature above twenty degrees, and that one of the young men who chose to scramble up the steep rock face on the far side in order to dive from the highest point was going to kill himself – sooner or later.

It took four firefighters to get the body out of the water. The bank was slippery and covered in sharp stones that made it difficult to get traction. On a couple of occasions one of the men stumbled and lost his footing, almost as if the water was putting up a fight, trying to retain the body for as long as possible.

Seen from a short distance away, the young man looked as if he was sleeping. He was lying on his back with his eyes closed, the pale features so peaceful that it was possible to believe that he would wake up at any moment.

But when the body landed on the stretcher with a horrible, heavy thud, the illusion was shattered. Cold water poured from his clothes and his long, fair hair, carrying with it blood from the back of his head, which had been crushed. It formed pink, shimmering puddles on the stretcher before it gathered enough weight to make its way down among the stones on the hard ground and disappear into the darkness.

Water always finds the lowest point, thought the police officer who was standing just a metre or so away. He wondered whether he ought to jot down that observation. Turn to the last page of his notebook where he collected such thoughts, small reflections that didn't really have anything to do with police work, but ought to be recorded anyway, possibly to balance out everything else he wrote. Instead, he stayed on the page he'd just started.

He had written the place, time and date only a minute or so after getting out of the police car.

Mörkaby quarry, 05.54, 29 August 1990.

Underneath he'd left space for the names of the four young people in front of him, one on each line. Their faces had taken on a greyish tinge and they were trying in vain to avoid looking at the body. He knew who they were, how old they were, where they lived; he even knew who their parents were and where they worked. Under normal circumstances, this was something he liked about his job out here in such a rural area – familiarity with the locals, the sense of community. But on this particular morning, he wished for the first time that he worked in a city.

Alexander Morell
Carina Pedersen
Bruno Sordi
Marie Andersson

They were all nineteen years old, as was the young man on the stretcher. As recently as June he'd seen all five of them careering through the village as they celebrated their graduation from high school – drinking cans of beer, blowing whistles, waving their white, peaked student caps and screaming with joy at the future that awaited them.

Simon Vidje, he wrote at the bottom of the list and underlined both words in black. He had known the identity of the victim for quite some time now, and yet there was something about seeing the name on paper that made the situation even more unpleasant. Everyone in Nedanås knew who Simon Vidje was. A child prodigy. One in a million. Someone who was destined to conquer the world, visit amazing places and take his home village and everyone in it along for the ride. Instead, his story had ended here, in cold black water in the middle of nowhere, not too far from the place where he'd grown up.

The police officer's radio crackled into life, then he heard a rough, familiar voice conveying instructions which he immediately carried out.

'Your father is on his way, Alex,' he said to the muscular boy with protruding wrestler's ears and broad shoulders. He received a brief nod in response.

The officer gazed at the four of them for a moment, then frowned and made a note below their names.

Marie Andersson's clothes are wet. Alexander Morell's, Carina Pedersen's and Bruno Sordi's clothes are dry.

Maybe it was a pointless observation, a fact with no value whatsoever. At least that was what he would claim later on, when it had somehow found its way into the official police report and people started asking him what those fifteen words actually meant.

However, he was currently unaware of the difficulties ahead. All he knew was that he had a job to do. Questions to ask, answers to write down in his notebook.

He began as gently as he could. 'So, what actually happened?' No one answered. The four of them had given up the struggle and were staring at the stretcher, where pale red water still dripped from Simon Vidje's crushed head and continued on its way to the lowest point, deep down in the darkness.

Rites of Spring

Sunday Times Crime Book of the Month

As new life blooms, old secrets stir . . .

Skåne, 1986: On the night of Walpurgis, the eve of May Day, where bonfires are lit to ward off evil spirits and preparations are made to celebrate the renewal of spring, a sixteen-year-old girl is ritualistically murdered in the woods beside a castle. Her stepbrother is convicted of the terrible deed and shortly after, the entire family vanishes without a trace.

Spring, 2019: Dr Thea Lind moves into the castle. After making a strange discovery in an ancient oak tree on the grounds, her fascination with the old tragedy deepens. As she uncovers more and more similarities between her own troubled past and the murdered girl, she begins to believe that the real truth of the killing was never uncovered.

What if the spring of 1986 claimed more than one victim?

Available now

End of Summer

You can always go home, but you can never go back . . .

Summer, 1983: Four-year-old Billy chases a rabbit in the fields behind his house. But when his mother goes to call him in, Billy has disappeared. Never to be seen again.

Today: Veronica is a bereavement counsellor. She's never fully come to terms with her mother's suicide after her brother Billy's disappearance. When a young man joins her group, he looks familiar and when he talks about the trauma of his friend's disappearance in 1983, Veronica feels a flicker of hope. Could Billy still be alive after all this time? Needing to know the truth, Veronica goes home – to the place where her life started to fall apart.

But is she prepared for the answers that wait for her there?

Available now